THE NECRONOMICON

THE NECRONOMICON

TALES OF ELDRITCH HORROR FROM THE MASTERS OF THE GENRE

H. P. LOVECRAFT

ARTHUR MACHEN • ROBERT E. HOWARD
ROBERT W. CHAMBERS • LAFCADIO HEARN

ARCTURUS

ARCTURUS
This edition published in 2025 by Arcturus Publishing Limited
26/27 Bickels Yard, 151–153 Bermondsey Street,
London SE1 3HA

ISBN: 978-1-3988-4967-9
AD012129US

Printed in China

CONTENTS

INTRODUCTION 7
THE HISTORY OF THE NECRONOMICON by H. P. Lovecraft 9
THE BLACK SEAL by Arthur Machen 13
THE CALL OF CTHULHU by H. P. Lovecraft 45
THE REPAIRER OF REPUTATIONS by Robert W. Chambers 71
THE DUNWICH HORROR by H. P. Lovecraft 99
THE MASK by Robert W. Chambers 137
SKULL-FACE by Robert E. Howard 153
THE WHISPERER IN DARKNESS by H. P. Lovecraft 229
NIGHTMARE-TOUCH by Lafcadio Hearn 285
THE HAUNTER OF THE RING by Robert E. Howard 291

INTRODUCTION

The *Necronomicon*, allegedly written by an Arab named 'Abdul Alhazred' (a pseudonym Lovecraft had adopted for himself as a child), is a fictional book of dark magic that appears in several of H. P. Lovecraft's stories. With its ancient evils and long-forgotten secrets, it symbolizes the essence of cosmic horror that is at the heart of Lovecraft's fiction. His tales of tentacled Elder Gods, nightmarish visions, and creeping insanity helped create the horror genre as we know it.

Yet Lovecraft was well aware of the debt he owed to the pioneering writers who inspired his unique creations. His extensive essay "Supernatural Horror in Literature" investigated the history of the horror story and tried to get to the bottom of what made one worth reading. He uncovered several different approaches, ranging from early gothic horror to turn-of-the-century ghost stories.

In this volume, you will find stories by Lovecraft himself as well as by four writers who influenced him and helped establish the conventions of horror literature: Arthur Machen, Lafcadio Hearn, Robert W. Chambers, and Robert E. Howard. These four writers took very different approaches to their fiction, and each are uniquely entertaining in their own way.

H. P. Lovecraft (1890–1937) was one of the most influential and important figures of horror literature ever. His writings spawned the "Cthulhu Mythos," a shared imaginative universe which began with the writings of close associates of his like August Derleth and has since found traction in film, television, music, and games. At the heart of his writing was the theme of the hubris of science and the dangers of human curiosity, as well as the possibility that there were immensely powerful and unknowable forces in the world.

Arthur Machen (1863–1947) was named by Lovecraft as one of the four "modern masters" of horror. He came from a religious family and had a deep interest in the rituals of Celtic Christianity. The publication of his novel *The Great God Pan* in 1894 shocked Victorian sensibilities, but it has since been acknowledged as a classic. Stephen King would later describe it as "maybe the best [horror story] in the English language." Machen's writing was infused with pagan symbolism and provided a very different style of horror to the gothic stories and ghost tales of his contemporaries. It was in many ways the beginning of the "weird," a genre that Lovecraft would develop to new heights.

A contemporary of Machen's, Lafcadio Hearn (1850–1904), approached the genre from a very different angle. At heart, Hearn was a recorder of folk tales – but not the folk tales of the Brothers Grimm or Hans Christian Andersen that a western audience would be familiar with, but rather the altogether more disturbing and unusual stories from the Caribbean and Japan. He is best known for his collections of Japanese ghost stories such as *In Ghostly Japan* (1899) and *Kwaidan: Stories and Studies of Strange Things* (1904). As a young man, Hearn had worked as a reporter for the *Cincinnati Daily Enquirer*, where he covered a series of gruesome murders for the paper. His talent for sensationalism served him well as a horror writer, though he always took care to treat the stories with as much authenticity as possible. His stories included bloodthirsty ghosts, spectral brides and priests with unnatural appetites that are uniquely terrifying.

Robert W. Chambers (1865–1933) was a great influence on Lovecraft and many of the elements of his stories would fit neatly into the Cthulhu Mythos. His most significant work was *The King in Yellow* (1895), a collection of weird and macabre stories that anticipated the cosmic horror that would prove so popular in the pulp magazines a few decades later. These stories are loosely tied together through their relation to a fictional play of the same name. Like the *Necronomicon*, it is a forbidden cursed text, and reading it can drive the reader insane. Its references to the mysterious city of Carcosa and the supernatural entities Hali and Hastur helped establish Chambers as one of the essential horror writers of his day. This volume includes a number of stories from *The King in Yellow*, including "The Repairer of Reputations" and "The Haunter of the Ring," as well as a number of other works of weird fiction from Chambers.

Robert E. Howard (1906–1936) was a contemporary of H. P. Lovecraft and a prolific short story writer. He was a key contributor to *Weird Tales* and many of the other pulp magazines of the interwar years. Howard also held an extensive correspondence with Lovecraft. Through their letters they discussed everything from the relative virtues of civilization and barbarism, contemporary politics, their travels through America, and of course, their writing. His life was a short and tragic one which ended in suicide at the age of 30, but his legacy has endured.

Howard is best known for his Conan the Barbarian stories, which have been adapted countless times for film, television and games, and his tales helped create the sword-and-sorcery genre, but he was also an accomplished horror writer. Some of his tales are considered part of the Cthulhu Mythos, while others share many of the elements that made Lovecraft's work so popular – from eldritch powers to forbidden knowledges and the dangers that await anyone who can't restrain their curiosity.

Together, these five writers helped shape the genre of supernatural horror as we know it today. Their stories blended the suspense and terror of earlier gothic writers and added supernatural elements and terrifying new imaginative creations to create a new wave of nerve-wracking fiction. Here, then, is a collection of tales to match the macabre madness of the *Necronomicon* itself...

THE HISTORY OF THE NECRONOMICON

BY

H. P. LOVECRAFT

Original title *Al Azif*—*azif* being the word used by Arabs to designate that nocturnal sound (made by insects) suppos'd to be the howling of daemons.

Composed by Abdul Alhazred, a mad poet of Sanaá, in Yemen, who is said to have flourished during the period of the Ommiade caliphs, circa 700 A.D. He visited the ruins of Babylon and the subterranean secrets of Memphis and spent ten years alone in the great southern desert of Arabia—the Roba el Khaliyeh or "Empty Space" of the ancients—and "Dahna" or "Crimson" desert of the modern Arabs, which is held to be inhabited by protective evil spirits and monsters of death. Of this desert many strange and unbelievable marvels are told by those who pretend to have penetrated it. In his last years Alhazred dwelt in Damascus, where the *Necronomicon* (*Al Azif*) was written, and of his final death or disappearance (738 A.D.) many terrible and conflicting things are told. He is said by Ebn Khallikan (12th cent. biographer) to have been seized by an invisible monster in broad daylight and devoured horribly before a large number of fright-frozen witnesses. Of his madness many things are told. He claimed to have seen fabulous Irem, or City of Pillars, and to have found beneath the ruins of a certain nameless desert town the shocking annals and secrets of a race older than mankind. He was only an indifferent Moslem, worshiping unknown entities whom he called Yog-Sothoth and Cthulhu.

In A.D. 950 the *Azif*, which had gained a considerable tho' surreptitious circulation amongst the philosophers of the age, was secretly translated into Greek by Theodorus Philetas of Constantinople under the title *Necronomicon*. For a century it impelled certain experimenters to terrible attempts, when it was suppressed and burned by the patriarch Michael. After this it is only heard of furtively, but (1228) Olaus Wormius made a Latin translation later in the Middle Ages, and the Latin text was printed twice—once in the fifteenth century in black-letter (evidently in Germany) and once in the seventeenth (prob. Spanish)—both editions being without identifying marks, and located as to time and place by internal typographical evidence only. The work both Latin and Greek was banned by Pope Gregory IX in 1232, shortly after its Latin translation, which called attention to it. The Arabic original was lost as early as Wormius' time, as indicated by his prefatory note; and no sight of the Greek copy—which was printed in Italy between 1500 and 1550—has been reported since the burning of a certain Salem man's library in 1692. An English translation made by Dr. Dee was never printed, and exists only in fragments recovered from the original manuscript. Of the Latin texts now existing one (15th cent.) is known to be in the British

Museum under lock and key, while another (17th cent.) is in the Bibliothèque Nationale at Paris. A seventeenth-century edition is in the Widener Library at Harvard, and in the library of Miskatonic University at Arkham. Also in the library of the University of Buenos Ayres. Numerous other copies probably exist in secret, and a fifteenth-century one is persistently rumored to form part of the collection of a celebrated American millionaire. A still vaguer rumor credits the preservation of a sixteenth-century Greek text in the Salem family of Pickman; but if it was so preserved, it vanished with the artist R.U. Pickman, who disappeared early in 1926. The book is rigidly suppressed by the authorities of most countries, and by all branches of organized ecclesiasticism. Reading leads to terrible consequences. It was from rumors of this book (of which relatively few of the general public know) that R.W. Chambers is said to have derived the idea of his early novel *The King in Yellow*.

CHRONOLOGY

Al Azif written circa A.D. 730 at Damascus by Abdul Alhazred.

Tr. to Greek A.D. 950 as *Necronomicon* by Theodorus Philetas.

Burned by Patriarch Michael 1050 (i.e., Greek text). Arabic text now lost.

Olaus translates Gr. to Latin 1228.

1232 Latin ed. (and Gr.) suppr. by Pope Gregory IX.

14... Black-letter printed edition (Germany).

15... Gr. text printed in Italy.

16... Spanish reprint of Latin text.

THE BLACK SEAL

BY

ARTHUR MACHEN

PROLOGUE

"I see you are a determined rationalist," said the lady. "Did you not hear me say that I have had experiences even more terrible? I too was once a sceptic, but after what I have known I can no longer affect to doubt."

"Madam," replied Mr. Phillipps, "no one shall make me deny my faith. I will never believe, nor will I pretend to believe, that two and two make five, nor will I on any pretences admit the existence of two-sided triangles."

"You are a little hasty," rejoined the lady. "But may I ask you if you ever heard the name of Professor Gregg, the authority on ethnology and kindred subjects?"

"I have done much more than merely hear of Professor Gregg," said Phillipps. "I always regarded him as one of our most acute and clear-headed observers; and his last publication, the *Textbook of Ethnology*, struck me as being quite admirable in its kind. Indeed, the book had but come into my hands when I heard of the terrible accident which cut short Gregg's career. He had, I think, taken a country house in the west of England for the summer, and is supposed to have fallen into a river. So far as I remember, his body was never recovered."

"Sir, I am sure that you are discreet. Your conversation seems to declare as much, and the very title of that little work of yours which you mentioned assures me that you are no empty trifler. In a word, I feel that I may depend on you. You appear to be under the impression that Professor Gregg is dead; I have no reason to believe that that is the case."

"What?" cried Phillipps, astonished and perturbed. "You do not hint that there was anything disgraceful? I cannot believe it. Gregg was a man of clearest character; his private life was one of great benevolence; and though I myself am free from delusions, I believe him to have been a sincere and devout Christian. Surely you cannot mean to insinuate that some disreputable history forced him to flee the country?"

"Again you are in a hurry." replied the lady. "I said nothing of all this. Briefly, then, I must tell you that Professor Gregg left this house one morning in full health both in mind and body. He never returned, but his watch and chain, a purse containing three sovereigns in gold, and some loose silver, with a ring that he wore habitually, were found three days later on a wild and savage hillside, many miles from the river. These articles were placed beside a limestone rock of fantastic form; they had been wrapped into a parcel with a kind of rough parchment which was secured with gut. The parcel was opened, and the inner side of the parchment bore an inscription done with some red substance; the characters were undecipherable, but seemed to be a corrupt cuneiform."

"You interest me intensely," said Phillipps. "Would you mind continuing your story? The circumstance you have mentioned seems to me of the most inexplicable character, and I thirst for an elucidation."

The young lady seemed to meditate for a moment, and she then proceeded to relate the

NOVEL OF THE BLACK SEAL

I must now give you some fuller particulars of my history. I am the daughter of a civil engineer, Steven Lally by name, who was so unfortunate as to die suddenly at the outset of his career, and before he had accumulated sufficient means to support his wife and her two children.

My mother contrived to keep the small household going on resources which must have been incredibly small; we lived in a remote country village, because most of the necessaries of life were cheaper than in a town, but even so we were brought up with the severest economy. My father was a clever and well-read man, and left behind him a small but select collection of books, containing the best Greek, Latin, and English classics, and these books were the only amusement we possessed. My brother, I remember, learnt Latin out of Descartes' *Meditationes*, and I, in place of the little tales which children are usually told to read, had nothing more charming than a translation of the *Gesta Romanorum*. We grew up thus, quiet and studious children, and in course of time my brother provided for himself in the manner I have mentioned. I continued to live at home: my poor mother had become an invalid, and demanded my continual care, and about two years ago she died after many months of painful illness. My situation was a terrible one; the shabby furniture barely sufficed to pay the debts I had been forced to contract, and the books I dispatched to my brother, knowing how he would value them. I was absolutely alone; I was aware how poorly my brother was paid; and though I came up to London in the hope of finding employment, with the understanding that he would defray my expenses, I swore it should only be for a month, and that if I could not in that time find some work I would starve rather than deprive him of the few miserable pounds he had laid by for his day of trouble. I took a little room in a distant suburb; the cheapest that I could find; I lived on bread and tea, and I spent my time in vain answering of advertisements, and vainer walks to addresses

I had noted. Day followed on day, and week on week, and still I was unsuccessful, till at last the term I had appointed drew to a close, and I saw before me the grim prospect of slowly dying of starvation. My landlady was good-natured in her way; she knew the slenderness of my means, and I am sure that she would not have turned me out of doors; it remained for me then to go away, and to try to die in some quiet place. It was winter then, and a thick white fog gathered in the early part of the afternoon, becoming more dense as the day wore on; it was a Sunday, I remember, and the people of the house were at chapel. At about three o'clock I crept out and walked away as quickly as I could, for I was weak from abstinence. The white mist wrapped all the streets in silence, a hard frost had gathered thick upon the bare branches of the trees, and frost crystals glittered on the wooden fences, and on the cold, cruel ground beneath my feet. I walked on, turning to right and left in utter haphazard, without caring to look up at the names of the streets, and all that I remember of my walk on that Sunday afternoon seems but the broken fragments of an evil dream. In a confused vision I stumbled on, through roads half town and half country, grey fields melting into the cloudy world of mist on one side of me, and on the other comfortable villas with a glow of firelight flickering on the walls, but all unreal; red brick walls and lighted windows, vague trees, and glimmering country, gas-lamps beginning to star the white shadows, the vanishing perspectives of the railway line beneath high embankments, the green and red of the signal lamps—all these were but momentary pictures flashed on my tired brain and senses numbed by hunger. Now and then I would hear a quick step ringing on the iron road, and men would pass me well wrapped up, walking fast for the sake of warmth, and no doubt eagerly foretasting the pleasures of a glowing hearth, with curtains tightly drawn about the frosted panes, and the welcomes of their friends, but as the early evening darkened and night approached, foot-passengers got fewer and fewer, and I passed through street after street alone. In the white silence I stumbled on, as desolate as if I trod the streets of a buried city; and as I grew more weak and exhausted, something of the horror of death was folding thickly round my heart. Suddenly, as I turned a corner, some one accosted me courteously beneath the lamp-post, and I heard a voice asking if I could kindly point the way to Avon Road. At the sudden shock of human accents I was prostrated, and my strength gave way; I fell all huddled on the sidewalk, and wept and sobbed and laughed in violent hysteria. I had gone out prepared to die, and as I stepped across the threshold that had sheltered me, I consciously bade adieu to all hopes and all remembrances; the door clanged behind me with the noise of thunder, and I felt that an iron curtain had fallen on the brief passage of my life, that henceforth I was to walk a little way in a world of gloom and shadow; I entered on the stage of the first act of death. Then came my wandering in the mist, the whiteness wrapping all things, the void streets, and muffled silence, till when that voice spoke to me it was as if I had died and life returned to me. In a few minutes I was able to compose my feelings, and as I rose I saw that I was confronted by a middle-aged gentleman of pleasing appearance, neatly and correctly dressed. He looked at me with an expression of great pity, but before I could stammer out my ignorance of the neighbourhood, for indeed I had not the slightest notion of where I had wandered, he spoke.

"My dear madam," he said, "you seem in some terrible distress. You cannot think how you alarmed me. But may I inquire the nature of your trouble? I assure you that you can safely confide in me."

"You are very kind," I replied. "But I fear there is nothing to be done. My condition seems a hopeless one."

"Oh, nonsense, nonsense! You are too young to talk like that. Come, let us walk down here and you must tell me your difficulty. Perhaps I may be able to help you."

There was something very soothing and persuasive in his manner, and as we walked together I gave him an outline of my story, and told of the despair that had oppressed me almost to death.

"You were wrong to give in so completely," he said, when I was silent. "A month is too short a time in which to feel one's way in London. London, let me tell you, Miss Lally, does not lie open and undefended; it is a fortified place, fossed and double-moated with curious intricacies. As must always happen in large towns, the conditions of life have become hugely artificial, no mere simple palisade is run up to oppose the man or woman who would take the place by storm, but serried lines of subtle contrivances, mines, and pitfalls which it needs a strange skill to overcome. You, in your simplicity, fancied you had only to shout for these walls to sink into nothingness, but the time is gone for such startling victories as these. Take courage; you will learn the secret of success before very long."

"Alas! sir," I replied, "I have no doubt your conclusions are correct, but at the present moment I seem to be in a fair way to die of starvation. You spoke of a secret; for Heaven's sake tell it me, if you have any pity for my distress."

He laughed genially. "There lies the strangeness of it all. Those who know the secret cannot tell it if they would; it is positively as ineffable as the central doctrine of freemasonry. But I may say this, that you yourself have penetrated at least the outer husk of the mystery," and he laughed again.

"Pray do not jest with me," I said. "What have I done, *que sçais-je?* I am so far ignorant that I have not the slightest idea of how my next meal is to be provided."

"Excuse me. You ask what you have done. You have met me. Come, we will fence no longer.

I see you have self-education, the only education which is not infinitely pernicious, and I am in want of a governess for my two children. I have been a widower for some years; my name is Gregg. I offer you the post I have named, and shall we say a salary of a hundred a year?"

I could only stutter out my thanks, and slipping a card with his address, and a banknote by way of earnest, into my hand, Mr. Gregg bade me good-bye, asking me to call in a day or two.

Such was my introduction to Professor Gregg, and can you wonder that the remembrance of despair and the cold blast that had blown from the gates of death upon me made me regard him as a second father?

Before the close of the week I was installed in my new duties. The Professor had leased an old brick manor-house in a western suburb of London, and here, surrounded by pleasant lawns and orchards, and soothed with the murmur of ancient elms that rocked their boughs above the roof, the new chapter of my life began. Knowing as you do the nature of the professor's occupation, you will not be surprised to hear that the house teemed with books, and cabinets full of strange, and even hideous, objects filled every available nook in the vast low rooms. Gregg was a man whose one thought was for knowledge, and I too before long caught something of his enthusiasm, and strove to enter into his passion of research. In a few months I was perhaps more his secretary than the governess of the two children, and many a night I have sat at the desk in the glow of the shaded lamp while he, pacing up and down in the rich gloom of the firelight, dictated to me the substance of his *Textbook of Ethnology*. But amidst these more sober and accurate studies I always detected a something hidden, a longing and desire for some object to which he did not allude; and now and then he would break short in what he was saying and lapse into reverie, entranced, as it seemed to me, by some distant prospect of adventurous discovery. The textbook was at last finished, and we began to receive proofs from the printers, which were entrusted to me for a first reading, and then underwent the final revision of the professor. All the while his weariness of the actual business he was engaged on increased, and it was with the joyous laugh of a schoolboy when term is over that he one day handed me a copy of the book. "There," he said, "I have kept my word; I promised to write it, and it is done with. Now I shall be free to live for stranger things; I confess it, Miss Lally, I covet the renown of Columbus; you will, I hope, see me play the part of an explorer."

"Surely," I said, "there is little left to explore. You have been born a few hundred years too late for that."

"I think you are wrong," he replied; "there are still, depend upon it, quaint, undiscovered countries and continents of strange extent. Ah, Miss Lally! believe me, we stand amidst sacraments and mysteries full of awe, and it doth not yet appear what we shall be. Life, believe me, is no simple thing, no mass of gray matter and congeries of veins and muscles to be laid naked by the surgeon's knife; man is the secret which I am about to explore, and before I can discover him I must cross over weltering seas indeed, and oceans and the mists of many thousand years. You know the myth of the lost Atlantis; what if it be true, and I am destined to be called the discoverer of that wonderful land?"

I could see excitement boiling beneath his words, and in his face was the heat of the hunter; before me stood a man who believed himself summoned to tourney with the unknown. A pang of joy possessed me when I reflected that I was to be in a way associated with him in the adventure, and I, too, burned with the lust of the chase, not pausing to consider that I knew not what we were to unshadow.

The next morning Professor Gregg took me into his inner study, where, ranged against the wall, stood a nest of pigeonholes, every drawer neatly labelled, and the results of years of toil classified in a few feet of space.

"Here," he said, "is my life; here are all the facts which I have gathered together with so much pains, and yet it is all nothing. No, nothing to what I am about to attempt. Look at this"; and he took me to an old bureau, a piece fantastic and faded, which stood in a corner of the room. He unlocked the front and opened one of the drawers.

"A few scraps of paper," he went on, pointing to the drawer, "and a lump of black stone, rudely annotated with queer marks and scratches—that is all that the drawer holds. Here you see is an old envelope with the dark red stamp of twenty years ago, but I have pencilled a few lines at the back; here is a sheet of manuscript, and here some cuttings from obscure local journals. And if you ask me the subject-matter of the collection, it will not seem extraordinary—a servant-girl at a farmhouse, who disappeared from her place and has never been heard of, a child supposed to have slipped down some old working on the mountains, some queer scribbling on a limestone rock, a man murdered with a blow from a strange weapon; such is the scent I have to go upon. Yes, as you say, there is a ready explanation for all this; the girl may have run away to London, or Liverpool, or New York; the child may be at the bottom of the disused shaft; and the letters on the rock may be the idle whims of some vagrant. Yes, yes, I admit all that; but I know I hold the true key. Look!" and he held out a slip of yellow paper.

Characters found inscribed on a limestone rock on the Grey Hills, I read, and then there was a word erased, presumably the name of a county, and a date some fifteen years back. Beneath was traced a number of uncouth characters, shaped somewhat like wedges or daggers, as strange and outlandish as the Hebrew alphabet.

"Now the seal," said Professor Gregg, and he handed me the black stone, a thing about two inches long, and something like an old-fashioned tobacco-stopper, much enlarged.

I held it up to the light, and saw to my surprise the characters on the paper repeated on the seal.

"Yes," said the professor, "they are the same. And the marks on the limestone rock were made fifteen years ago, with some red substance. And the characters on the seal are four thousand years old at least. Perhaps much more."

"Is it a hoax?" I said.

"No, I anticipated that. I was not to be led to give my life to a practical joke. I have tested the matter very carefully. Only one person besides myself knows of the mere existence of that black seal. Besides, there are other reasons which I cannot enter into now."

"But what does it all mean?" I said. "I cannot understand to what conclusion all this leads."

"My dear Miss Lally, that is a question that I would rather leave unanswered for some little time. Perhaps I shall never be able to say what secrets are held here in solution; a few vague hints, the outlines of village tragedies, a few marks done with red earth upon a rock, and an ancient seal. A queer set of data to go upon? Half a dozen pieces of evidence, and twenty years before even so much could be got together; and who knows what mirage or *terra incognita* may be beyond all this? I look across deep waters, Miss Lally, and the land beyond may be but a haze after all. But still I believe it is not so, and a few months will show whether I am right or wrong."

He left me, and alone I endeavoured to fathom the mystery, wondering to what goal such eccentric odds and ends of evidence could lead. I myself am not wholly devoid of imagination, and I had reason to respect the professor's solidity of intellect; yet I saw in the contents of the drawers but the materials of fantasy, and vainly tried to conceive what theory could be founded on the fragments that had been placed before me. Indeed, I could discover in what I had heard and seen but the first chapter of an extravagant romance; and yet deep in my heart I burned with curiosity, and day after day I looked eagerly in Professor Gregg's face for some hint of what was to happen.

It was one evening after dinner that the word came.

"I hope you can make your preparations without much trouble," he said suddenly to me. "We shall be leaving here in a week's time."

"Really!" I said in astonishment. "Where are we going?"

"I have taken a country house in the west of England, not far from Caermaen, a quiet little town, once a city, and the headquarters of a Roman legion. It is very dull there, but the country is pretty, and the air is wholesome."

I detected a glint in his eyes, and guessed that this sudden move had some relation to our conversation of a few days before.

"I shall just take a few books with me," said Professor Gregg, "that is all. Everything else will remain here for our return. I have got a holiday," he went on, smiling at me, "and I shan't be sorry to be quit for a time of my old bones and stones and rubbish. Do you know," he went on, "I have been grinding away at facts for thirty years; it is time for fancies."

The days passed quickly; I could see that the professor was all quivering with suppressed excitement, and I could scarce credit the eager appetence of his glance as we left the old manor-house behind us and began our journey. We set out at midday, and it was in the dusk of the evening that we arrived at a little country station. I was tired and excited, and the drive through the lanes seems all a dream. First the deserted streets of a forgotten village, while I heard Professor Gregg's voice talking of the Augustan Legion and the clash of arms, and all the tremendous pomp that followed the eagles; then the broad river swimming to full tide with the last afterglow glimmering duskily in the yellow water, the wide meadows, the cornfields whitening, and the deep lane winding on the slope between the hills and the water. At last we began to ascend, and the air grew rarer. I looked down and saw the pure white mist tracking the outline of the river like a shroud, and a vague and shadowy country; imaginations and fantasy of swelling hills and hanging woods, and half-shaped outlines of hills beyond, and in the distance the glare of the furnace fire on the mountain, glowing by turns a pillar of shining flame and fading to a dull point of red. We were slowly mounting a carriage drive, and then there came to me the cool breath and the secret of the great wood that was above us; I seemed to wander in its deepest depths, and there was the sound of trickling water, the scent of the green leaves, and the breath of the summer night. The carriage stopped at last, and I could scarcely distinguish the form of the house, as I waited a moment at the pillared porch. The rest of the evening seemed a dream of strange things bounded by the great silence of the wood and the valley and the river.

The next morning, when I awoke and looked out of the bow window of the big, old-fashioned bedroom, I saw under a grey sky a country that was still all mystery. The long, lovely valley, with the river winding in and out below, crossed in mid-vision by a mediæval bridge of vaulted and buttressed stone, the clear presence of the rising ground beyond, and the woods that I had only seen in shadow the night before, seemed tinged with enchantment, and the soft breath of air that sighed in at the opened pane was like no other wind. I looked across the valley, and beyond, hill followed on hill as wave on wave, and here a faint blue pillar of smoke rose still in the morning air from the chimney of an ancient grey farmhouse, there was a rugged height crowned with dark firs, and in the distance I saw the white streak of a road that climbed and vanished into some unimagined country. But the boundary of all was a great wall of mountain, vast in the west, and ending like a fortress with a steep ascent and a domed tumulus clear against the sky.

I saw Professor Gregg walking up and down the terrace path below the windows, and it was evident that he was revelling in the sense of liberty, and the thought that he had for a while bidden good-bye to task-work. When I joined him there was exultation in his voice as he pointed out the sweep of valley and the river that wound beneath the lovely hills.

"Yes," he said, "it is a strangely beautiful country; and to me, at least, it seems full of mystery. You have not forgotten the drawer I showed you, Miss Lally? No; and you have guessed that I have come here not merely for the sake of the children and the fresh air?"

"I think I have guessed as much as that," I replied; "but you must remember I do not know the mere nature of your investigations; and as for the connection between the search and this wonderful valley, it is past my guessing."

He smiled queerly at me. "You must not think I am making a mystery for the sake of mystery," he said. "I do not speak out because, so far, there is nothing to be spoken, nothing definite, I mean, nothing that can be set down in hard black and white, as dull and sure and irreproachable as any blue-book. And then I have another reason: Many years ago a chance paragraph in a newspaper caught my attention, and focussed in an instant the vagrant thoughts and half-formed fancies of many idle and speculative hours into a certain hypothesis. I saw at once that I was treading on a thin crust; my theory was wild and fantastic in the extreme, and I would not for any consideration have written a hint of it for publication. But I thought that in the company of scientific men like myself, men who knew the course of discovery, and were aware that the gas that blazes and flares in the gin-palace was once a wild hypothesis—I thought that with such men as these I might hazard my dream—let us say Atlantis, or the philosopher's stone, or what you like—without danger of ridicule. I found I was grossly mistaken; my friends looked blankly at me and at one another, and I could see something of pity, and something also of insolent contempt, in the glances they exchanged. One of them called on me next day, and hinted that I must be suffering from overwork and brain exhaustion. 'In plain terms,' I said, 'you think I am going mad. I think not;' and I showed him out with some little appearance of heat. Since that day I vowed that I would never whisper the nature of my theory to any living soul; to no one but yourself have I ever shown the contents of that drawer. After all, I may be following a rainbow; I may have been misled by the play of coincidence; but as I stand here in this mystic hush and silence, amidst the woods and wild hills, I am more than ever sure that I am hot on the scent. Come, it is time we went in."

To me in all this there was something both of wonder and excitement; I knew how in his ordinary work Professor Gregg moved step by step, testing every inch of the way, and never venturing on assertion without proof that was impregnable. Yet I divined, more from his glance and the vehemence of his tone than from the spoken word, that he had in his every thought the vision of the almost incredible continually with him; and I, who was with some share of imagination no little of a sceptic, offended at a hint of the marvellous, could not help asking myself whether he were cherishing a monomania, and barring out from this one subject all the scientific method of his other life.

Yet, with this image of mystery haunting my thoughts, I surrendered wholly to the charm of the country. Above the faded house on the hillside began the great forest—a long, dark line seen from the opposing hills, stretching above the river for many a mile from north to south, and yielding in the north to even wilder country, barren and savage hills, and ragged commonland, a territory all strange and unvisited, and more unknown to Englishmen than the very heart of Africa. The space of a couple of steep fields alone separated the house from the woods, and the children were delighted to follow me up the long alleys of undergrowth, between smooth pleached walls of shining beech, to the highest point in the wood, whence one looked on one side across the river and the rise and fall of the country to the great western mountain wall, and on the other over the surge and dip of the myriad trees of the forest, over level meadows and the shining yellow sea to the faint coast beyond. I used to sit at this point on the warm sunlit turf which marked the track of the Roman Road, while the two children raced about hunting for the whinberries that grew here and there on the banks. Here, beneath the deep blue sky and the great clouds rolling, like olden galleons with sails full-bellied, from the sea to the hills, as I listened to the whispered charm of the great and ancient wood, I lived solely for delight, and only remembered strange things when we would return to the house and find Professor Gregg either shut up in the little room he had made his study, or else pacing the terrace with the look, patient and enthusiastic, of the determined seeker.

One morning, some eight or nine days after our arrival, I looked out of my window and saw the whole landscape transmuted before me. The clouds had dipped low and hidden the mountain in the west; a southern wind was driving the rain in shifting pillars up the valley, and the little brooklet that burst the hill below the house now raged, a red torrent, down to the river. We were perforce obliged to keep snug within-doors; and when I had attended to my pupils, I sat down in the morning-room, where the ruins of a library still encumbered an old-fashioned bookcase. I had inspected the shelves once or twice, but their contents had failed to attract me; volumes of eighteenth-century sermons, an old book on farriery, a collection of poems by "persons of quality," Prideaus's *Connection*, and an odd volume of Pope, were the boundaries of the library, and there seemed little doubt that everything of interest or value had been removed. Now, however, in desperation, I began to re-examine the musty sheepskin and calf bindings, and found, much to my delight, a fine old quarto printed by the Stephani, containing the three books of Pomponius Mela, *De Situ Orbis*, and other of the ancient geographers. I knew enough of Latin to steer my way through an ordinary sentence, and I soon became absorbed in the odd mixture of fact and fancy—light shining on a little of the space of the world, and beyond, mist and shadow and awful forms. Glancing over the clear-printed pages, my attention was caught by the heading of a chapter in Solinus, and I read the words:

> MIRA DE INTIMIS GENTIBUS LIBYAE. DE LAPIDE HEXECONTALITHO,—

"The wonders of the people that inhabit the inner parts of Libya, and of the stone called Sixtystone."

The odd title attracted me, and I read on:

> *Gens ista avia et secreta habitat, in montibus horrendis foeda mysteria celebrat. De hominibus nihil aliud illi praeferunt quam figuram, ab humano ritu prorsus exulant, oderunt deum lucis.*
>
> *Stridunt potius quam loquuntur; vox absona nec sine horrore auditur. Lapide quodam gloriantur, quem Hexecontalithon vocant; dicunt enim hunc lapidem sexaginta notas ostendere.*
>
> *Cujus lapidis nomen secretum ineffabile colunt: quod Ixaxar.*

"This folk," I translated to myself, "dwells in remote and secret places, and celebrates foul mysteries on savage hills. Nothing have they in common with men save the face, and the customs of humanity are wholly strange to them; and they hate the sun. They hiss rather than speak; their voices are harsh, and not to be heard without fear. They boast of a certain stone, which they call Sixtystone; for they say that it displays sixty characters. And this stone has a secret unspeakable name; which is Ixaxar."

I laughed at the queer inconsequence of all this, and thought it fit for "Sinbad the Sailor," or other of the supplementary *Nights*. When I saw Professor Gregg in the course of the day, I told him of my find in the bookcase, and the fantastic rubbish I had been reading. To my surprise he looked up at me with an expression of great interest.

"That is really very curious," he said. "I have never thought it worth while to look into the old geographers, and I dare say I have missed a good deal. Ah, that is the passage, is it? It seems a shame to rob you of your entertainment, but I really think I must carry off the book."

The next day the professor called me to come to the study. I found him sitting at a table in the full light of the window, scrutinizing something very attentively with a magnifying glass.

"Ah, Miss Lally," he began, "I want to use your eyes. This glass is pretty good, but not like my old one that I left in town. Would you mind examining the thing yourself, and telling me how many characters are cut on it?"

He handed me the object in his hand. I saw that it was the black seal he had shown me in London, and my heart began to beat with the thought that I was presently to know something. I took the seal, and, holding it up to the light, checked off the grotesque dagger-shaped characters one by one.

"I make sixty-two," I said at last.

"Sixty-two? Nonsense; it's impossible. Ah, I see what you have done, you have counted that and that," and he pointed to two marks which I had certainly taken as letters with the rest.

"Yes, yes," Professor Gregg went on, "but those are obviously scratches, done accidentally; I saw that at once. Yes, then that's quite right. Thank you very much, Miss Lally."

I was going away, rather disappointed at my having been called in merely to count the number of marks on the black seal, when suddenly there flashed into my mind what I had read in the morning.

"But, Professor Gregg," I cried, breathless, "the seal, the seal. Why, it is the stone Hexecontalithos that Solinus writes of; it is Ixaxar."

"Yes," he said, "I suppose it is. Or it may be a mere coincidence. It never does to be too sure, you know, in these matters. Coincidence killed the professor."

I went away puzzled by what I had heard, and as much as ever at a loss to find the ruling clue in this maze of strange evidence. For three days the bad weather lasted, changing from driving rain to a dense mist, fine and dripping, and we seemed to be shut up in a white cloud that veiled all the world away from us. All the while Professor Gregg was darkling in his room, unwilling, it appeared, to dispense confidences or talk of any kind, and I heard him walking to and fro with a quick, impatient step, as if he were in some way wearied of inaction. The fourth morning was fine, and at breakfast the professor said briskly:

"We want some extra help about the house; a boy of fifteen or sixteen, you know. There are a lot of little odd jobs that take up the maids' time which a boy could do much better."

"The girls have not complained to me in any way," I replied. "Indeed, Anne said there was much less work than in London, owing to there being so little dust;"

"Ah, yes, they are very good girls. But I think we shall do much better with a boy. In fact, that is what has been bothering me for the last two days."

"Bothering you?" I said in astonishment, for as a matter of fact the professor never took the slightest interest in the affairs of the house.

"Yes," he said, "the weather, you know. I really couldn't go out in that Scotch mist; I don't know the country very well, and I should have lost my way. But I am going to get the boy this morning."

"But how do you know there is such a boy as you want anywhere about?"

"Oh, I have no doubt as to that. I may have to walk a mile or two at the most, but I am sure to find just the boy I require."

I thought the professor was joking, but, though his tone was airy enough, there was something grim and set about his features that puzzled me. He got his stick, and stood at the door looking meditatively before him, and as I passed through the hall he called to me.

"By the way, Miss Lally, there was one thing I wanted to say to you. I dare say you may have heard that some of these country lads are not over-bright; 'idiotic' would be a harsh word to use, and they are usually called 'naturals', or something of the kind. I hope you won't mind if the boy I am after should turn out not too keen-witted; he will be perfectly harmless, of course, and blacking boots doesn't need much mental effort."

With that he was gone, striding up the road that led to the wood, and I remained stupefied; and then for the first time my astonishment was mingled with a sudden note of terror, arising I knew not whence, and all unexplained even to myself, and yet I felt about my heart for an instant something of the chill of death, and that shapeless, formless dread of the unknown that is worse than death itself. I tried to find courage in the sweet air that blew up from the sea, and in the sunlight after rain, but the mystic woods seemed to darken around me; and the vision of the river coiling between the reeds, and the silver grey of the ancient bridge, fashioned in my mind symbols of vague dread, as the mind of a child fashions terror from things harmless and familiar.

Two hours later Professor Gregg returned. I met him as he came down the road, and asked quietly if he had been able to find a boy.

"Oh, yes." he answered; "I found one easily enough. His name is Jervase Cradock, and I expect he will make himself very useful. His father has been dead for many years, and the mother, whom I saw, seemed very glad at the prospect of a few shillings extra coming in on Saturday nights. As I expected, he is not too sharp, has fits at times, the mother said; but as he will not be trusted with the china, that doesn't much matter, does it? And he is not in any way dangerous, you know, merely a little weak."

"When is he coming?"

"Tomorrow morning at eight o'clock. Anne will show him what he has to do, and how to do it. At first he will go home every night, but perhaps it may ultimately turn out more convenient for him to sleep here, and only go home for Sundays."

I found nothing to say to all this; Professor Gregg spoke in a quiet tone of matter-of-fact, as indeed was warranted by the circumstance; and yet I could not quell my sensation of astonishment at the whole affair. I knew that in reality no assistance was wanted in the housework, and the professor's prediction that the boy he was to engage might prove a little "simple," followed by so exact a fulfilment, struck me as bizarre in the extreme. The next morning I heard from the housemaid that the boy Cradock had come at eight, and that she had been trying to make him useful. "He doesn't seem quite all there, I don't think, miss," was her comment, and later in the day I saw him helping the old man who worked in the garden. He was a youth of about fourteen, with black hair and black eyes and an olive skin, and I saw at once from the curious vacancy of his expression that he was mentally weak. He touched his forehead awkwardly as I went by, and I heard him answering the gardener in a queer, harsh voice that caught my attention; it gave me the impression of some one speaking deep below under the earth, and there was a strange sibilance, like the hissing of the phonograph as the pointer travels over the cylinder. I heard that he seemed anxious to do what he could, and was quite docile and obedient, and Morgan the gardener, who knew his mother, assured me he was perfectly harmless. "He's always been a bit queer," he said, "and no wonder, after what his mother went through before he was born. I did know his father, Thomas Cradock, well, and a very fine workman he was too, indeed. He got something wrong with his lungs owing to working in the wet woods, and never got over it, and went off quite sudden like. And they do say as how Mrs. Cradock was quite off her head: anyhow, she was found by Mr. Hillyer, Ty Coch, all crouched up on the Grey Hills, over there, crying and weeping like a lost soul. And Jervase, he was born about eight months afterwards, and, as I was saying, he was a bit queer always; and they do say when he could scarcely walk he would frighten the other children into fits with the noises he would make."

A word in the story had stirred up some remembrance within me, and, vaguely curious, I asked the old man where the Grey Hills were.

"Up there," he said, with the same gesture he had used before; "you go past the 'Fox and Hounds,' and through the forest, by the old ruins. It's a good five mile from here, and a strange sort of a place. The poorest soil between this and Monmouth, they do say, though it's good feed for sheep. Yes, it was a sad thing for poor Mrs. Cradock."

The old man turned to his work, and I strolled on down the path between the espaliers, gnarled and gouty with age, thinking of the story I had heard, and groping for the point in it that had some key to my memory. In an instant it came before me; I had seen the phrase "Grey Hills" on the slip of yellowed paper that Professor Gregg had taken from the drawer in his cabinet. Again I was seized with pangs of mingled curiosity and fear; I remembered the strange characters copied from the limestone rock, and then again their identity with the inscription of the age-old seal, and the fantastic fables of the Latin geographer. I saw beyond doubt that, unless coincidence had set all the scene and disposed all these bizarre events with curious art, I was to be a spectator of things far removed from the usual and customary traffic and jostle of life. Professor Gregg I noted day by day; he was hot on his trail, growing lean with eagerness; and in the evenings, when the sun was swimming on the verge of the mountain, he would pace the terrace to and fro with his eyes on the ground, while the mist grew white in the valley, and the stillness of the evening brought far voices near, and the blue smoke rose a straight column from the diamond-shaped chimney of the grey farmhouse, just as I had seen it on the first morning. I have told you I was of sceptical habit; but though I understood little or nothing, I began to dread, vainly proposing to myself the iterated dogmas of science that all life is material, and that in the system of things there is no undiscovered land, even beyond the remotest stars, where the supernatural can find a footing. Yet there struck in on this the thought that matter is as really awful and unknown as spirit, that science itself but dallies on the threshold, scarcely gaining more than a glimpse of the wonders of the inner place.

There is one day that stands up from amidst the others as a grim red beacon, betokening evil to come. I was sitting on a bench in the garden, watching the boy Cradock weeding, when I was suddenly alarmed by a harsh and choking sound, like the cry of a wild beast in anguish, and I was unspeakably shocked to see the unfortunate lad standing in full view before me, his whole body quivering and shaking at short intervals as though shocks of electricity were passing through him, his teeth grinding, foam gathering on his lips, and his face all swollen and blackened to a hideous mask of humanity. I shrieked with terror, and Professor Gregg came running; and as I pointed to Cradock, the boy with one convulsive shudder fell face forward, and lay on the wet earth, his body writhing like a wounded blind-worm, and an inconceivable babble of sounds bursting and rattling and hissing from his lips. He seemed to pour forth an infamous jargon, with words, or what seemed words, that might have belonged to a tongue dead since untold ages and buried deep beneath Nilotic mud, or in the inmost recesses of the Mexican forest. For a moment the thought passed through my mind, as my ears were still revolted with that infernal clamour, "Surely this is the very speech of hell," and then I cried out again and again, and ran away shuddering to my inmost soul. I had seen Professor Gregg's face as he stooped over the wretched boy and raised him, and I was appalled by the glow of exultation that shone on every lineament and feature. As I sat in my room with drawn blinds, and my eyes hidden in my hands, I heard heavy steps beneath, and I was told afterwards that Professor Gregg had carried Cradock to his study, and had locked the door. I heard voices murmur indistinctly, and I trembled to think of what might be passing within a few feet of where I sat; I longed to escape to the woods and sunshine, and yet I dreaded the sights that might confront me on the way; and at last, as I held the handle of the door nervously, I heard Professor Gregg's voice calling to me with a cheerful ring. "It's all right now, Miss Lally," he said. "The poor fellow has got over it, and I have been arranging for him to sleep here after tomorrow. Perhaps I may be able to do something for him."

"Yes," he said later, "it was a very painful sight, and I don't wonder you were alarmed. We may hope that good food will build him up a little, but I am afraid he will never be really cured," and he affected the dismal and conventional air with which one speaks of hopeless illness; and yet beneath it I detected the delight that leapt up rampant within him, and fought and struggled to find utterance. It was as if one glanced down on the even surface of the sea, clear and immobile, and saw beneath raging depths and a storm of contending billows. It was indeed to me a torturing and offensive problem that this man, who had so bounteously rescued me from the sharpness of death, and showed himself in all the relations of life full of benevolence, and pity, and kindly forethought, should so manifestly be for once on the side of the demons, and take a ghastly pleasure in the torments of an afflicted fellow creature. Apart, I struggled with the horned difficulty, and strove to find the solution; but without the hint of a clue, beset by mystery and contradiction. I saw nothing that might help me, and began to wonder whether, after all, I had not escaped from the white mist of the suburb at too dear a rate. I hinted something of my thought to the professor; I said enough to let him know that I was in the most acute perplexity, but the moment after regretted what I had done when I saw his face contort with a spasm of pain.

"My dear Miss Lally," he said, "you surely do not wish to leave us? No, no, you would not do it. You do not know how I rely on you; how confidently I go forward, assured that you are here to watch over my children. You, Miss Lally, are my rear-guard; for let me tell you the business in which I am engaged is not wholly devoid of peril. You have not forgotten what I said the first morning here; my lips are shut by an old and firm resolve till they can open to utter no ingenious hypothesis or vague surmise, but irrefragable fact, as certain as a demonstration in mathematics. Think over it, Miss Lally; not for a moment would I endeavour to keep you here against your own instincts, and yet I tell you frankly that I am persuaded it is here, here amidst the woods, that your duty lies."

I was touched by the eloquence of his tone, and by the remembrance that the man, after all, had been my salvation, and I gave him my hand on a promise to serve him loyally and without question. A few days later the rector of our church—a little church, grey and severe and quaint, that hovered on the very banks of the river and watched the tides swim and return—came to see us, and Professor Gregg easily persuaded him to stay and share our dinner. Mr. Meyrick was a member of an antique family of squires, whose old manor-house stood amongst the hills some seven miles away, and thus rooted in the soil, the rector was a living store of all the old fading customs and lore of the country. His manner, genial, with a deal of retired oddity, won on Professor Gregg; and towards the cheese, when a curious Burgundy had begun its incantations, the two men glowed like the wine, and talked of philology with the enthusiasm of a burgess over the peerage. The parson was expounding the pronunciation of the Welsh *ll*, and producing sounds like the gurgle of his native brooks, when Professor Gregg struck in.

"By the way," he said, "that was a very odd word I met with the other day. You know my boy, poor Jervase Cradock? Well, he has got the bad habit of talking to himself, and the day before yesterday I was walking in the garden here and heard him; he was evidently quite unconscious of my presence. A lot of what he said I couldn't make out, but one word struck me distinctly. It was such an odd sound, half sibilant, half guttural, and as quaint as those double *l*'s you have been demonstrating. I do not know whether I can give you an idea of the sound; 'Ishakshar' is perhaps as near as I can get. But the *k* ought to be a Greek *chi* or a Spanish *j*. Now what does it mean in Welsh?"

"In Welsh?" said the parson. "There is no such word in Welsh, nor any word remotely resembling it. I know the book-Welsh, as they call it, and the colloquial dialects as well as any man, but there's no word like that from Anglesea to Usk. Besides, none of the Cradocks speak a word of Welsh; it's dying out about here."

"Really. You interest me extremely, Mr. Meyrick. I confess the word didn't strike me as having the Welsh ring. But I thought it might be some local corruption."

"No, I never heard such a word, or anything like it. Indeed," he added, smiling whimsically, "if it belongs to any language, I should say it must be that of the fairies—the Tylwydd Têg, as we call them."

The talk went on to the discovery of a Roman villa in the neighbourhood; and soon after I left the room, and sat down apart to wonder at the drawing together of such strange clues of evidence. As the professor had spoken of the curious word, I had caught the glint in his eye upon me; and though the pronunciation he gave was grotesque in the extreme, I recognized the name of the stone of sixty characters mentioned by Solinus, the black seal shut up in some secret drawer of the study, stamped for ever by a vanished race with signs that no man could read, signs that might, for all I knew, be the veils of awful things done long ago, and forgotten before the hills were moulded into form.

When the next morning I came down, I found Professor Gregg pacing the terrace in his eternal walk.

"Look at that bridge," he said, when he saw me; "observe the quaint and Gothic design, the angles between the arches, and the silvery grey of the stone in the awe of the morning light. I confess it seems to me symbolic; it should illustrate a mystical allegory of the passage from one world to another."

"Professor Gregg," I said quietly, "it is time that I knew something of what has happened, and of what is to happen."

For the moment he put me off, but I returned again with the same question in the evening, and then Professor Gregg flamed with excitement. "Don't you understand yet?" he cried. "But I have told you a good deal; yes, and shown you a good deal; you have heard pretty nearly all that I have heard, and seen what I have seen; or at least," and his voice chilled as he spoke, "enough to make a good deal clear as noonday. The servants told you, I have no doubt, that the wretched boy Cradock had another seizure the night before last; he awoke me with cries in that voice you heard in the garden, and I went to him, and God forbid you should see what I saw that night. But all this is useless; my time here is drawing to a close; I must be back in town in three weeks, as I have a course of lectures to prepare, and need all my books about me. In a very few days it will be all over, and I shall no longer hint, and no longer be liable to ridicule as a madman and a quack. No, I shall speak plainly, and I shall be heard with such emotions as perhaps no other man has ever drawn from the breasts of his fellows."

He paused, and seemed to grow radiant with the joy of great and wonderful discovery.

"But all that is for the future, the near future certainly, but still the future," he went on at length. "There is something to be done yet; you will remember my telling you that my researches were not altogether devoid of peril? Yes, there, is a certain amount of danger to be faced; I did not know how much when I spoke on the subject before, and to a certain extent I am still in the dark. But it will be a strange adventure, the last of all, the last demonstration in the chain."

He was walking up and down the room as he spoke, and I could hear in his voice the contending tones of exultation and despondence, or perhaps I should say awe, the awe of a man who goes forth on unknown waters, and I thought of his allusion to Columbus on the night he had laid his book before me. The evening was a little chilly, and a fire of logs had been lighted in the study where we were; the remittent flame and the glow on the walls reminded me of the old days. I was sitting silent in an armchair by the fire, wondering over all I had heard, and still vainly speculating as to the secret springs concealed from me under all the phantasmagoria I had witnessed, when I became suddenly aware of a sensation that change of some sort had been at work in the room, and that there was something unfamiliar in its aspect. For some time I looked about me, trying in vain to localize the alteration that I knew had been made; the table by the window, the chairs, the faded settee were all as I had known them. Suddenly, as a sought-for recollection flashes into the mind, I knew what was amiss. I was facing the professor's desk, which stood on the other side of the fire, and above the desk was a grimy-looking bust of Pitt, that I had never seen there before. And then I remembered the true position of this work of art; in the furthest corner by the door was an old cupboard, projecting into the room, and on the top of the cupboard, fifteen feet from the floor, the bust had been, and there, no doubt, it had delayed, accumulating dirt, since the early days of the century.

I was utterly amazed, and sat silent, still in a confusion of thought. There was, so far as I knew, no such thing as a stepladder in the house, for I had asked for one to make some alteration in the curtains of my room, and a tall man standing on a chair would have found it impossible to take down the bust. It had been placed, not on the edge of the cupboard, but far back against the wall; and Professor Gregg was, if anything, under the average height.

"How on earth did you manage to get down Pitt?" I said at last.

The professor looked curiously at me, and seemed to hesitate a little.

"They must have found you a step-ladder, or perhaps the gardener brought in a short ladder from outside?"

"No, I have had no ladder of any kind. Now, Miss Lally," he went on with an awkward simulation of jest, "there is a little puzzle for you; a problem in the manner of the inimitable Holmes; there are the facts, plain and patent: summon your acuteness to the solution of the puzzle. For Heaven's sake," he cried with a breaking voice, "say no more about it! I tell you, I never touched the thing," and he went out of the room with horror manifest on his face, and his hand shook and jarred the door behind him.

I looked round the room in vague surprise, not at all realizing what had happened, making vain and idle surmises by way of explanation, and wondering at the stirring of black waters by an idle word and the trivial change of an ornament. "This is some petty business, some whim on which I have jarred." I reflected; "the professor is perhaps scrupulous and superstitious over trifles, and my question may have outraged unacknowledged fears, as though one killed a spider or spilled the salt before the very eyes of a practical Scotchwoman." I was immersed in these fond suspicions, and began to plume myself a little on my immunity from such empty fears, when the truth fell heavily as lead upon my heart, and I recognized with cold terror that some awful influence had been at work. The bust was simply inaccessible; without a ladder no one could have touched it.

I went out to the kitchen and spoke as quietly as I could to the housemaid.

"Who moved that bust from the top of the cupboard, Anne?" I said to her. "Professor Gregg says he has not touched it. Did you find an old step-ladder in one of the outhouses?"

The girl looked at me blankly.

"I never touched it," she said. "I found it where it is now the other morning when I dusted the room. I remember now, it was Wednesday morning, because it was the morning after Cradock was taken bad in the night. My room is next to his, you know, miss," the girl went on piteously, "and it was awful to hear how he cried and called out names that I couldn't understand. It made me feel all afraid; and then master came, and I heard him speak, and he took down Cradock to the study and gave him something."

"And you found that bust moved the next morning?"

"Yes, miss. There was a queer sort of smell in the study when I came down and opened the windows; a bad smell it was, and I wondered what it could be. Do you know, miss, I went a long time ago to the Zoo in London with my cousin Thomas Barker, one afternoon that I had off, when I was at Mrs. Prince's in Stanhope Gate, and we went into the snake-house to see the snakes, and it was just the same sort of smell; very sick it made me feel, I remember, and I got Barker to take me out. And it was just the same kind of smell in the study, as I was saying, and I was wondering what it could be from, when I see that bust with Pitt cut in it, standing on the master's desk, and I thought to myself, 'Now who has done that, and how have they done it?' And when I came to dust the things, I looked at the bust, and I saw a great mark on it where the dust was gone, for I don't think it can have been touched with a duster for years and years, and it wasn't like finger-marks, but a large patch like, broad and spread out. So I passed my hand over it, without thinking what I was doing, and where that patch was it was all sticky and slimy, as if a snail had crawled over it. Very strange, isn't it, miss? and I wonder who can have done it, and how that mess was made."

The well-meant gabble of the servant touched me to the quick; I lay down upon my bed, and bit my lip that I should not cry out loud in the sharp anguish of my terror and bewilderment. Indeed, I was almost mad with dread; I believe that if it had been daylight I should have fled hot foot, forgetting all courage and all the debt of gratitude that was due to Professor Gregg, not caring whether my fate were that I must starve slowly, so long as

I might escape from the net of blind and panic fear that every day seemed to draw a little closer round me. If I knew, I thought, if I knew what there was to dread, I could guard against it; but here, in this lonely house, shut in on all sides by the olden woods and the vaulted hills, terror seems to spring inconsequent from every covert, and the flesh is aghast at the half-hearted murmurs of horrible things. All in vain I strove to summon scepticism to my aid, and endeavoured by cool common sense to buttress my belief in a world of natural order, for the air that blew in at the open window was a mystic breath, and in the darkness I felt the silence go heavy and sorrowful as a mass of requiem, and I conjured images of strange shapes gathering fast amidst the reeds, beside the wash of the river.

In the morning from the moment that I set foot in the breakfast-room, I felt that the unknown plot was drawing to a crisis; the professor's face was firm and set, and he seemed hardly to hear our voices when we spoke.

"I am going out for a rather long walk," he said, when the meal was over. "You mustn't be expecting me, now, or thinking anything has happened if I don't turn up to dinner. I have been getting stupid lately, and I dare say a miniature walking tour will do me good. Perhaps I may even spend the night in some little inn, if I find any place that looks clean and comfortable."

I heard this, and knew by my experience of Professor Gregg's manner that it was no ordinary business of pleasure that impelled him. I knew not, nor even remotely guessed, where he was bound, nor had I the vaguest notion of his errand, but all the fear of the night before returned; and as he stood, smiling, on the terrace, ready to set out, I implored him to stay, and to forget all his dreams of the undiscovered continent.

"No, no, Miss Lally," he replied, still smiling, "it's too late now. *Vestigia nulla retrorsum*, you know, is the device of all true explorers, though I hope it won't be literally true in my case. But, indeed, you are wrong to alarm yourself so; I look upon my little expedition as quite commonplace; no more exciting than a day with the geological hammers. There is a risk, of course, but so there is on the commonest excursion. I can afford to be jaunty; I am doing nothing so hazardous as 'Arry does a hundred times over in the course of every Bank Holiday. Well, then, you must look more cheerfully; and so good-bye till tomorrow at latest."

He walked briskly up the road, and I saw him open the gate that marks the entrance of the wood, and then he vanished in the gloom of the trees.

All the day passed heavily with a strange darkness in the air, and again I felt as if imprisoned amidst the ancient woods, shut in an olden land of mystery and dread, and as if all was long ago and forgotten by the living outside. I hoped and dreaded; and when the dinner-hour came I waited, expecting to hear the professor's step in the hall, and his voice exulting at I knew not what triumph. I composed my face to welcome him gladly, but the night descended dark, and he did not come.

In the morning, when the maid knocked at my door, I called out to her, and asked if her master had returned; and when she replied that his bedroom door stood open and empty, I felt the cold clasp of despair. Still, I fancied he might have discovered genial company, and would return for luncheon, or perhaps in the afternoon, and I took the children for a walk in the forest, and tried my best to play and laugh with them, and to shut out the thoughts of mystery and veiled terror.

Hour after hour I waited, and my thoughts grew darker; again the night came and found me watching, and at last, as I was making much ado to finish my dinner, I heard steps outside and the sound of a man's voice.

The maid came in and looked oddly at me. "Please, miss," she began, "Mr. Morgan, the gardener, wants to speak to you for a minute, if you didn't mind."

"Show him in, please," I answered, and set my lips tight.

The old man came slowly into the room, and the servant shut the door behind him.

"Sit down, Mr. Morgan," I said; "what is it that you want to say to me?"

"Well, miss, Mr. Gregg he gave me something for you yesterday morning, just before he went off, and he told me particular not to hand it up before eight o'clock this evening exactly, if so be as he wasn't back again home before, and if he should come home before I was just to return it to him in his own hands. So, you see, as Mr. Gregg isn't here yet, I suppose I'd better give you the parcel directly."

He pulled out something from his pocket, and gave it to me, half rising. I took it silently, and seeing that Morgan seemed doubtful as to what he was to do next. I thanked him and bade him good night, and he went out. I was left alone in the room with the parcel in my hand—a paper parcel, neatly sealed and directed to me, with the instructions Morgan had quoted, all written in the professor's large, loose hand. I broke the seals with a choking at my heart, and found an envelope inside, addressed also, but open, and I took the letter out.

My dear Miss Lally, it began—*To quote the old logic manual, the case of your reading this note is a case of my having made a blunder of some sort, and, I am afraid, a blunder that turns these lines into a farewell. It is practically certain that neither you nor any one else will ever see me again. I have made my will with provision for this eventuality, and I hope you will consent to accept the small remembrance addressed to you, and my sincere thanks for the way in which you joined your fortunes to mine. The fate which has come upon me is desperate and terrible beyond the remotest dreams of man; but this fate you have a right to know—if you please. If you look in the left-hand drawer of my dressing-table, you will find the key of the escritoire, properly labelled. In the well of the escritoire is a large envelope sealed and addressed to your name. I advise you to throw it forthwith into the fire; you will sleep better of nights if you do so. But if you must know the history of what has happened, it is all written down for you to read.*

The signature was firmly written below, and again I turned the page and read out the words one by one, aghast and white to the lips, my hands cold as ice, and sickness choking me. The dead silence of the room, and the thought of the dark woods and hills closing me in on every side, oppressed me, helpless and without capacity, and not knowing where to turn for counsel. At last I resolved that though knowledge should haunt my whole life and all the days to come, I must know the meaning of the strange terrors that had so long tormented me, rising grey, dim, and awful, like the shadows in the wood at dusk. I carefully carried out Professor Gregg's directions, and not without reluctance broke the seal of the envelope, and spread out his manuscript before me. That manuscript I always carry with me, and I see that I cannot deny your unspoken request to read it. This, then, was what I read that night, sitting at the desk, with a shaded lamp beside me.

The young lady who called herself Miss Lally then proceeded to recite

THE STATEMENT OF WILLIAM GREGG. F.R.S., etc.

It is many years since the first glimmer of the theory which is now almost, if not quite, reduced to fact dawned on my mind. A somewhat extensive course of miscellaneous and obsolete reading had done a great deal to prepare the way, and, later, when I became somewhat of a specialist, and immersed myself in the studies known as ethnological, I was now and then startled by facts that would not square with orthodox scientific opinion, and by discoveries that seemed to hint at something still hidden for all our research. More particularly I became convinced that much of the folk-lore of the world is but an exaggerated account of events that really happened, and I was especially drawn to consider the stories of the fairies, the good folk of the Celtic races. Here, I thought I could detect the fringe of embroidery and exaggeration, the fantastic guise, the little people dressed in green and gold sporting in the flowers, and I thought I saw a distinct analogy between the name given to this race (supposed to be imaginary) and the description of their appearance and manners. Just as our remote ancestors called the dreaded beings "fair" and "good" precisely because they dreaded them, so they had dressed them up in charming forms, knowing the truth to be the very reverse. Literature, too, had gone early to work, and had lent a powerful hand in the transformation, so that the playful elves of Shakespere are already far removed from the true original, and the real horror is disguised in a form of prankish mischief. But in the older tales, the stories that used to make men cross themselves as they sat around the burning logs, we tread a different stage; I saw a widely opposed spirit in certain histories of children and of men and women who vanished strangely from the earth. They would be seen by a peasant in the fields walking towards some green and rounded hillock, and seen no more on earth; and there are stories of mothers who have left a child quietly sleeping, with the cottage door rudely barred with a piece of wood, and have returned, not to find the plump and rosy little Saxon, but a thin and wizened creature, with sallow skin and black, piercing eyes, the child of another race. Then, again, there were myths darker still; the dread of witch and wizard, the lurid evil of the Sabbath, and the hint of demons who mingled with the daughters of men. And just as we have turned the terrible "fair folk" into a company of benignant, if freakish elves, so we have hidden from us the black foulness of the witch and her companions under a popular *diablerie* of old women and broomsticks, and a comic cat with tail on end. So the Greeks called the hideous furies benevolent ladies, and thus the northern nations have followed their example. I pursued my investigations, stealing odd hours from other and more imperative labours, and I asked myself the question: Supposing these traditions to be true, who were the demons who are reported to have attended the Sabbaths? I need not say that I laid aside what I may call the supernatural hypothesis of the Middle Ages, and came to the conclusion that fairies and devils were of one and the same race and origin; invention, no doubt, and the Gothic fancy of old days, had done much in the way of exaggeration and distortion; yet I firmly believe that beneath all this imagery there was a black background of truth. As for some of the alleged wonders, I hesitated. While I should be very loath to receive any one specific instance of modern spiritualism as containing even a grain of the genuine, yet I was not wholly prepared to deny that human flesh may now and then, once perhaps in ten millions cases, be the veil of powers which seem magical to us—powers which, so far from proceeding from the heights and leading men thither, are in reality survivals from the depths of being. The amoeba and the snail have powers which we do not possess; and I thought it possible that the theory of reversion might explain many things which seem wholly inexplicable.

Thus stood my position; I saw good reason to believe that much of the tradition, a vast deal of the earliest and uncorrupted tradition of the so-called fairies, represented solid fact, and I thought that the purely supernatural element in these traditions was to be accounted for on the hypothesis that a race which had fallen out of the grand march of evolution might have retained, as a survival, certain powers which would be to us wholly miraculous. Such was my theory as it stood conceived in my mind; and working with this in view, I seemed to gather confirmation from every side, from the spoils of a tumulus or a barrow, from a local paper reporting an antiquarian meeting in the country, and from general literature of all kinds. Amongst other instances, I remember being struck by the phrase "articulate-speaking men" in Homer, as if the writer knew or had heard of men whose speech was so rude that it could hardly be termed articulate; and on my hypothesis of a race who had lagged far behind the rest, I could easily conceive that such a folk would speak a jargon but little removed from the inarticulate noises of brute beasts.

Thus I stood, satisfied that my conjecture was at all events not far removed from fact, when a chance paragraph in a small country print one day arrested my attention. It was a short account of what was to all appearance the usual sordid tragedy of the village—a young girl unaccountably missing, and evil rumour blatant and busy with her reputation. Yet I could read between the lines that all this scandal was purely hypothetical, and in all probability invented to account for what was in any other manner unaccountable. A flight to London or Liverpool, or an undiscovered body lying with a weight about its neck in the foul depths of a woodland pool, or perhaps murder—such were the theories of the wretched girl's neighbours. But as I idly scanned the paragraph, a flash of thought passed through me with the violence of an electric shock: what if the obscure and horrible race of the hills still survived, still remained haunting wild places and barren hills, and now and then repeating the evil of Gothic legend, unchanged and unchangeable as the Turanian Shelta, or the Basques of Spain? I have said that the thought came with violence; and indeed I drew in my breath sharply, and clung with both hands to my elbow-chair, in a strange confusion of horror and elation. It was as if one of my *confrères* of physical science, roaming in a quiet English wood, had been suddenly stricken aghast by the presence of the slimy and loathsome terror of the ichthyosaurus, the original of the stories of the awful worms killed by valorous knights, or had seen the sun darkened by the pterodactyl, the dragon of tradition. Yet as a resolute explorer of knowledge, the thought of such a discovery threw me into a passion of joy, and I cut out the slip from the paper and put it in a drawer in my old bureau, resolved that it should be but the first piece in a collection of the strangest significance. I sat long that evening dreaming of the conclusions I should establish, nor did cooler reflection at first dash my confidence. Yet as I began to put the case fairly, I saw that I might be building on an unstable foundation; the facts might possibly be in accordance with local opinion, and I regarded the affair with a mood of some reserve. Yet I resolved to remain perched on the look-out, and I hugged to myself the thought that I alone was watching and wakeful, while the great crowd of thinkers and searchers stood heedless and indifferent, perhaps letting the most prerogative facts pass by unnoticed.

Several years elapsed before I was enabled to add to the contents of the drawer; and the second find was in reality not a valuable one, for it was a mere repetition of the first, with only the variation of another and distant locality. Yet I gained something; for in the second case, as in the first, the tragedy took place in a desolate and lonely country, and so far my theory seemed justified. But the third piece was to me far more decisive. Again, amongst outland hills, far even from a main road of traffic, an old man was found done to death, and the instrument of execution was left beside him. Here, indeed, there were rumour and conjecture, for the deadly tool was a primitive stone axe, bound by gut to the wooden handle, and surmises the most extravagant and improbable were indulged in. Yet, as I thought with a kind of glee, the wildest conjectures went far astray; and I took the pains to enter into correspondence with the local doctor, who was called at the inquest. He, a man of some acuteness, was dumbfounded. "It will not do to speak of these things in country places," he wrote to me; "but frankly, there is some hideous mystery here. I have obtained possession of the stone axe, and have been so curious as to test its powers. I took it into the back garden of my house one Sunday afternoon when my family and the servants were all out, and there, sheltered by the poplar hedges, I made my experiments. I found the thing utterly unmanageable; whether there is some peculiar balance, some nice adjustment of weights, which require incessant practice, or whether an effectual blow can be struck only by a certain trick of the muscles, I do not know; but I can assure you that I went into the house with but a sorry opinion of my athletic capacities. I was like an inexperienced man trying 'putting the hammer;' the force exerted seemed to return on oneself, and I found myself hurled backwards with violence, while the axe fell harmless to the ground. On another occasion I tried the experiment with a clever woodman of the place; but this man, who had handled his axe for forty years, could do nothing with the stone implement, and missed every stroke most ludicrously. In short, if it were not so supremely absurd, I should say that for four thousand years no one on earth could have struck an effective blow with the tool that undoubtedly was used to murder the old man." This, as may be imagined, was to me rare news; and afterwards, when I heard the whole story, and learned that the unfortunate old man had babbled tales of what might be seen at night on a certain wild hillside, hinting at unheard-of wonders, and that he had been found cold one morning on the very hill in question, my exultation was extreme, for I felt I was leaving conjecture far behind me. But the next step was of still greater importance. I had possessed for many years an extraordinary stone seal—a piece of dull black stone, two inches long from the handle to the stamp, and the stamping end a rough hexagon an inch and a quarter in diameter. Altogether, it presented the appearance of an enlarged tobacco stopper of an old-fashioned make. It had been sent to me by an agent in the East, who informed me that it had been found near the site of the ancient Babylon. But the characters engraved on the seal were to me an intolerable puzzle. Somewhat of the cuneiform pattern, there were yet striking differences, which I detected at the first glance, and all efforts to read the inscription on the hypothesis that the rules for deciphering the arrow-headed writing would apply proved futile. A riddle such as this stung my pride, and at odd moments I would take the Black Seal out of the cabinet, and scrutinize it with so much idle perseverance that every letter was familiar to my mind, and I could have drawn the inscription from memory without the slightest error. Judge, then, of my surprise when I one day received from a correspondent in the west of England a letter and an enclosure that positively left me thunderstruck. I saw carefully traced on a large piece of paper the very characters of the Black Seal, without alteration of any kind, and above the inscription my friend had written: *Inscription found on a limestone rock on the Grey Hills, Monmouthshire. Done in some red earth, and quite recent.* I turned to the letter. My friend wrote: "I send you the enclosed inscription with all due reserve. A shepherd who passed by the stone a week ago swears that there was then no mark of any kind. The characters, as I have noted, are formed by drawing some red earth over the stone, and are of an average height of one inch. They look to me like a kind of cuneiform character, a good deal altered, but this, of course, is impossible. It may be either a hoax, or more probably some scribble of the gipsies, who are plentiful enough in this wild country. They have, as you are aware, many hieroglyphics which they use in communicating with one another. I happened to visit the stone in question two days ago in connection with a rather painful incident which has occurred here."

As it may be supposed, I wrote immediately to my friends, thanking him for the copy of the inscription, and asking him in a casual manner the history of the incident he mentioned. To be brief, I heard that a woman named Cradock, who had lost her husband a day before, had set out to communicate the sad news to a cousin who lived some five miles away. She took a short cut which led by the Grey Hills. Mrs. Cradock, who was then quite a young woman, never arrived at her relative's house. Late that night a farmer, who had lost a couple of sheep, supposed to have wandered from the flock, was walking over the Grey Hills, with a lantern and his dog. His attention was attracted by a noise, which he described as a kind of wailing, mournful and pitiable to hear; and, guided by the sound, he found the unfortunate Mrs. Cradock crouched on the ground by the limestone rock, swaying her body to and fro, and lamenting and crying in so heart-rending a manner that the farmer was, as he says, at first obliged to stop his ears, or he would have run away. The woman allowed herself to be taken home, and a neighbour came to see to her necessities. All the night she never ceased her crying, mixing her lament with words of some unintelligible jargon, and when the doctor arrived he pronounced her insane. She lay on her bed for a week, now wailing, as people said, like one lost and damned for eternity, and now sunk in a heavy coma; it was thought that grief at the loss of her husband had unsettled her mind, and the medical man did not at one time expect her to live. I need not say that I was deeply interested in this story, and I made my friend write to me at intervals with all the particulars of the case. I heard then that in the course of six weeks the woman gradually recovered the use of her faculties, and some months later she gave birth to a son, christened Jervase, who unhappily proved to be of weak intellect. Such were the facts known to the village; but to me, while I whitened at the suggested thought of the hideous enormities that had doubtless been committed, all this was nothing short of conviction, and I incautiously hazarded a hint of something like the truth to some scientific friends. The moment the words had left my lips I bitterly regretted having spoken, and thus given away the great secret of my life, but with a good deal of relief mixed with indignation I found my fears altogether misplaced, for my friends ridiculed me to my face, and I was regarded as a madman; and beneath a natural anger I chuckled to myself, feeling as secure amidst these blockheads as if I had confided what I knew to the desert sands.

But now, knowing so much, I resolved I would know all, and I concentrated my efforts on the task of deciphering the inscription on the Black Seal. For many years I made this puzzle the sole object of my leisure moments, for the greater portion of my time was, of course, devoted to other duties, and it was only now and then that I could snatch a week of clear research. If I were to tell the full history of this curious investigation, this statement would be wearisome in the extreme, for it would contain simply the account of long and tedious failure. But with what I knew already of ancient scripts I was well equipped for the chase, as I always termed it to myself. I had correspondents amongst all the scientific men in Europe, and, indeed, in the world, and I could not believe that in these days any character, however ancient and however perplexed, could long resist the search-light I should bring to bear upon it. Yet in point of fact, it was fully fourteen years before I succeeded. With every year my professional duties increased and my leisure became smaller. This no doubt retarded me a good deal; and yet, when I look back on those years, I am astonished at the vast scope of my investigation of the Black Seal. I made my bureau a centre, and from all the world and from all the ages I gathered transcripts of ancient writing.

Nothing, I resolved, should pass me unawares, and the faintest hint should be welcomed and followed up. But as one covert after another was tried and proved empty of result, I began in the course of years to despair, and to wonder whether the Black Seal were the sole relic of some race that had vanished from the world, and left no other trace of its existence—had perished, in fine, as Atlantis is said to have done, in some great cataclysm, its secrets perhaps drowned beneath the ocean or moulded into the heart of the hills. The thought chilled my warmth a little, and though I still persevered, it was no longer with the same certainty of faith. A chance came to the rescue. I was staying in a considerable town in the north of England, and took the opportunity of going over the very creditable museum that had for some time been established in the place. The curator was one of my correspondents; and, as we were looking through one of the mineral cases, my attention was struck by a specimen, a piece of black stone some four inches square, the appearance of which reminded me in a measure of the Black Seal. I took it up carelessly, and was turning it over in my hand, when I saw, to my astonishment, that the under side was inscribed. I said, quietly enough, to my friend the curator that the specimen interested me, and that I should be much obliged if he would allow me to take it with me to my hotel for a couple of days. He, of course, made no objection, and I hurried to my rooms and found that my first glance had not deceived me. There were two inscriptions; one in the regular cuneiform character, another in the character of the Black Seal, and I realized that my task was accomplished. I made an exact copy of the two inscriptions; and when I got to my London study, and had the seal before me, I was able seriously to grapple with the great problem. The interpreting inscription on the museum specimen, though in itself curious enough, did not bear on my quest, but the transliteration made me master of the secret of the Black Seal. Conjecture, of course, had to enter into my calculations; there was here and there uncertainty about a particular ideograph, and one sign recurring again and again on the seal baffled me for many successive nights. But at last the secret stood open before me in plain English, and I read the key of the awful transmutation of the hills. The last word was hardly written, when with fingers all trembling and unsteady I tore the scrap of paper into the minutest fragments, and saw them flame and blacken in the red hollow of the fire, and then I crushed the grey films that remained into finest powder. Never since then have I written those words; never will I write the phrases which tell how man can be reduced to the slime from which he came, and be forced to put on the flesh of the reptile and the snake.

There was now but one thing remaining. I knew, but I desired to see, and I was after some time able to take a house in the neighbourhood of the Grey Hills, and not far from the cottage where Mrs. Cradock and her son Jervase resided. I need not go into a full and detailed account of the apparently inexplicable events which have occurred here, where I am writing this. I knew that I should find in Jervase Cradock something of the blood of the "Little People," and I found later that he had more than once encountered his kinsmen in lonely places in that lonely land. When I was summoned one day to the garden, and found him in a seizure speaking or hissing the ghastly jargon of the Black Seal, I am afraid that exultation prevailed over pity. I heard bursting from his lips the secrets of the underworld, and the word of dread, "Ishakshar," signification of which I must be excused from giving.

But there is one incident I cannot pass over unnoticed. In the waste hollow of the night I awoke at the sound of those hissing syllables I knew so well; and on going to the wretched boy's room, I found him convulsed and foaming at the mouth, struggling on the bed as if he strove to escape the grasp of writhing demons. I took him down to my room and lit the lamp, while he lay twisting on the floor, calling on the power within his flesh to leave him. I saw his body swell and become distended as a bladder, while the face blackened before my eyes; and then at the crisis I did what was necessary according to the directions on the Seal, and putting all scruple on one side, I became a man of science, observant of what was passing. Yet the sight I had to witness was horrible, almost beyond the power of human conception and the most fearful fantasy. Something pushed out from the body there on the floor, and stretched forth a slimy, wavering tentacle, across the room, grasped the bust upon the cupboard, and laid it down on my desk.

> When it was over, and I was left to walk up and down all the rest of the night, white and shuddering, with sweat pouring from my flesh, I vainly tried to reason within myself: I said, truly enough, that I had seen nothing really supernatural, that a snail pushing out his horns and drawing them in was but an instance on a smaller scale of what I had witnessed; and yet horror broke through all such reasonings and left me shattered and loathing myself for the share I had taken in the night's work.
>
> There is little more to be said. I am going now to the final trial and encounter; for I have determined that there shall be nothing wanting, and I shall meet the "Little People" face to face. I shall have the Black Seal and the knowledge of its secrets to help me, and if I unhappily do not return from my journey, there is no need to conjure up here a picture of the awfulness of my fate.

Pausing a little at the end of Professor Gregg's statement, Miss Lally continued her tale in the following words:

Such was the almost incredible story that the professor had left behind him. When I had finished reading it, it was late at night, but the next morning I took Morgan with me, and we proceeded to search the Grey Hills for some trace of the lost professor. I will not weary you with a description of the savage desolation of that tract of country, a tract of utterest loneliness, of bare green hills dotted over with grey limestone boulders, worn by the ravages of time into fantastic semblances of men and beast. Finally, after many hours of weary searching, we found what I told you—the watch and chain, and purse, and the ring—wrapped in a piece of coarse parchment. When Morgan cut the gut that bound the parcel together, and I saw the professor's property, I burst into tears, but the sight of the dreaded characters of the Black Seal repeated on the parchment froze me to silent horror, and I think I understood for the first time the awful fate that had come upon my late employer.

I have only to add that Professor Gregg's lawyer treated my account of what had happened as a fairy tale, and refused even to glance at the documents I laid before him. It was he who was responsible for the statement that appeared in the public press, to the effect that Professor Gregg had been drowned, and that his body must have been swept into the open sea.

Miss Lally stopped speaking, and looked at Mr. Phillipps, with a glance of some inquiry. He, for his part, was sunken in a deep reverie of thought; and when he looked up and saw the bustle of the evening gathering in the square, men and women hurrying to partake of dinner, and crowds already besetting the music-halls, all the hum and press of actual life seemed unreal and visionary, a dream in the morning after an awakening.

THE CALL OF CTHULHU

BY

H. P. LOVECRAFT

(Found Among the Papers of the Late Francis Wayland Thurston, of Boston)

Of such great powers or beings there may be conceivably a survival... a survival of a hugely remote period when... consciousness was manifested, perhaps, in shapes and forms long since withdrawn before the tide of advancing humanity... forms of which poetry and legend alone have caught a flying memory and called them gods, monsters, mythical beings of all sorts and kinds....

—Algernon Blackwood

I
THE HORROR IN CLAY

The most merciful thing in the world, I think, is the inability of the human mind to correlate all its contents. We live on a placid island of ignorance in the midst of black seas of infinity, and it was not meant that we should voyage far. The sciences, each straining in its own direction, have hitherto harmed us little; but some day the piecing together of dissociated knowledge will open up such terrifying vistas of reality, and of our frightful position therein, that we shall either go mad from the revelation or flee from the deadly light into the peace and safety of a new dark age.

Theosophists have guessed at the awesome grandeur of the cosmic cycle wherein our world and human race form transient incidents. They have hinted at strange survivals in terms which would freeze the blood if not masked by a bland optimism. But it is not from them that there came the single glimpse of forbidden eons which chills me when I think of it and maddens me when I dream of it. That glimpse, like all dread glimpses of truth, flashed out from an accidental piecing together of separated things—in this case an old newspaper item and the notes of a dead professor. I hope that no one else will accomplish this piecing out; certainly, if I live, I shall never knowingly supply a link in so hideous a chain. I think that the professor, too, intended to keep silent regarding the part he knew, and that he would have destroyed his notes had not sudden death seized him.

THE CALL OF CTHULHU

My knowledge of the thing began in the winter of 1926–27 with the death of my great-uncle George Gammell Angell, Professor Emeritus of Semitic Languages in Brown University, Providence, Rhode Island. Professor Angell was widely known as an authority on ancient inscriptions, and had frequently been resorted to by the heads of prominent museums; so that his passing at the age of ninety-two may be recalled by many. Locally, interest was intensified by the obscurity of the cause of death. The professor had been stricken whilst returning from the Newport boat; falling suddenly, as witnesses said, after having been jostled by a nautical-looking negro who had come from one of the queer dark courts on the precipitous hillside which formed a short cut from the waterfront to the deceased's home in Williams Street. Physicians were unable to find any visible disorder, but concluded after perplexed debate that some obscure lesion of the heart, induced by the brisk ascent of so steep a hill by so elderly a man, was responsible for the end. At the time I saw no reason to dissent from this dictum, but latterly I am inclined to wonder—and more than wonder.

As my grand-uncle's heir and executor, for he died a childless widower, I was expected to go over his papers with some thoroughness; and for that purpose moved his entire set of files and boxes to my quarters in Boston. Much of the material which I correlated will be later published by the American Archaeological Society, but there was one box which I found exceedingly puzzling, and which I felt much averse from showing to other eyes. It had been locked, and I did not find the key till it occurred to me to examine the personal ring which the professor carried always in his pocket. Then indeed I succeeded in opening it, but when I did so seemed only to be confronted by a greater and more closely locked barrier. For what could be the meaning of the queer clay bas-relief and the disjointed jottings, ramblings, and cuttings which I found? Had my uncle, in his latter years, become credulous of the most superficial impostures? I resolved to search out the eccentric sculptor responsible for this apparent disturbance of an old man's peace of mind.

The bas-relief was a rough rectangle less than an inch thick and about five by six inches in area; obviously of modern origin. Its designs, however, were far from modern in atmosphere and suggestion; for although the vagaries of cubism and futurism are many and wild, they do not often reproduce that cryptic regularity which lurks in prehistoric writing. And writing of some kind the bulk of these designs seemed certainly to be; though my memory, despite much familiarity with the papers and collections of my uncle, failed in any way to identify this particular species, or even to hint at its remotest affiliations.

Above these apparent hieroglyphics was a figure of evidently pictorial intent, though its impressionistic execution forbade a very clear idea of its nature. It seemed to be a sort of monster, or symbol representing a monster, of a form which only a diseased fancy could conceive. If I say that my somewhat extravagant imagination yielded simultaneous pictures of an octopus, a dragon, and a human caricature, I shall not be unfaithful to the spirit of the thing. A pulpy, tentacled head surmounted a grotesque and scaly body with rudimentary wings; but it was the *general outline* of the whole which made it most shockingly frightful. Behind the figure was a vague suggestion of a Cyclopean architectural background.

The writing accompanying this oddity was, aside from a stack of press cuttings, in Professor Angell's most recent hand; and made no pretence to literary style. What seemed to be the main document was headed "CTHULHU CULT" in characters painstakingly printed to avoid the erroneous reading of a word so unheard-of. The manuscript was divided into two sections, the first of which was headed "1925—Dream and Dream Work of H. A. Wilcox, 7 Thomas St, Providence, RI," and the second, "Narrative of Inspector John R. Legrasse, 121 Bienville St, New Orleans, La, at 1908 A. A. S. Mtg—Notes on Same, & Prof. Webb's Acct." The other manuscript papers were all brief notes, some of them accounts of the queer dreams of different persons, some of them citations from theosophical books and magazines (notably W. Scott-Elliot's *Atlantis and the Lost Lemuria*), and the rest comments on long-surviving secret societies and hidden cults, with references to passages in such mythological and anthropological source-books as Frazer's *Golden Bough* and Miss Murray's *Witch-Cult in Western Europe*. The cuttings largely alluded to *outré* mental illnesses and outbreaks of group folly or mania in the spring of 1925.

The first half of the principal manuscript told a very peculiar tale. It appears that on March 1st, 1925, a thin, dark young man of neurotic and excited aspect had called upon Professor Angell bearing the singular clay bas-relief, which was then exceedingly damp and fresh. His card bore the name of Henry Anthony Wilcox, and my uncle had recognized him as the youngest son of an excellent family slightly known to him, who had latterly been studying sculpture at the Rhode Island School of Design and living alone at the Fleur-de-Lys Building near that institution. Wilcox was a precocious youth of known genius but great eccentricity, and had from childhood excited attention through the strange stories and odd dreams he was in the habit of relating. He called himself "psychically hypersensitive," but the staid folk of the ancient commercial city dismissed him as merely "queer." Never mingling much with his kind, he had dropped gradually from social visibility, and was now known only to a small group of aesthetes from other towns. Even the Providence Art Club, anxious to preserve its conservatism, had found him quite hopeless.

On the occasion of the visit, ran the professor's manuscript, the sculptor abruptly asked for the benefit of his host's archeological knowledge in identifying the hieroglyphics on the bas-relief. He spoke in a dreamy, stilted manner which suggested pose and alienated sympathy; and my uncle showed some sharpness in replying, for the conspicuous freshness of the tablet implied kinship with anything but archeology. Young Wilcox's rejoinder, which impressed my uncle enough to make him recall and record it verbatim, was of a fantastically poetic cast which must have typified his whole conversation, and which I have since found highly characteristic of him. He said, "It is new, indeed, for I made it last night in a dream of strange cities; and dreams are older than brooding Tyre, or the contemplative Sphinx, or garden-girdled Babylon."

It was then that he began that rambling tale which suddenly played upon a sleeping memory and won the fevered interest of my uncle. There had been a slight earthquake tremor the night before, the most considerable felt in New England for some years; and Wilcox's imagination had been keenly affected. Upon retiring, he had had an unprecedented dream of great Cyclopean cities of titan blocks and sky-flung monoliths, all dripping with green ooze and sinister with latent horror. Hieroglyphics had covered the walls and pillars, and from some undetermined point below had come a voice that was not a voice; a chaotic sensation which only fancy could transmute into sound, but which he attempted to render by the almost unpronounceable jumble of letters "*Cthulhu fhtagn.*"

This verbal jumble was the key to the recollection which excited and disturbed Professor Angell. He questioned the sculptor with scientific minuteness; and studied with almost frantic intensity the bas-relief on which the youth had found himself working, chilled and clad only in his night-clothes, when waking had stolen bewilderingly over him. My uncle blamed his old age, Wilcox afterward said, for his slowness in recognizing both hieroglyphics and pictorial design. Many of his questions seemed highly out-of-place to his visitor, especially those which tried to connect the latter with strange cults or societies; and Wilcox could not understand the repeated promises of silence which he was offered in exchange for an admission of membership in some widespread mystical or paganly religious body. When Professor Angell became convinced that the sculptor was indeed ignorant of any cult or system of cryptic lore, he besieged his visitor with demands for future reports of dreams. This bore regular fruit, for after the first interview the manuscript records daily calls of the young man, during which he related startling fragments of nocturnal imagery whose burden was always some terrible Cyclopean vista of dark and dripping stone, with a subterrene voice or intelligence shouting monotonously in enigmatical sense-impacts uninscribable save as gibberish. The two sounds most frequently repeated are those rendered by the letters "*Cthulhu*" and "*R'lyeh.*"

On March 23rd, the manuscript continued, Wilcox failed to appear; and inquiries at his quarters revealed that he had been stricken with an obscure sort of fever and taken to the home of his family in Waterman Street. He had cried out in the night, arousing several other artists in the building, and had manifested since then only alternations of unconsciousness and delirium. My uncle at once telephoned the family, and from that time forward kept close watch of the case; calling often at the Thayer Street office of Dr. Tobey, whom he learned to be in charge. The youth's febrile mind, apparently, was dwelling on strange things; and the doctor shuddered now and then as he spoke of them. They included not only a repetition of what he had formerly dreamed, but touched wildly on a gigantic thing "miles high" which walked or lumbered about.

He at no time fully described this object, but occasional frantic words, as repeated by Dr. Tobey, convinced the professor that it must be identical with the nameless monstrosity he had sought to depict in his dream-sculpture. Reference to this object, the doctor added, was invariably a prelude to the young man's subsidence into lethargy. His temperature, oddly enough, was not greatly above normal; but his whole condition was otherwise such as to suggest true fever rather than mental disorder.

On April 2nd at about 3 p.m. every trace of Wilcox's malady suddenly ceased. He sat upright in bed, astonished to find himself at home and completely ignorant of what had happened in dream or reality since the night of March 22nd. Pronounced well by his physician, he returned to his quarters in three days; but to Professor Angell he was of no further assistance. All traces of strange dreaming had vanished with his recovery, and my uncle kept no record of his night-thoughts after a week of pointless and irrelevant accounts of thoroughly usual visions.

Here the first part of the manuscript ended, but references to certain of the scattered notes gave me much material for thought—so much, in fact, that only the ingrained skepticism then forming my philosophy can account for my continued distrust of the artist. The notes in question were those descriptive of the dreams of various persons covering the same period as that in which young Wilcox had had his strange visitations. My uncle, it seems, had quickly instituted a prodigiously far-flung body of inquiries amongst nearly all the friends whom he could question without impertinence, asking for nightly reports of their dreams, and the dates of any notable visions for some time past. The reception of his request seems to have been varied; but he must, at the very least, have received more responses than any ordinary man could have handled without a secretary. This original correspondence was not preserved, but his notes formed a thorough and really significant digest. Average people in society and business—New England's traditional "salt of the earth"—gave an almost completely negative result, though scattered cases of uneasy but formless nocturnal impressions appear here and there, always between March 23rd and April 2nd—the period of young Wilcox's delirium. Scientific men were little more affected, though four cases of vague description suggest fugitive glimpses of strange landscapes, and in one case there is mentioned a dread of something abnormal.

It was from the artists and poets that the pertinent answers came, and I know that panic would have broken loose had they been able to compare notes. As it was, lacking their original letters, I half suspected the compiler of having asked leading questions, or of having edited the correspondence in corroboration of what he had latently resolved to see. That is why I continued to feel that Wilcox, somehow cognizant of the old data which my uncle had possessed, had been imposing on the veteran scientist. These responses from aesthetes told a disturbing tale. From February 28th to April 2nd a large proportion of them had dreamed very bizarre things, the intensity of the dreams being immeasurably the stronger during the period of the sculptor's delirium. Over a fourth of those who reported anything, reported scenes and half-sounds not unlike those which Wilcox had described; and some of the dreamers confessed acute fear of the gigantic nameless thing visible toward the last. One case, which the note describes with emphasis, was very sad. The subject, a widely known architect with leanings toward theosophy and occultism, went violently insane on the date of young Wilcox's seizure, and expired several months later after incessant screamings to be saved from some escaped denizen of hell. Had my uncle referred to these cases by name instead of merely by number, I should have attempted some corroboration and personal investigation; but as it was, I succeeded in tracing down only a few. All of these, however, bore out the notes in full. I have often wondered if all the objects of the professor's questioning felt as puzzled as did this fraction. It is well that no explanation shall ever reach them.

The press cuttings, as I have intimated, touched on cases of panic, mania, and eccentricity during the given period. Professor Angell must have employed a cutting bureau, for the number of extracts was tremendous and the sources scattered throughout the globe. Here was a nocturnal suicide in London, where a lone sleeper had leaped from a window after a shocking cry. Here likewise a rambling letter to the editor of a paper in South America, where a fanatic deduces a dire future from visions he has seen. A dispatch from California describes a theosophist colony as donning white robes en masse for some "glorious fulfillment" which never arrives, whilst items from India speak guardedly of serious native unrest toward the end of March. Voodoo orgies multiply in Haiti, and African outposts report ominous mutterings. American officers in the Philippines find certain tribes bothersome about this time, and New York policemen are mobbed by hysterical Levantines on the night of March 22nd–23rd. The west of Ireland, too, is full of wild rumor and legendry, and a fantastic painter named Ardois-Bonnot hangs a blasphemous "Dream Landscape" in the Paris spring salon of 1926. And so numerous are the recorded troubles in insane asylums, that only a miracle can have stopped the medical fraternity from noting strange parallelisms and drawing mystified conclusions. A weird bunch of cuttings, all told; and I can at this date scarcely envisage the callous rationalism with which I set them aside. But I was then convinced that young Wilcox had known of the older matters mentioned by the professor.

II
THE TALE OF INSPECTOR LEGRASSE

The older matters which had made the sculptor's dream and bas-relief so significant to my uncle formed the subject of the second half of his long manuscript. Once before, it appears, Professor Angell had seen the hellish outlines of the nameless monstrosity, puzzled over the unknown hieroglyphics, and heard the ominous syllables which can be rendered only as "*Cthulhu*"; and all this in so stirring and horrible a connection that it is small wonder he pursued young Wilcox with queries and demands for data.

The earlier experience had come in 1908, seventeen years before, when the American Archaeological Society held its annual meeting in St Louis. Professor Angell, as befitted one of his authority and attainments, had had a prominent part in all the deliberations; and was one of the first to be approached by the several outsiders who took advantage of the convocation to offer questions for correct answering and problems for expert solution.

The chief of these outsiders, and in a short time the focus of interest for the entire meeting, was a commonplace-looking middle-aged man who had traveled all the way from New Orleans for certain special information unobtainable from any local source. His name was John Raymond Legrasse, and he was by profession an Inspector of Police. With him he bore the subject of his visit, a grotesque, repulsive, and apparently very ancient stone statuette whose origin he was at a loss to determine. It must not be fancied that Inspector Legrasse had the least interest in archeology. On the contrary, his wish for enlightenment was prompted by purely professional considerations. The statuette, idol, fetish, or whatever it was, had been captured some months before in the wooded swamps south of New Orleans during a raid on a supposed voodoo meeting; and so singular and hideous were the rites connected with it, that the police could not but realize that they had stumbled on a dark cult totally unknown to them, and infinitely more diabolic than even the blackest of the African voodoo circles. Of its origin, apart from the erratic and unbelievable tales extorted from the captured members, absolutely nothing was to be discovered; hence the anxiety of the police for any antiquarian lore which might help them to place the frightful symbol, and through it track down the cult to its fountain-head.

Inspector Legrasse was scarcely prepared for the sensation which his offering created. One sight of the thing had been enough to throw the assembled men of science into a state of tense excitement, and they lost no time in crowding around him to gaze at the diminutive figure whose utter strangeness and air of genuinely abysmal antiquity hinted so potently at unopened and archaic vistas. No recognized school of sculpture had animated this terrible object, yet centuries and even thousands of years seemed recorded in its dim and greenish surface of unplaceable stone.

The figure, which was finally passed slowly from man to man for close and careful study, was between seven and eight inches in height, and of exquisitely artistic workmanship. It represented a monster of vaguely anthropoid outline, but with an octopus-like head whose face was a mass of feelers, a scaly, rubbery-looking body, prodigious claws on hind and fore feet, and long, narrow wings behind. This thing, which seemed instinct with a fearsome and unnatural malignancy, was of a somewhat bloated corpulence, and squatted evilly on a rectangular block or pedestal covered with undecipherable characters. The tips of the wings touched the back edge of the block, the seat occupied the center, whilst the long, curved claws of the doubled-up, crouching hind legs gripped the front edge and extended a quarter of the way down toward the bottom of the pedestal. The cephalopod head was bent forward, so that the ends of the facial feelers brushed the backs of huge fore paws which clasped the croucher's elevated knees. The aspect of the whole was abnormally life-like, and the more subtly fearful because its source was so totally unknown. Its vast, awesome, and incalculable age was unmistakable; yet not one link did it show with any known type of art belonging to civilization's youth—or indeed to any other time. Totally separate and apart, its very material was a mystery; for the soapy, greenish-black stone with its golden or iridescent flecks and striations resembled nothing familiar to geology or mineralogy. The characters along the base were equally baffling; and no member present, despite a representation of half the world's expert learning in this field, could form the least notion of even their remotest linguistic kinship. They, like the subject and material, belonged to something horribly remote and distinct from mankind as we know it; something frightfully suggestive of old and unhallowed cycles of life in which our world and our conceptions have no part.

And yet, as the members severally shook their heads and confessed defeat at the Inspector's problem, there was one man in that gathering who suspected a touch of bizarre familiarity in the monstrous shape and writing, and who presently told with some diffidence of the odd trifle he knew. This person was the late William Channing Webb, Professor of Anthropology in Princeton University, and an explorer of no slight note. Professor Webb had been engaged, forty-eight years before, in a tour of Greenland and Iceland in search of some Runic inscriptions which he failed to unearth; and whilst high up on the West Greenland coast had encountered a singular tribe or cult of degenerate Eskimos whose religion, a curious form of devil-worship, chilled him with its deliberate bloodthirstiness and repulsiveness. It was a faith of which other Eskimos knew little, and which they mentioned only with shudders, saying that it had come down from horribly ancient eons before ever the world was made. Besides nameless rites and human sacrifices there were certain queer hereditary rituals addressed to a supreme elder devil or *tornasuk;* and of this Professor Webb had taken a careful phonetic copy from an aged *angekok* or wizard-priest, expressing the sounds in Roman letters as best he knew how. But just now of prime significance was the fetish which this cult had cherished, and around which they danced when the aurora leaped high over the ice cliffs. It was, the professor stated, a very crude bas-relief of stone, comprising a hideous picture and some cryptic writing. And so far as he could tell, it was a rough parallel in all essential features of the bestial thing now lying before the meeting.

This data, received with suspense and astonishment by the assembled members, proved doubly exciting to Inspector Legrasse; and he began at once to ply his informant with questions. Having noted and copied an oral ritual among the swamp cult-worshipers his men had arrested, he besought the professor to remember as best he might the syllables taken down amongst the diabolist Eskimos. There then followed an exhaustive comparison of details, and a moment of really awed silence when both detective and scientist agreed on the virtual identity of the phrase common to two hellish rituals so many worlds of distance apart. What, in substance, both the Eskimo wizards and the Louisiana swamp-priests had chanted to their kindred idols was something very like this—the word-divisions being guessed at from traditional breaks in the phrase as chanted aloud:

Ph'nglui mglw'nafh Cthulhu R'lyeh wgah'nagl fhtagn.

Legrasse had one point in advance of Professor Webb, for several among his mongrel prisoners had repeated to him what older celebrants had told them the words meant. This text, as given, ran something like this:

"In his house at R'lyeh dead Cthulhu waits dreaming."

And now, in response to a general and urgent demand, Inspector Legrasse related as fully as possible his experience with the swamp worshipers; telling a story to which I could see my uncle attached profound significance. It savored of the wildest dreams of myth-maker and theosophist, and disclosed an astonishing degree of cosmic imagination among such half-castes and pariahs as might be least expected to possess it.

On November 1st, 1907, there had come to the New Orleans police a frantic summons from the swamp and lagoon country to the south. The squatters there, mostly primitive but good-natured descendants of Lafitte's men, were in the grip of stark terror from an unknown thing which had stolen upon them in the night. It was voodoo, apparently, but voodoo of a more terrible sort than they had ever known; and some of their women and children had disappeared since the malevolent tom-tom had begun its incessant beating far within the black haunted woods where no dweller ventured. There were insane shouts and harrowing screams, soul-chilling chants and dancing devil-flames; and, the frightened messenger added, the people could stand it no more.

So a body of twenty police, filling two carriages and an automobile, had set out in the late afternoon with the shivering squatter as a guide. At the end of the passable road they alighted, and for miles splashed on in silence through the terrible cypress woods where day never came. Ugly roots and malignant hanging nooses of Spanish moss beset them, and now and then a pile of dank stones or fragment of a rotting wall intensified by its hint of morbid habitation a depression which every malformed tree and every fungous islet combined to create. At length the squatter settlement, a miserable huddle of huts, hove in sight; and hysterical dwellers ran out to cluster around the group of bobbing lanterns. The muffled beat of tom-toms was now faintly audible far, far ahead; and a curdling shriek came at infrequent intervals when the wind shifted. A reddish glare, too, seemed to filter through the pale undergrowth beyond endless avenues of forest night. Reluctant even to be left alone again, each one of the cowed squatters refused point-blank to advance another inch toward the scene of unholy worship, so Inspector Legrasse and his nineteen colleagues plunged on unguided into black arcades of horror that none of them had ever trod before.

The region now entered by the police was one of traditionally evil repute, substantially unknown and untraversed by white men. There were legends of a hidden lake unglimpsed by mortal sight, in which dwelt a huge, formless white polypous thing with luminous eyes; and squatters whispered that bat-winged devils flew up out of caverns in inner earth to worship it at midnight. They said it had been there before D'Iberville, before La Salle, before the Indians, and before even the wholesome beasts and birds of the woods. It was nightmare itself, and to see it was to die. But it made men dream, and so they knew enough to keep away. The present voodoo orgy was, indeed, on the merest fringe of this abhorred area, but that location was bad enough; hence perhaps the very place of the worship had terrified the squatters more than the shocking sounds and incidents.

Only poetry or madness could do justice to the noises heard by Legrasse's men as they plowed on through the black morass toward the red glare and the muffled tom-toms. There are vocal qualities peculiar to men, and vocal qualities peculiar to beasts; and it is terrible to hear the one when the source should yield the other. Animal fury and orgiastic license here whipped themselves to daemoniac heights by howls and squawking ecstasies that tore and reverberated through those nighted woods like pestilential tempests from the gulfs of hell. Now and then the less organized ululation would cease, and from what seemed a well-drilled chorus of hoarse voices would rise in sing-song chant that hideous phrase or ritual:

Ph'nglui mglw'nafh Cthulhu R'lyeh wgah'nagl fhtagn.

Then the men, having reached a spot where the trees were thinner, came suddenly in sight of the spectacle itself. Four of them reeled, one fainted, and two were shaken into a frantic cry which the mad cacophony of the orgy fortunately deadened. Legrasse dashed swamp water on the face of the fainting man, and all stood trembling and nwearly hypnotized with horror.

In a natural glade of the swamp stood a grassy island of perhaps an acre's extent, clear of trees and tolerably dry. On this now leaped and twisted a more indescribable horde of human abnormality than any but a Sime or an Angarola could paint. Void of clothing, this hybrid spawn were braying, bellowing, and writhing about a monstrous ring-shaped bonfire; in the center of which, revealed by occasional rifts in the curtain of flame, stood a great granite monolith some eight feet in height; on top of which, incongruous with its diminutiveness, rested the noxious carven statuette. From a wide circle of ten scaffolds set up at regular intervals with the flame-girt monolith as a center hung, head downward, the oddly marred bodies of the helpless squatters who had disappeared. It was inside this circle that the ring of worshipers jumped and roared, the general direction of the mass motion being from left to right in endless Bacchanal between the ring of bodies and the ring of fire.

It may have been only imagination and it may have been only echoes which induced one of the men, an excitable Spaniard, to fancy he heard antiphonal responses to the ritual from some far and unillumined spot deeper within the wood of ancient legendry and horror. This man, Joseph D. Galvez, I later met and questioned; and he proved distractingly imaginative. He indeed went so far as to hint of the faint beating of great wings, and of a glimpse of shining eyes and a mountainous white bulk beyond the remotest trees—but I suppose he had been hearing too much native superstition.

Actually, the horrified pause of the men was of comparatively brief duration. Duty came first; and although there must have been nearly a hundred mongrel celebrants in the throng, the police relied on their firearms and plunged determinedly into the nauseous rout. For five minutes the resultant din and chaos were beyond description. Wild blows were struck, shots were fired, and escapes were made; but in the end Legrasse was able to count some forty-seven sullen prisoners, whom he forced to dress in haste and fall into line between two rows of policemen. Five of the worshipers lay dead, and two severely wounded ones were carried away on improvised stretchers by their fellow—prisoners. The image on the monolith, of course, was carefully removed and carried back by Legrasse.

Examined at headquarters after a trip of intense strain and weariness, the prisoners all proved to be men of a very low, mixed-blooded, and mentally aberrant type. Most were seamen, and a sprinkling of negroes and mulattoes, largely West Indians or Brava Portuguese from the Cape Verde Islands, gave a coloring of voodooism to the heterogeneous cult. But before many questions were asked, it became manifest that something far deeper and older than negro fetishism was involved. Degraded and ignorant as they were, the creatures held with surprising consistency to the central idea of their loathsome faith.

They worshiped, so they said, the Great Old Ones who lived ages before there were any men, and who came to the young world out of the sky. Those Old Ones were gone now, inside the earth and under the sea; but their dead bodies had told their secrets in dreams to the first men, who formed a cult which had never died. This was that cult, and the prisoners said it had always existed and always would exist, hidden in distant wastes and dark places all over the world until the time when the great priest Cthulhu, from his dark house in the mighty city of R'lyeh under the waters, should rise and bring the earth again beneath his sway. Some day he would call, when the stars were ready, and the secret cult would always be waiting to liberate him.

Meanwhile no more must be told. There was a secret which even torture could not extract. Mankind was not absolutely alone among the conscious things of earth, for shapes came out of the dark to visit the faithful few. But these were not the Great Old Ones. No man had ever seen the Old Ones. The carven idol was great Cthulhu, but none might say whether or not the others were precisely like him. No one could read the old writing now, but things were told by word of mouth. The chanted ritual was not the secret—that was never spoken aloud, only whispered. The chant meant only this: *In his house at R'lyeh dead Cthulhu waits dreaming.*

Only two of the prisoners were found sane enough to be hanged, and the rest were committed to various institutions. All denied a part in the ritual murders, and averred that the killing had been done by Black Winged Ones which had come to them from their immemorial meeting-place in the haunted wood. But of those mysterious allies no coherent account could ever be gained. What the police did extract, came mainly from an immensely aged mestizo named Castro, who claimed to have sailed to strange ports and talked with undying leaders of the cult in the mountains of China.

Old Castro remembered bits of hideous legend that paled the speculations of theosophists and made man and the world seem recent and transient indeed. There had been eons when other Things ruled on the earth, and They had had great cities. Remains of Them, he said the deathless Chinamen had told him, were still to be found as Cyclopean stones on islands in the Pacific. They all died vast epochs of time before men came, but there were arts which could revive Them when the stars had come round again to the right positions in the cycle of eternity. They had, indeed, come themselves from the stars, and brought Their images with Them.

These Great Old Ones, Castro continued, were not composed altogether of flesh and blood. They had shape—for did not this star-fashioned image prove it?—but that shape was not made of matter. When the stars were right, They could plunge from world to world through the sky; but when the stars were wrong, They could not live. But although They no longer lived, They would never really die. They all lay in stone houses in Their great city of R'lyeh, preserved by the spells of mighty Cthulhu for a glorious resurrection when the stars and the earth might once more be ready for Them. But at that time some force from outside must serve to liberate Their bodies. The spells that preserved Them intact likewise prevented Them from making an initial move, and They could only lie awake in the dark and think whilst uncounted millions of years rolled by. They knew all that was occurring in the universe, but Their mode of speech was transmitted thought. Even now They talked in Their tombs. When, after infinities of chaos, the first men came, the Great Old Ones spoke to the sensitive among them by molding their dreams; for only thus could Their language reach the fleshly minds of mammals.

Then, whispered Castro, those first men formed the cult around small idols which the Great Ones showed them; idols brought in dim eras from dark stars. That cult would never die till the stars came right again, and the secret priests would take great Cthulhu from His tomb to revive His subjects and resume His rule of earth. The time would be easy to know, for then mankind would have become as the Great Old Ones; free and wild and beyond good and evil, with laws and morals thrown aside and all men shouting and killing and reveling in joy. Then the liberated Old Ones would teach them new ways to shout and kill and revel and enjoy themselves, and all the earth would flame with a holocaust of ecstasy and freedom. Meanwhile the cult, by appropriate rites, must keep alive the memory of those ancient ways and shadow forth the prophecy of their return.

In the elder time chosen men had talked with the entombed Old Ones in dreams, but then something had happened. The great stone city R'lyeh, with its monoliths and sepulchers, had sunk beneath the waves; and the deep waters, full of the one primal mystery through which not even thought can pass, had cut off the spectral intercourse. But memory never died, and high-priests said that the city would rise again when the stars were right. Then came out of the earth the black spirits of earth, moldy and shadowy, and full of dim rumors picked up in caverns beneath forgotten sea-bottoms. But of them old Castro dared not speak much. He cut himself off hurriedly, and no amount of persuasion or subtlety could elicit more in this direction. The *size* of the Old Ones, too, he curiously declined to mention. Of the cult, he said that he thought the center lay amid the pathless deserts of Arabia, where Irem, the City of Pillars, dreams hidden and untouched. It was not allied to the European witch-cult, and was virtually unknown beyond its members. No book had ever really hinted of it, though the deathless Chinamen said that there were double meanings in the *Necronomicon* of the mad Arab Abdul Alhazred which the initiated might read as they chose, especially the much-discussed couplet:

> That is not dead which can eternal lie,
> And with strange eons even death may die.

Legrasse, deeply impressed and not a little bewildered, had inquired in vain concerning the historic affiliations of the cult. Castro, apparently, had told the truth when he said that it was wholly secret. The authorities at Tulane University could shed no light upon either cult or image, and now the detective had come to the highest authorities in the country and met with no more than the Greenland tale of Professor Webb.

The feverish interest aroused at the meeting by Legrasse's tale, corroborated as it was by the statuette, is echoed in the subsequent correspondence of those who attended; although scant mention occurs in the formal publications of the society. Caution is the first care of those accustomed to face occasional charlatanry and imposture. Legrasse for some time lent the image to Professor Webb, but at the latter's death it was returned to him and remains in his possession, where I viewed it not long ago. It is truly a terrible thing, and unmistakably akin to the dream-sculpture of young Wilcox.

That my uncle was excited by the tale of the sculptor I did not wonder, for what thoughts must arise upon hearing, after a knowledge of what Legrasse had learned of the cult, of a sensitive young man who had *dreamed* not only the figure and exact hieroglyphics of the swamp-found image and the Greenland devil tablet, but had come *in his dreams* upon at least three of the precise words of the formula uttered alike by Eskimo diabolists and mongrel Louisianans? Professor Angell's instant start on an investigation of the utmost thoroughness was eminently natural; though privately I suspected young Wilcox of having heard of the cult in some indirect way, and of having invented a series of dreams to heighten and continue the mystery at my uncle's expense. The dream-narratives and cuttings collected by the professor were, of course, strong corroboration; but the rationalism of my mind and the extravagance of the whole subject led me to adopt what I thought the most sensible conclusions. So, after thoroughly studying the manuscript again and correlating the theosophical and anthropological notes with the cult narrative of Legrasse, I made a trip to Providence to see the sculptor and give him the rebuke I thought proper for so boldly imposing upon a learned and aged man.

Wilcox still lived alone in the Fleur-de-Lys Building in Thomas Street, a hideous Victorian imitation of seventeenth-century Breton architecture which flaunts its stuccoed front amidst the lovely colonial houses on the ancient hill, and under the very shadow of the finest Georgian steeple in America. I found him at work in his rooms, and at once conceded from the specimens scattered about that his genius is indeed profound and authentic. He will, I believe, some time be heard from as one of the great decadents; for he has crystallized in clay and will one day mirror in marble those nightmares and fantasies which Arthur Machen evokes in prose, and Clark Ashton Smith makes visible in verse and in painting.

Dark, frail, and somewhat unkempt in aspect, he turned languidly at my knock and asked me my business without rising. When I told him who I was, he displayed some interest; for my uncle had excited his curiosity in probing his strange dreams, yet had never explained the reason for the study. I did not enlarge his knowledge in this regard, but sought with some subtlety to draw him out. In a short time I became convinced of his absolute sincerity, for he spoke of the dreams in a manner none could mistake. They and their subconscious residuum had influenced his art profoundly, and he showed me a morbid statue whose contours almost made me shake with the potency of its black suggestion. He could not recall having seen the original of this thing except in his own dream bas-relief, but the outlines had formed themselves insensibly under his hands. It was, no doubt, the giant shape he had raved of in delirium. That he really knew nothing of the hidden cult, save from what my uncle's relentless catechism had let fall, he soon made clear; and again I strove to think of some way in which he could possibly have received the weird impressions.

He talked of his dreams in a strangely poetic fashion; making me see with terrible vividness the damp Cyclopean city of slimy green stone—whose *geometry,* he oddly said, was *all wrong*—and hear with frightened expectancy the ceaseless, half-mental calling from underground: *Cthulhu fhtagn, Cthulhu fhtagn.*

These words had formed part of that dread ritual which told of dead Cthulhu's dream-vigil in his stone vault at R'lyeh, and I felt deeply moved despite my rational beliefs. Wilcox, I was sure, had heard of the cult in some casual way, and had soon forgotten it amidst the mass of his equally weird reading and imagining. Later, by virtue of its sheer impressiveness, it had found subconscious expression in dreams, in the bas-relief, and in the terrible statue I now beheld; so that his imposture upon my uncle had been a very innocent one. The youth was of a type, at once slightly affected and slightly ill-mannered, which I could never like; but I was willing enough now to admit both his genius and his honesty. I took leave of him amicably, and wish him all the success his talent promises.

The matter of the cult still remained to fascinate me, and at times I had visions of personal fame from researches into its origin and connections. I visited New Orleans, talked with Legrasse and others of that old-time raiding-party, saw the frightful image, and even questioned such of the mongrel prisoners as still survived. Old Castro, unfortunately, had been dead for some years. What I now heard so graphically at first-hand, though it was really no more than a detailed confirmation of what my uncle had written, excited me afresh; for I felt sure that I was on the track of a very real, very secret, and very ancient religion whose discovery would make me an anthropologist of note. My attitude was still one of absolute materialism, as I wish it still were, and I discounted with almost inexplicable perversity the coincidence of the dream notes and odd cuttings collected by Professor Angell.

One thing I began to suspect, and which I now fear I *know,* is that my uncle's death was far from natural. He fell on a narrow hill street leading up from an ancient waterfront swarming with foreign mongrels, after a careless push from a negro sailor. I did not forget the mixed blood and marine pursuits of the cult-members in Louisiana, and would not be surprised to learn of secret methods and poison needles as ruthless and as anciently known as the cryptic rites and beliefs. Legrasse and his men, it is true, have been let alone; but in Norway a certain seaman who saw things is dead. Might not the deeper inquiries of my uncle after encountering the sculptor's data have come to sinister ears? I think Professor Angell died because he knew too much, or because he was likely to learn too much. Whether I shall go as he did remains to be seen, for I have learned much now.

III
THE MADNESS FROM THE SEA

If heaven ever wishes to grant me a boon, it will be a total effacing of the results of a mere chance which fixed my eye on a certain stray piece of shelf-paper. It was nothing on which I would naturally have stumbled in the course of my daily round, for it was an old number of an Australian journal, the *Sydney Bulletin* for April 18th, 1925. It had escaped even the cutting bureau which had at the time of its issuance been avidly collecting material for my uncle's research.

I had largely given over my inquiries into what Professor Angell called the "Cthulhu Cult," and was visiting a learned friend in Paterson, New Jersey; the curator of a local museum and a mineralogist of note. Examining one day the reserve specimens roughly set on the storage shelves in a rear room of the museum, my eye was caught by an odd picture in one of the old papers spread beneath the stones. It was the *Sydney Bulletin* I have mentioned, for my friend has wide affiliations in all conceivable foreign parts; and the picture was a half-tone cut of a hideous stone image almost identical with that which Legrasse had found in the swamp.

Eagerly clearing the sheet of its precious contents, I scanned the item in detail; and was disappointed to find it of only moderate length. What it suggested, however, was of portentous significance to my flagging quest; and I carefully tore it out for immediate action. It read as follows:

MYSTERY DERELICT FOUND AT SEA

Vigilant Arrives With Helpless
Armed New Zealand Yacht in Tow.

One Survivor and Dead Man Found Aboard.

Tale of Desperate Battle and Deaths at Sea.

Rescued Seaman Refuses
Particulars of Strange Experience.

Odd Idol Found in His Possession. Inquiry to Follow.

The Morrison Co.'s freighter *Vigilant*, bound from Valparaiso, arrived this morning at its wharf in Darling Harbour, having in tow the battled and disabled but heavily armed steam yacht *Alert* of Dunedin, NZ, which was sighted April 12th in S. Latitude 34° 21', W. Longitude 152° 17' with one living and one dead man aboard.

The *Vigilant* left Valparaiso March 25th, and on April 2nd was driven considerably south of her course by exceptionally heavy storms and monster waves. On April 12th the derelict was sighted; and though apparently deserted, was found upon boarding to contain one survivor in a half-delirious condition and one man who had evidently been dead for more than a week. The living man was clutching a horrible stone idol of unknown origin, about a foot in height, regarding whose nature authorities at Sydney University, the Royal Society, and the Museum in College Street all profess complete bafflement, and which the survivor says he found in the cabin of the yacht, in a small carved shrine of common pattern.

This man, after recovering his senses, told an exceedingly strange story of piracy and slaughter. He is Gustaf Johansen, a Norwegian of some intelligence, and had been second mate of the two-masted schooner *Emma* of Auckland, which sailed for Callao February 20th with a complement of eleven men. The *Emma*, he says, was delayed and thrown widely south of her course by the great storm of March 1st, and on March 22nd, in S. Latitude 49° 51', W. Longitude 128° 34', encountered the *Alert*, manned by a queer and evil-looking crew of Kanakas and half-castes. Being ordered peremptorily to turn back, Capt. Collins refused; whereupon the strange crew began to fire savagely and without warning upon the schooner with a peculiarly heavy battery of brass cannon forming part of the yacht's equipment. The *Emma*'s men showed fight, says the survivor, and though the schooner began to sink from shots beneath the waterline they managed to heave alongside their enemy and board her, grappling with the savage crew on the yacht's deck, and being forced to kill them all, the number being slightly superior, because of their particularly abhorrent and desperate though rather clumsy mode of fighting.

Three of the *Emma*'s men, including Capt. Collins and First Mate Green, were killed; and the remaining eight under Second Mate Johansen proceeded to navigate the captured yacht, going ahead in their original direction to see if any reason for their ordering back had existed. The next day, it appears, they raised and landed on a small island, although none is known to exist in that part of the ocean; and six of the men somehow died ashore, though Johansen is queerly reticent about this part of his story, and speaks only of their falling into a rock chasm. Later, it seems, he and one companion boarded the yacht and tried to manage her, but were beaten about by the storm of April 2nd. From that time till his rescue on the 12th the man remembers little, and he does not even recall when William Briden, his companion, died. Briden's death reveals no apparent cause, and was probably due to excitement or exposure. Cable advices from Dunedin report that the *Alert* was well known there as an island trader, and bore an evil reputation along the waterfront. It was owned by a curious group of half-castes whose frequent meetings and night trips to the woods attracted no little curiosity; and it had set sail in great haste just after the storm and earth tremors of March 1st. Our Auckland correspondent gives the *Emma* and her crew an excellent reputation, and Johansen is described as a sober and worthy man. The admiralty will institute an inquiry on the whole matter beginning tomorrow, at which every effort will be made to induce Johansen to speak more freely than he has done hitherto.

This was all, together with the picture of the hellish image; but what a train of ideas it started in my mind! Here were new treasuries of data on the Cthulhu Cult, and evidence that it had strange interests at sea as well as on land. What motive prompted the hybrid crew to order back the *Emma* as they sailed about with their hideous idol? What was the unknown island on which six of the *Emma*'s crew had died, and about which the mate Johansen was so secretive? What had the vice-admiralty's investigation brought out, and what was known of the noxious cult in Dunedin? And most marvelous of all, what deep and more than natural linkage of dates was this which gave a malign and now undeniable significance to the various turns of events so carefully noted by my uncle?

March 1st—our February 28th according to the International Date Line—the earthquake and storm had come. From Dunedin the *Alert* and her noisome crew had darted eagerly forth as if imperiously summoned, and on the other side of the earth poets and artists had begun to dream of a strange, dank Cyclopean city whilst a young sculptor had molded in his sleep the form of the dreaded Cthulhu. March 23rd the crew of the *Emma* landed on an unknown island and left six men dead; and on that date the dreams of sensitive men assumed a heightened vividness and darkened with dread of a giant monster's malign pursuit, whilst an architect had gone mad and a sculptor had lapsed suddenly into delirium! And what of this storm of April 2nd—the date on which all dreams of the dank city ceased, and Wilcox emerged unharmed from the bondage of strange fever? What of all this—and of those hints of old Castro about the sunken, star-born Old Ones and their coming reign; their faithful cult *and their mastery of dreams?* Was I tottering on the brink of cosmic horrors beyond man's power to bear? If so, they must be horrors of the mind alone, for in some way April 2nd had put a stop to whatever monstrous menace had begun its siege of mankind's soul.

That evening, after a day of hurried cabling and arranging, I bade my host adieu and took a train for San Francisco. In less than a month I was in Dunedin; where, however, I found that little was known of the strange cult-members who had lingered in the old sea-taverns. Waterfront scum was far too common for special mention; though there was vague talk about one inland trip these mongrels had made, during which faint drumming and red flame were noted on the distant hills. In Auckland I learned that Johansen had returned *with yellow hair turned white* after a perfunctory and inconclusive questioning at Sydney, and had thereafter sold his cottage in West Street and sailed with his wife to his old home in Oslo. Of his stirring experience he would tell his friends no more than he had told the admiralty officials, and all they could do was to give me his Oslo address.

After that I went to Sydney and talked profitlessly with seamen and members of the vice-admiralty court. I saw the *Alert*, now sold and in commercial use, at Circular Quay in Sydney Cove, but gained nothing from its non-committal bulk. The crouching image with its cuttlefish head, dragon body, scaly wings, and hieroglyphed pedestal, was preserved in the Museum at Hyde Park; and I studied it long and well, finding it a thing of balefully exquisite workmanship, and with the same utter mystery, terrible antiquity, and unearthly strangeness of material which I had noted in Legrasse's smaller specimen. Geologists, the curator told me, had found it a monstrous puzzle; for they vowed that the world held no rock like it. Then I thought with a shudder of what old Castro had told Legrasse about the primal Great Ones: "They had come from the stars, and had brought Their images with Them."

Shaken with such a mental revolution as I had never before known, I now resolved to visit Mate Johansen in Oslo. Sailing for London, I re-embarked at once for the Norwegian capital; and one autumn day landed at the trim wharves in the shadow of the Egeberg. Johansen's address, I discovered, lay in the Old Town of King Harold Haardrada, which kept alive the name of Oslo during all the centuries that the greater city masqueraded as "Christiana." I made the brief trip by taxicab, and knocked with palpitant heart at the door of a neat and ancient building with plastered front. A sad-faced woman in black answered my summons, and I was stung with disappointment when she told me in halting English that Gustaf Johansen was no more.

He had not survived his return, said his wife, for the doings at sea in 1925 had broken him. He had told her no more than he had told the public, but had left a long manuscript—of "technical matters" as he said—written in English, evidently in order to safeguard her from the peril of casual perusal. During a walk through a narrow lane near the Gothenburg dock, a bundle of papers falling from an attic window had knocked him down. Two Lascar sailors at once helped him to his feet, but before the ambulance could reach him he was dead. Physicians found no adequate cause for the end, and laid it to heart trouble and a weakened constitution.

I now felt gnawing at my vitals that dark terror which will never leave me till I, too, am at rest; "accidentally" or otherwise. Persuading the widow that my connection with her husband's "technical matters" was sufficient to entitle me to his manuscript, I bore the document away and began to read it on the London boat. It was a simple, rambling thing—a naive sailor's effort at a *post-facto* diary—and strove to recall day by day that last awful voyage. I cannot attempt to transcribe it verbatim in all its cloudiness and redundance, but I will tell its gist enough to show why the sound of the water against the vessel's sides became so unendurable to me that I stopped my ears with cotton.

Johansen, thank God, did not know quite all, even though he saw the city and the Thing, but I shall never sleep calmly again when I think of the horrors that lurk ceaselessly behind life in time and in space, and of those unhallowed blasphemies from elder stars which dream beneath the sea, known and favored by a nightmare cult ready and eager to loose them on the world whenever another earthquake shall heave their monstrous stone city again to the sun and air.

Johansen's voyage had begun just as he told it to the vice-admiralty. The *Emma*, in ballast, had cleared Auckland on February 20th, and had felt the full force of that earthquake-born tempest which must have heaved up from the sea-bottom the horrors that filled men's dreams. Once more under control, the ship was making good progress when held up by the *Alert* on March 22nd, and I could feel the mate's regret as he wrote of her bombardment and sinking. Of the swarthy cult-fiends on the *Alert* he speaks with significant horror. There was some peculiarly abominable quality about them which made their destruction seem almost a duty, and Johansen shows ingenuous wonder at the charge of ruthlessness brought against his party during the proceedings of the court of inquiry. Then, driven ahead by curiosity in their captured yacht under Johansen's command, the men sight a great stone pillar sticking out of the sea, and in S. Latitude 47° 9', W. Longitude 123° 43' come upon a coastline of mingled mud, ooze, and weedy Cyclopean masonry which can be nothing less than the tangible substance of earth's supreme terror—the nightmare corpse-city of R'lyeh, that was built in measureless eons behind history by the vast, loathsome shapes that seeped down from the dark stars. There lay great Cthulhu and his hordes, hidden in green slimy vaults and sending out at last, after cycles incalculable, the thoughts that spread fear to the dreams of the sensitive and called imperiously to the faithful to come on a pilgrimage of liberation and restoration. All this Johansen did not suspect, but God knows he soon saw enough!

I suppose that only a single mountaintop, the hideous monolith-crowned citadel whereon great Cthulhu was buried, actually emerged from the waters. When I think of the extent of all that may be brooding down there I almost wish to kill myself forthwith. Johansen and his men were awed by the cosmic majesty of this dripping Babylon of elder daemons, and must have guessed without guidance that it was nothing of this or of any sane planet. Awe at the unbelievable size of the greenish stone blocks, at the dizzying height of the great carven monolith, and at the stupefying identity of the colossal statues and bas-reliefs with the queer image found in the shrine on the *Alert*, is poignantly visible in every line of the mate's frightened description.

Without knowing what futurism is like, Johansen achieved something very close to it when he spoke of the city; for instead of describing any definite structure or building, he dwells only on broad impressions of vast angles and stone surfaces—surfaces too great to belong to any thing right or proper for this earth, and impious with horrible images and hieroglyphs. I mention his talk about *angles* because it suggests something Wilcox had told me of his awful dreams. He had said that the *geometry* of the dream-place he saw was abnormal, non-Euclidean, and loathsomely redolent of spheres and dimensions apart from ours. Now an unlettered seaman felt the same thing whilst gazing at the terrible reality.

Johansen and his men landed at a sloping mud-bank on this monstrous Acropolis, and clambered slipperily up over titan oozy blocks which could have been no mortal staircase. The very sun of heaven seemed distorted when viewed through the polarizing miasma welling out from this sea-soaked perversion, and twisted menace and suspense lurked leeringly in those crazily elusive angles of carven rock where a second glance showed concavity after the first showed convexity.

Something very like fright had come over all the explorers before anything more definite than rock and ooze and weed was seen. Each would have fled had he not feared the scorn of the others, and it was only half-heartedly that they searched—vainly, as it proved—for some portable souvenir to bear away.

It was Rodriguez the Portuguese who climbed up the foot of the monolith and shouted of what he had found. The rest followed him, and looked curiously at the immense carved door with the now familiar squid-dragon bas-relief. It was, Johansen said, like a great barn-door; and they all felt that it was a door because of the ornate lintel, threshold, and jambs around it, though they could not decide whether it lay flat like a trap-door or slantwise like an outside cellar-door. As Wilcox would have said, the geometry of the place was all wrong. One could not be sure that the sea and the ground were horizontal, hence the relative position of everything else seemed phantasmally variable.

Briden pushed at the stone in several places without result. Then Donovan felt over it delicately around the edge, pressing each point separately as he went. He climbed interminably along the grotesque stone molding—that is, one would call it climbing if the thing was not after all horizontal—and the men wondered how any door in the universe could be so vast. Then, very softly and slowly, the acre-great panel began to give inward at the top; and they saw that it was balanced. Donovan slid or somehow propelled himself down or along the jamb and rejoined his fellows, and everyone watched the queer recession of the monstrously carven portal. In this fantasy of prismatic distortion it moved anomalously in a diagonal way, so that all the rules of matter and perspective seemed upset.

The aperture was black with a darkness almost material. That tenebrousness was indeed a *positive quality*; for it obscured such parts of the inner walls as ought to have been revealed, and actually burst forth like smoke from its eon-long imprisonment, visibly darkening the sun as it slunk away into the shrunken and gibbous sky on flapping membranous wings. The odor arising from the newly opened depths was intolerable, and at length the quick-eared Hawkins thought he heard a nasty, slopping sound down there. Everyone listened, and everyone was listening still when It lumbered slobberingly into sight and gropingly squeezed Its gelatinous green immensity through the black doorway into the tainted outside air of that poison city of madness.

Poor Johansen's handwriting almost gave out when he wrote of this. Of the six men who never reached the ship, he thinks two perished of pure fright in that accursed instant. The Thing cannot be described—there is no language for such abysms of shrieking and immemorial lunacy, such eldritch contradictions of all matter, force, and cosmic order. A mountain walked or stumbled. God! What wonder that across the earth a great architect went mad, and poor Wilcox raved with fever in that telepathic instant? The Thing of the idols, the green, sticky spawn of the stars, had awaked to claim his own. The stars were right again, and what an age-old cult had failed to do by design, a band of innocent sailors had done by accident. After vigintillions of years great Cthulhu was loose again, and ravening for delight.

Three men were swept up by the flabby claws before anybody turned. God rest them, if there be any rest in the universe. They were Donovan, Guerrera, and Ångstrom. Parker slipped as the other three were plunging frenziedly over endless vistas of green-crusted rock to the boat, and Johansen swears he was swallowed up by an angle of masonry which shouldn't have been there; an angle which was acute, but behaved as if it were obtuse. So only Briden and Johansen reached the boat, and pulled desperately for the *Alert* as the mountainous monstrosity flopped down the slimy stones and hesitated floundering at the edge of the water.

Steam had not been suffered to go down entirely, despite the departure of all hands for the shore; and it was the work of only a few moments of feverish rushing up and down between wheel and engines to get the *Alert* under way. Slowly, amidst the distorted horrors of that indescribable scene, she began to churn the lethal waters; whilst on the masonry of that charnel shore that was not of earth the titan Thing from the stars slavered and gibbered like Polypheme cursing the fleeing ship of Odysseus. Then, bolder than the storied Cyclops, great Cthulhu slid greasily into the water and began to pursue with vast wave-raising strokes of cosmic potency. Briden looked back and went mad, laughing shrilly as he kept on laughing at intervals till death found him one night in the cabin whilst Johansen was wandering deliriously.

But Johansen had not given out yet. Knowing that the Thing could surely overtake the

Alert until steam was fully up, he resolved on a desperate chance; and, setting the engine for full speed, ran lightning-like on deck and reversed the wheel. There was a mighty eddying and foaming in the noisome brine, and as the steam mounted higher and higher the brave Norwegian drove his vessel head on against the pursuing jelly which rose above the unclean froth like the stern of a daemon galleon. The awful squid-head with writhing feelers came nearly up to the bowsprit of the sturdy yacht, but Johansen drove on relentlessly. There was a bursting as of an exploding bladder, a slushy nastiness as of a cloven sunfish, a stench as of a thousand opened graves, and a sound that the chronicler would not put on paper. For an instant the ship was befouled by an acrid and blinding green cloud, and then there was only a venomous seething astern; where—God in heaven!—the scattered plasticity of that nameless sky-spawn was nebulously *recombining* in its hateful original form, whilst its distance widened every second as the *Alert* gained impetus from its mounting steam.

That was all. After that Johansen only brooded over the idol in the cabin and attended to a few matters of food for himself and the laughing maniac by his side. He did not try to navigate after the first bold flight, for the reaction had taken something out of his soul. Then came the storm of April 2nd, and a gathering of the clouds about his consciousness. There is a sense of spectral whirling through liquid gulfs of infinity, of dizzying rides through reeling universes on a comet's tail, and of hysterical plunges from the pit to the moon and from the moon back again to the pit, all livened by a cachinnating chorus of the distorted, hilarious elder gods and the green, bat-winged mocking imps of Tartarus.

Out of that dream came rescue—the *Vigilant,* the vice-admiralty court, the streets of Dunedin, and the long voyage back home to the old house by the Egeberg. He could not tell—they would think him mad. He would write of what he knew before death came, but his wife must not guess. Death would be a boon if only it could blot out the memories.

That was the document I read, and now I have placed it in the tin box beside the bas-relief and the papers of Professor Angell. With it shall go this record of mine—this test of my own sanity, wherein is pieced together that which I hope may never be pieced together again. I have looked upon all that the universe has to hold of horror, and even the skies of spring and the flowers of summer must ever afterward be poison to me. But I do not think my life will be long. As my uncle went, as poor Johansen went, so I shall go. I know too much, and the cult still lives.

Cthulhu still lives, too, I suppose, again in that chasm of stone which has shielded him since the sun was young. His accursed city is sunken once more, for the *Vigilant* sailed over the spot after the April storm; but his ministers on earth still bellow and prance and slay around idol-capped monoliths in lonely places. He must have been trapped by the sinking whilst within his black abyss, or else the world would by now be screaming with fright and frenzy. Who knows the end? What has risen may sink, and what has sunk may rise. Loathsomeness waits and dreams in the deep, and decay spreads over the tottering cities of men. A time will come—but I must not and cannot think! Let me pray that, if I do not survive this manuscript, my executors may put caution before audacity and see that it meets no other eye.

THE REPAIRER OF REPUTATIONS

BY

ROBERT W. CHAMBERS

"Ne raillons pas les fous; leur folie dure plus longtemps que la nôtre.... Voila toute la différence."

I

Toward the end of the year 1920 the Government of the United States had practically completed the programme, adopted during the last months of President Winthrop's administration. The country was apparently tranquil. Everybody knows how the Tariff and Labor questions were settled. The war with Germany, incident on that country's seizure of the Samoan Islands, had left no visible scars upon the republic, and the temporary occupation of Norfolk by the invading army had been forgotten in the joy over repeated naval victories, and the subsequent ridiculous plight of General Von Gartenlaube's forces in the State of New Jersey. The Cuban and Hawaiian investments had paid one hundred per cent and the territory of Samoa was well worth its cost as a coaling station. The country was in a superb state of defence. Every coast city had been well supplied with land fortifications; the army under the parental eye of the General Staff, organized according to the Prussian system, had been increased to 300,000 men, with a territorial reserve of a million; and six magnificent squadrons of cruisers and battle-ships patrolled the six stations of the navigable seas, leaving a steam reserve amply fitted to control home waters. The gentlemen from the West had at last been constrained to acknowledge that a college for the training of diplomats was as necessary as law schools are for the training of barristers; consequently we were no longer represented abroad by incompetent patriots. The nation was prosperous; Chicago, for a moment paralyzed after a second great fire, had risen from its ruins, white and imperial, and more beautiful than the white city which had been built for its plaything in 1893. Everywhere good architecture was replacing bad, and even in New York, a sudden craving for decency had swept away a great portion of the existing horrors. Streets had been widened, properly paved and lighted, trees had been planted, squares laid out, elevated structures demolished and underground roads built to replace them. The new government buildings and barracks were fine bits of architecture, and the long system of stone quays which completely surrounded the island had been turned into parks which proved a god-send to the population. The subsidizing of the state theatre and state opera brought its own reward. The United States National Academy of Design was much like European institutions of the same kind. Nobody envied the Secretary of Fine Arts, either his cabinet position or his portfolio. The Secretary of Forestry and Game Preservation had a much easier time, thanks to the new system of National Mounted Police. We had profited well by the latest treaties with France and England; the exclusion of foreign-born Jews as a measure of self-preservation, the settlement of the new independent negro state of Suanee, the checking of immigration, the new laws concerning naturalization, and the gradual centralization of power in the executive all contributed to national calm and prosperity. When the Government solved the Indian problem and squadrons of Indian cavalry scouts in native costume were substituted for the pitiable organizations tacked on to the tail of skeletonized regiments by a former Secretary of War, the nation drew a long sigh of relief. When, after the colossal Congress of Religions, bigotry and intolerance were laid in their graves and kindness and charity began to draw warring sects together, many thought the millennium had arrived, at least in the new world which after all is a world by itself.

But self-preservation is the first law, and the United States had to look on in helpless sorrow as Germany, Italy, Spain and Belgium writhed in the throes of Anarchy, while Russia, watching from the Caucasus, stooped and bound them one by one.

In the city of New York the summer of 1899 was signalized by the dismantling of the Elevated Railroads. The summer of 1900 will live in the memories of New York people for many a cycle; the Dodge Statue was removed in that year. In the following winter began that agitation for the repeal of the laws prohibiting suicide which bore its final fruit in the month of April, 1920, when the first Government Lethal Chamber was opened on Washington Square.

I had walked down that day from Dr. Archer's house on Madison Avenue, where I had been as a mere formality. Ever since that fall from my horse, four years before, I had been troubled at times with pains in the back of my head and neck, but now for months they had been absent, and the doctor sent me away that day saying there was nothing more to be cured in me. It was hardly worth his fee to be told that; I knew it myself. Still I did not grudge him the money. What I minded was the mistake which he made at first. When they picked me up from the pavement where I lay unconscious, and somebody had mercifully sent a bullet through my horse's head, I was carried to Dr. Archer, and he, pronouncing my brain affected, placed me in his private asylum where I was obliged to endure treatment for insanity. At last he decided that I was well, and I, knowing that my mind had always been as sound as his, if not sounder, "paid my tuition" as he jokingly called it, and left. I told him, smiling, that I would get even with him for his mistake, and he laughed heartily, and asked me to call once in a while. I did so, hoping for a chance to even up accounts, but he gave me none, and I told him I would wait.

The fall from my horse had fortunately left no evil results; on the contrary it had changed my whole character for the better. From a lazy young man about town, I had become active, energetic, temperate, and above all—oh, above all else—ambitious. There was only one thing which troubled me, I laughed at my own uneasiness, and yet it troubled me.

During my convalescence I had bought and read for the first time, *The King in Yellow*. I remember after finishing the first act that it occurred to me that I had better stop. I started up and flung the book into the fireplace; the volume struck the barred grate and fell open on the hearth in the firelight. If I had not caught a glimpse of the opening words in the second act I should never have finished it, but as I stooped to pick it up, my eyes became riveted to the open page, and with a cry of terror, or perhaps it was of joy so poignant that I suffered in every nerve, I snatched the thing out of the coals and crept shaking to my bedroom, where I read it and reread it, and wept and laughed and trembled with a horror which at times assails me yet. This is the thing that troubles me, for I cannot forget Carcosa where black stars hang in the heavens; where the shadows of men's thoughts lengthen in the afternoon, when the twin suns sink into the lake of Hali; and my mind will bear for ever the memory of the Pallid Mask. I pray God will curse the writer, as the writer has cursed the world with this beautiful, stupendous creation, terrible in its simplicity, irresistible in its truth—a world which now trembles before the King in Yellow. When the French Government seized the translated copies which had just arrived in Paris, London, of course, became eager to read it. It is well known how the book spread like an infectious disease, from city to city, from continent to continent, barred out here, confiscated there, denounced by Press and pulpit, censured even by the most advanced of literary anarchists. No definite principles had been violated in those wicked pages, no doctrine promulgated, no convictions outraged. It could not be judged by any known standard, yet, although it was acknowledged that the supreme note of art had been struck in *The King in Yellow*, all felt that human nature could not bear the strain, nor thrive on words in which the essence of purest poison lurked. The very banality and innocence of the first act only allowed the blow to fall afterward with more awful effect.

It was, I remember, the 13th day of April, 1920, that the first Government Lethal Chamber was established on the south side of Washington Square, between Wooster Street and South Fifth Avenue. The block which had formerly consisted of a lot of shabby old buildings, used as cafés and restaurants for foreigners, had been acquired by the Government in the winter of 1898. The French and Italian cafés and restaurants were torn down; the whole block was enclosed by a gilded iron railing, and converted into a lovely garden with lawns, flowers and fountains. In the centre of the garden stood a small, white building, severely classical in architecture, and surrounded by thickets of flowers. Six Ionic columns supported the roof, and the single door was of bronze. A splendid marble group of the "Fates" stood before the door, the work of a young American sculptor, Boris Yvain, who had died in Paris when only twenty-three years old.

The inauguration ceremonies were in progress as I crossed University Place and entered the square. I threaded my way through the silent throng of spectators, but was stopped at Fourth Street by a cordon of police. A regiment of United States lancers were drawn up in a hollow square round the Lethal Chamber. On a raised tribune facing Washington Park stood the Governor of New York, and behind him were grouped the Mayor of New York and Brooklyn, the Inspector-General of Police, the Commandant of the state troops, Colonel Livingston, military aid to the President of the United States, General Blount, commanding at Governor's Island, Major-General Hamilton, commanding the garrison of New York and Brooklyn, Admiral Buffby of the fleet in the North River, Surgeon-General Lanceford, the staff of the National Free Hospital, Senators Wyse and Franklin of New York, and the Commissioner of Public Works. The tribune was surrounded by a squadron of hussars of the National Guard.

The Governor was finishing his reply to the short speech of the Surgeon-General. I heard him say: "The laws prohibiting suicide and providing punishment for any attempt at self-destruction have been repealed. The Government has seen fit to acknowledge the right of man to end an existence which may have become intolerable to him, through physical suffering or mental despair. It is believed that the community will be benefited by the removal of such people from their midst. Since the passage of this law, the number of suicides in the United States has not increased. Now the Government has determined to establish a Lethal Chamber in every city, town and village in the country, it remains to be seen whether or not that class of human creatures from whose desponding ranks new victims of self-destruction fall daily will accept the relief thus provided." He paused, and turned to the white Lethal Chamber. The silence in the street was absolute. "There a painless death awaits him who can no longer bear the sorrows of this life. If death is welcome let him seek it there." Then quickly turning to the military aid of the President's household, he said, "I declare the Lethal Chamber open," and again facing the vast crowd he cried in a clear voice: "Citizens of New York and of the United States of America, through me the Government declares the Lethal Chamber to be open."

The solemn hush was broken by a sharp cry of command, the squadron of hussars filed after the Governor's carriage, the lancers wheeled and formed along Fifth Avenue to wait for the commandant of the garrison, and the mounted police followed them. I left the crowd to gape and stare at the white marble Death Chamber, and, crossing South Fifth Avenue, walked along the western side of that thoroughfare to Bleecker Street. Then I turned to the right and stopped before a dingy shop which bore the sign:

HAWBERK, ARMORER.

I glanced in at the doorway and saw Hawberk busy in his little shop at the end of the hall. He looked up, and catching sight of me cried in his deep, hearty voice, "Come in, Mr. Castaigne!" Constance, his daughter, rose to meet me as I crossed the threshold, and held out her pretty hand, but I saw the blush of disappointment on her cheeks, and knew that it was another Castaigne she had expected, my cousin Louis. I smiled at her confusion and complimented her on the banner she was embroidering from a colored plate. Old Hawberk sat riveting the worn greaves of some ancient suit of armor, and the ting! ting! ting! of his little hammer sounded pleasantly in the quaint shop. Presently he dropped his hammer, and fussed about for a moment with a tiny wrench. The soft clash of the mail sent a thrill of pleasure through me. I loved to hear the music of steel brushing against steel, the mellow shock of the mallet on thigh pieces, and the jingle of chain armor. That was the only reason I went to see Hawberk. He had never interested me personally, nor did Constance, except for the fact of her being in love with Louis. This did occupy my attention, and sometimes even kept me awake at night. But I knew in my heart that all would come right, and that I should arrange their future as I expected to arrange that of my kind doctor, John Archer. However, I should never have troubled myself about visiting them just then, had it not been, as I say, that the music of the tinkling hammer had for me this strong fascination. I would sit for hours, listening and listening, and when a stray sunbeam struck the inlaid steel, the sensation it gave me was almost too keen to endure. My eyes would become fixed, dilating with a pleasure that stretched every nerve almost to breaking, until some movement of the old armorer cut off the ray of sunlight, then, still thrilling secretly, I leaned back and listened again to the sound of the polishing rag, swish! swish! rubbing rust from the rivets.

Constance worked with the embroidery over her knees, now and then pausing to examine more closely the pattern in the colored plate from the Metropolitan Museum.

"Who is this for?" I asked.

Hawberk explained, that in addition to the treasures of armor in the Metropolitan Museum of which he had been appointed armorer, he also had charge of several collections belonging to rich amateurs. This was the missing greave of a famous suit which a client of his had traced to a little shop in Paris on the Quai d'Orsay. He, Hawberk, had negotiated for and secured the greave, and now the suit was complete. He laid down his hammer and read me the history of the suit, traced since 1450 from owner to owner until it was acquired by Thomas Stainbridge. When his superb collection was sold, this client of Hawberk's bought the suit, and since then the search for the missing greave had been pushed until it was, almost by accident, located in Paris.

"Did you continue the search so persistently without any certainty of the greave being still in existence?" I demanded.

"Of course," he replied coolly.

Then for the first time I took a personal interest in Hawberk.

"It was worth something to you," I ventured.

"No," he replied, laughing, "my pleasure in finding it was my reward."

"Have you no ambition to be rich?" I asked, smiling.

"My one ambition is to be the best armorer in the world," he answered gravely.

Constance asked me if I had seen the ceremonies at the Lethal Chamber. She herself had noticed cavalry passing up Broadway that morning, and had wished to see the inauguration, but her father wanted the banner finished, and she had stayed at his request.

"Did you see your cousin, Mr. Castaigne, there?" she asked, with the slightest tremor of her soft eyelashes.

"No," I replied carelessly. "Louis' regiment is manœuvring out in Westchester County." I rose and picked up my hat and cane.

"Are you going upstairs to see the lunatic again?" laughed old Hawberk. If Hawberk knew how I loathe that word "lunatic," he would never use it in my presence. It rouses certain feelings within me which I do not care to explain. However, I answered him quietly: "I think I shall drop in and see Mr. Wilde for a moment or two."

"Poor fellow," said Constance, with a shake of the head, "it must be hard to live alone year after year poor, crippled and almost demented. It is very good of you, Mr. Castaigne, to visit him as often as you do."

"I think he is vicious," observed Hawberk, beginning again with his hammer. I listened to the golden tinkle on the greave plates; when he had finished I replied:

"No, he is not vicious, nor is he in the least demented. His mind is a wonder chamber, from which he can extract treasures that you and I would give years of our life to acquire."

Hawberk laughed.

I continued a little impatiently: "He knows history as no one else could know it. Nothing, however trivial, escapes his search, and his memory is so absolute, so precise in details, that were it known in New York that such a man existed, the people could not honor him enough."

"Nonsense," muttered Hawberk, searching on the floor for a fallen rivet.

"Is it nonsense," I asked, managing to suppress what I felt, "is it nonsense when he says that the tassets and cuissards of the enamelled suit of armor commonly known as the 'Prince's Emblazoned' can be found among a mass of rusty theatrical properties, broken stoves and ragpicker's refuse in a garret in Pell Street?"

Hawberk's hammer fell to the ground, but he picked it up and asked, with a great deal of calm, how I knew that the tassets and left cuissard were missing from the "Prince's Emblazoned."

"I did not know until Mr. Wilde mentioned it to me the other day. He said they were in the garret of 998 Pell Street."

"Nonsense," he cried, but I noticed his hand trembling under his leathern apron.

"Is this nonsense too?" I asked pleasantly, "is it nonsense when Mr. Wilde continually speaks of you as the Marquis of Avonshire and of Miss Constance—"

I did not finish, for Constance had started to her feet with terror written on every feature. Hawberk looked at me and slowly smoothed his leathern apron.

"That is impossible," he observed, "Mr. Wilde may know a great many things—"

"About armor, for instance, and the 'Prince's Emblazoned,'" I interposed, smiling.

"Yes," he continued, slowly, "about armor also—may be—but he is wrong in regard to the Marquis of Avonshire, who, as you know, killed his wife's traducer years ago, and went to Australia where he did not long survive his wife."

"Mr. Wilde is wrong," murmured Constance. Her lips were blanched, but her voice was sweet and calm.

"Let us agree, if you please, that in this one circumstance Mr. Wilde is wrong," I said.

II

I climbed the three dilapidated flights of stairs, which I had so often climbed before, and knocked at a small door at the end of the corridor. Mr. Wilde opened the door and I walked in.

When he had double-locked the door and pushed a heavy chest against it, he came and sat down beside me, peering up into my face with his little light-colored eyes. Half a dozen new scratches covered his nose and cheeks, and the silver wires which supported his artificial ears had become displaced. I thought I had never seen him so hideously fascinating. He had no ears. The artificial ones, which now stood out at an angle from the fine wire, were his one weakness. They were made of wax and painted a shell pink, but the rest of his face was yellow. He might better have revelled in the luxury of some artificial fingers for his left hand, which was absolutely fingerless, but it seemed to cause him no inconvenience, and he was satisfied with his wax ears. He was very small, scarcely higher than a child of ten, but his arms were magnificently developed, and his thighs as thick as any athlete's. Still, the most remarkable thing about Mr. Wilde was that a man of his marvellous intelligence and knowledge should have such a head. It was flat and pointed, like the heads of many of those unfortunates whom people imprison in asylums for the weak-minded. Many called him insane, but I knew him to be as sane as I was.

I do not deny that he was eccentric; the mania he had for keeping that cat and teasing her until she flew at his face like a demon was certainly eccentric. I never could understand why he kept the creature, nor what pleasure he found in shutting himself up in his room with this surly, vicious beast. I remember once, glancing up from the manuscript I was studying by the light of some tallow dips, and seeing Mr. Wilde squatting motionless on his high chair, his eyes fairly blazing with excitement, while the cat, which had risen from her place before the stove, came creeping across the floor right at him. Before I could move she flattened her belly to the ground, crouched, trembled, and sprang into his face. Howling and foaming they rolled over and over on the floor, scratching and clawing, until the cat screamed and fled under the cabinet, and Mr. Wilde turned over on his back, his limbs contracting and curling up like the legs of a dying spider. He *was* eccentric.

Mr. Wilde had climbed into his high chair, and, after studying my face, picked up a dog's-eared ledger and opened it.

"Henry B. Matthews," he read, "book-keeper with Whysot Whysot and Company, dealers in church ornaments. Called April 3rd. Reputation damaged on the race-track. Known as a welcher. Reputation to be repaired by August 1st. Retainer Five Dollars." He turned the page and ran his fingerless knuckles down the closely-written columns.

"P. Greene Dusenberry, Minister of the Gospel, Fairbeach, New Jersey. Reputation damaged in the Bowery. To be repaired as soon as possible. Retainer $100."

He coughed and added, "Called, April 6th."

"Then you are not in need of money, Mr. Wilde," I inquired.

"Listen," he coughed again.

"Mrs. C. Hamilton Chester, of Chester Park, New York City. Called April 7th. Reputation damaged at Dieppe, France. To be repaired by October 1st Retainer $500.

"Note.—C. Hamilton Chester, Captain U.S.S. 'Avalanche', ordered home from South Sea Squadron October 1st."

"Well," I said, "the profession of a Repairer of Reputations is lucrative."

His colorless eyes sought mine, "I only wanted to demonstrate that I was correct. You said it was impossible to succeed as a Repairer of Reputations; that even if I did succeed in certain cases it would cost me more than I would gain by it. Today I have five hundred men in my employ, who are poorly paid, but who pursue the work with an enthusiasm which possibly may be born of fear. These men enter every shade and grade of society; some even are pillars of the most exclusive social temples; others are the prop and pride of the financial world; still others, hold undisputed sway among the 'Fancy and the Talent.' I choose them at my leisure from those who reply to my advertisements. It is easy enough, they are all cowards. I could treble the number in twenty days if I wished. So you see, those who have in their keeping the reputations of their fellow-citizens, I have in my pay."

"They may turn on you," I suggested.

He rubbed his thumb over his cropped ears, and adjusted the wax substitutes. "I think not," he murmured thoughtfully, "I seldom have to apply the whip, and then only once. Besides they like their wages."

"How do you apply the whip?" I demanded.

His face for a moment was awful to look upon. His eyes dwindled to a pair of green sparks.

"I invite them to come and have a little chat with me," he said in a soft voice.

A knock at the door interrupted him, and his face resumed its amiable expression.

"Who is it?" he inquired.

"Mr. Steylette," was the answer.

"Come tomorrow," replied Mr. Wilde.

"Impossible," began the other, but was silenced by a sort of bark from Mr. Wilde.

"Come tomorrow," he repeated.

We heard somebody move away from the door and turn the corner by the stairway.

"Who is that?" I asked.

"Arnold Steylette, Owner and Editor in Chief of the great New York daily."

He drummed on the ledger with his fingerless hand adding: "I pay him very badly, but he thinks it a good bargain."

"Arnold Steylette!" I repeated amazed.

"Yes," said Mr. Wilde, with a self-satisfied cough.

The cat, which had entered the room as he spoke, hesitated, looked up at him and snarled. He climbed down from the chair and, squatting on the floor, took the creature into his arms and caressed her. The cat ceased snarling and presently began a loud purring which seemed to increase in timbre as he stroked her. "Where are the notes?" I asked. He pointed to the table, and for the hundredth time I picked up the bundle of manuscript entitled—

"THE IMPERIAL DYNASTY OF AMERICA."

One by one I studied the well-worn pages, worn only by my own handling, and although I knew all by heart, from the beginning, "When from Carcosa, the Hyades, Hastur, and Aldebaran," to "Castaigne, Louis de Calvados, born December 19th, 1877," I read it with an eager, rapt attention, pausing to repeat parts of it aloud, and dwelling especially on "Hildred de Calvados, only son of Hildred Castaigne and Edythe Landes Castaigne, first in succession," etc., etc.

When I finished, Mr. Wilde nodded and coughed.

"Speaking of your legitimate ambition," he said, "how do Constance and Louis get along?"

"She loves him," I replied simply.

The cat on his knee suddenly turned and struck at his eyes, and he flung her off and climbed on to the chair opposite me.

"And Dr. Archer! But that's a matter you can settle any time you wish," he added.

"Yes," I replied, "Dr. Archer can wait, but it is time I saw my cousin Louis."

"It is time," he repeated. Then he took another ledger from the table and ran over the leaves rapidly. "We are now in communication with ten thousand men," he muttered. "We can count on one hundred thousand within the first twenty-eight hours, and in forty-eight hours the state will rise *en masse*. The country follows the state, and the portion that will not, I mean California and the Northwest, might better never have been inhabited. I shall not send them the Yellow Sign."

The blood rushed to my head, but I only answered, "A new broom sweeps clean."

"The ambition of Caesar and of Napoleon pales before that which could not rest until it had seized the minds of men and controlled even their unborn thoughts," said Mr. Wilde.

"You are speaking of the King in Yellow," I groaned, with a shudder.

"He is a king whom emperors have served."

"I am content to serve him," I replied.

Mr. Wilde sat rubbing his ears with his crippled hand. "Perhaps Constance does not love him," he suggested.

I started to reply, but a sudden burst of military music from the street below drowned my voice. The twentieth dragoon regiment, formerly in garrison at Mount St. Vincent, was returning from the manœuvres in Westchester County, to its new barracks on East

Washington Square. It was my cousin's regiment. They were a fine lot of fellows, in their pale blue, tight-fitting jackets, jaunty busbys and white riding breeches with the double yellow stripe, into which their limbs seemed moulded. Every other squadron was armed with lances, from the metal points of which fluttered yellow and white pennons. The band passed, playing the regimental march, then came the colonel and staff, the horses crowding and trampling, while their heads bobbed in unison, and the pennons fluttered from their lance points. The troopers, who rode with the beautiful English seat, looked brown as berries from their bloodless campaign among the farms of Westchester, and the music of their sabres against the stirrups, and the jingle of spurs and carbines was delightful to me. I saw Louis riding with his squadron. He was as handsome an officer as I have ever seen. Mr. Wilde, who had mounted a chair by the window, saw him too, but said nothing. Louis turned and looked straight at Hawberk's shop as he passed, and I could see the flush on his brown cheeks. I think Constance must have been at the window. When the last troopers had clattered by, and the last pennons vanished into South Fifth Avenue, Mr. Wilde clambered out of his chair and dragged the chest away from the door.

"Yes," he said, "it is time that you saw your cousin Louis."

He unlocked the door and I picked up my hat and stick and stepped into the corridor. The stairs were dark. Groping about, I set my foot on something soft, which snarled and spit, and I aimed a murderous blow at the cat, but my cane shivered to splinters against the balustrade, and the beast scurried back into Mr. Wilde's room.

Passing Hawberk's door again I saw him still at work on the armor, but I did not stop, and stepping out into Bleecker Street, I followed it to Wooster, skirted the grounds of the Lethal Chamber, and crossing Washington Park went straight to my rooms in the Benedick. Here I lunched comfortably, read the *Herald* and the *Meteor*, and finally went to the steel safe in my bedroom and set the time combination. The three and three-quarter minutes which it is necessary to wait, while the time lock is opening, are to me golden moments. From the instant I set the combination to the moment when I grasp the knobs and swing back the solid steel doors, I live in an ecstasy of expectation. Those moments must be like moments passed in Paradise. I know what I am to find at the end of the time limit. I know what the massive safe holds secure for me, for me alone, and the exquisite pleasure of waiting is hardly enhanced when the safe opens and I lift, from its velvet crown, a diadem of purest gold, blazing with diamonds. I do this every day, and yet the joy of waiting and at last touching again the diadem, only seems to increase as the days pass. It is a diadem fit for a King among kings, an Emperor among emperors. The King in Yellow might scorn it, but it shall be worn by his royal servant.

I held it in my arms until the alarm in the safe rang harshly, and then tenderly, proudly, I replaced it and shut the steel doors. I walked slowly back into my study, which faces Washington Square, and leaned on the window sill. The afternoon sun poured into my windows, and a gentle breeze stirred the branches of the elms and maples in the park, now covered with buds and tender foliage. A flock of pigeons circled about the tower of the Memorial Church; sometimes alighting on the purple tiled roof, sometimes wheeling downward to the lotos fountain in front of the marble arch. The gardeners were busy with the flower beds around the fountain, and the freshly turned earth smelled sweet and spicy. A lawn mower, drawn by a fat white horse, clinked across the green sward, and watering-carts poured showers of spray over the asphalt drives. Around the statue of Peter Stuyvesant, which in 1897 had replaced the monstrosity supposed to represent Garibaldi, children played in the spring sunshine, and nurse girls wheeled elaborate baby carriages with a reckless disregard for the pasty-faced occupants, which could probably be explained by the presence of half a dozen trim dragoon troopers languidly lolling on the benches. Through the trees, the Washington Memorial Arch glistened like silver in the sunshine, and beyond, on the eastern extremity of the square the grey stone barracks of the dragoons, and the white granite artillery stables were alive with color and motion.

I looked at the Lethal Chamber on the corner of the square opposite. A few curious people still lingered about the gilded iron railing, but inside the grounds the paths were deserted. I watched the fountains ripple and sparkle; the sparrows had already found this new bathing nook, and the basins were covered with the dusty-feathered little things. Two or three white peacocks picked their way across the lawns, and a drab-colored pigeon sat so motionless on the arm of one of the "Fates," that it seemed to be a part of the sculptured stone.

As I was turning carelessly away, a slight commotion in the group of curious loiterers around the gates attracted my attention. A young man had entered, and was advancing with nervous strides along the gravel path which leads to the bronze doors of the Lethal Chamber. He paused a moment before the "Fates," and as he raised his head to those three mysterious faces, the pigeon rose from its sculptured perch, circled about for a moment and wheeled to the east. The young man pressed his hand to his face, and then with an undefinable gesture sprang up the marble steps, the bronze doors closed behind him, and half an hour later the loiterers slouched away, and the frightened pigeon returned to its perch in the arms of Fate.

I put on my hat and went out into the park for a little walk before dinner. As I crossed the central driveway a group of officers passed, and one of them called out, "Hello, Hildred," and came back to shake hands with me. It was my cousin Louis, who stood smiling and tapping his spurred heels with his riding-whip.

"Just back from Westchester," he said; "been doing the bucolic; milk and curds, you know, dairy-maids in sunbonnets, who say 'haeow' and 'I don't think' when you tell them they are pretty. I'm nearly dead for a square meal at Delmonico's. What's the news?"

"There is none," I replied pleasantly. "I saw your regiment coming in this morning."

"Did you? I didn't see you. Where were you?"

"In Mr. Wilde's window."

"Oh, hell!" he began impatiently, "that man is stark mad! I don't understand why you—"

He saw how annoyed I felt by this outburst, and begged my pardon.

"Really, old chap," he said, "I don't mean to run down a man you like, but for the life of me I can't see what the deuce you find in common with Mr. Wilde. He's not well bred, to put it generously; he is hideously deformed; his head is the head of a criminally insane person. You know yourself he's been in an asylum—"

"So have I," I interrupted calmly.

Louis looked startled and confused for a moment, but recovered and slapped me heartily on the shoulder. "You were completely cured," he began; but I stopped him again.

"I suppose you mean that I was simply acknowledged never to have been insane."

"Of course that—that's what I meant," he laughed.

I disliked his laugh because I knew it was forced, but I nodded gaily and asked him where he was going. Louis looked after his brother officers who had now almost reached Broadway.

"We had intended to sample a Brunswick cocktail, but to tell you the truth I was anxious for an excuse to go and see Hawberk instead. Come along, I'll make you my excuse."

We found old Hawberk, neatly attired in a fresh spring suit, standing at the door of his shop and sniffing the air.

"I had just decided to take Constance for a little stroll before dinner," he replied to the impetuous volley of questions from Louis. "We thought of walking on the park terrace along the North River."

At that moment Constance appeared and grew pale and rosy by turns as Louis bent over her small gloved fingers. I tried to excuse myself, alleging an engagement uptown, but Louis and Constance would not listen, and I saw I was expected to remain and engage old Hawberk's attention. After all it would be just as well if I kept my eye on Louis, I thought, and when they hailed a Spring Street horse-car, I got in after them and took my seat beside the armorer.

The beautiful line of parks and granite terraces overlooking the wharves along the North

River, which were built in 1910 and finished in the autumn of 1917, had become one of the most popular promenades in the metropolis. They extended from the battery to 190th Street, overlooking the noble river and affording a fine view of the Jersey shore and the Highlands opposite. Cafés and restaurants were scattered here and there among the trees, and twice a week military bands from the garrison played in the kiosks on the parapets.

We sat down in the sunshine on the bench at the foot of the equestrian statue of General Sheridan. Constance tipped her sunshade to shield her eyes, and she and Louis began a murmuring conversation which was impossible to catch. Old Hawberk, leaning on his ivory headed cane, lighted an excellent cigar, the mate to which I politely refused, and smiled at vacancy. The sun hung low above the Staten Island woods, and the bay was dyed with golden hues reflected from the sun-warmed sails of the shipping in the harbor.

Brigs, schooners, yachts, clumsy ferry-boats, their decks swarming with people, railroad transports carrying lines of brown, blue and white freight cars, stately sound steamers, déclassé tramp steamers, coasters, dredgers, scows, and everywhere pervading the entire bay impudent little tugs puffing and whistling officiously;—these were the craft which churned the sunlight waters as far as the eye could reach. In calm contrast to the hurry of sailing vessel and steamer a silent fleet of white warships lay motionless in midstream.

Constance's merry laugh aroused me from my reverie.

"What *are* you staring at?" she inquired.

"Nothing—the fleet," I smiled.

Then Louis told us what the vessels were, pointing out each by its relative position to the old Red Fort on Governor's Island.

"That little cigar-shaped thing is a torpedo boat," he explained; "there are four more lying close together. They are the *Tarpon*, the *Falcon*, the *Sea Fox*, and the *Octopus*. The gun-boats just above are the *Princeton*, the *Champlain*, the *Still Water* and the *Erie*. Next to them lie the cruisers *Faragut* and *Los Angeles*, and above them the battle ships *California*, and *Dakota*, and the *Washington* which is the flag ship. Those two squatty looking chunks of metal which are anchored there off Castle William are the double-turreted monitors *Terrible* and *Magnificent*; behind them lies the ram, *Osceola*."

Constance looked at him with deep approval in her beautiful eyes. "What loads of things you know for a soldier," she said, and we all joined in the laugh which followed.

Presently Louis rose with a nod to us and offered his arm to Constance, and they strolled away along the river wall. Hawberk watched them for a moment and then turned to me.

"Mr. Wilde was right," he said. "I have found the missing tassets and left cuissard of the 'Prince's Emblazoned,' in a vile old junk garret in Pell Street."

"998?" I inquired, with a smile.

"Yes."

"Mr. Wilde is a very intelligent man," I observed.

"I want to give him the credit of this most important discovery," continued Hawberk. "And I intend it shall be known that he is entitled to the fame of it."

"He won't thank you for that," I answered sharply; "please say nothing about it."

"Do you know what it is worth?" said Hawberk.

"No, fifty dollars, perhaps."

"It is valued at five hundred, but the owner of the 'Prince's Emblazoned' will give two thousand dollars to the person who completes his suit; that reward also belongs to Mr. Wilde."

"He doesn't want it! He refuses it!" I answered angrily. "What do you know about Mr. Wilde? He doesn't need the money. He is rich—or will be—richer than any living man except myself. What will we care for money then—what will we care, he and I, when—when—"

"When what?" demanded Hawberk, astonished.

"You will see," I replied, on my guard again.

He looked at me narrowly, much as Doctor Archer used to, and I knew he thought I was mentally unsound. Perhaps it was fortunate for him that he did not use the word lunatic just then.

"No," I replied to his unspoken thought, "I am not mentally weak; my mind is as healthy as Mr. Wilde's. I do not care to explain just yet what I have on hand, but it is an investment which will pay more than mere gold, silver and precious stones. It will secure the happiness and prosperity of a continent—yes, a hemisphere!"

"Oh," said Hawberk.

"And eventually," I continued more quietly, "it will secure the happiness of the whole world."

"And incidentally your own happiness and prosperity as well as Mr. Wilde's?"

"Exactly," I smiled. But I could have throttled him for taking that tone.

He looked at me in silence for a while and then said very gently, "Why don't you give up your books and studies, Mr. Castaigne, and take a tramp among the mountains somewhere or other? You used to be fond of fishing. Take a cast or two at the trout in the Rangelys."

"I don't care for fishing any more," I answered, without a shade of annoyance in my voice.

"You used to be fond of everything," he continued; "athletics, yachting, shooting, riding—"

"I have never cared to ride since my fall," I said quietly.

"Ah, yes, your fall," he repeated, looking away from me.

I thought this nonsense had gone far enough, so I brought the conversation back to Mr. Wilde; but he was scanning my face again in a manner highly offensive to me.

"Mr. Wilde," he repeated, "do you know what he did this afternoon? He came downstairs and nailed a sign over the hall door next to mine; it read:

MR. WILDE,
REPAIRER OF REPUTATIONS.
Third Bell.

"Do you know what a Repairer of Reputations can be?"

"I do," I replied, suppressing the rage within.

"Oh," he said again.

Louis and Constance came strolling by and stopped to ask if we would join them. Hawberk looked at his watch. At the same moment a puff of smoke shot from the casemates of Castle William, and the boom of the sunset gun rolled across the water and was re-echoed from the Highlands opposite. The flag came running down from the flag-pole, the bugles sounded on the white decks of the warships, and the first electric light sparkled out from the Jersey shore.

As I turned into the city with Hawberk I heard Constance murmur something to Louis which I did not understand; but Louis whispered "My darling," in reply; and again, walking ahead with Hawberk through the square I heard a murmur of "sweetheart," and "my own Constance," and I knew the time had nearly arrived when I should speak of important matters with my cousin Louis.

III

One morning early in May I stood before the steel safe in my bedroom, trying on the golden jewelled crown. The diamonds flashed fire as I turned to the mirror, and the heavy beaten gold burned like a halo about my head. I remembered Camilla's agonized scream and the awful words echoing through the dim streets of Carcosa. They were the last lines in the first act, and I dared not think of what followed—dared not, even in the spring sunshine, there in my own room, surrounded with familiar objects, reassured by the bustle from the street and the voices of the servants in the hallway outside. For those poisoned words had dropped slowly into my heart, as death-sweat drops upon a bed-sheet and is absorbed. Trembling, I put the diadem from my head and wiped my forehead, but I thought of Hastur and of my own rightful ambition, and I remembered Mr. Wilde as I had last left him, his face all torn and bloody from the claws of that devil's creature, and what he said—ah, what he said. The alarm bell in the safe began to whirr harshly, and I knew my time was up; but I would not heed it, and replacing the flashing circlet upon my head I turned defiantly to the mirror. I stood for a long time absorbed in the changing expression of my own eyes. The mirror reflected a face which was like my own, but whiter, and so thin that I hardly recognized it. And all the time I kept repeating between my clenched teeth, "The day has come! the day has come!" while the alarm in the safe whirred and clamored, and the diamonds sparkled and flamed above my brow. I heard a door open but did not heed it. It was only when I saw two faces in the mirror:—it was only when another face rose over my shoulder, and two other eyes met mine. I wheeled like a flash and seized a long knife from my dressing-table, and my cousin sprang back very pale, crying: "Hildred! for God's sake!" then as my hand fell, he said: "It is I, Louis, don't you know me?" I stood silent. I could not have spoken for my life. He walked up to me and took the knife from my hand.

"What is all this?" he inquired, in a gentle voice. "Are you ill?"

"No," I replied. But I doubt if he heard me.

"Come, come, old fellow," he cried, "take off that brass crown and toddle into the study. Are you going to a masquerade? What's all this theatrical tinsel anyway?"

I was glad he thought the crown was made of brass and paste, yet I didn't like him any the better for thinking so. I let him take it from my hand, knowing it was best to humor him. He tossed the splendid diadem in the air, and catching it, turned to me smiling.

"It's dear at fifty cents," he said. "What's it for?"

I did not answer, but took the circlet from his hands, and placing it in the safe shut the massive steel door. The alarm ceased its infernal din at once. He watched me curiously, but did not seem to notice the sudden ceasing of the alarm. He did, however, speak of the safe as a biscuit box. Fearing lest he might examine the combination I led the way into my study. Louis threw himself on the sofa and flicked at flies with his eternal riding-whip. He wore his fatigue uniform with the braided jacket and jaunty cap, and I noticed that his riding-boots were all splashed with red mud.

"Where have you been?" I inquired.

"Jumping mud creeks in Jersey," he said. "I haven't had time to change yet; I was rather in a hurry to see you. Haven't you got a glass of something? I'm dead tired; been in the saddle twenty-four hours."

I gave him some brandy from my medicinal store, which he drank with a grimace.

"Damned bad stuff," he observed. "I'll give you an address where they sell brandy that is brandy."

"It's good enough for my needs," I said indifferently. "I use it to rub my chest with." He stared and flicked at another fly.

"See here, old fellow," he began, "I've got something to suggest to you. It's four years now that you've shut yourself up here like an owl, never going anywhere, never taking any healthy exercise, never doing a damn thing but poring over those books up there on the mantelpiece."

He glanced along the row of shelves. "Napoleon, Napoleon, Napoleon!" he read. "For heaven's sake, have you nothing but Napoleons there?"

"I wish they were bound in gold," I said. "But wait, yes, there is another book, *The King in Yellow*." I looked him steadily in the eye.

"Have you never read it?" I asked.

"I? No, thank God! I don't want to be driven crazy."

I saw he regretted his speech as soon as he had uttered it. There is only one word which I loathe more than I do lunatic and that word is crazy. But I controlled myself and asked him why he thought *The King in Yellow* dangerous.

"Oh, I don't know," he said, hastily. "I only remember the excitement it created and the denunciations from pulpit and Press. I believe the author shot himself after bringing forth this monstrosity, didn't he?"

"I understand he is still alive," I answered.

"That's probably true," he muttered; "bullets couldn't kill a fiend like that."

"It is a book of great truths," I said.

"Yes," he replied, "of 'truths' which send men frantic and blast their lives. I don't care if the thing is, as they say, the very supreme essence of art. It's a crime to have written it, and I for one shall never open its pages."

"Is that what you have come to tell me?" I asked.

"No," he said, "I came to tell you that I am going to be married."

I believe for a moment my heart ceased to beat, but I kept my eyes on his face.

"Yes," he continued, smiling happily, "married to the sweetest girl on earth."

"Constance Hawberk," I said mechanically.

"How did you know?" he cried, astonished. "I didn't know it myself until that evening last April, when we strolled down to the embankment before dinner."

"When is it to be?" I asked.

"It was to have been next September, but an hour ago a despatch came ordering our regiment to the Presidio, San Francisco. We leave at noon tomorrow. Tomorrow," he repeated. "Just think, Hildred, tomorrow I shall be the happiest fellow that ever drew breath in this jolly world, for Constance will go with me."

I offered him my hand in congratulation, and he seized and shook it like the good-natured fool he was—or pretended to be.

"I am going to get my squadron as a wedding present," he rattled on. "Captain and Mrs. Louis Castaigne, eh, Hildred?"

Then he told me where it was to be and who were to be there, and made me promise to come and be best man. I set my teeth and listened to his boyish chatter without showing what I felt, but—

I was getting to the limit of my endurance, and when he jumped up, and, switching his spurs till they jingled, said he must go, I did not detain him.

"There's one thing I want to ask of you," I said quietly.

"Out with it, it's promised," he laughed.

"I want you to meet me for a quarter of an hour's talk tonight."

"Of course, if you wish," he said, somewhat puzzled. "Where?"

"Anywhere, in the park there."

"What time, Hildred?"

"Midnight."

"What in the name of—" he began, but checked himself and laughingly assented. I watched him go down the stairs and hurry away, his sabre banging at every stride. He turned into Bleecker Street, and I knew he was going to see Constance. I gave him ten minutes to disappear and then followed in his footsteps, taking with me the jewelled crown and the silken robe embroidered with the Yellow Sign. When I turned into Bleecker Street, and entered the doorway which bore the sign—

MR. WILDE,
REPAIRER OF REPUTATIONS.
Third Bell.

I saw old Hawberk moving about in his shop, and imagined I heard Constance's voice in the parlor; but I avoided them both and hurried up the trembling stairways to Mr. Wilde's apartment. I knocked and entered without ceremony. Mr. Wilde lay groaning on the floor, his face covered with blood, his clothes torn to shreds. Drops of blood were scattered about over the carpet, which had also been ripped and frayed in the evidently recent struggle.

"It's that cursed cat," he said, ceasing his groans, and turning his colorless eyes to me; "she attacked me while I was asleep. I believe she will kill me yet."

This was too much, so I went into the kitchen, and, seizing a hatchet from the pantry, started to find the infernal beast and settle her then and there. My search was fruitless, and after a while I gave it up and came back to find Mr. Wilde squatting on his high chair by the table. He had washed his face and changed his clothes. The great furrows which the cat's claws had ploughed up in his face he had filled with collodion, and a rag hid the wound in his throat. I told him I should kill the cat when I came across her, but he only shook his head and turned to the open ledger before him. He read name after name of the people who had come to him in regard to their reputation, and the sums he had amassed were startling.

"I put on the screws now and then," he explained.

"One day or other some of these people will assassinate you," I insisted.

"Do you think so?" he said, rubbing his mutilated ears.

It was useless to argue with him, so I took down the manuscript entitled *Imperial Dynasty of America*, for the last time I should ever take it down in Mr. Wilde's study. I read it through, thrilling and trembling with pleasure. When I had finished Mr. Wilde took the manuscript and, turning to the dark passage which leads from his study to his bed-chamber, called out in a loud voice, "Vance." Then for the first time, I noticed a man crouching there in the shadow. How I had overlooked him during my search for the cat, I cannot imagine.

"Vance, come in," cried Mr. Wilde.

The figure rose and crept towards us, and I shall never forget the face that he raised to mine, as the light from the window illuminated it.

"Vance, this is Mr. Castaigne," said Mr. Wilde. Before he had finished speaking, the man threw himself on the ground before the table, crying and grasping, "Oh, God! Oh, my God! Help me! Forgive me! Oh, Mr. Castaigne, keep that man away. You cannot, you cannot mean it! You are different—save me! I am broken down—I was in a madhouse and now—when all was coming right—when I had forgotten the King—the King in Yellow and—but I shall go mad again—I shall go mad—"

His voice died into a choking rattle, for Mr. Wilde had leapt on him and his right hand encircled the man's throat. When Vance fell in a heap on the floor, Mr. Wilde clambered nimbly into his chair again, and rubbing his mangled ears with the stump of his hand, turned to me and asked me for the ledger. I reached it down from the shelf and he opened it. After a moment's searching among the beautifully written pages, he coughed complacently, and pointed to the name Vance.

"Vance," he read aloud, "Osgood Oswald Vance." At the sound of his name, the man on the floor raised his head and turned a convulsed face to Mr. Wilde. His eyes were injected with blood, his lips tumefied. "Called April 28th," continued Mr. Wilde. "Occupation, cashier in the Seaforth National Bank; has served a term of forgery at Sing Sing, from whence he was transferred to the Asylum for the Criminal Insane. Pardoned by the Governor of New York, and discharged from the Asylum, January 19, 1918. Reputation damaged at Sheepshead Bay. Rumors that he lives beyond his income. Reputation to be repaired at once. Retainer $1,500.

"Note.—Has embezzled sums amounting to $30,000 since March 20, 1919, excellent family, and secured present position through uncle's influence. Father, President of Seaforth Bank."

I looked at the man on the floor.

"Get up, Vance," said Mr. Wilde in a gentle voice. Vance rose as if hypnotized. "He will do as we suggest now," observed Mr. Wilde, and opening the manuscript, he read the entire history of the Imperial Dynasty of America. Then in a kind and soothing murmur he ran over the important points with Vance, who stood like one stunned. His eyes were so blank and vacant that I imagined he had become half-witted, and remarked it to Mr. Wilde who replied that it was of no consequence anyway. Very patiently we pointed out to Vance what his share in the affair would be, and he seemed to understand after a while. Mr. Wilde explained the manuscript, using several volumes on Heraldry, to substantiate the result of his researches. He mentioned the establishment of the Dynasty in Carcosa, the lakes which connected Hastur, Aldebaran and the mystery of the Hyades. He spoke of Cassilda and Camilla, and sounded the cloudy depths of Demhe, and the Lake of Hali. "The scolloped tatters of the King in Yellow must hide Yhtill forever," he muttered, but I do not believe Vance heard him. Then by degrees he led Vance along the ramifications of the Imperial family, to Uoht and Thale, from Naotalba and Phantom of Truth, to Aldones, and then tossing aside his manuscript and notes, he began the wonderful story of the Last King. Fascinated and thrilled I watched him. He threw up his head, his long arms were stretched out in a magnificent gesture of pride and power, and his eyes blazed deep in their sockets like two emeralds. Vance listened stupefied. As for me, when at last Mr. Wilde had finished, and pointing to me, cried, "The cousin of the King!" my head swam with excitement.

Controlling myself with a superhuman effort, I explained to Vance why I alone was worthy of the crown and why my cousin must be exiled or die. I made him understand that my cousin must never marry, even after renouncing all his claims, and how that least of all he should marry the daughter of the Marquis of Avonshire and bring England into the question. I showed him a list of thousands of names which Mr. Wilde had drawn up; every man whose name was there had received the Yellow Sign which no living human being dared disregard. The city, the state, the whole land, were ready to rise and tremble before the Pallid Mask.

The time had come, the people should know the son of Hastur, and the whole world bow to the black stars which hang in the sky over Carcosa.

Vance leaned on the table, his head buried in his hands. Mr. Wilde drew a rough sketch on the margin of yesterday's *Herald* with a bit of lead pencil. It was a plan of Hawberk's rooms. Then he wrote out the order and affixed the seal, and shaking like a palsied man I signed my first writ of execution with my name Hildred-Rex.

Mr. Wilde clambered to the floor and, unlocking the cabinet, took a long square box from the first shelf. This he brought to the table and opened. A new knife lay in the tissue paper inside and I picked it up and handed it to Vance, along with the order and the plan of Hawberk's apartment. Then Mr. Wilde told Vance he could go; and he went, shambling like an outcast of the slums.

I sat for a while watching the daylight fade behind the square tower of the Judson Memorial Church, and finally, gathering up the manuscript and notes, took my hat and started for the door.

Mr. Wilde watched me in silence. When I had stepped into the hall I looked back. Mr. Wilde's small eyes were still fixed on me. Behind him, the shadows gathered in the fading light. Then I closed the door behind me and went out into the darkening streets.

I had eaten nothing since breakfast, but I was not hungry. A wretched, half-starved creature, who stood looking across the street at the Lethal Chamber, noticed me and came up to tell me a tale of misery. I gave him money, I don't know why, and he went away without thanking me. An hour later another outcast approached and whined his story. I had a blank bit of paper in my pocket, on which was traced the Yellow Sign, and I handed it to him. He looked at it stupidly for a moment, and then with an uncertain glance at me, folded it with what seemed to me exaggerated care and placed it in his bosom.

The electric lights were sparkling among the trees, and the new moon shone in the sky above the Lethal Chamber. It was tiresome waiting in the square; I wandered from the Marble Arch to the artillery stables and back again to the lotos fountain. The flowers and grass exhaled a fragrance which troubled me. The jet of the fountain played in the moonlight, and the musical splash of falling drops reminded me of the tinkle of chained mail in Hawberk's shop. But it was not so fascinating, and the dull sparkle of the moonlight on the water brought no such sensations of exquisite pleasure, as when the sunshine played over the polished steel of a corselet on Hawberk's knee. I watched the bats darting and turning above the water plants in the fountain basin, but their rapid, jerky flight set my nerves on edge, and I went away again to walk aimlessly to and fro among the trees.

The artillery stables were dark, but in the cavalry barracks the officers' windows were brilliantly lighted, and the sallyport was constantly filled with troopers in fatigue, carrying straw and harness and baskets filled with tin dishes.

Twice the mounted sentry at the gates was changed while I wandered up and down the asphalt walk. I looked at my watch. It was nearly time. The lights in the barracks went out one by one, the barred gate was closed, and every minute or two an officer passed in through the side wicket, leaving a rattle of accoutrements and a jingle of spurs on the night air. The square had become very silent. The last homeless loiterer had been driven away by the gray-coated park policeman, the car tracks along Wooster Street were deserted, and the only sound which broke the stillness was the stamping of the sentry's horse and the ring of his sabre against the saddle pommel. In the barracks, the officers' quarters were still lighted, and military servants passed and repassed before the bay windows. Twelve o'clock sounded from the new spire of St. Francis Xavier, and at the last stroke of the sad-toned bell a figure passed through the wicket beside the portcullis, returned the salute of the sentry, and crossing the street entered the square and advanced toward the Benedick apartment house.

"Louis," I called.

The man pivoted on his spurred heels and came straight toward me.

"Is that you, Hildred?"

"Yes, you are on time."

I took his offered hand, and we strolled toward the Lethal Chamber.

He rattled on about his wedding and the graces of Constance, and their future prospects, calling my attention to his captain's shoulder-straps, and the triple gold arabesque on his sleeve and fatigue cap. I believe I listened as much to the music of his spurs and sabre as I did to his boyish babble, and at last we stood under the elms on the Fourth Street corner of the square opposite the Lethal Chamber. Then he laughed and asked me what I wanted with him. I motioned him to a seat on a bench under the electric light, and sat down beside him. He looked at me curiously, with that same searching glance which I hate and fear so in doctors. I felt the insult of his look, but he did not know it, and I carefully concealed my feelings.

"Well, old chap," he inquired, "what can I do for you?"

I drew from my pocket the manuscript and notes of the *Imperial Dynasty of America*, and looking him in the eye said:

"I will tell you. On your word as a soldier, promise me to read this manuscript from beginning to end, without asking me a question. Promise me to read these notes in the same way, and promise me to listen to what I have to tell later."

"I promise, if you wish it," he said pleasantly. "Give me the paper, Hildred."

He began to read, raising his eyebrows with a puzzled, whimsical air, which made me tremble with suppressed anger. As he advanced his, eyebrows contracted, and his lips seemed to form the word "rubbish."

Then he looked slightly bored, but apparently for my sake read, with an attempt at interest, which presently ceased to be an effort. He started when in the closely written pages he came to his own name, and when he came to mine he lowered the paper, and looked sharply at me for a moment. But he kept his word, and resumed his reading, and I let the half-formed question die on his lips unanswered. When he came to the end and read the signature of Mr. Wilde, he folded the paper carefully and returned it to me. I handed him the notes, and he settled back, pushing his fatigue cap up to his forehead, with a boyish gesture, which I remembered so well in school. I watched his face as he read, and when he finished I took the notes with the manuscript, and placed them in my pocket. Then I unfolded a scroll marked with the Yellow Sign. He saw the sign, but he did not seem to recognize it, and I called his attention to it somewhat sharply.

"Well," he said, "I see it. What is it?"

"It is the Yellow Sign," I said angrily.

"Oh, that's it, is it?" said Louis, in that flattering voice, which Doctor Archer used to employ with me, and would probably have employed again, had I not settled his affair for him.

I kept my rage down and answered as steadily as possible, "Listen, you have engaged your word?"

"I am listening, old chap," he replied soothingly.

I began to speak very calmly.

"Dr. Archer, having by some means become possessed of the secret of the Imperial Succession, attempted to deprive me of my right, alleging that because of a fall from my horse four years ago, I had become mentally deficient. He presumed to place me under restraint in his own house in hopes of either driving me insane or poisoning me. I have not forgotten it. I visited him last night and the interview was final."

Louis turned quite pale, but did not move. I resumed triumphantly, "There are yet three people to be interviewed in the interests of Mr. Wilde and myself. They are my cousin Louis, Mr. Hawberk, and his daughter Constance."

Louis sprang to his feet and I arose also, and flung the paper marked with the Yellow Sign to the ground.

"Oh, I don't need that to tell you what I have to say," I cried, with a laugh of triumph. "You must renounce the crown to me, do you hear, to *me*."

Louis looked at me with a startled air, but recovering himself said kindly, "Of course I renounce the—what is it I must renounce?"

"The crown," I said angrily.

"Of course," he answered, "I renounce it. Come, old chap, I'll walk back to your rooms with you."

"Don't try any of your doctor's tricks on me," I cried, trembling with fury. "Don't act as if you think I am insane."

"What nonsense," he replied. "Come, it's getting late, Hildred."

"No," I shouted, "you must listen. You cannot marry, I forbid it. Do you hear? I forbid it. You shall renounce the crown, and in reward I grant you exile, but if you refuse you shall die."

He tried to calm me, but I was roused at last, and drawing my long knife barred his way.

Then I told him how they would find Dr. Archer in the cellar with his throat open, and I laughed in his face when I thought of Vance and his knife, and the order signed by me.

"Ah, you are the King," I cried, "but I shall be King. Who are you to keep me from Empire over all the habitable earth! I was born the cousin of a king, but I shall be King!"

Louis stood white and rigid before me. Suddenly a man came running up Fourth Street, entered the gate of the Lethal Temple, traversed the path to the bronze doors at full speed, and plunged into the death chamber with the cry of one demented, and I laughed until I wept tears, for I had recognized Vance, and knew that Hawberk and his daughter were no longer in my way.

"Go," I cried to Louis, "you have ceased to be a menace. You will never marry Constance now, and if you marry anyone else in your exile, I will visit you as I did my doctor last night. Mr. Wilde takes charge of you tomorrow." Then I turned and darted into South Fifth Avenue, and with a cry of terror Louis dropped his belt and sabre and followed me like the wind. I heard him close behind me at the corner of Bleecker Street, and I dashed into the doorway under Hawberk's sign. He cried, "Halt, or I fire!" but when he saw that I flew up the stairs leaving Hawberk's shop below, he left me, and I heard him hammering and shouting at their door as though it were possible to arouse the dead.

Mr. Wilde's door was open, and I entered crying, "It is done, it is done! Let the nations rise and look upon their King!" but I could not find Mr. Wilde, so I went to the cabinet and took the splendid diadem from its case. Then I drew on the white silk robe, embroidered with the Yellow Sign, and placed the crown upon my head. At last I was King, King by my right in Hastur, King because I knew the mystery of the Hyades, and my mind had sounded the depths of the Lake of Hali. I was King! The first grey pencillings of dawn would raise a tempest which would shake two hemispheres. Then as I stood, my every nerve pitched to the highest tension, faint with the joy and splendor of my thought, without, in the dark passage, a man groaned.

I seized the tallow dip and sprang to the door. The cat passed me like a demon, and the tallow dip went out, but my long knife flew swifter than she, and I heard her screech, and I knew that my knife had found her. For a moment I listened to her tumbling and thumping about in the darkness, and then when her frenzy ceased, I lighted a lamp and raised it over my head. Mr. Wilde lay on the floor with his throat torn open. At first I thought he was dead, but as I looked, a green sparkle came into his sunken eyes, his mutilated hand trembled, and then a spasm stretched his mouth from ear to ear. For a moment my terror and despair gave place to hope, but as I bent over him his eyeballs rolled clean around in his head, and he died. Then while I stood, transfixed with rage and despair, seeing my crown, my empire, every hope and every ambition, my very life, lying prostrate there with the dead master, *they* came, seized me from behind, and bound me until my veins stood out like cords, and my voice failed with the paroxysms of my frenzied screams. But I still raged, bleeding and infuriated among them, and more than one policeman felt my sharp teeth. Then when I could no longer move they came nearer; I saw old Hawberk, and behind him my cousin Louis' ghastly face, and farther away, in the corner, a woman, Constance, weeping softly.

"Ah! I see it now!" I shrieked. "You have seized the throne and the empire. Woe! woe to you who are crowned with the crown of the King in Yellow!"

[EDITOR'S NOTE.—Mr. Castaigne died yesterday in the Asylum for Criminally Insane.]

THE DUNWICH HORROR

BY

H. P. LOVECRAFT

Gorgons, and Hydras, and Chimaeras—dire stories of Celaeno and the Harpies—may reproduce themselves in the brain of superstition—*but they were there before.* They are transcripts, types—the archetypes are in us, and eternal. How else should the recital of that which we know in a waking sense to be false come to affect us at all? Is it that we naturally conceive terror from such objects, considered in their capacity of being able to inflict upon us bodily injury? O, least of all! *These terrors are of older standing. They date beyond body*—or without the body, they would have been the same... That the kind of fear here treated is purely spiritual—that it is strong in proportion as it is objectless on earth, that it predominates in the period of our sinless infancy—are difficulties the solution of which might afford some probable insight into our ante-mundane condition, and a peep at least into the shadowland of pre-existence.

—Charles Lamb: *Witches and Other Night-Fears*

I

When a traveler in north central Massachusetts takes the wrong fork at the junction of the Aylesbury pike just beyond Dean's Corners he comes upon a lonely and curious country. The ground gets higher, and the brier-bordered stone walls press closer and closer against the ruts of the dusty, curving road. The trees of the frequent forest belts seem too large, and the wild weeds, brambles, and grasses attain a luxuriance not often found in settled regions. At the same time the planted fields appear singularly few and barren; while the sparsely scattered houses wear a surprisingly uniform aspect of age, squalor, and dilapidation. Without knowing why, one hesitates to ask directions from the gnarled, solitary figures spied now and then on crumbling doorsteps or on the sloping, rock-strewn meadows. Those figures are so silent and furtive that one feels somehow confronted by forbidden things, with which it would be better to have nothing to do. When a rise in the road brings the mountains in view above the deep woods, the feeling of strange uneasiness is increased. The summits are too rounded and symmetrical to give a sense of comfort and naturalness, and sometimes the sky silhouettes with especial clearness the queer circles of tall stone pillars with which most of them are crowned.

Gorges and ravines of problematical depth intersect the way, and the crude wooden bridges always seem of dubious safety. When the road dips again there are stretches of marshland that one instinctively dislikes, and indeed almost fears at evening when unseen whippoorwills chatter and the fireflies come out in abnormal profusion to dance to the raucous, creepily insistent rhythms of stridently piping bull-frogs. The thin, shining line of the Miskatonic's upper reaches has an oddly serpent-like suggestion as it winds close to the feet of the domed hills among which it rises.

As the hills draw nearer, one heeds their wooded sides more than their stone-crowned tops. Those sides loom up so darkly and precipitously that one wishes they would keep their distance, but there is no road by which to escape them. Across a covered bridge one sees a small village huddled between the stream and the vertical slope of Round Mountain, and wonders at the cluster of rotting gambrel roofs bespeaking an earlier architectural period than that of the neighboring region. It is not reassuring to see, on a closer glance, that most of the houses are deserted and falling to ruin, and that the broken-steepled church now harbors the one slovenly mercantile establishment of the hamlet. One dreads to trust the tenebrous tunnel of the bridge, yet there is no way to avoid it. Once across, it is hard to prevent the impression of a faint, malign odor about the village street, as of the massed mold and decay of centuries. It is always a relief to get clear of the place, and to follow the narrow road around the base of the hills and across the level country beyond till it rejoins the Aylesbury pike. Afterward one sometimes learns that one has been through Dunwich.

Outsiders visit Dunwich as seldom as possible, and since a certain season of horror all the signboards pointing toward it have been taken down. The scenery, judged by any ordinary aesthetic canon, is more than commonly beautiful; yet there is no influx of artists or summer tourists. Two centuries ago, when talk of witch-blood, Satan-worship, and strange forest presences was not laughed at, it was the custom to give reasons for avoiding the locality. In our sensible age—since the Dunwich horror of 1928 was hushed up by those who had the town's and the world's welfare at heart—people shun it without knowing exactly why. Perhaps one reason—though it cannot apply to uninformed strangers—is that the natives are now repellently decadent, having gone far along that path of retrogression so common in many New England backwaters. They have come to form a race by themselves, with the well-defined mental and physical stigmata of degeneracy and inbreeding. The average of their intelligence is woefully low, whilst their annals reek of overt viciousness and of half-hidden murders, incests, and deeds of almost unnamable violence and perversity. The old gentry, representing the two or three armigerous families which came from Salem in 1692, have kept somewhat above the general level of decay; though many branches are sunk into the sordid populace so deeply that only their names remain as a key to the origin they disgrace. Some of the Whateleys and Bishops still send their eldest sons to Harvard and Miskatonic, though those sons seldom return to the moldering gambrel roofs under which they and their ancestors were born.

No one, even those who have the facts concerning the recent horror, can say just what is the matter with Dunwich; though old legends speak of unhallowed rites and conclaves of the Indians, amidst which they called forbidden shapes of shadow out of the great rounded hills, and made wild orgiastic prayers that were answered by loud crackings and rumblings from the ground below. In 1747 the Reverend Abijah Hoadley, newly come to the Congregational Church at Dunwich Village, preached a memorable sermon on the close presence of Satan and his imps; in which he said:

> *It must be allow'd, that these Blasphemies of an infernall Train of Daemons are Matters of too common Knowledge to be deny'd; the cursed Voices of Azazel and Buzrael, of Beelzebub and Belial, being heard now from under Ground by above a Score of credible Witnesses now living. I myself did not more than a Fortnight ago catch a very plain Discourse of evill Powers in the Hill behind my House; wherein there were a Rattling and Rolling, Groaning, Screeching, and Hissing, such as no Things of this Earth cou'd raise up, and which must needs have come from those Caves that only black Magick can discover, and only the Divell unlock.*

Mr. Hoadley disappeared soon after delivering this sermon; but the text, printed in Springfield, is still extant. Noises in the hills continued to be reported from year to year, and still form a puzzle to geologists and physiographers.

Other traditions tell of foul odors near the hill-crowning circles of stone pillars, and of rushing airy presences to be heard faintly at certain hours from stated points at the bottom of the great ravines; while still others try to explain the Devil's Hop Yard—a bleak, blasted hillside where no tree, shrub, or grass-blade will grow. Then too, the natives are mortally afraid of the numerous whippoorwills which grow vocal on warm nights. It is vowed that the birds are psychopomps lying in wait for the souls of the dying, and that they time their eerie cries in unison with the sufferer's struggling breath. If they can catch the fleeing soul when it leaves the body, they instantly flutter away chittering in daemoniac laughter; but if they fail, they subside gradually into a disappointed silence.

These tales, of course, are obsolete and ridiculous; because they come down from very old times. Dunwich is indeed ridiculously old—older by far than any of the communities within thirty miles of it. South of the village one may still spy the cellar walls and chimney of the ancient Bishop house, which was built before 1700; whilst the ruins of the mill at the falls, built in 1806, form the most modern piece of architecture to be seen. Industry did not flourish here, and the nineteenth-century factory movement proved short-lived. Oldest of all are the great rings of rough-hewn stone columns on the hilltops, but these are more generally attributed to the Indians than to the settlers. Deposits of skulls and bones, found within these circles and around the sizeable table-like rock on Sentinel Hill, sustain the popular belief that such spots were once the burial-places of the Pocumtucks; even though many ethnologists, disregarding the absurd improbability of such a theory, persist in believing the remains Caucasian.

II

It was in the township of Dunwich, in a large and partly inhabited farmhouse set against a hillside four miles from the village and a mile and a half from any other dwelling, that Wilbur Whateley was born at 5 a.m. on Sunday, February 2nd, 1913. This date was recalled because it was Candlemas, which people in Dunwich curiously observe under another name; and because the noises in the hills had sounded, and all the dogs of the countryside had barked persistently, throughout the night before. Less worthy of notice was the fact that the mother was one of the decadent Whateleys, a somewhat deformed, unattractive albino woman of thirty-five, living with an aged and half-insane father about whom the most frightful tales of wizardry had been whispered in his youth. Lavinia Whateley had no known husband, but according to the custom of the region made no attempt to disavow the child; concerning the other side of whose ancestry the country folk might—and did—speculate as widely as they chose. On the contrary, she seemed strangely proud of the dark, goatish-looking infant who formed such a contrast to her own sickly and pink-eyed albinism, and was heard to mutter many curious prophecies about its unusual powers and tremendous future.

Lavinia was one who would be apt to mutter such things, for she was a lone creature given to wandering amidst thunderstorms in the hills and trying to read the great odorous books which her father had inherited through two centuries of Whateleys, and which were fast falling to pieces with age and worm-holes. She had never been to school, but was filled with disjointed scraps of ancient lore that Old Whateley had taught her. The remote farmhouse had always been feared because of Old Whateley's reputation for black magic, and the unexplained death by violence of Mrs. Whateley when Lavinia was twelve years old had not helped to make the place popular. Isolated among strange influences, Lavinia was fond of wild and grandiose day-dreams and singular occupations; nor was her leisure much taken up by household cares in a home from which all standards of order and cleanliness had long since disappeared.

There was a hideous screaming which echoed above even the hill noises and the dogs' barking on the night Wilbur was born, but no known doctor or midwife presided at his coming. Neighbors knew nothing of him till a week afterward, when Old Whateley drove his sleigh through the snow into Dunwich Village and discoursed incoherently to the group of loungers at Osborn's general store. There seemed to be a change in the old man—an added element of furtiveness in the clouded brain which subtly transformed him from an object to a subject of fear—though he was not one to be perturbed by any common family event. Amidst it all he showed some trace of the pride later noticed in his daughter, and what he said of the child's paternity was remembered by many of his hearers years afterward.

"I dun't keer what folks think—ef Lavinny's boy looked like his pa, he wouldn't look like nothin' ye expeck. Ye needn't think the only folks is the folks hereabaouts. Lavinny's read some, an' has seed some things the most o' ye only tell abaout. I calc'late her man is as good a husban' as ye kin find this side of Aylesbury; an' ef ye knowed as much abaout the hills as I dew, ye wouldn't ast no better church weddin' nor her'n. Let me tell ye suthin'—*some day yew folks'll hear a child o' Lavinny's a-callin' its father's name on the top o' Sentinel Hill!*"

The only persons who saw Wilbur during the first month of his life were old Zechariah Whateley, of the undecayed Whateleys, and Earl Sawyer's common-law wife, Mamie Bishop. Mamie's visit was frankly one of curiosity, and her subsequent tales did justice to her observations; but Zechariah came to lead a pair of Alderney cows which Old Whateley had bought of his son Curtis. This marked the beginning of a course of cattle-buying on the part of small Wilbur's family which ended only in 1928, when the Dunwich horror came and went; yet at no time did the ramshackle Whateley barn seem overcrowded with livestock. There came a period when people were curious enough to steal up and count the herd that grazed precariously on the steep hillside above the old farmhouse, and they could never find more than ten or twelve anemic, bloodless-looking specimens. Evidently some blight or distemper, perhaps sprung from the unwholesome pasturage or the diseased fungi and timbers of the filthy barn, caused a heavy mortality amongst the Whateley animals. Odd wounds or sores, having something of the aspect of incisions, seemed to afflict the visible cattle; and once or twice during the earlier months certain callers fancied they could discern similar sores about the throats of the gray, unshaven old man and his slatternly, crinkly-haired albino daughter.

In the spring after Wilbur's birth Lavinia resumed her customary rambles in the hills, bearing in her misproportioned arms the swarthy child. Public interest in the Whateleys subsided after most of the country folk had seen the baby, and no one bothered to comment on the swift development which that newcomer seemed every day to exhibit. Wilbur's growth was indeed phenomenal, for within three months of his birth he had attained a size and muscular power not usually found in infants under a full year of age. His motions and even his vocal sounds showed a restraint and deliberateness highly peculiar in an infant, and no one was really unprepared when, at seven months, he began to walk unassisted, with falterings which another month was sufficient to remove.

It was somewhat after this time—on Hallowe'en—that a great blaze was seen at midnight on the top of Sentinel Hill where the old table-like stone stands amidst its tumulus of ancient bones. Considerable talk was started when Silas Bishop—of the undecayed Bishops—mentioned having seen the boy running sturdily up that hill ahead of his mother about an hour before the blaze was remarked. Silas was rounding up a stray heifer, but he nearly forgot his mission when he fleetingly spied the two figures in the dim light of his lantern. They darted almost noiselessly through the underbrush, and the astonished watcher seemed to think they were entirely unclothed. Afterward he could not be sure about the boy, who may have had some kind of a fringed belt and a pair of dark trunks or trousers on. Wilbur was never subsequently seen alive and conscious without complete and tightly buttoned attire, the disarrangement or threatened disarrangement of which always seemed to fill him with anger and alarm. His contrast with his squalid mother and grandfather in this respect was thought very notable until the horror of 1928 suggested the most valid of reasons.

The next January gossips were mildly interested in the fact that "Lavinny's black brat" had commenced to talk, and at the age of only eleven months. His speech was somewhat remarkable both because of its difference from the ordinary accents of the region, and because it displayed a freedom from infantile lisping of which many children of three or four might well be proud. The boy was not talkative, yet when he spoke he seemed to reflect some elusive element wholly unpossessed by Dunwich and its denizens. The strangeness did not reside in what he said, or even in the simple idioms he used; but seemed vaguely linked with his intonation or with the internal organs that produced the spoken sounds. His facial aspect, too, was remarkable for its maturity; for though he shared his mother's and grandfather's chinlessness, his firm and precociously shaped nose united with the expression of his large, dark, almost Latin eyes to give him an air of quasi-adulthood and well-nigh preternatural intelligence. He was, however, exceedingly ugly despite his appearance of brilliancy; there being something almost goatish or animalistic about his thick lips, large-pored, yellowish skin, coarse crinkly hair, and oddly elongated ears. He was soon disliked even more decidedly than his mother and grandsire, and all conjectures about him were spiced with references to the bygone magic of Old Whateley, and how the hills once shook when he shrieked the dreadful name of *Yog-Sothoth* in the midst of a circle of stones with a great book open in his arms before him. Dogs abhorred the boy, and he was always obliged to take various defensive measures against their barking menace.

III

Meanwhile Old Whateley continued to buy cattle without measurably increasing the size of his herd. He also cut timber and began to repair the unused parts of his house—a spacious, peaked-roofed affair whose rear end was buried entirely in the rocky hillside, and whose three least-ruined ground-floor rooms had always been sufficient for himself and his daughter.

There must have been prodigious reserves of strength in the old man to enable him to accomplish so much hard labor; and though he still babbled dementedly at times, his carpentry seemed to show the effects of sound calculation. It had already begun as soon as Wilbur was born, when one of the many tool-sheds had been put suddenly in order, clapboarded, and fitted with a stout fresh lock. Now, in restoring the abandoned upper story of the house, he was a no less thorough craftsman. His mania showed itself only in his tight boarding-up of all the windows in the reclaimed section—though many declared that it was a crazy thing to bother with the reclamation at all.

Less inexplicable was his fitting up of another downstairs room for his new grandson—a room which several callers saw, though no one was ever admitted to the closely boarded upper story. This chamber he lined with tall, firm shelving; along which he began gradually to arrange, in apparently careful order, all the rotting ancient books and parts of books which during his own day had been heaped promiscuously in odd corners of the various rooms.

"I made some use of 'em," he would say as he tried to mend a torn black-letter page with paste prepared on the rusty kitchen stove, "but the boy's fitten to make better use of 'em. He'd orter hev 'em as well sot as he kin, for they're goin' to be all of his larnin'."

When Wilbur was a year and seven months old—in September of 1914—his size and accomplishments were almost alarming. He had grown as large as a child of four, and was a fluent and incredibly intelligent talker. He ran freely about the fields and hills, and accompanied his mother on all her wanderings. At home he would pore diligently over the queer pictures and charts in his grandfather's books, while Old Whateley would instruct and catechize him through long, hushed afternoons. By this time the restoration of the house was finished, and those who watched it wondered why one of the upper windows had been made into a solid plank door. It was a window in the rear of the east gable end, close against the hill; and no one could imagine why a cleated wooden runway was built up to it from the ground. About the period of this work's completion people noticed that the old tool-house, tightly locked and windowlessly clapboarded since Wilbur's birth, had been abandoned again. The door swung listlessly open, and when Earl Sawyer once stepped within after a cattle-selling call on Old Whateley he was quite discomposed by the singular odor he encountered—such a stench, he averred, as he had never before smelled in all his life except near the Indian circles on the hills, and which could not come from anything sane or of this earth. But then, the homes and sheds of Dunwich folk have never been remarkable for olfactory immaculateness.

The following months were void of visible events, save that everyone swore to a slow but steady increase in the mysterious hill noises. On May Eve of 1915 there were tremors which even the Aylesbury people felt, whilst the following Hallowe'en produced an underground rumbling queerly synchronized with bursts of flame—"them witch Whateleys' doin's"—from the summit of Sentinel Hill. Wilbur was growing up uncannily, so that he looked like a boy of ten as he entered his fourth year. He read avidly by himself now; but talked much less than formerly. A settled taciturnity was absorbing him, and for the first time people began to speak specifically of the dawning look of evil in his goatish face. He would sometimes mutter an unfamiliar jargon, and chant in bizarre rhythms which chilled the listener with a sense of unexplainable terror. The aversion displayed toward him by dogs had now become a matter of wide remark, and he was obliged to carry a pistol in order to traverse the countryside in safety. His occasional use of the weapon did not enhance his popularity amongst the owners of canine guardians.

The few callers at the house would often find Lavinia alone on the ground floor, while odd cries and footsteps resounded in the boarded-up second story. She would never tell what her father and the boy were doing up there, though once she turned pale and displayed an abnormal degree of fear when a jocose fish-peddler tried the locked door leading to the stairway. That peddler told the store loungers at Dunwich Village that he thought he heard a horse stamping on that floor above. The loungers reflected, thinking of the door and runway, and of the cattle that so swiftly disappeared. Then they shuddered as they recalled tales of Old Whateley's youth, and of the strange things that are called out of the earth when a bullock is sacrificed at the proper time to certain heathen gods. It had for some time been noticed that dogs had begun to hate and fear the whole Whateley place as violently as they hated and feared young Wilbur personally.

In 1917 the war came, and Squire Sawyer Whateley, as chairman of the local draft board, had hard work finding a quota of young Dunwich men fit even to be sent to a development camp. The government, alarmed at such signs of wholesale regional decadence, sent several officers and medical experts to investigate; conducting a survey which New England newspaper readers may still recall. It was the publicity attending this investigation which set reporters on the track of the Whateleys, and caused the *Boston Globe* and *Arkham Advertiser* to print flamboyant Sunday stories of young Wilbur's precociousness, Old Whateley's black magic, the shelves of strange books, the sealed second story of the ancient farmhouse, and the weirdness of the whole region and its hill noises. Wilbur was four and a half then, and looked like a lad of fifteen. His lips and cheeks were fuzzy with a coarse dark down, and his voice had begun to break.

Earl Sawyer went out to the Whateley place with both sets of reporters and camera men, and called their attention to the queer stench which now seemed to trickle down from the sealed upper spaces. It was, he said, exactly like a smell he had found in the tool-shed abandoned when the house was finally repaired; and like the faint odors which he sometimes thought he caught near the stone circles on the mountains. Dunwich folk read the stories when they appeared, and grinned over the obvious mistakes. They wondered, too, why the writers made so much of the fact that Old Whateley always paid for his cattle in gold pieces of extremely ancient date. The Whateleys had received their visitors with ill-concealed distaste, though they did not dare court further publicity by a violent resistance or refusal to talk.

IV

For a decade the annals of the Whateleys sink indistinguishably into the general life of a morbid community used to their queer ways and hardened to their May Eve and All-Hallows orgies. Twice a year they would light fires on the top of Sentinel Hill, at which times the mountain rumblings would recur with greater and greater violence; while at all seasons there were strange and portentous doings at the lonely farmhouse. In the course of time callers professed to hear sounds in the sealed upper story even when all the family were downstairs, and they wondered how swiftly or how lingeringly a cow or bullock was usually sacrificed. There was talk of a complaint to the Society for the Prevention of Cruelty to Animals; but nothing ever came of it, since Dunwich folk are never anxious to call the outside world's attention to themselves.

About 1923, when Wilbur was a boy of ten whose mind, voice, stature, and bearded face gave all the impressions of maturity, a second great siege of carpentry went on at the old house. It was all inside the sealed upper part, and from bits of discarded lumber people concluded that the youth and his grandfather had knocked out all the partitions and even removed the attic floor, leaving only one vast open void between the ground story and the peaked roof. They had torn down the great central chimney, too, and fitted the rusty range with a flimsy outside tin stovepipe.

In the spring after this event Old Whateley noticed the growing number of whippoorwills that would come out of Cold Spring Glen to chirp under his window at night. He seemed to regard the circumstance as one of great significance, and told the loungers at Osborn's that he thought his time had almost come.

"They whistle jest in tune with my breathin' naow," he said, "an' I guess they're gittin' ready to ketch my soul. They know it's a-goin' aout, an' dun't calc'late to miss it. Yew'll know, boys, arter I'm gone, whether they git me er not. Ef they dew, they'll keep up a-singin' an' laffin' till break o' day. Ef they dun't they'll kinder quiet daown like. I expeck them an' the souls they hunts fer hev some pretty tough tussles sometimes."

On Lammas Night, 1924, Dr. Houghton of Aylesbury was hastily summoned by Wilbur Whateley, who had lashed his one remaining horse through the darkness and telephoned from Osborn's in the village. He found Old Whateley in a very grave state, with a cardiac action and stertorous breathing that told of an end not far off. The shapeless albino daughter and oddly bearded grandson stood by the bedside, whilst from the vacant abyss overhead there came a disquieting suggestion of rhythmical surging or lapping, as of the waves on some level beach. The doctor, though, was chiefly disturbed by the chattering night birds outside; a seemingly limitless legion of whippoorwills that cried their endless message in repetitions timed diabolically to the wheezing gasps of the dying man. It was uncanny and unnatural—too much, thought Dr. Houghton, like the whole of the region he had entered so reluctantly in response to the urgent call.

Toward one o'clock Old Whateley gained consciousness, and interrupted his wheezing to choke out a few words to his grandson.

"More space, Willy, more space soon. Yew grows—an' *that* grows faster. It'll be ready to sarve ye soon, boy. Open up the gates to Yog-Sothoth with the long chant that ye'll find on page 751 *of the complete edition,* an' *then* put a match to the prison. Fire from airth can't burn it nohaow."

He was obviously quite mad. After a pause, during which the flock of whippoorwills outside adjusted their cries to the altered tempo while some indications of the strange hill noises came from afar off, he added another sentence or two.

"Feed it reg'lar, Willy, an' mind the quantity; but dun't let it grow too fast fer the place, fer ef it busts quarters or gits aout afore ye opens to Yog-Sothoth, it's all over an' no use. Only them from beyont kin make it multiply an' work... Only them, the old uns as wants to come back..."

But speech gave place to gasps again, and Lavinia screamed at the way the whippoorwills followed the change. It was the same for more than an hour, when the final throaty rattle came. Dr. Houghton drew shrunken lids over the glazing gray eyes as the tumult of birds faded imperceptibly to silence. Lavinia sobbed, but Wilbur only chuckled whilst the hill noises rumbled faintly.

"They didn't git him," he muttered in his heavy bass voice.

Wilbur was by this time a scholar of really tremendous erudition in his one-sided way, and was quietly known by correspondence to many librarians in distant places where rare and forbidden books of old days are kept. He was more and more hated and dreaded around Dunwich because of certain youthful disappearances which suspicion laid vaguely at his door; but was always able to silence inquiry through fear or through use of that fund of old-time gold which still, as in his grandfather's time, went forth regularly and increasingly for cattle-buying. He was now tremendously mature of aspect, and his height, having reached the normal adult limit, seemed inclined to wax beyond that figure. In 1925, when a scholarly correspondent from Miskatonic University called upon him one day and departed pale and puzzled, he was fully six-and-three-quarters feet tall.

Through all the years Wilbur had treated his half-deformed albino mother with a growing contempt, finally forbidding her to go to the hills with him on May Eve and Hallowmass; and in 1926 the poor creature complained to Mamie Bishop of being afraid of him.

"They's more abaout him as I knows than I kin tell ye, Mamie," she said, "an' naowadays they's more nor what I know myself. I vaow afur Gawd, I dun't know what he wants nor what he's a-tryin' to dew."

That Hallowe'en the hill noises sounded louder than ever, and fire burned on Sentinel Hill as usual; but people paid more attention to the rhythmical screaming of vast flocks of unnaturally belated whippoorwills which seemed to be assembled near the unlighted Whateley farmhouse. After midnight their shrill notes burst into a kind of pandemoniac cachinnation which filled all the countryside, and not until dawn did they finally quiet down. Then they vanished, hurrying southward where they were fully a month overdue. What this meant, no one could quite be certain till later. None of the country folk seemed to have died—but poor Lavinia Whateley, the twisted albino, was never seen again.

In the summer of 1927 Wilbur repaired two sheds in the farmyard and began moving his books and effects out to them. Soon afterward Earl Sawyer told the loungers at Osborn's that more carpentry was going on in the Whateley farmhouse. Wilbur was closing all the doors and windows on the ground floor, and seemed to be taking out partitions as he and his grandfather had done upstairs four years before. He was living in one of the sheds, and Sawyer thought he seemed unusually worried and tremulous. People generally suspected him of knowing something about his mother's disappearance, and very few ever approached his neighborhood now. His height had increased to more than seven feet, and showed no signs of ceasing its development.

V

The following winter brought an event no less strange than Wilbur's first trip outside the Dunwich region. Correspondence with the Widener Library at Harvard, the Bibliothèque Nationale in Paris, the British Museum, the University of Buenos Aires, and the Library of Miskatonic University of Arkham had failed to get him the loan of a book he desperately wanted; so at length he set out in person, shabby, dirty, bearded, and uncouth of dialect, to consult the copy at Miskatonic, which was the nearest to him geographically. Almost eight feet tall, and carrying a cheap new valise from Osborn's general store, this dark and goatish gargoyle appeared one day in Arkham in quest of the dreaded volume kept under lock and key at the college library—the hideous *Necronomicon* of the mad Arab Abdul Alhazred in Olaus Wormius's Latin version, as printed in Spain in the seventeenth century. He had never seen a city before, but had no thought save to find his way to the university grounds; where, indeed, he passed heedlessly by the great white-fanged watchdog that barked with unnatural fury and enmity, and tugged frantically at its stout chain.

Wilbur had with him the priceless but imperfect copy of Dr. Dee's English version which his grandfather had bequeathed him, and upon receiving access to the Latin copy he at once began to collate the two texts with the aim of discovering a certain passage which would have come on the 751st page of his own defective volume. This much he could not civilly refrain from telling the librarian—the same erudite Henry Armitage (A.M. Miskatonic, Ph. D. Princeton, Litt. D. Johns Hopkins) who had once called at the farm, and who now politely plied him with questions. He was looking, he had to admit, for a kind of formula or incantation containing the frightful name *Yog-Sothoth,* and it puzzled him to find discrepancies, duplications, and ambiguities which made the matter of determination far from easy. As he copied the formula he finally chose, Dr. Armitage looked involuntarily over his shoulder at the open pages; the left-hand one of which, in the Latin version, contained such monstrous threats to the peace and sanity of the world.

> *Nor is it to be thought* (ran the text as Armitage mentally translated it) *that man is either the oldest or the last of earth's masters, or that the common bulk of life and substance walks alone. The Old Ones were, the Old Ones are, and the Old Ones shall be. Not in the spaces we know, but between them, They walk serene and primal, undimensioned and to us unseen. Yog-Sothoth knows the gate. Yog-Sothoth is the gate. Yog-Sothoth is the key and guardian of the gate. Past, present, future, all are one in Yog-Sothoth. He knows where the Old Ones broke through of old, and where They shall break through again. He knows where They have trod earth's fields, and where They still tread them, and why no one can behold Them as They tread. By Their smell can men sometimes know Them near, but of Their semblance can no man know, saving only in the features of those They have begotten on mankind; and of those are there many sorts, differing in likeness from man's truest eidolon to that shape without sight or substance which is Them. They walk unseen and foul in lonely places where the Words have been spoken and the Rites howled through at their Seasons. The wind gibbers with Their voices, and the earth mutters with Their consciousness. They bend the forest and crush the city, yet may not forest or city behold the hand that smites. Kadath in the cold waste hath known Them, and what man knows Kadath? The ice desert of the South and the sunken isles of Ocean hold stones whereon Their seal is engraven, but who hath seen the deep frozen city or the sealed tower long garlanded with seaweed and barnacles? Great Cthulhu is Their cousin, yet can he spy Them only dimly. Iä! Shub-Niggurath! As a foulness shall ye know Them. Their hand is at your throats, yet ye see Them not; and Their habitation is even one with your guarded threshold. Yog-Sothoth is the key to the gate, whereby the spheres meet. Man rules now where They ruled once; They shall soon rule where man rules now. After summer is winter, and after winter summer. They wait patient and potent, for here shall They reign again.*

Dr. Armitage, associating what he was reading with what he had heard of Dunwich and its brooding presences, and of Wilbur Whateley and his dim, hideous aura that stretched from a dubious birth to a cloud of probable matricide, felt a wave of fright as tangible as a draft of the tomb's cold clamminess. The bent, goatish giant before him seemed like the spawn of another planet or dimension; like something only partly of mankind, and linked to black gulfs of essence and entity that stretch like titan phantasms beyond all spheres of force and matter, space and time. Presently Wilbur raised his head and began speaking in that strange, resonant fashion which hinted at sound-producing organs unlike the run of mankind's.

"Mr. Armitage," he said, "I calc'late I've got to take that book home. They's things in it I've got to try under sarten conditions that I can't git here, an' it 'ud be a mortal sin to let a red-tape rule hold me up. Let me take it along, Sir, an' I'll swar they wun't nobody know the difference. I dun't need to tell ye I'll take good keer of it. It wa'n't me that put this Dee copy in the shape it is..."

He stopped as he saw firm denial on the librarian's face, and his own goatish features grew crafty. Armitage, half-ready to tell him he might make a copy of what parts he needed, thought suddenly of the possible consequences and checked himself. There was too much responsibility in giving such a being the key to such blasphemous outer spheres. Whateley saw how things stood, and tried to answer lightly.

"Wal, all right, ef ye feel that way abaout it. Maybe Harvard wun't be so fussy as yew be." And without saying more he rose and strode out of the building, stooping at each doorway.

Armitage heard the savage yelping of the great watchdog, and studied Whateley's gorilla-like lope as he crossed the bit of campus visible from the window. He thought of the wild tales he had heard, and recalled the old Sunday stories in the *Advertiser;* these things, and the lore he had picked up from Dunwich rustics and villagers during his one visit there. Unseen things not of earth—or at least not of tri-dimensional earth—rushed fetid and horrible through New England's glens, and brooded obscenely on the mountain tops. Of this he had long felt certain. Now he seemed to sense the close presence of some terrible part of the intruding horror, and to glimpse a hellish advance in the black dominion of the ancient and once passive nightmare. He locked away the *Necronomicon* with a shudder of disgust, but the room still reeked with an unholy and unidentifiable stench. "As a foulness shall ye know them," he quoted. Yes—the odor was the same as that which had sickened him at the Whateley farmhouse less than three years before. He thought of Wilbur, goatish and ominous, once again, and laughed mockingly at the village rumors of his parentage.

"Inbreeding?" Armitage muttered half-aloud to himself. "Great God, what simpletons! Show them Arthur Machen's Great God Pan and they'll think it a common Dunwich scandal! But what thing—what cursed shapeless influence on or off this three—dimensioned earth—was Wilbur Whateley's father? Born on Candlemas—nine months after May Eve of 1912, when the talk about the queer earth noises reached clear to Arkham—what walked on the mountains that May-Night? What Roodmas horror fastened itself on the world in half-human flesh and blood?"

During the ensuing weeks Dr. Armitage set about to collect all possible data on Wilbur Whateley and the formless presences around Dunwich. He got in communication with Dr. Houghton of Aylesbury, who had attended Old Whateley in his last illness, and found much to ponder over in the grandfather's last words as quoted by the physician. A visit to Dunwich Village failed to bring out much that was new; but a close survey of the *Necronomicon,* in those parts which Wilbur had sought so avidly, seemed to supply new and terrible clues to the nature, methods, and desires of the strange evil so vaguely threatening this planet. Talks with several students of archaic lore in Boston, and letters to many others elsewhere, gave him a growing amazement which passed slowly through varied degrees of alarm to a state of really acute spiritual fear. As the summer drew on he felt dimly that something ought to be done about the lurking terrors of the upper Miskatonic valley, and about the monstrous being known to the human world as Wilbur Whateley.

VI

The Dunwich horror itself came between Lammas and the equinox in 1928, and Dr. Armitage was among those who witnessed its monstrous prologue. He had heard, meanwhile, of Whateley's grotesque trip to Cambridge, and of his frantic efforts to borrow or copy from the *Necronomicon* at the Widener Library. Those efforts had been in vain, since Armitage had issued warnings of the keenest intensity to all librarians having charge of the dreaded volume. Wilbur had been shockingly nervous at Cambridge; anxious for the book, yet almost equally anxious to get home again, as if he feared the results of being away long.

Early in August the half-expected outcome developed, and in the small hours of the 3rd Dr. Armitage was awakened suddenly by the wild, fierce cries of the savage watchdog on the college campus. Deep and terrible, the snarling, half-mad growls and barks continued; always in mounting volume, but with hideously significant pauses. Then there rang out a scream from a wholly different throat—such a scream as roused half the sleepers of Arkham and haunted their dreams ever afterward—such a scream as could come from no being born of earth, or wholly of earth.

Armitage, hastening into some clothing and rushing across the street and lawn to the college buildings, saw that others were ahead of him; and heard the echoes of a burglar-alarm still shrilling from the library. An open window showed black and gaping in the moonlight.

What had come had indeed completed its entrance; for the barking and the screaming, now fast fading into a mixed low growling and moaning, proceeded unmistakably from within. Some instinct warned Armitage that what was taking place was not a thing for unfortified eyes to see, so he brushed back the crowd with authority as he unlocked the vestibule door. Among the others he saw Professor Warren Rice and Dr. Francis Morgan, men to whom he had told some of his conjectures and misgivings; and these two he motioned to accompany him inside. The inward sounds, except for a watchful, droning whine from the dog, had by this time quite subsided; but Armitage now perceived with a sudden start that a loud chorus of whippoorwills among the shrubbery had commenced a damnably rhythmical piping, as if in unison with the last breaths of a dying man.

The building was full of a frightful stench which Dr. Armitage knew too well, and the three men rushed across the hall to the small genealogical reading-room whence the low whining came. For a second nobody dared to turn on the light, then Armitage summoned up his courage and snapped the switch. One of the three—it is not certain which—shrieked aloud at what sprawled before them among disordered tables and overturned chairs. Professor Rice declares that he wholly lost consciousness for an instant, though he did not stumble or fall.

The thing that lay half-bent on its side in a fetid pool of greenish-yellow ichor and tarry stickiness was almost nine feet tall, and the dog had torn off all the clothing and some of the skin. It was not quite dead, but twitched silently and spasmodically while its chest heaved in monstrous unison with the mad piping of the expectant whippoorwills outside. Bits of shoe-leather and fragments of apparel were scattered about the room, and just inside the window an empty canvas sack lay where it had evidently been thrown. Near the central desk a revolver had fallen, a dented but undischarged cartridge later explaining why it had not been fired. The thing itself, however, crowded out all other images at the time. It would be trite and not wholly accurate to say that no human pen could describe it, but one may properly say that it could not be vividly visualized by anyone whose ideas of aspect and contour are too closely bound up with the common life-forms of this planet and of the three known dimensions. It was partly human, beyond a doubt, with very man-like hands and head, and the goatish, chinless face had the stamp of the Whateleys upon it. But the torso and lower parts of the body were teratologically fabulous, so that only generous clothing could ever have enabled it to walk on earth unchallenged or uneradicated.

Above the waist it was semi-anthropomorphic; though its chest, where the dog's rending paws still rested watchfully, had the leathery, reticulated hide of a crocodile or alligator. The back was piebald with yellow and black, and dimly suggested the squamous covering of certain snakes. Below the waist, though, it was the worst; for here all human resemblance left off and sheer fantasy began. The skin was thickly covered with coarse black fur, and from the abdomen a score of long greenish-gray tentacles with red sucking mouths protruded limply. Their arrangement was odd, and seemed to follow the symmetries of some cosmic geometry unknown to earth or the solar system. On each of the hips, deep set in a kind of pinkish, ciliated orbit, was what seemed to be a rudimentary eye; whilst in lieu of a tail there depended a kind of trunk or feeler with purple annular markings, and with many evidences of being an undeveloped mouth or throat. The limbs, save for their black fur, roughly resembled the hind legs of prehistoric earth's giant saurians; and terminated in ridgy-veined pads that were neither hooves nor claws. When the thing breathed, its tail and tentacles rhythmically changed color, as if from some circulatory cause normal to the non-human side of its ancestry. In the tentacles this was observable as a deepening of the greenish tinge, whilst in the tail it was manifest as a yellowish appearance which alternated with a sickly grayish-white in the spaces between the purple rings. Of genuine blood there was none; only the fetid greenish-yellow ichor which trickled along the painted floor beyond the radius of the stickiness, and left a curious discoloration behind it.

As the presence of the three men seemed to rouse the dying thing, it began to mumble without turning or raising its head. Dr. Armitage made no written record of its mouthings, but asserts confidently that nothing in English was uttered. At first the syllables defied all correlation with any speech of earth, but toward the last there came some disjointed fragments evidently taken from the *Necronomicon,* that monstrous blasphemy in quest of which the thing had perished. These fragments, as Armitage recalls them, ran something like *"N'gai, n'gha'ghaa, bugg-shoggog, y'hah; Yog-Sothoth, Yog-Sothoth..."* They trailed off into nothingness as the whippoorwills shrieked in rhythmical crescendos of unholy anticipation.

Then came a halt in the gasping, and the dog raised its head in a long, lugubrious howl. A change came over the yellow, goatish face of the prostrate thing, and the great black eyes fell in appallingly. Outside the window the shrilling of the whippoorwills had suddenly ceased, and above the murmurs of the gathering crowd there came the sound of a panic-struck whirring and fluttering. Against the moon vast clouds of feathery watchers rose and raced from sight, frantic at that which they had sought for prey.

All at once the dog started up abruptly, gave a frightened bark, and leaped nervously out of the window by which it had entered. A cry rose from the crowd, and Dr. Armitage shouted to the men outside that no one must be admitted till the police or medical examiner came. He was thankful that the windows were just too high to permit of peering in, and drew the dark curtains carefully down over each one. By this time two policemen had arrived; and Dr. Morgan, meeting them in the vestibule, was urging them for their own sakes to postpone entrance to the stench-filled reading-room till the examiner came and the prostrate thing could be covered up.

Meanwhile frightful changes were taking place on the floor. One need not describe the kind and rate of shrinkage and disintegration that occurred before the eyes of Dr. Armitage and Professor Rice; but it is permissible to say that, aside from the external appearance of face and hands, the really human element in Wilbur Whateley must have been very small. When the medical examiner came, there was only a sticky whitish mass on the painted boards, and the monstrous odor had nearly disappeared. Apparently Whateley had had no skull or bony skeleton; at least, in any true or stable sense. He had taken somewhat after his unknown father.

VII

Yet all this was only the prologue of the actual Dunwich horror. Formalities were gone through by bewildered officials, abnormal details were duly kept from press and public, and men were sent to Dunwich and Aylesbury to look up property and notify any who might be heirs of the late Wilbur Whateley. They found the countryside in great agitation, both because of the growing rumblings beneath the domed hills, and because of the unwonted stench and the surging, lapping sounds which came increasingly from the great empty shell formed by Whateley's boarded-up farmhouse. Earl Sawyer, who tended the horse and cattle during Wilbur's absence, had developed a woefully acute case of nerves. The officials devised excuses not to enter the noisome boarded place; and were glad to confine their survey of the deceased's living quarters, the newly mended sheds, to a single visit. They filed a ponderous report at the court-house in Aylesbury, and litigations concerning heirship are said to be still in progress amongst the innumerable Whateleys, decayed and undecayed, of the upper Miskatonic valley.

An almost interminable manuscript in strange characters, written in a huge ledger and adjudged a sort of diary because of the spacing and the variations in ink and penmanship, presented a baffling puzzle to those who found it on the old bureau which served as its owner's desk. After a week of debate it was sent to Miskatonic University, together with the deceased's collection of strange books, for study and possible translation; but even the best linguists soon saw that it was not likely to be unriddled with ease. No trace of the ancient gold with which Wilbur and Old Whateley always paid their debts has yet been discovered.

It was in the dark of September 9th that the horror broke loose. The hill noises had been very pronounced during the evening, and dogs barked frantically all night. Early risers on the 10th noticed a peculiar stench in the air. About seven o'clock Luther Brown, the hired boy at George Corey's, between Cold Spring Glen and the village, rushed frenziedly back from his morning trip to Ten-Acre Meadow with the cows. He was almost convulsed with fright as he stumbled into the kitchen; and in the yard outside the no less frightened herd were pawing and lowing pitifully, having followed the boy back in the panic they shared with him. Between gasps Luther tried to stammer out his tale to Mrs. Corey.

"Up thar in the rud beyont the glen, Mis' Corey—they's suthin' ben thar! It smells like thunder, an' all the bushes an' little trees is pushed back from the rud like they'd a haouse ben moved along of it. An' that ain't the wust, nuther. They's *prints* in the rud, Mis' Corey—great raound prints as big as barrel-heads, all sunk daown deep like a elephant had ben along, *only they's a sight more nor four feet could make!* I looked at one or two afore I run, an' I see every one was covered with lines spreadin' aout from one place, like as if big palm-leaf fans—twict or three times as big as any they is—hed of ben paounded daown into the rud. An' the smell was awful, like what it is araound Wizard Whateley's ol' haouse..."

Here he faltered, and seemed to shiver afresh with the fright that had sent him flying home. Mrs. Corey, unable to extract more information, began telephoning the neighbors; thus starting on its rounds the overture of panic that heralded the major terrors. When she got Sally Sawyer, housekeeper at Seth Bishop's, the nearest place to Whateley's, it became her turn to listen instead of transmit; for Sally's boy Chauncey, who slept poorly, had been up on the hill toward Whateley's, and had dashed back in terror after one look at the place, and at the pasturage where Mr. Bishop's cows had been left out all night.

"Yes, Mis' Corey," came Sally's tremulous voice over the party wire, "Cha'ncey he just come back a-postin', and couldn't haff talk fer bein' scairt! He says Ol' Whateley's haouse is all blowed up, with the timbers scattered raound like they'd ben dynamite inside; only the bottom floor ain't through, but is all covered with a kind o' tar-like stuff that smells awful an' drips daown offen the aidges onto the graoun' whar the side timbers is blown away. An' they's awful kinder marks in the yard, tew—great raound marks bigger raound than a hogshead, an' all sticky with stuff like is on the blowed-up haouse. Cha'ncey he says they leads off into the medders, whar a great swath wider'n a barn is matted daown, an' all the stun walls tumbled every whichway wherever it goes.

"An' he says, says he, Mis' Corey, as haow he sot to look fer Seth's caows, frighted ez he was; an' faound 'em in the upper pasture nigh the Devil's Hop Yard in an awful shape. Haff on 'em's clean gone, an' nigh haff o' them that's left is sucked most dry o' blood, with sores on 'em like they's ben on Whateley's cattle ever senct Lavinny's black brat was born. Seth he's gone aout naow to look at 'em, though I'll vaow he wun't keer ter git very nigh Wizard Whateley's! Cha'ncey didn't look keerful ter see whar the big matted-daown swath led arter it leff the pasturage, but he says he thinks it p'inted towards the glen rud to the village.

"I tell ye, Mis' Corey, they's suthin' abroad as hadn't orter be abroad, an' I for one think that black Wilbur Whateley, as come to the bad eend he desarved, is at the bottom of the breedin' of it. He wa'n't all human hisself, I allus says to everybody; an' I think he an' Ol' Whateley must a raised suthin' in that there nailed-up haouse as ain't even so human as he was. They's allus ben unseen things araound Dunwich—livin' things—as ain't human an' ain't good fer human folks.

"The graoun' was a-talkin' lass night, an' towards mornin' Cha'ncey he heerd the whippoorwills so laoud in Col' Spring Glen he couldn't sleep nun. Then he thought he heerd another faint-like saound over towards Wizard Whateley's—a kinder rippin' or tearin' o' wood, like some big box er crate was bein' opened fur off. What with this an' that, he didn't git to sleep at all till sunup, an' no sooner was he up this mornin', but he's got to go over to Whateley's an' see what's the matter. He see enough, I tell ye, Mis' Corey! This dun't mean no good, an' I think as all the men-folks ought to git up a party an' do suthin'. I know suthin' awful's abaout, an' feel my time is nigh, though only Gawd knows jest what it is.

"Did your Luther take accaount o' whar them big tracks led tew? No? Wal, Mis' Corey, ef they was on the glen rud this side o' the glen, an' ain't got to your haouse yet, I calc'late they must go into the glen itself. They would do that. I allus says Col' Spring Glen ain't no healthy nor decent place. The whippoorwills an' fireflies there never did act like they was creaters o' Gawd, an' they's them as says ye kin hear strange things a-rushin' an' a-talkin' in the air daown thar ef ye stand in the right place, atween the rock falls an' Bear's Den."

By that noon fully three-quarters of the men and boys of Dunwich were trooping over the roads and meadows between the new-made Whateley ruins and Cold Spring Glen, examining in horror the vast, monstrous prints, the maimed Bishop cattle, the strange, noisome wreck of the farmhouse, and the bruised, matted vegetation of the fields and roadsides. Whatever had burst loose upon the world had assuredly gone down into the great sinister ravine; for all the trees on the banks were bent and broken, and a great avenue had been gouged in the precipice-hanging underbrush. It was as though a house, launched by an avalanche, had slid down through the tangled growths of the almost vertical slope. From below no sound came, but only a distant, undefinable fetor; and it is not to be wondered at that the men preferred to stay on the edge and argue, rather than descend and beard the unknown Cyclopean horror in its lair. Three dogs that were with the party had barked furiously at first, but seemed cowed and reluctant when near the glen. Someone telephoned the news to the *Aylesbury Transcript;* but the editor, accustomed to wild tales from Dunwich, did no more than concoct a humorous paragraph about it; an item soon afterward reproduced by the Associated Press.

That night everyone went home, and every house and barn was barricaded as stoutly as possible. Needless to say, no cattle were allowed to remain in open pasturage. About two in the morning a frightful stench and the savage barking of the dogs awakened the household at Elmer Frye's, on the eastern edge of Cold Spring Glen, and all agreed that they could hear a sort of muffled swishing or lapping sound from somewhere outside. Mrs. Frye proposed telephoning the neighbors, and Elmer was about to agree when the noise of splintering wood burst in upon their deliberations. It came, apparently, from the barn; and was quickly followed by a hideous screaming and stamping amongst the cattle. The dogs slavered and crouched close to the feet of the fear-numbed family. Frye lit a lantern through force of habit, but knew it would be death to go out into that black farmyard. The children and the womenfolk whimpered, kept from screaming by some obscure, vestigial instinct of defense which told them their lives depended on silence. At last the noise of the cattle subsided to a pitiful moaning, and a great snapping, crashing, and crackling ensued. The Fryes, huddled together in the sitting-room, did not dare to move until the last echoes died away far down in Cold Spring Glen. Then, amidst the dismal moans from the stable and the daemoniac piping of late whippoorwills in the glen, Selina Frye tottered to the telephone and spread what news she could of the second phase of the horror.

The next day all the countryside was in a panic; and cowed, uncommunicative groups came and went where the fiendish thing had occurred. Two titan swaths of destruction stretched from the glen to the Frye farmyard, monstrous prints covered the bare patches of ground, and one side of the old red barn had completely caved in. Of the cattle, only a quarter could be found and identified. Some of these were in curious fragments, and all that survived had to be shot. Earl Sawyer suggested that help be asked from Aylesbury or Arkham, but others maintained it would be of no use. Old Zebulon Whateley, of a branch that hovered about half way between soundness and decadence, made darkly wild suggestions about rites that ought to be practiced on the hilltops. He came of a line where tradition ran strong, and his memories of chantings in the great stone circles were not altogether connected with Wilbur and his grandfather.

Darkness fell upon a stricken countryside too passive to organize for real defense. In a few cases closely related families would band together and watch in the gloom under one roof; but in general there was only a repetition of the barricading of the night before, and a futile, ineffective gesture of loading muskets and setting pitchforks handily about. Nothing, however, occurred except some hill noises; and when the day came there were many who hoped that the new horror had gone as swiftly as it had come. There were even bold souls who proposed an offensive expedition down in the glen, though they did not venture to set an actual example to the still reluctant majority.

When night came again the barricading was repeated, though there was less huddling together of families. In the morning both the Frye and the Seth Bishop households reported excitement among the dogs and vague sounds and stenches from afar, while early explorers noted with horror a fresh set of the monstrous tracks in the road skirting Sentinel Hill. As before, the sides of the road showed a bruising indicative of the blasphemously stupendous bulk of the horror; whilst the conformation of the tracks seemed to argue a passage in two directions, as if the moving mountain had come from Cold Spring Glen and returned to it along the same path. At the base of the hill a thirty-foot swath of crushed shrubbery saplings led steeply upward, and the seekers gasped when they saw that even the most perpendicular places did not deflect the inexorable trail. Whatever the horror was, it could scale a sheer stony cliff of almost complete verticality; and as the investigators climbed around to the hill's summit by safer routes they saw that the trail ended—or rather, reversed—there.

It was here that the Whateleys used to build their hellish fires and chant their hellish rituals by the table-like stone on May Eve and Hallowmass. Now that very stone formed the center of a vast space thrashed around by the mountainous horror, whilst upon its slightly concave surface was a thick and fetid deposit of the same tarry stickiness observed on the floor of the ruined Whateley farmhouse when the horror escaped. Men looked at one another and muttered. Then they looked down the hill. Apparently the horror had descended by a route much the same as that of its ascent. To speculate was futile. Reason, logic, and normal ideas of motivation stood confounded. Only old Zebulon, who was not with the group, could have done justice to the situation or suggested a plausible explanation.

Thursday night began much like the others, but it ended less happily. The whippoorwills in the glen had screamed with such unusual persistence that many could not sleep, and about 3 a.m. all the party telephones rang tremulously. Those who took down their receivers heard a fright-mad voice shriek out, "Help, oh, my Gawd!..." and some thought a crashing sound followed the breaking off of the exclamation. There was nothing more. No one dared do anything, and no one knew till morning whence the call came. Then those who had heard it called everyone on the line, and found that only the Fryes did not reply. The truth appeared an hour later, when a hastily assembled group of armed men trudged out to the Frye place at the head of the glen. It was horrible, yet hardly a surprise. There were more swaths and monstrous prints, but there was no longer any house. It had caved in like an eggshell, and amongst the ruins nothing living or dead could be discovered. Only a stench and a tarry stickiness. The Elmer Fryes had been erased from Dunwich.

VIII

In the meantime a quieter yet even more spiritually poignant phase of the horror had been blackly unwinding itself behind the closed door of a shelf-lined room in Arkham. The curious manuscript record or diary of Wilbur Whateley, delivered to Miskatonic University for translation, had caused much worry and bafflement among the experts in languages both ancient and modern; its very alphabet, notwithstanding a general resemblance to the heavily shaded Arabic used in Mesopotamia, being absolutely unknown to any available authority. The final conclusion of the linguists was that the text represented an artificial alphabet, giving the effect of a cipher; though none of the usual methods of cryptographic solution seemed to furnish any clue, even when applied on the basis of every tongue the writer might conceivably have used. The ancient books taken from Whateley's quarters, while absorbingly interesting and in several cases promising to open up new and terrible lines of research among philosophers and men of science, were of no assistance whatever in this matter. One of them, a heavy tome with an iron clasp, was in another unknown alphabet—this one of a very different cast, and resembling Sanskrit more than anything else. The old ledger was at length given wholly into the charge of Dr. Armitage, both because of his peculiar interest in the Whateley matter, and because of his wide linguistic learning and skill in the mystical formulae of antiquity and the Middle Ages.

Armitage had an idea that the alphabet might be something esoterically used by certain forbidden cults which have come down from old times, and which have inherited many forms and traditions from the wizards of the Saracenic world. That question, however, he did not deem vital; since it would be unnecessary to know the origin of the symbols if, as he suspected, they were used as a cipher in a modern language. It was his belief that, considering the great amount of text involved, the writer would scarcely have wished the trouble of using another speech than his own, save perhaps in certain special formulae and incantations. Accordingly he attacked the manuscript with the preliminary assumption that the bulk of it was in English.

Dr. Armitage knew, from the repeated failures of his colleagues, that the riddle was a deep and complex one; and that no simple mode of solution could merit even a trial. All through late August he fortified himself with the massed lore of cryptography; drawing upon the fullest resources of his own library, and wading night after night amidst the arcana of Trithemius's *Poligraphia,* Giambattista Porta's *De Furtivis Literarum Notis,* De Vigenère's *Traité des Chiffres,* Falconer's *Cryptomenysis Patefacta,* Davys's and Thicknesse's eighteenth-century treatises, and such fairly modern authorities as Blair, von Marten, and Klüber's *Kryptographik.* He interspersed his study of the books with attacks on the manuscript itself, and in time became convinced that he had to deal with one of those subtlest and most ingenious of cryptograms, in which many separate lists of corresponding letters are arranged like the multiplication table, and the message built up with arbitrary key-words known only to the initiated. The older authorities seemed rather more helpful than the newer ones, and Armitage concluded that the code of the manuscript was one of great antiquity, no doubt handed down through a long line of mystical experimenters. Several times he seemed near daylight, only to be set back by some unforeseen obstacle. Then, as September approached, the clouds began to clear. Certain letters, as used in certain parts of the manuscript, emerged definitely and unmistakably; and it became obvious that the text was indeed in English.

On the evening of September 2nd the last major barrier gave way, and Dr. Armitage read for the first time a continuous passage of Wilbur Whateley's annals. It was in truth a diary, as all had thought; and it was couched in a style clearly showing the mixed occult erudition and general illiteracy of the strange being who wrote it. Almost the first long passage that Armitage deciphered, an entry dated November 26th, 1916, proved highly startling and disquieting. It was written, he remembered, by a child of three and a half who looked like a lad of twelve or thirteen.

> *Today learned the Aklo for the Sabaoth* (it ran), *which did not like, it being answerable from the hill and not from the air. That upstairs more ahead of me than I had thought it would be, and is not like to have much earth brain. Shot Elam Hutchins's collie Jack when he went to bite me, and Elam says he would kill me if he dast. I guess he won't. Grandfather kept me saying the Dho formula last night, and I think I saw the inner city at the 2 magnetic poles. I shall go to those poles when the earth is cleared off, if I can't break through with the Dho-Hna formula when I commit it. They from the air told me at Sabbat that it will be years before I can clear off the earth, and I guess grandfather will be dead then, so I shall have to learn all the angles of the planes and all the formulas between the Yr and the Nhhngr. They from outside*

will help, but they cannot take body without human blood. That upstairs looks it will have the right cast. I can see it a little when I make the Voorish sign or blow the powder of Ibn Ghazi at it, and it is near like them at May Eve on the Hill. The other face may wear off some. I wonder how I shall look when the earth is cleared and there are no earth beings on it. He that came with the Aklo Sabaoth said I may be transfigured, there being much of outside to work on.

Morning found Dr. Armitage in a cold sweat of terror and a frenzy of wakeful concentration. He had not left the manuscript all night, but sat at his table under the electric light turning page after page with shaking hands as fast as he could decipher the cryptic text. He had nervously telephoned his wife he would not be home, and when she brought him a breakfast from the house he could scarcely dispose of a mouthful. All that day he read on, now and then halted maddeningly as a reapplication of the complex key became necessary. Lunch and dinner were brought him, but he ate only the smallest fraction of either. Toward the middle of the next night he drowsed off in his chair, but soon woke out of a tangle of nightmares almost as hideous as the truths and menaces to man's existence that he had uncovered.

On the morning of September 4th Professor Rice and Dr. Morgan insisted on seeing him for a while, and departed trembling and ashen-gray. That evening he went to bed, but slept only fitfully. Wednesday—the next day—he was back at the manuscript, and began to take copious notes both from the current sections and from those he had already deciphered. In the small hours of that night he slept a little in an easy-chair in his office, but was at the manuscript again before dawn. Some time before noon his physician, Dr. Hartwell, called to see him and insisted that he cease work. He refused; intimating that it was of the most vital importance for him to complete the reading of the diary, and promising an explanation in due course of time. That evening, just as twilight fell, he finished his terrible perusal and sank back exhausted. His wife, bringing his dinner, found him in a half-comatose state; but he was conscious enough to warn her off with a sharp cry when he saw her eyes wander toward the notes he had taken. Weakly rising, he gathered up the scribbled papers and sealed them all in a great envelope, which he immediately placed in his inside coat pocket. He had sufficient strength to get home, but was so clearly in need of medical aid that Dr. Hartwell was summoned at once. As the doctor put him to bed he could only mutter over and over again, *"But what, in God's name, can we do?"*

Dr. Armitage slept, but was partly delirious the next day. He made no explanations to Hartwell, but in his calmer moments spoke of the imperative need of a long conference with Rice and Morgan. His wilder wanderings were very startling indeed, including frantic appeals that something in a boarded-up farmhouse be destroyed, and fantastic references to some plan for the extirpation of the entire human race and all animal and vegetable life from the earth by some terrible elder race of beings from another dimension. He would shout that the world was in danger, since the Elder Things wished to strip it and drag it away from the solar system and cosmos of matter into some other plane or phase of entity from which it had once fallen, vigintillions of eons ago. At other times he would call for the dreaded *Necronomicon* and the *Daemonolatreia* of Remigius, in which he seemed hopeful of finding some formula to check the peril he conjured up.

"Stop them, stop them!" he would shout. "Those Whateleys meant to let them in, and the worst of all is left! Tell Rice and Morgan we must do something—it's a blind business, but I know how to make the powder... It hasn't been fed since the second of August, when Wilbur came here to his death, and at that rate..."

But Armitage had a sound physique despite his seventy-three years, and slept off his disorder that night without developing any real fever. He woke late Friday, clear of head, though sober with a gnawing fear and tremendous sense of responsibility. Saturday afternoon he felt able to go over to the library and summon Rice and Morgan for a conference, and the rest of that day and evening the three men tortured their brains in the wildest speculation and the most desperate debate. Strange and terrible books were drawn voluminously from the stack shelves and from secure places of storage; and diagrams and formulae were copied with feverish haste and in bewildering abundance. Of skepticism there was none. All three had seen the body of Wilbur Whateley as it lay on the floor in a room of that very building, and after that not one of them could feel even slightly inclined to treat the diary as a madman's raving.

Opinions were divided as to notifying the Massachusetts State Police, and the negative finally won. There were things involved which simply could not be believed by those who had not seen a sample, as indeed was made clear during certain subsequent investigations. Late at night the conference disbanded without having developed a definite plan, but all day Sunday Armitage was busy comparing formulae and mixing chemicals obtained from the college laboratory. The more he reflected on the hellish diary, the more he was inclined to doubt the efficacy of any material agent in stamping out the entity which Wilbur Whateley had left behind him—the earth-threatening entity which, unknown to him, was to burst forth in a few hours and become the memorable Dunwich horror.

Monday was a repetition of Sunday with Dr. Armitage, for the task in hand required an infinity of research and experiment. Further consultations of the monstrous diary brought about various changes of plan, and he knew that even in the end a large amount of uncertainty must remain. By Tuesday he had a definite line of action mapped out, and believed he would try a trip to Dunwich within a week. Then, on Wednesday, the great shock came. Tucked obscurely away in a corner of the *Arkham Advertiser* was a facetious little item from the Associated Press, telling what a record-breaking monster the bootleg whiskey of Dunwich had raised up. Armitage, half stunned, could only telephone for Rice and Morgan. Far into the night they discussed, and the next day was a whirlwind of preparation on the part of them all. Armitage knew he would be meddling with terrible powers, yet saw that there was no other way to annul the deeper and more malign meddling which others had done before him.

IX

Friday morning Armitage, Rice, and Morgan set out by motor for Dunwich, arriving at the village about one in the afternoon. The day was pleasant, but even in the brightest sunlight a kind of quiet dread and portent seemed to hover about the strangely domed hills and the deep, shadowy ravines of the stricken region. Now and then on some mountain-top a gaunt circle of stones could be glimpsed against the sky. From the air of hushed fright at Osborn's store they knew something hideous had happened, and soon learned of the annihilation of the Elmer Frye house and family. Throughout that afternoon they rode around Dunwich; questioning the natives concerning all that had occurred, and seeing for themselves with rising pangs of horror the drear Frye ruins with their lingering traces of the tarry stickiness, the blasphemous tracks in the Frye yard, the wounded Seth Bishop cattle, and the enormous swaths of disturbed vegetation in various places. The trail up and down Sentinel Hill seemed to Armitage of almost cataclysmic significance, and he looked long at the sinister altar-like stone on the summit.

At length the visitors, apprised of a party of State Police which had come from Aylesbury that morning in response to the first telephone reports of the Frye tragedy, decided to seek out the officers and compare notes as far as practicable. This, however, they found more easily planned than performed; since no sign of the party could be found in any direction. There had been five of them in a car, but now the car stood empty near the ruins in the Frye yard. The natives, all of whom had talked with the policemen, seemed at first as perplexed as Armitage and his companions. Then old Sam Hutchins thought of something and turned pale, nudging Fred Farr and pointing to the dank, deep hollow that yawned close by.

"Gawd," he gasped, "I telled 'em not ter go daown into the glen, an' I never thought nobody'd dew it with them tracks an' that smell an' the whippoorwills a-screechin' daown thar in the dark o' noonday..."

A cold shudder ran through natives and visitors alike, and every ear seemed strained in a kind of instinctive, unconscious listening. Armitage, now that he had actually come upon the horror and its monstrous work, trembled with the responsibility he felt to be his. Night would soon fall, and it was then that the mountainous blasphemy lumbered upon its eldritch course. *Negotium perambulans in tenebris...* The old librarian rehearsed the formulae he had memorized, and clutched the paper containing the alternative one he had not memorized. He saw that his electric flashlight was in working order. Rice, beside him, took from a valise a metal sprayer of the sort used in combating insects; whilst Morgan uncased the big-game rifle on which he relied despite his colleague's warnings that no material weapon would be of help.

Armitage, having read the hideous diary, knew painfully well what kind of a manifestation to expect; but he did not add to the fright of the Dunwich people by giving any hints or clues. He hoped that it might be conquered without any revelation to the world of the monstrous thing it had escaped. As the shadows gathered, the natives commenced to disperse homeward, anxious to bar themselves indoors despite the present evidence that all human locks and bolts were useless before a force that could bend trees and crush houses when it chose. They shook their heads at the visitors' plan to stand guard at the Frye ruins near the glen; and as they left, had little expectancy of ever seeing the watchers again.

There were rumblings under the hills that night, and the whippoorwills piped threateningly. Once in a while a wind, sweeping up out of Cold Spring Glen, would bring a touch of ineffable fetor to the heavy night air; such a fetor as all three of the watchers had smelled once before, when they stood above a dying thing that had passed for fifteen years and a half as a human being. But the looked-for terror did not appear. Whatever was down there in the glen was biding its time, and Armitage told his colleagues it would be suicidal to try to attack it in the dark.

Morning came wanly, and the night-sounds ceased. It was a gray, bleak day, with now and then a drizzle of rain; and heavier and heavier clouds seemed to be piling themselves up beyond the hills to the northwest. The men from Arkham were undecided what to do. Seeking shelter from the increasing rainfall beneath one of the few undestroyed Frye outbuildings, they debated the wisdom of waiting, or of taking the aggressive and going down into the glen in quest of their nameless, monstrous quarry. The downpour waxed in heaviness, and distant peals of thunder sounded from far horizons. Sheet lightning shimmered, and then a forky bolt flashed near at hand, as if descending into the accursed glen itself. The sky grew very dark, and the watchers hoped that the storm would prove a short, sharp one followed by clear weather.

It was still gruesomely dark when, not much over an hour later, a confused babel of voices sounded down the road. Another moment brought to view a frightened group of more than a dozen men, running, shouting, and even whimpering hysterically. Someone in the lead began sobbing out words, and the Arkham men started violently when those words developed a coherent form.

"Oh, my Gawd, my Gawd," the voice choked out. "It's a-goin' agin, *an' this time by day!* It's aout—it's aout an' a-movin' this very minute, an' only the Lord knows when it'll be on us all!"

The speaker panted into silence, but another took up his message.

"Nigh on a haour ago Zeb Whateley here heerd the 'phone a-ringin', an' it was Mis' Corey, George's wife, that lives daown by the junction. She says the hired boy Luther was aout drivin' in the caows from the storm arter the big bolt, when he see all the trees a-bendin' at the maouth o' the glen—opposite side ter this—an' smelt the same awful smell like he smelt when he faound the big tracks las' Monday mornin'. An' she says he says they was a swishin', lappin' saound, more nor what the bendin' trees an' bushes could make, an' all on a suddent the trees along the rud begun ter git pushed one side, an' they was a awful stompin' an' splashin' in the mud. But mind ye, Luther he didn't see nothin' at all, only just the bendin' trees an' underbrush.

"Then fur ahead where Bishop's Brook goes under the rud he heerd a awful creakin' an' strainin' on the bridge, an' says he could tell the saound o' wood a-startin' to crack an' split. An' all the whiles he never see a thing, only them trees an' bushes a-bendin'. An' when the swishin' saound got very fur off—on the rud towards Wizard Whateley's an' Sentinel Hill—Luther he had the guts ter step up whar he'd heerd it furst an' look at the graound. It was all mud an' water, an' the sky was dark, an' the rain was wipin' aout all tracks abaout as fast as could be; but beginnin' at the glen maouth, whar the trees had moved, they was still some o' them awful prints big as bar'ls like he seen Monday."

At this point the first excited speaker interrupted.

"But *that* ain't the trouble naow—that was only the start. Zeb here was callin' folks up an' everybody was a-listenin' in when a call from Seth Bishop's cut in. His haousekeeper Sally was carryin' on fit ter kill—she'd jest seed the trees a-bendin' beside the rud, an' says they was a kind o' mushy saound, like a elephant puffin' an' treadin', a-headin' fer the haouse. Then she up an' spoke suddent of a fearful smell, an' says her boy Cha'ncey was a-screamin' as haow it was jest like what he smelt up to the Whateley rewins Monday mornin'. An' the dogs was all barkin' an' whinin' awful.

"An' then she let aout a turrible yell, an' says the shed daown the rud had jest caved in like the storm hed blowed it over, only the wind wa'n't strong enough to dew that. Everybody was a-listenin', an' we could hear lots o' folks on the wire a-gaspin'. All to onct Sally she yelled agin, an' says the front yard picket fence hed just crumbled up, though they wa'n't no sign o' what done it. Then everybody on the line could hear Cha'ncey an' ol' Seth Bishop a-yellin' tew, an' Sally was shriekin' aout that suthin' heavy hed struck the haouse—not lightnin' nor nothin', but suthin' heavy agin the front, that kep' a-launchin' itself agin an' agin, though ye couldn't see nothin' aout the front winders. An' then... an' then..."

Lines of fright deepened on every face; and Armitage, shaken as he was, had barely poise enough to prompt the speaker.

"An' then... Sally she yelled aout, 'O help, the haouse is a-cavin' in'... an' on the wire we could hear a turrible crashin', an' a hull flock o' screamin'... jest like when Elmer Frye's place was took, only wuss..."

The man paused, and another of the crowd spoke.

"That's all—not a saound nor squeak over the 'phone arter that. Jest still-like. We that heerd it got aout Fords an' wagons an' raounded up as many able-bodied menfolks as we could git, at Corey's place, an' come up here ter see what yew thought best ter dew. Not but what I think it's the Lord's jedgment fer our iniquities, that no mortal kin ever set aside."

Armitage saw that the time for positive action had come, and spoke decisively to the faltering group of frightened rustics.

"We must follow it, boys." He made his voice as reassuring as possible. "I believe there's a chance of putting it out of business. You men know that those Whateleys were wizards—well, this thing is a thing of wizardry, and must be put down by the same means. I've seen Wilbur Whateley's diary and read some of the strange old books he used to read; and I think I know the right kind of spell to recite to make the thing fade away. Of course, one can't be sure, but we can always take a chance. It's invisible—I knew it would be—but there's a powder in this long-distance sprayer that might make it show up for a second. Later on we'll try it. It's a frightful thing to have alive, but it isn't as bad as what Wilbur would have let in if he'd lived longer. You'll never know what the world has escaped. Now we've only this one thing to fight, and it can't multiply. It can, though, do a lot of harm; so we mustn't hesitate to rid the community of it.

"We must follow it—and the way to begin is to go to the place that has just been wrecked. Let somebody lead the way—I don't know your roads very well, but I've an idea there might be a shorter cut across lots. How about it?"

The men shuffled about a moment, and then Earl Sawyer spoke softly, pointing with a grimy finger through the steadily lessening rain.

"I guess ye kin git to Seth Bishop's quickest by cuttin' acrost the lower medder here, wadin' the brook at the low place, an' climbin' through Carrier's mowin' and the timber-lot beyont. That comes aout on the upper rud mighty nigh Seth's—a leetle t'other side."

Armitage, with Rice and Morgan, started to walk in the direction indicated; and most of the natives followed slowly. The sky was growing lighter, and there were signs that the storm had worn itself away. When Armitage inadvertently took a wrong direction, Joe Osborn warned him and walked ahead to show the right one. Courage and confidence were mounting; though the twilight of the almost perpendicular wooded hill which lay toward the end of their short cut, and among whose fantastic ancient trees they had to scramble as if up a ladder, put these qualities to a severe test.

At length they emerged on a muddy road to find the sun coming out. They were a little beyond the Seth Bishop place, but bent trees and hideously unmistakable tracks showed what had passed by. Only a few moments were consumed in surveying the ruins just around the bend. It was the Frye incident all over again, and nothing dead or living was found in either of the collapsed shells which had been the Bishop house and barn. No one cared to remain there amidst the stench and tarry stickiness, but all turned instinctively to the line of horrible prints leading on toward the wrecked Whateley farmhouse and the altar-crowned slopes of Sentinel Hill.

As the men passed the site of Wilbur Whateley's abode they shuddered visibly, and seemed again to mix hesitancy with their zeal. It was no joke tracking down something as big as a house that one could not see, but that had all the vicious malevolence of a daemon. Opposite the base of Sentinel Hill the tracks left the road, and there was a fresh bending and matting visible along the broad swath marking the monster's former route to and from the summit.

Armitage produced a pocket telescope of considerable power and scanned the steep green side of the hill. Then he handed the instrument to Morgan, whose sight was keener. After a moment of gazing Morgan cried out sharply, passing the glass to Earl Sawyer and indicating a certain spot on the slope with his finger. Sawyer, as clumsy as most non-users of optical devices are, fumbled a while; but eventually focused the lenses with Armitage's aid. When he did so his cry was less restrained than Morgan's had been.

"Gawd almighty, the grass an' bushes is a-movin'! It's a-goin' up—slow-like—creepin' up ter the top this minute, heaven only knows what fur!"

Then the germ of panic seemed to spread among the seekers. It was one thing to chase the nameless entity, but quite another to find it. Spells might be all right—but suppose they weren't? Voices began questioning Armitage about what he knew of the thing, and no reply seemed quite to satisfy. Everyone seemed to feel himself in close proximity to phases of Nature and of being utterly forbidden, and wholly outside the sane experience of mankind.

X

In the end the three men from Arkham—old, white-bearded Dr. Armitage, stocky, iron-gray Professor Rice, and lean, youngish Dr. Morgan—ascended the mountain alone. After much patient instruction regarding its focusing and use, they left the telescope with the frightened group that remained in the road; and as they climbed they were watched closely by those among whom the glass was passed around. It was hard going, and Armitage had to be helped more than once. High above the toiling group the great swath trembled as its hellish maker re-passed with snail-like deliberateness. Then it was obvious that the pursuers were gaining.

Curtis Whateley—of the undecayed branch—was holding the telescope when the Arkham party detoured radically from the swath. He told the crowd that the men were evidently trying to get to a subordinate peak which overlooked the swath at a point considerably ahead of where the shrubbery was now bending. This, indeed, proved to be true; and the party were seen to gain the minor elevation only a short time after the invisible blasphemy had passed it.

Then Wesley Corey, who had taken the glass, cried out that Armitage was adjusting the sprayer which Rice held, and that something must be about to happen. The crowd stirred uneasily, recalling that this sprayer was expected to give the unseen horror a moment of visibility. Two or three men shut their eyes, but Curtis Whateley snatched back the telescope and strained his vision to the utmost. He saw that Rice, from the party's point of vantage above and behind the entity, had an excellent chance of spreading the potent powder with marvelous effect.

Those without the telescope saw only an instant's flash of gray cloud—a cloud about the size of a moderately large building—near the top of the mountain. Curtis, who had held the instrument, dropped it with a piercing shriek into the ankle-deep mud of the road.

He reeled, and would have crumpled to the ground had not two or three others seized and steadied him. All he could do was moan half-inaudibly.

"Oh, oh, great Gawd... that... that..."

There was a pandemonium of questioning, and only Henry Wheeler thought to rescue the fallen telescope and wipe it clean of mud. Curtis was past all coherence, and even isolated replies were almost too much for him.

"Bigger'n a barn... all made o' squirmin' ropes... hull thing sort o' shaped like a hen's egg bigger'n anything, with dozens o' legs like hogsheads that haff shut up when they step... nothin' solid abaout it—all like jelly, an' made o' sep'rit wrigglin' ropes pushed clost together... great bulgin' eyes all over it... ten or twenty maouths or trunks a-stickin' aout all along the sides, big as stovepipes, an' all a-tossin' an' openin' an' shuttin'... all gray, with kinder blue or purple rings... *an' Gawd in heaven—that haff face on top!...*"

This final memory, whatever it was, proved too much for poor Curtis; and he collapsed completely before he could say more. Fred Farr and Will Hutchins carried him to the roadside and laid him on the damp grass. Henry Wheeler, trembling, turned the rescued telescope on the mountain to see what he might. Through the lenses were discernible three tiny figures, apparently running toward the summit as fast as the steep incline allowed. Only these—nothing more. Then everyone noticed a strangely unseasonable noise in the deep valley behind, and even in the underbrush of Sentinel Hill itself. It was the piping of unnumbered whippoorwills, and in their shrill chorus there seemed to lurk a note of tense and evil expectancy.

Earl Sawyer now took the telescope and reported the three figures as standing on the topmost ridge, virtually level with the altar-stone but at a considerable distance from it. One figure, he said, seemed to be raising its hands above its head at rhythmic intervals; and as Sawyer mentioned the circumstance the crowd seemed to hear a faint, half-musical sound from the distance, as if a loud chant were accompanying the gestures. The weird silhouette on that remote peak must have been a spectacle of infinite grotesqueness and impressiveness, but no observer was in a mood for aesthetic appreciation. "I guess he's sayin' the spell," whispered Wheeler as he snatched back the telescope. The whippoorwills were piping wildly, and in a singularly curious irregular rhythm quite unlike that of the visible ritual.

Suddenly the sunshine seemed to lessen without the intervention of any discernible cloud. It was a very peculiar phenomenon, and was plainly marked by all. A rumbling sound seemed brewing beneath the hills, mixed strangely with a concordant rumbling which clearly came from the sky. Lightning flashed aloft, and the wondering crowd looked in vain for the portents of storm. The chanting of the men from Arkham now became unmistakable, and Wheeler saw through the glass that they were all raising their arms in the rhythmic incantation. From some farmhouse far away came the frantic barking of dogs.

The change in the quality of the daylight increased, and the crowd gazed about the horizon in wonder. A purplish darkness, born of nothing more than a spectral deepening of the sky's blue, pressed down upon the rumbling hills. Then the lightning flashed again, somewhat brighter than before, and the crowd fancied that it had showed a certain mistiness around the altar-stone on the distant height. No one, however, had been using the telescope at that instant. The whippoorwills continued their irregular pulsation, and the men of Dunwich braced themselves tensely against some imponderable menace with which the atmosphere seemed surcharged.

Without warning came those deep, cracked, raucous vocal sounds which will never leave the memory of the stricken group who heard them. Not from any human throat were they born, for the organs of man can yield no such acoustic perversions. Rather would one have said they came from the pit itself, had not their source been so unmistakably the altar-stone on the peak. It is almost erroneous to call them *sounds* at all, since so much of their ghastly, infra-bass timbre spoke to dim seats of consciousness and terror far subtler than the ear; yet one must do so, since their form was indisputably though vaguely that of half-articulate *words*. They were loud—loud as the rumblings and the thunder above which they echoed—yet did they come from no visible being. And because imagination might suggest a conjectural source in the world of non-visible beings, the huddled crowd at the mountain's base huddled still closer, and winced as if in expectation of a blow.

"*Ygnaiih... ygnaiih... thflthkh'ngha... Yog-Sothoth...*" rang the hideous croaking out of space. "*Y'bthnk... h'ehye—n'grkdl'lh...*"

The speaking impulse seemed to falter here, as if some frightful psychic struggle were going on. Henry Wheeler strained his eye at the telescope, but saw only the three grotesquely silhouetted human figures on the peak, all moving their arms furiously in strange gestures as their incantation drew near its culmination. From what black wells of Acherontic fear or feeling, from what unplumbed gulfs of extra-cosmic consciousness or obscure, long-latent heredity, were those half-articulate thunder-croakings drawn? Presently they began to gather renewed force and coherence as they grew in stark, utter, ultimate frenzy.

"Eh-ya-ya-ya-yahaah—e'yayayayaaaa... ngh'aaaaa... ngh'aaaa... h'yuh... h'yuh... HELP! HELP!... ff—ff—ff—FATHER! FATHER! YOG-SOTHOTH!..."

But that was all. The pallid group in the road, still reeling at the *indisputably English* syllables that had poured thickly and thunderously down from the frantic vacancy beside that shocking altar-stone, were never to hear such syllables again. Instead, they jumped violently at the terrific report which seemed to rend the hills; the deafening, cataclysmic peal whose source, be it inner earth or sky, no hearer was ever able to place. A single lightning-bolt shot from the purple zenith to the altar-stone, and a great tidal wave of viewless force and indescribable stench swept down from the hill to all the countryside. Trees, grass, and underbrush were whipped into a fury; and the frightened crowd at the mountain's base, weakened by the lethal fetor that seemed about to asphyxiate them, were almost hurled off their feet. Dogs howled from the distance, green grass and foliage wilted to a curious, sickly yellow-gray, and over field and forest were scattered the bodies of dead whippoorwills.

The stench left quickly, but the vegetation never came right again. To this day there is something queer and unholy about the growths on and around that fearsome hill. Curtis Whateley was only just regaining consciousness when the Arkham men came slowly down the mountain in the beams of a sunlight once more brilliant and untainted. They were grave and quiet, and seemed shaken by memories and reflections even more terrible than those which had reduced the group of natives to a state of cowed quivering. In reply to a jumble of questions they only shook their heads and reaffirmed one vital fact.

"The thing has gone forever," Armitage said. "It has been split up into what it was originally made of, and can never exist again. It was an impossibility in a normal world. Only the least fraction was really matter in any sense we know. It was like its father—and most of it has gone back to him in some vague realm or dimension outside our material universe; some vague abyss out of which only the most accursed rites of human blasphemy could ever have called him for a moment on the hills."

There was a brief silence, and in that pause the scattered senses of poor Curtis Whateley began to knit back into a sort of continuity; so that he put his hands to his head with a moan. Memory seemed to pick itself up where it had left off, and the horror of the sight that had prostrated him burst in upon him again.

"Oh, oh, my Gawd, that haff face—that haff face on top of it... that face with the red eyes an' crinkly albino hair, an' no chin, like the Whateleys... It was a octopus, centipede, spider kind o' thing, but they was a haff-shaped man's face on top of it, an' it looked like Wizard Whateley's, only it was yards an' yards acrost..."

He paused exhausted, as the whole group of natives stared in a bewilderment not quite crystallized into fresh terror. Only old Zebulon Whateley, who wanderingly remembered ancient things but who had been silent heretofore, spoke aloud.

"Fifteen year' gone," he rambled, "I heerd Ol' Whateley say as haow some day we'd hear a child o' Lavinny's a-callin' its father's name on the top o' Sentinel Hill..."

But Joe Osborn interrupted him to question the Arkham men anew.

"What was it anyhaow, an' haowever did young Wizard Whateley call it aout o' the air it come from?"

Armitage chose his words very carefully.

"It was—well, it was mostly a kind of force that doesn't belong in our part of space; a kind of force that acts and grows and shapes itself by other laws than those of our sort of Nature. We have no business calling in such things from outside, and only very wicked people and very wicked cults ever try to. There was some of it in Wilbur Whateley himself—enough to make a devil and a precocious monster of him, and to make his passing out a pretty terrible sight. I'm going to burn his accursed diary, and if you men are wise you'll dynamite that altar-stone up there, and pull down all the rings of standing stones on the other hills. Things like that brought down the beings those Whateleys were so fond of—the beings they were going to let in tangibly to wipe out the human race and drag the earth off to some nameless place for some nameless purpose.

"But as to this thing we've just sent back—the Whateleys raised it for a terrible part in the doings that were to come. It grew fast and big from the same reason that Wilbur grew fast and big—but it beat him because it had a greater share of the outsideness in it. You needn't ask how Wilbur called it out of the air. He didn't call it out. *It was his twin brother, but it looked more like the father than he did.*"

THE MASK

BY

ROBERT W. CHAMBERS

Camilla: You, sir, should unmask.
Stranger: Indeed?
Cassilda: Indeed it's time. We all have laid aside disguise but you.
Stranger: I wear no mask.
Camilla: (Terrified, aside to Cassilda.) No mask? No mask!

THE KING IN YELLOW, ACT I, SCENE 2.

I

Although I knew nothing of chemistry, I listened fascinated. He picked up an Easter lily which Geneviève had brought that morning from Notre Dame, and dropped it into the basin. Instantly the liquid lost its crystalline clearness. For a second the lily was enveloped in a milk-white foam, which disappeared, leaving the fluid opalescent. Changing tints of orange and crimson played over the surface, and then what seemed to be a ray of pure sunlight struck through from the bottom where the lily was resting. At the same instant he plunged his hand into the basin and drew out the flower. "There is no danger," he explained, "if you choose the right moment. That golden ray is the signal."

He held the lily toward me, and I took it in my hand. It had turned to stone, to the purest marble.

"You see," he said, "it is without a flaw. What sculptor could reproduce it?"

The marble was white as snow, but in its depths the veins of the lily were tinged with palest azure, and a faint flush lingered deep in its heart.

"Don't ask me the reason of that," he smiled, noticing my wonder. "I have no idea why the veins and heart are tinted, but they always are. Yesterday I tried one of Geneviève's gold-fish,—there it is."

The fish looked as if sculptured in marble. But if you held it to the light the stone was beautifully veined with a faint blue, and from somewhere within came a rosy light like the tint which slumbers in an opal. I looked into the basin. Once more it seemed filled with clearest crystal.

"If I should touch it now?" I demanded.

"I don't know," he replied, "but you had better not try."

"There is one thing I'm curious about," I said, "and that is where the ray of sunlight came from."

"It looked like a sunbeam true enough," he said. "I don't know, it always comes when I immerse any living thing. Perhaps," he continued, smiling, "perhaps it is the vital spark of the creature escaping to the source from whence it came."

I saw he was mocking, and threatened him with a mahl-stick, but he only laughed and changed the subject.

"Stay to lunch. Geneviève will be here directly."

"I saw her going to early mass," I said, "and she looked as fresh and sweet as that lily—before you destroyed it."

"Do you think I destroyed it?" said Boris gravely.

"Destroyed, preserved, how can we tell?"

We sat in the corner of a studio near his unfinished group of the "Fates." He leaned back on the sofa, twirling a sculptor's chisel and squinting at his work.

"By the way," he said, "I have finished pointing up that old academic Ariadne, and I suppose it will have to go to the Salon. It's all I have ready this year, but after the success the 'Madonna' brought me I feel ashamed to send a thing like that."

The "Madonna," an exquisite marble for which Geneviève had sat, had been the sensation of last year's Salon. I looked at the Ariadne. It was a magnificent piece of technical work, but I agreed with Boris that the world would expect something better of him than that. Still, it was impossible now to think of finishing in time for the Salon that splendid terrible group half shrouded in the marble behind me. The "Fates" would have to wait.

We were proud of Boris Yvain. We claimed him and he claimed us on the strength of his having been born in America, although his father was French and his mother was a Russian. Every one in the Beaux Arts called him Boris. And yet there were only two of us whom he addressed in the same familiar way—Jack Scott and myself.

Perhaps my being in love with Geneviève had something to do with his affection for me. Not that it had ever been acknowledged between us. But after all was settled, and she had told me with tears in her eyes that it was Boris whom she loved, I went over to his house and congratulated him. The perfect cordiality of that interview did not deceive either of us, I always believed, although to one at least it was a great comfort. I do not think he and Geneviève ever spoke of the matter together, but Boris knew.

Geneviève was lovely. The Madonna-like purity of her face might have been inspired by the Sanctus in Gounod's Mass. But I was always glad when she changed that mood for what we called her "April Manœuvres." She was often as variable as an April day. In the morning grave, dignified and sweet, at noon laughing, capricious, at evening whatever one least expected. I preferred her so rather than in that Madonna-like tranquillity which stirred the depths of my heart. I was dreaming of Geneviève when he spoke again.

"What do you think of my discovery, Alec?"

"I think it wonderful."

"I shall make no use of it, you know, beyond satisfying my own curiosity so far as may be, and the secret will die with me."

"It would be rather a blow to sculpture, would it not? We painters lose more than we ever gain by photography."

Boris nodded, playing with the edge of the chisel.

"This new vicious discovery would corrupt the world of art. No, I shall never confide the secret to any one," he said slowly.

It would be hard to find any one less informed about such phenomena than myself; but of course I had heard of mineral springs so saturated with silica that the leaves and twigs which fell into them were turned to stone after a time. I dimly comprehended the process, how the silica replaced the vegetable matter, atom by atom, and the result was a duplicate of the object in stone. This, I confess, had never interested me greatly, and as for the ancient fossils thus produced, they disgusted me. Boris, it appeared, feeling curiosity instead of repugnance, had investigated the subject, and had accidentally stumbled on a solution which, attacking the immersed object with a ferocity unheard of, in a second did the work of years. This was all I could make out of the strange story he had just been telling me. He spoke again after a long silence.

"I am almost frightened when I think what I have found. Scientists would go mad over the discovery. It was so simple too; it discovered itself. When I think of that formula, and that new element precipitated in metallic scales—"

"What new element?"

"Oh, I haven't thought of naming it, and I don't believe I ever shall. There are enough precious metals now in the world to cut throats over."

I pricked up my ears. "Have you struck gold, Boris?"

"No, better;—but see here, Alec!" he laughed, starting up. "You and I have all we need in this world. Ah! how sinister and covetous you look already!" I laughed too, and told him I was devoured by the desire for gold, and we had better talk of something else; so when Geneviève came in shortly after, we had turned our backs on alchemy.

Geneviève was dressed in silvery gray from head to foot. The light glinted along the soft curves of her fair hair as she turned her cheek to Boris; then she saw me and returned my greeting. She had never before failed to blow me a kiss from the tips of her white fingers, and I promptly complained of the omission. She smiled and held out her hand, which dropped almost before it had touched mine; then she said, looking at Boris—

"You must ask Alec to stay for luncheon." This also was something new. She had always asked me herself until today.

"I did," said Boris shortly.

"And you said yes, I hope?" She turned to me with a charming conventional smile. I might have been an acquaintance of the day before yesterday. I made her a low bow. "*J'avais bien l'honneur, madame*," but refusing to take up our usual bantering tone, she murmured a hospitable commonplace and disappeared. Boris and I looked at one another.

"I had better go home, don't you think?" I asked.

"Hanged if I know," he replied frankly.

While we were discussing the advisability of my departure Geneviève reappeared in the doorway without her bonnet. She was wonderfully beautiful, but her color was too deep and her lovely eyes were too bright. She came straight up to me and took my arm.

"Luncheon is ready. Was I cross, Alec? I thought I had a headache, but I haven't. Come here, Boris;" and she slipped her other arm through his. "Alec knows that after you there is no one in the world whom I like as well as I like him, so if he sometimes feels snubbed it won't hurt him."

"*À la bonheur!*" I cried, "who says there are no thunderstorms in April?"

"Are you ready?" chanted Boris. "Aye ready;" and arm-in-arm we raced into the dining-room, scandalizing the servants. After all we were not so much to blame; Geneviève was eighteen, Boris was twenty-three, and I not quite twenty-one.

II

Some work that I was doing about this time on the decorations for Geneviève's boudoir kept me constantly at the quaint little hotel in the Rue Sainte-Cécile. Boris and I in those days labored hard but as we pleased, which was fitfully, and we all three, with Jack Scott, idled a great deal together.

One quiet afternoon I had been wandering alone over the house examining curios, prying into odd corners, bringing out sweetmeats and cigars from strange hiding-places, and at last

I stopped in the bathing-room. Boris, all over clay, stood there washing his hands.

The room was built of rose-colored marble excepting the floor, which was tessellated in rose and gray. In the centre was a square pool sunken below the surface of the floor; steps led down into it, sculptured pillars supported a frescoed ceiling. A delicious marble Cupid appeared to have just alighted on his pedestal at the upper end of the room. The whole interior was Boris' work and mine. Boris, in his working-clothes of white canvas, scraped the traces of clay and red modelling wax from his handsome hands, and coquetted over his shoulder with the Cupid.

"I see you," he insisted, "don't try to look the other way and pretend not to see me. You know who made you, little humbug!"

It was always my rôle to interpret Cupid's sentiments in these conversations, and when my turn came I responded in such a manner, that Boris seized my arm and dragged me toward the pool, declaring he would duck me. Next instant he dropped my arm and turned pale. "Good God!" he said, "I forgot the pool is full of the solution!"

I shivered a little, and dryly advised him to remember better where he had stored the precious liquid.

"In Heaven's name, why do you keep a small lake of that gruesome stuff here of all places?" I asked.

"I want to experiment on something large," he replied.

"On me, for instance?"

"Ah! that came too close for jesting; but I do want to watch the action of that solution on a more highly organized living body; there is that big white rabbit," he said, following me into the studio.

Jack Scott, wearing a paint-stained jacket, came wandering in, appropriated all the Oriental sweetmeats he could lay his hands on, looted the cigarette case, and finally he and Boris disappeared together to visit the Luxembourg Gallery, where a new silver bronze by Rodin and a landscape of Monet's were claiming the exclusive attention of artistic France. I went back to the studio, and resumed my work. It was a Renaissance screen, which Boris wanted me to paint for Geneviève's boudoir. But the small boy who was unwillingly dawdling through a series of poses for it, today refused all bribes to be good. He never rested an instant in the same position, and inside of five minutes I had as many different outlines of the little beggar.

"Are you posing, or are you executing a song and dance, my friend?" I inquired.

"Whichever monsieur pleases," he replied, with an angelic smile.

Of course I dismissed him for the day, and of course I paid him for the full time, that being the way we spoil our models.

THE MASK

After the young imp had gone, I made a few perfunctory daubs at my work, but was so thoroughly out of humor, that it took me the rest of the afternoon to undo the damage I had done, so at last I scraped my palette, stuck my brushes in a bowl of black soap, and strolled into the smoking-room. I really believe that, excepting Geneviève's apartments, no room in the house was so free from the perfume of tobacco as this one. It was a queer chaos of odds and ends, hung with threadbare tapestry. A sweet-toned old spinet in good repair stood by the window. There were stands of weapons, some old and dull, others bright and modern, festoons of Indian and Turkish armor over the mantel, two or three good pictures, and a pipe-rack. It was here that we used to come for new sensations in smoking. I doubt if any type of pipe ever existed which was not represented in that rack. When we had selected one, we immediately carried it somewhere else and smoked it; for the place was, on the whole, more gloomy and less inviting than any in the house. But this afternoon, the twilight was very soothing, the rugs and skins on the floor looked brown and soft and drowsy; the big couch was piled with cushions—I found my pipe and curled up there for an unaccustomed smoke in the smoking-room. I had chosen one with a long flexible stem, and lighting it fell to dreaming. After a while it went out, but I did not stir. I dreamed on and presently fell asleep.

I awoke to the saddest music I had ever heard. The room was quite dark, I had no idea what time it was. A ray of moonlight silvered one edge of the old spinet, and the polished wood seemed to exhale the sounds as perfume floats above a box of sandalwood. Some one rose in the darkness, and came away weeping quietly, and I was fool enough to cry out "Geneviève!"

She dropped at my voice, and, I had time to curse myself while I made a light and tried to raise her from the floor. She shrank away with a murmur of pain. She was very quiet, and asked for Boris. I carried her to the divan, and went to look for him, but he was not in the house, and the servants were gone to bed. Perplexed and anxious, I hurried back to Geneviève. She lay where I had left her, looking very white.

"I can't find Boris nor any of the servants," I said.

"I know," she answered faintly, "Boris has gone to Ept with Mr. Scott. I did not remember when I sent you for him just now."

"But he can't get back in that case before tomorrow afternoon, and—are you hurt? Did I frighten you into falling? What an awful fool I am, but I was only half awake."

"Boris thought you had gone home before dinner. Do please excuse us for letting you stay here all this time."

"I have had a long nap," I laughed, "so sound that I did not know whether I was still asleep or not when I found myself staring at a figure that was moving toward me, and called out your name. Have you been trying the old spinet? You must have played very softly."

I would tell a thousand more lies worse than that one to see the look of relief that came into her face. She smiled adorably, and said in her natural voice: "Alec, I tripped on that wolf's head, and I think my ankle is sprained. Please call Marie, and then go home."

I did as she bade me, and left her there when the maid came in.

III

At noon next day when I called, I found Boris walking restlessly about his studio.

"Geneviève is asleep just now," he told me, "the sprain is nothing, but why should she have such a high fever? The doctor can't account for it; or else he will not," he muttered.

"Geneviève has a fever?" I asked.

"I should say so, and has actually been a little light-headed at intervals all night. The idea!—gay little Geneviève, without a care in the world,—and she keeps saying her heart's broken, and she wants to die!"

My own heart stood still.

Boris leaned against the door of his studio, looking down, his hands in his pockets, his kind, keen eyes clouded, a new line of trouble drawn "over the mouth's good mark, that made the smile." The maid had orders to summon him the instant Geneviève opened her eyes. We waited and waited, and Boris, growing restless, wandered about, fussing with modelling wax and red clay. Suddenly he started for the next room. "Come and see my rose-colored bath full of death!" he cried.

"Is it death?" I asked, to humor his mood.

"You are not prepared to call it life, I suppose," he answered. As he spoke he plucked a solitary gold-fish squirming and twisting out of its globe. "We'll send this one after the other—wherever that is," he said. There was feverish excitement in his voice. A dull weight of fever lay on my limbs and on my brain as I followed him to the fair crystal pool with its pink-tinted sides; and he dropped the creature in. Falling, its scales flashed with a hot orange gleam in its angry twistings and contortions; the moment it struck the liquid it became rigid and sank heavily to the bottom. Then came the milky foam, the splendid hues radiating on the surface and then the shaft of pure serene light broke through from seemingly infinite depths. Boris plunged in his hand and drew out an exquisite marble thing, blue-veined, rose-tinted, and glistening with opalescent drops.

"Child's play," he muttered, and looked wearily, longingly at me,—as if I could answer such questions! But Jack Scott came in and entered into the "game," as he called it, with ardor. Nothing would do but to try the experiment on the white rabbit then and there. I was willing that Boris should find distraction from his cares, but I hated to see the life go out of a warm, living creature and I declined to be present. Picking up a book at random, I sat down in the studio to read. Alas! I had found *The King in Yellow*. After a few moments, which seemed ages, I was putting it away with a nervous shudder, when Boris and Jack came in bringing their marble rabbit. At the same time the bell rang above, and a cry came from the sick-room. Boris was gone like a flash, and the next moment he called, "Jack, run for the doctor; bring him back with you. Alec, come here."

I went and stood at her door. A frightened maid came out in haste and ran away to fetch some remedy. Geneviève, sitting bolt upright, with crimson cheeks and glittering eyes, babbled incessantly and resisted Boris' gentle restraint. He called me to help. At my first touch she sighed and sank back, closing her eyes, and then—then—as we still bent above her, she opened them again, looked straight into Boris' face—poor fever-crazed girl!—and told her secret. At the same instant our three lives turned into new channels; the bond that held us so long together snapped for ever and a new bond was forged in its place, for she had spoken my name, and as the fever tortured her, her heart poured out its load of hidden sorrow. Amazed and dumb I bowed my head, while my face burned like a live coal, and the blood surged in my ears, stupefying me with its clamor. Incapable of movement, incapable of speech, I listened to her feverish words in an agony of shame and sorrow. I could not silence her, I could not look at Boris. Then I felt an arm upon my shoulder, and Boris turned a bloodless face to mine.

"It is not your fault, Alec; don't grieve so if she loves you—" but he could not finish; and as the doctor stepped swiftly into the room, saying—"Ah, the fever!" I seized Jack Scott and hurried him to the street, saying, "Boris would rather be alone." We crossed the street to our own apartments, and that night, seeing I was going to be ill too, he went for the doctor again. The last thing I recollect with any distinctness was hearing Jack say, "For Heaven's sake, doctor, what ails him, to wear a face like that?" and I thought of *The King in Yellow* and the Pallid Mask.

I was very ill, for the strain of two years which I had endured since that fatal May morning when Geneviève murmured, "I love you, but I think I love Boris best," told on me at last. I had never imagined that it could become more than I could endure. Outwardly tranquil, I had deceived myself. Although the inward battle raged night after night, and I, lying alone in my room, cursed myself for rebellious thoughts unloyal to Boris and unworthy of Geneviève, the morning always brought relief, and I returned to Geneviève and to my dear Boris with a heart washed clean by the tempests of the night.

Never in word or deed or thought while with them had I betrayed my sorrow even to myself.

The mask of self-deception was no longer a mask for me, it was a part of me. Night lifted it, laying bare the stifled truth below; but there was no one to see except myself, and when the day broke the mask fell back again of its own accord. These thoughts passed through my troubled mind as I lay sick, but they were hopelessly entangled with visions of white creatures, heavy as stone, crawling about in Boris' basin,—of the wolf's head on the rug, foaming and snapping at Geneviève, who lay smiling beside it. I thought, too, of the King in Yellow wrapped in the fantastic colors of his tattered mantle, and that bitter cry of Cassilda, "Not upon us, oh King, not upon us!" Feverishly I struggled to put it from me, but I saw the lake of Hali, thin and blank, without a ripple or wind to stir it, and I saw the towers of Carcosa behind the moon. Aldebaran, the Hyades, Alar, Hastur, glided through the cloud-rifts which fluttered and flapped as they passed like the scolloped tatters of the King in Yellow. Among all these, one sane thought persisted. It never wavered, no matter what else was going on in my disordered mind, that my chief reason for existing was to meet some requirement of Boris and Geneviève. What this obligation was, its nature, was never clear; sometimes it seemed to be protection, sometimes support, through a great crisis. Whatever it seemed to be for the time, its weight rested only on me, and I was never so ill or so weak that I did not respond with my whole soul. There were always crowds of faces about me, mostly strange, but a few I recognized, Boris among them. Afterward they told me that this could not have been, but I know that once at least he bent over me. It was only a touch, a faint echo of his voice, then the clouds settled back on my senses, and I lost him, but he *did* stand there and bend over me *once* at least.

At last, one morning I awoke to find the sunlight falling across my bed, and Jack Scott reading beside me. I had not strength enough to speak aloud, neither could I think, much less remember, but I could smile feebly, as Jack's eye met mine, and when he jumped up and asked eagerly if I wanted anything, I could whisper, "Yes—Boris." Jack moved to the head of my bed, and leaned down to arrange my pillow: I did not see his face, but he answered heartily, "You must wait, Alec; you are too weak to see even Boris."

I waited and I grew strong; in a few days I was able to see whom I would, but meanwhile I had thought and remembered. From the moment when all the past grew clear again in my mind, I never doubted what I should do when the time came, and I felt sure that Boris would have resolved upon the same course so far as he was concerned; as for what pertained to me alone, I knew he would see that also as I did. I no longer asked for any one. I never inquired why no message came from them; why during the week I lay there, waiting and growing stronger, I never heard their name spoken. Preoccupied with my own searchings for the right way, and with my feeble but determined fight against despair, I simply acquiesced in Jack's reticence, taking for granted that he was afraid to speak of them, lest I should turn unruly and insist on seeing them. Meanwhile I said over and over to myself, how would it be when life began again for us all? We would take up our relations exactly as they were before Geneviève fell ill. Boris and I would look into each other's eyes, and there would be neither rancour nor cowardice nor mistrust in that glance. I would be with them again for a little while in the dear intimacy of their home, and then, without pretext or explanation, I would disappear from their lives for ever. Boris would know; Geneviève—the only comfort was that she would never know. It seemed, as I thought it over, that I had found the meaning of that sense of obligation which had persisted all through my delirium, and the only possible answer to it. So, when I was quite ready, I beckoned Jack to me one day, and said—

"Jack, I want Boris at once; and take my dearest greeting to Geneviève...."

When at last he made me understand that they were both dead, I fell into a wild rage that tore all my little convalescent strength to atoms. I raved and cursed myself into a relapse, from which I crawled forth some weeks afterward a boy of twenty-one who believed that his youth was gone for ever. I seemed to be past the capability of further suffering, and one day when Jack handed me a letter and the keys to Boris' house, I took them without a tremor and asked him to tell me all. It was cruel of me to ask him, but there was no help for it, and he leaned wearily on his thin hands, to reopen the wound which could never entirely heal. He began very quietly—

"Alec, unless you have a clue that I know nothing about, you will not be able to explain any more than I what has happened. I suspect that you would rather not hear these details, but you must learn them, else I would spare you the relation. God knows I wish I could be spared the telling. I shall use few words.

"That day when I left you in the doctor's care and came back to Boris, I found him working on the 'Fates.' Geneviève, he said, was sleeping under the influence of drugs. She had been quite out of her mind, he said. He kept on working, not talking any more, and I watched him. Before long, I saw that the third figure of the group—the one looking straight ahead, out over the world—bore his face; not as you ever saw it, but as it looked then and to the end. This is one thing for which I should like to find an explanation, but I never shall.

"Well, he worked and I watched him in silence, and we went on that way until nearly midnight. Then we heard the door open and shut sharply, and a swift rush in the next room. Boris sprang through the doorway and I followed; but we were too late. She lay at the bottom of the pool, her hands across her breast. Then Boris shot himself through the heart." Jack stopped speaking, drops of sweat stood under his eyes, and his thin cheeks twitched. "I carried Boris to his room. Then I went back and let that hellish fluid out of the pool, and turning on all the water, washed the marble clean of every drop. When at length I dared descend the steps, I found her lying there as white as snow. At last, when I had decided what was best to do, I went into the laboratory, and first emptied the solution in the basin into the waste-pipe; then I poured the contents of every jar and bottle after it. There was wood in the fireplace, so I built a fire, and breaking the locks of Boris' cabinet I burnt every paper, notebook and letter that I found there. With a mallet from the studio I smashed to pieces all the empty bottles, then loading them into a coal-scuttle, I carried them to the cellar and threw them over the red-hot bed of the furnace. Six times I made the journey, and at last, not a vestige remained of anything which might again aid in seeking for the formula which Boris had found. Then at last I dared call the doctor. He is a good man, and together we struggled to keep it from the public. Without him I never could have succeeded. At last we got the servants paid and sent away into the country, where old Rosier keeps them quiet with stories of Boris' and Geneviève's travels in distant lands, from whence they will not return for years. We buried Boris in the little cemetery of Sèvres. The doctor is a good creature, and knows when to pity a man who can bear no more. He gave his certificate of heart disease and asked no questions of me."

Then, lifting his head from his hands, he said, "Open the letter, Alec; it is for us both."

I tore it open. It was Boris' will dated a year before. He left everything to Geneviève, and in case of her dying childless, I was to take control of the house in the Rue Sainte-Cécile, and Jack Scott the management at Ept. On our deaths the property reverted to his mother's family in Russia, with the exception of the sculptured marbles executed by himself. These he left to me.

The page blurred under our eyes, and Jack got up and walked to the window. Presently he returned and sat down again. I dreaded to hear what he was going to say, but he spoke with the same simplicity and gentleness.

"Geneviève lies before the Madonna in the marble room. The Madonna bends tenderly above her, and Geneviève smiles back into that calm face that never would have been except for her."

His voice broke, but he grasped my hand, saying, "Courage, Alec." Next morning he left for Ept to fulfil his trust.

IV

The same evening I took the keys and went into the house I had known so well. Everything was in order, but the silence was terrible. Though I went twice to the door of the marble room, I could not force myself to enter. It was beyond my strength. I went into the smoking-room and sat down before the spinet. A small lace handkerchief lay on the keys, and I turned away, choking. It was plain I could not stay, so I locked every door, every window, and the three front and back gates, and went away. Next morning Alcide packed my valise, and leaving him in charge of my apartments I took the Orient express for Constantinople. During the two years that I wandered through the East, at first, in our letters, we never mentioned Geneviève and Boris, but gradually their names crept in. I recollect particularly a passage in one of Jack's letters replying to one of mine—

"What you tell me of seeing Boris bending over you while you lay ill, and feeling his touch on your face, and hearing his voice, of course troubles me. This that you describe must have happened a fortnight after he died. I say to myself that you were dreaming, that it was part of your delirium, but the explanation does not satisfy me, nor would it you."

Toward the end of the second year a letter came from Jack to me in India so unlike anything that I had ever known of him that I decided to return at once to Paris. He wrote: "I am well, and sell all my pictures as artists do who have no need of money. I have not a care of my own, but I am more restless than if I had. I am unable to shake off a strange anxiety about you. It is not apprehension, it is rather a breathless expectancy—of what, God knows! I can only say it is wearing me out. Nights I dream always of you and Boris. I can never recall anything afterward, but I wake in the morning with my heart beating, and all day the excitement increases until I fall asleep at night to recall the same experience. I am quite exhausted by it, and have determined to break up this morbid condition. I must see you. Shall I go to Bombay, or will you come to Paris?"

I telegraphed him to expect me by the next steamer.

When we met I thought he had changed very little; I, he insisted, looked in splendid health. It was good to hear his voice again, and as we sat and chatted about what life still held for us, we felt that it was pleasant to be alive in the bright spring weather.

We stayed in Paris together a week, and then I went for a week to Ept with him, but first of all we went to the cemetery at Sèvres, where Boris lay.

"Shall we place the 'Fates' in the little grove above him?" Jack asked, and I answered—

"I think only the 'Madonna' should watch over Boris' grave." But Jack was none the better for my home-coming. The dreams of which he could not retain even the least definite outline continued, and he said that at times the sense of breathless expectancy was suffocating.

"You see I do you harm and not good," I said. "Try a change without me." So he started alone for a ramble among the Channel Islands, and I went back to Paris. I had not yet entered Boris' house, now mine, since my return, but I knew it must be done. It had been kept in order by Jack; there were servants there, so I gave up my own apartment and went there to live. Instead of the agitation I had feared, I found myself able to paint there tranquilly. I visited all the rooms—all but one. I could not bring myself to enter the marble room where Geneviève lay, and yet I felt the longing growing daily to look upon her face, to kneel beside her.

One April afternoon, I lay dreaming in the smoking-room, just as I had lain two years before, and mechanically I looked among the tawny Eastern rugs for the wolf-skin. At last I distinguished the pointed ears and flat cruel head, and I thought of my dream where I saw Geneviève lying beside it. The helmets still hung against the threadbare tapestry, among them the old Spanish morion which I remembered Geneviève had once put on when we were amusing ourselves with the ancient bits of mail. I turned my eyes to the spinet; every yellow key seemed eloquent of her caressing hand, and I rose, drawn by the strength of my life's passion to the sealed door of the marble room. The heavy doors swung inward under my trembling hands. Sunlight poured through the window, tipping with gold the wings of Cupid, and lingered like a nimbus over the brows of the Madonna. Her tender face bent in compassion over a marble form so exquisitely pure that I knelt and signed myself. Geneviève lay in the shadow under the Madonna, and yet, through her white arms, I saw the pale azure vein, and beneath her softly clasped hands the folds of her dress were tinged with rose, as if from some faint warm light within her breast.

Bending, with a breaking heart, I touched the marble drapery with my lips, then crept back into the silent house.

A maid came and brought me a letter, and I sat down in the little conservatory to read it; but as I was about to break the seal, seeing the girl lingering, I asked her what she wanted.

She stammered something about a white rabbit that had been caught in the house, and asked what should be done with it. I told her to let it loose in the walled garden behind the house, and opened my letter. It was from Jack, but so incoherent that I thought he must have lost his reason. It was nothing but a series of prayers to me not to leave the house until he could get back; he could not tell me why, there were the dreams, he said—he could explain nothing, but he was sure that I must not leave the house in the Rue Sainte-Cécile.

As I finished reading I raised my eyes and saw the same maid-servant standing in the doorway holding a glass dish in which two gold-fish were swimming: "Put them back into the tank and tell me what you mean by interrupting me," I said.

With a half-suppressed whimper she emptied water and fish into an aquarium at the end of the conservatory, and turning to me asked my permission to leave my service. She said people were playing tricks on her, evidently with a design of getting her into trouble; the marble rabbit had been stolen and a live one had been brought into the house; the two beautiful marble fish were gone, and she had just found those common live things flopping on the dining-room floor. I reassured her and sent her away, saying I would look about myself. I went into the studio; there was nothing there but my canvases and some casts, except the marble of the Easter lily. I saw it on a table across the room. Then I strode angrily over to it. But the flower I lifted from the table was fresh and fragile and filled the air with perfume.

Then suddenly I comprehended, and sprang through the hallway to the marble room. The doors flew open, the sunlight streamed into my face, and through it, in a heavenly glory, the Madonna smiled, as Geneviève lifted her flushed face from her marble couch and opened her sleepy eyes.

SKULL-FACE

BY

ROBERT E. HOWARD

CHAPTER ONE

THE FACE IN THE MIST

"We are no other than a moving row
Of Magic Shadow-shapes that come and go."
—Omar Khayyam

The horror first took concrete form amid that most unconcrete of all things—a hashish dream. I was off on a timeless, spaceless journey through the strange lands that belong to this state of being, a million miles away from earth and all things earthly; yet I became cognizant that something was reaching across the unknown voids—something that tore ruthlessly at the separating curtains of my illusions and intruded itself into my visions.

I did not exactly return to ordinary waking life, yet I was conscious of a seeing and a recognizing that was unpleasant and seemed out of keeping with the dream I was at that time enjoying. To one who has never known the delights of hashish, my explanation must seem chaotic, and impossible. Still, I was aware of a rending of mists and then the Face intruded itself into my sight. I thought at first it was merely a skull; then I saw that it was a hideous yellow instead of white, and was endowed with some horrid form of life. Eyes glimmered deep in the sockets and the jaws moved as if in speech. The body, except for the high, thin shoulders, was vague and indistinct, but the hands, which floated in the mists before and below the skull, were horribly vivid and filled me crawling fears. They were like the hands of a mummy, long, lean and yellow, with knobby joints and cruel curving talons.

Then, to complete the vague horror which was swiftly taking possession of me, a voice spoke—imagine a man so long dead that his vocal organ had grown rusty and unaccustomed to speech. This was the thought which made my flesh crawl as I listened.

"A strong brute and one who might be useful somehow. See that he is given all the hashish he requires."

Then the face began to recede, even as I sensed that I was the subject of conversation, and the mists billowed and began to close again. Yet for a single instant a scene stood out with startling clarity. I gasped—or sought to. For over the high, strange shoulder of the apparition another face stood out clearly for an instant, as if the owner peered at me. Red lips, half parted, long dark eyelashes. shading vivid eyes, a shimmery cloud of hair. Over the shoulder of Horror, breath-taking beauty for an instant looked at me.

CHAPTER TWO
THE HASHISH SLAVE

"Up from Earth's center through the Seventh Gate
I rose, and on the Throne of Saturn sate."
—Omar Khayyam

My dream of the skull-face was borne over that usually uncrossable gap that lies between hashish enchantment and humdrum reality. I sat cross-legged on a mat in Yun Shatu's Temple of Dreams and gathered the fading forces of my decaying brain to the task of remembering events and faces.

This last dream was so entirely different from any I had ever had before, that my waning interest was roused to the point of inquiring as to its origin. When I first began to experiment with hashish, I sought to find a physical or psychic basis for the wild flights of illusion pertaining thereto, but of late I had been content to enjoy without seeking cause and effect.

Whence this unaccountable sensation of familiarity in regard to that vision? I took my throbbing head between my hands and laboriously sought a clue. A living dead man and a girl of rare beauty who had looked over his shoulder. Then I remembered.

Back in the fog of days and nights which veils a hashish addict's memory, my money had given out. It seemed years or possibly centuries, but my stagnant reason told me that it had probably been only a few days. At any rate, I had presented myself at Yun Shatu's sordid dive as usual and had been thrown out by the great Negro, Hassim, when it was learned I had no more money.

My universe crashing to pieces about me, and my nerves humming like taut piano wires for the vital need that was mine, I crouched in the gutter and gibbered bestially, till Hassim swaggered out and stilled my yammerings with a blow that felled me, half stunned.

Then as I presently rose, staggeringly and with no thought save of the river; which flowed with cool murmur so near me—as I rose, a light hand was laid like the touch of a rose on my arm. I turned with a frightened start, and stood spellbound before the vision of loveliness which met my gaze. Dark eyes, limpid with pity surveyed me and the little hand on my ragged sleeve drew me toward the door of the Dream Temple. I shrank back, but a low voice, soft and musical, urged me, and filled with a trust that was strange. I shambled along with my beautiful guide.

At the door Hassim met us, cruel hands lifted and a dark scowl on his ape-like brow, but as I cowered there, expecting a blow, he halted before the girl's upraised hand and her word of command which had taken on an imperious note.

I did not understand what she said, but I saw dimly, as in a fog, that she gave the black man money, and she led me to a couch where she had me recline and arranged the cushions as if I were king of Egypt instead of a ragged, dirty renegade who lived only for hashish. Her slim hand was cool on my brow for a moment, and then she was gone and Yussef Ali came bearing the stuff for which my very soul shrieked—and soon I was wandering again through those strange and exotic countries that only a hashish slave knows.

Now as I sat on the mat and pondered the dream of the skull-face I wondered more. Since the unknown girl had led me back into the dive, I had come and gone as before, when I had plenty of money to pay Yun Shatu. Someone certainly was paying him for me, and while my subconscious mind had told me it was the girl, my rusty brain had failed to grasp the fact entirely, or to wonder why. What need of wondering? So someone paid and the vivid-hued dreams continued, what cared I? But now I wondered. For the girl who had protected me from Hassim and had brought the hashish for me was the same girl I had seen in the skull-face dream.

Through the soddenness of my degradation the lure of her struck like a knife piercing my heart and strangely revived the memories of the days when I was a man like other men—not yet a sullen, cringing slave of dreams. Far and dim they were, shimmery islands in the mist of years—and what a dark sea lay between!

I looked at my ragged sleeve and the dirty, claw-like hand protruding from it; I gazed through the hanging smoke which fogged the sordid room, at the low bunks along the wall whereon lay the blankly staring dreamers—slaves, like me, of hashish or of opium. I gazed at the slippered Chinamen gliding softly to and fro bearing pipes or roasting balls of concentrated purgatory over tiny flickering fires. I gazed at Hassim standing, arms folded, beside the door like a great statue of black basalt.

And I shuddered and hid my face in my hands because with the faint dawning of returning manhood, I knew that this last and most cruel dream was futile—I had crossed an ocean over which I could never return, had cut myself off from the world of normal men or women. Naught remained now but to drown this dream as I had drowned all my others—swiftly and with hope that I should soon attain that Ultimate Ocean which lies beyond all dreams.

So these fleeting moments of lucidity, of lodging, that tear aside the veils of all dope slaves—unexplainable, without hope of attainment.

So I went back to my empty dreams, to my fantasmagoria of illusions; but sometimes, like a sword cleaving a mist, through the high lands and the low lands and seas of my visions floated, like half-forgotten music, the sheen of dark eyes and shimmery hair.

You ask how I, Stephen Costigan, American and a man of some attainments and culture, came to lie in a filthy dive of London's Limehouse? The answer is simple—no jaded debauchee, I, seeking new sensations in the mysteries of the Orient. I answer—Argonne! Heavens, what deeps and heights of horror lurk in that one word alone! Shell-shocked—shell-torn. Endless days and nights without end and roaring red hell over No Man's Land where I lay shot and bayoneted to shreds of gory flesh. My body recovered, how I know not; my mind never did.

And the leaping fires and shifting shadows in my tortured brain drove me down and down, along the stairs of degradation, uncaring until at last I found surcease in Yun Shatu's Temple of Dreams, where I slew my red dreams in other dreams—the dreams of hashish whereby a man may descend to the lower pits of the reddest hells or soar into those unnamable heights where the stars are diamond pinpoints beneath his feet.

Not the visions of the sot, the beasts, were mine. I attained the unattainable, stood face to face with the unknown and in cosmic calmness knew the unguessable. And was content after a fashion, until the sight of burnished hair and scarlet lips swept away my dream-built universe and left me shuddering among its ruins.

CHAPTER THREE
THE MASTER OF DOOM

"And He that toss'd you down into the Field,
He knows about it all—He knows! He knows!"
—Omar Khayyam

A hand shook me roughly as I emerged languidly from my latest debauch.

"The master wishes you! Up! Swine!"

Hassim it was who spoke.

"To hell with the Master!" I answered, for I hated Hassim—and feared him.

"Up with you or you get no more hashish," was the brutal response, and I rose in trembling haste.

I followed the huge black man and he led the way to the rear of the building, stepping in and out among the wretched dreamers on the floor.

"Muster all hands on deck!" droned a sailor in a bunk. "All hands!"

Hassim flung open the door at the rear and motioned me to enter. I had never before passed through that door and had supposed it led into Yun Shatu's private quarters. But it was furnished only with a cot, a bronze idol of some sort before which incense burned, and a heavy table.

Hassim gave me a sinister glance and seized the table as if to spin it about. It turned as if it stood on a revolving platform and a section of the floor turned with it, revealing a hidden doorway in the floor. Steps led downward in the darkness.

Hassim lighted a candle and with a brusk gesture invited me to descend. I did so, with the sluggish obedience of the dope addict, and he followed, closing the door above us by means of an iron lever fastened to the underside of the floor. In the semi-darkness we went down the rickety steps, some nine or ten I should say, and then came upon a narrow corridor.

Here Hassim again took the lead, holding the candle high in front of him. I could scarcely see the sides of this cave-like passage-way but knew that it was not wide. The flickering light showed it to be bare of any sort of furnishings save for a number of strange-looking chests which lined the walls—receptacles containing opium and other dope, I thought.

A continuous scurrying and the occasional glint of small red eyes haunted the shadows, betraying the presence of vast numbers of the great rats which infest the Thames waterfront of that section.

Then more steps loomed out of the dark in front of us as the corridor came to an abrupt end. Hassim led the way up and at the top knocked four times against what seemed the underside of a floor. A hidden door opened and a flood of soft, illusive light streamed through.

Hassim hustled me up roughly and I stood blinking in such a setting as I had never seen in my wildest flights of vision. I stood in a jungle of palm-trees through which wriggled a million vivid-hued dragons! Then, as my startled eyes became accustomed to the light, I saw that I had not been suddenly transferred to some other planet, as I had at first thought. The palm-trees were there, and the dragons, but the trees were artificial and stood in great pots and the dragons writhed across heavy tapestries which hid the walls.

The room itself was a monstrous affair—inhumanly large, it seemed to me. A thick smoke, yellowish and tropical in suggestion, seemed to hang over all, veiling the ceiling and baffling upward glances. This smoke, I saw, emanated from an altar in front of the wall to my left. I started. Through the saffron billowing fog two eyes, hideously large and vivid, glittered at me. The vague outlines of some bestial idol took indistinct shape. I flung an uneasy glance about, marking the Oriental divans and couches and the bizarre furnishings, and then my eyes halted and rested on a lacquer screen just in front of me.

I could not pierce it and no sound came from beyond it, yet I felt eyes searing into my consciousness through it, eyes that burned through my very soul. A strange aura of evil flowed from that strange screen with its weird carvings and unholy decorations.

Hassim salaamed profoundly before it and then, without speaking, stepped back and folded his arms, statue-like.

A voice suddenly broke the heavy and oppressive silence.

"You who are a swine, would you like to be a man again?"

I started. The tone was inhuman, cold—more, there was a suggestion of long disuse of the vocal organs—the voice I had heard in my dream!

"Yes," I replied, trance-like, "I would like to be a man again."

Silence ensued for a space; then the voice came again with a sinister whispering undertone at the back of its sound like bats flying through a cavern.

"I shall make you a man again because I am a friend to all broken men. Not for a price shall I do it, nor for gratitude. And I give you a sign to seal my promise and my vow. Thrust your hand through the screen."

At these strange and almost unintelligible words I stood perplexed, and then, as the unseen one repeated the last command, I stepped forward and thrust my hand through a slit which opened silently in the screen. I felt my wrist seized in an iron grip and something seven times colder than ice touched the inside of my hand. Then my wrist was released, and drawing forth my hand I saw a strange symbol traced in blue close to the base of my thumb—a thing that resembled a scorpion.

The voice spoke again in a sibilant language I did not understand, and Hassim stepped forward deferentially. He reached about the screen and then turned to me, holding a goblet of some amber-colored liquid which he proffered me with an ironical bow. I took it hesitatingly.

"Drink and fear not," said the unseen one. "It is only an Egyptian wine with life-giving qualities."

So I raised the goblet and emptied it; the taste was not unpleasant, and even as I handed the beaker to Hassim again, I seemed to feel new life and vigor whip along my jaded veins.

"Remain at Yun Shatu's house," said the voice. "You will be given food and a bed until you are strong enough to work for yourself. You will use no hashish nor will you require any. Go!"

As in a daze, I followed Hassim back through the hidden door, down the steps, along the dark corridor and up through the other door that led us into the Temple of Dreams.

An we steppec from the rear chamber into the main room of the dreamers, I turned to the Negro wonderingly.

"Master? Master of what? Of Life?"

Hassim laughed, fiercely and sardonically.

"Master of Doom!"

CHAPTER FOUR
THE SPIDER AND THE FLY

"There was the Door to which I found no Key;
There was the Veil through which I might not see."
—Omar Khayyam

I sat on Yun Shatu's cushions and pondered with a clearness of mind new and strange to me. As for that, all my sensations were new and strange. I felt as if I had wakened from a monstrously long sleep, and though my thoughts were sluggish, I felt as though the cobwebs which had clogged them for so long had been partly brushed away.

I drew my hand across my brow, noting how it trembled. I was weak and shaky and felt the stirrings of hunger—not for dope but for food. What had been in the draft I had quaffed in the chamber of mystery? And why had the "Master" chosen me, out of all the other wretches of Yun Shatu's, for regeneration?

And who was this Master? Somehow the word sounded vaguely familiar—I sought laboriously to remember. Yes—I had heard it, lying half-waking in the bunks or on the floor—whispered sibilantly by Yun Shatu or by Hassim or by Yussef Ali, the Moor, muttered in their low-voiced conversation and mingled always with words I could not understand. Was not Yun Shatu, then, master of the Temple of Dreams?

I had thought and the other addicts thought that the withered Chinaman held undisputed sway over this drab kingdom and that Hassim and Yussef Ali were his servants. And the four China boys who roasted opium with Yun Shatu and Yar Khan the Afghan and Santiago the Haitian and Ganra Singh the renegade Sikh—all in the pay of Yun Shatu, we supposed—bound to the opium lord by bonds of gold or fear.

For Yun Shatu was a power in London's Chinatown and I had heard that his tentacles reached across the seas into high places of mighty and mysterious tongues. Was that Yun Shatu behind the lacquer screen? No; I knew the Chinaman's voice and besides I had seen him puttering about in the front of the Temple just as I went through the back door.

Another thought came to me. Often, lying half torpid, in the late hours of night or in the early grayness of dawn, I had seen men and women steal into the Temple, whose dress and bearing were strangely out of place and incongruous. Tall, erect men, often in evening dress, with their hats drawn low about their brows, and fine ladies, veiled, in silks and furs. Never two of them came together, but always they came separately and, hiding their features, hurried to the rear door, where they entered and presently came forth again, hours later sometimes.

Knowing that the lust for dope finds resting-place in high positions sometimes, I had never wondered overmuch, supposing that these were wealthy men and women of society who had fallen victims to the craving, and that somewhere in the back of the building there was a private chamber for such. Yet now I wondered—sometimes these persons had remained only a few moments—was it always opium for which they came, or did they, too, traverse that strange corridor and converse with the One behind the screen?

My mind dallied with the idea of a great specialist to whom came all classes of people to find surcease from the dope habit. Yet it was strange that such a one should select a dope-joint from which to work—strange, too, that the owner of that house should apparently look on him with so much reverence.

I gave it up as my head began to hurt with the unwonted effort of thinking, and shouted for food. Yussef Ali brought it to me on a tray, with a promptness which was surprising. More, he salaamed as he departed, leaving me to ruminate on the strange shift of my status in the Temple of Dreams.

I ate, wondering what the One of the screen wanted with me. Not for an instant did I suppose that his actions had been prompted by the reasons he pretended: the life of the underworld had taught me that none of its denizens leaned toward philanthropy. And underworld the chamber of mystery had been, in spite of its elaborate and bizarre nature. And where could it be located? How far had I walked along the corridor? I shrugged my shoulders, wondering if it were not all a hashish-induced dream; then my eye fell upon my hand—and the scorpion traced thereon.

"Muster all hands!" droned the sailor in the bunk. "All hands!"

To tell in detail of the next few days would be boresome to any who have not tasted the dire slavery of dope. I waited for the craving to strike me again—waited with sure sardonic hopelessness. All day, all night—another day—then the miracle was forced upon my doubting brain. Contrary to all theories and supposed facts of science and common sense the craving had left me as suddenly and completely as a bad dream!

At first I could not credit my senses but believed myself to be still in the grip of a dope nightmare. But it was true. From the time I quaffed the goblet in the room of mystery, I felt not the slightest desire for the stuff which had been life itself to me. This, I felt vaguely, was somehow unholy and certainly opposed to all rules of nature. If the dread being behind the screen had discovered the secret of breaking hashish's terrible power, what other monstrous secrets had he discovered and what unthinkable dominance was his? The suggestion of evil crawled serpent-like through my mind.

I remained at Yun Shatu's house, lounging in a bunk or on cushions spread upon the floor, eating and drinking at will, but now that I was becoming a normal man again, the atmosphere became most revolting to me and the sight of the wretches writhing in their dreams reminded me unpleasantly of what I myself had been, and it repelled, nauseated me.

So one day, when no one was watching me, I rose and went out on the street and walked along the waterfront. The air, burdened though it was with smoke and foul scents, filled my lungs with strange freshness and aroused new vigor in what had once been a powerful frame. I took new interest in the sounds of men living and working, and the sight of a vessel being unloaded at one of the wharfs actually thrilled me. The force of longshoremen was short, and presently I found myself heaving and lifting and carrying, and though the sweat coursed down my brow and my limbs trembled at the effort, I exulted in the thought that at last I was able to labor for myself again, no matter how low or drab the work might be. As I returned to the door of Yun Shatu's that evening—hideously weary but with the renewed feeling of manhood that comes of honest toil—Hassim met me at the door.

"You been where?" he demanded roughly.

"I've been working on the docks," I answered shortly.

"You don't need to work on docks," he snarled. "The Master got work for you."

He led the way, and again I traversed the dark stairs and the corridor under the earth. This time my faculties were alert and I decided that the passageway could not be over thirty or forty feet in length. Again I stood before the lacquer screen and again I heard the inhuman voice of living death.

"I can give you work," said the voice. "Are you willing to work for me?"

I quickly assented. After all, in spite of the fear which the voice inspired, I was deeply indebted to the owner.

"Good. Take these."

As I started toward the screen a sharp command halted me and Hassim stepped forward and, reaching behind, took what was offered. This was a bundle of pictures and papers, apparently.

"Study these," said the One behind the screen, "and learn all you can about the man portrayed thereby. Yun Shatu will give you money; buy yourself such clothes as seamen wear and take a room at the front of the Temple. At the end of two days, Hassim will bring you to me again. Go!"

The last impression I had, as the hidden door closed above me, was that the eyes of the idol, blinking through the everlasting smoke, leered mockingly at me.

The front of the Temple of Dreams consisted of rooms for rent, masking the true purpose of the building under the guise of a waterfront boarding-house. The police had made several visits to Yun Shatu but had never got any incriminating evidence against him.

So in one of these rooms I took up my abode and set to work studying the material given me.

The pictures were all of one man, a large man, not unlike me in build, and general facial outline, except that he wore a heavy beard and was inclined to blondness whereas I am dark. The name, as written on the accompanying papers, was Major Fairlan Morley, special commissioner to Natal and the Transvaal. This office and title were new to me and I wondered at the connection between an African commissioner and an opium house on the Thames waterfront.

The papers consisted of extensive data evidently copied from authentic sources and all dealing with Major Morley, and a number of private documents considerably illuminating on the major's private life.

An exhaustive description was given of the man's personal appearance and habits, some of which seemed very trivial to me. I wondered what the purpose could be, and how the One behind the screen had come in possession of papers of such intimate nature.

I could find no clue in answer to this question but bent all my energies to the task set out for me. I owed a deep debt of gratitude to the unknown man who required this of me and I was determined to repay him to the best of my ability. Nothing, at this time, suggested a snare to me.

CHAPTER FIVE
THE MAN ON THE COUCH

"What dam of lances sent thee forth
to jest at dawn with Death?"
—Kipling

At the expiration of two days, Hassim beckoned me as I stood in the opium room. I advanced with a springy, resilient tread, secure in the confidence that I had culled the Morley papers of all their worth. I was a new man; my mental swiftness and physical readiness surprised me—sometimes it seemed unnatural.

Hassim eyed me through narrowed lids and motioned me to follow, as usual. As we crossed the room, my gaze fell upon a man who lay on a couch close to the wall, smoking opium. There was nothing at all suspicious about his ragged, unkempt clothes, his dirty, bearded face or the blank stare, but my eyes, sharpened to an abnormal point, seemed to sense a certain incongruity in the clean-cut limbs which not even the slouchy garments could efface.

Hassim spoke impatiently and I turned away. We entered the rear room, and as he shut the door and turned to the table, it moved of itself and a figure bulked up through the hidden doorway. The Sikh, Ganra Singh, a lean sinister-eyed giant, emerged and proceeded to the door opening into the opium room, where he halted until we should have descended and closed the secret doorway.

Again I stood amid the billowing yellow smoke and listened to the hidden, voice.

"Do you think you know enough about Major Morley to impersonate him successfully?"

Startled, I answered, "No doubt I could, unless I met someone who was intimate with him."

"I will take care of that. Follow me closely. Tomorrow you sail on the first boat for Calais. There you will meet an agent of mine who will accost you the instant you step upon the wharfs, and give you further instructions. You will sail second class and avoid all conversation with strangers or anyone. Take the papers with you. The agent will aid you in making up and your masquerade will start in Calais. That is all. Go!"

I departed, my wonder growing. All this rigmarole evidently had a meaning, but one which I could not fathom. Back in the opium room Hassim bade me be seated on some cushions to await his return. To my question he snarled that he was going forth as he had been ordered, to buy me a ticket on the Channel boat. He departed and I sat down, leaning my back against the wall. As I ruminated, it seemed suddenly that eyes were fixed on me so intensely as to disturb my sub-mind. I glanced up quickly but no one seemed to be looking at me. The smoke drifted through the hot atmosphere as usual; Yussef Ali and the Chinese glided back and forth tending to the wants of the sleepers.

Suddenly the door to the rear room opened and a strange and hideous figure came haltingly out. Not all of those who found entrance to Yun Shatu's back room were aristocrats and society members. This was one of the exceptions, and one whom I remembered as having often entered and emerged therefrom—a tall, gaunt figure, shapeless and ragged wrappings and nondescript garments, face entirely hidden. Better that the face be hidden, I thought, for without doubt the wrapping concealed a grisly sight. The man was a leper, who had somehow managed to escape the attention of the public guardians and who was occasionally seen haunting the lower and more mysterious regions of East End—a mystery even to the lowest denizens of Limehouse.

Suddenly my supersensitive mind was aware of a swift tension in the air. The leper hobbled out the door, closed it behind him. My eyes instinctively sought the couch whereon lay the man who had aroused my suspicions earlier in the day. I could have sworn that cold steely eyes gleamed menacingly before they flickered shut. I crossed to the couch in one stride and bent over the prostrate man. Something about his face seemed unnatural—a healthy bronze seemed to underlie the pallor of complexion.

"Yun Shatu!" I shouted. "A spy is in the house!"

Things happened then with bewildering speed. The man on the couch with one tigerish movement leaped erect and a revolver gleamed in his hand. One sinewy arm flung me aside as I sought to grapple with him and a sharp decisive voice sounded over the babble which broke forth:

"You there! Halt! Halt!"

The pistol in the stranger's hand was leveled at the leper, who was making for the door in long strides!

All about was confusion; Yun Shatu was shrieking volubly in Chinese and the four China boys and Yussef Ali were rushing in from all sides, knives glittering in their hands.

All this I saw with unnatural clearness even as I marked the stranger's face. As the flying leper gave no evidence of halting, I saw the eyes harden to steely points of determination, sighting along the pistol barrel—the features set with the grim purpose of the slayer. The leper was almost to the outer door, but death would strike him down ere he could reach it.

And then, just as the finger of the stranger tightened on the trigger, I hurled myself forward and my right fist crashed against his chin. He went, down as though struck by a trip-hammer, the revolver exploding harmlessly in the air.

In that instant, with the blinding flare of light that sometimes comes to one, I knew that the leper was none other than the Man Behind the Screen!

I bent over the fallen man, who though not entirely senseless had been rendered temporarily helpless by that terrific blow. He was struggling dazedly to rise but I shoved him roughly down again and seizing the false beard he wore, tore it away. A lean bronzed face was revealed, the strong lines of which not even the artificial dirt and grease-paint could alter.

Yussef Ali leaned above him now, dagger in hand, eyes slits of murder. The brown sinewy hand went up—I caught the wrist.

"Not so fast, you black devil! What are you about to do?"

"This is John Gordon," he hissed, "the Master's greatest foe! He must die, curse you!"

John Gordon! The name was familiar somehow, and yet I did not seem to connect it with the London police nor account for the man's presence in Yun Shatu's dope-joint.

The false leper had vanished. Yun Shatu stood gazing at me as immobile as an idol, hands in his wide sleeves, and Yussef Ali stood back, muttering murderously and thumbing his dagger edge, as I led Gordon out of the opium room and through the innocent-appearing bar which lay between that room and the street.

Out in the street I said to him: "I have no idea as to who you are or what you are doing here, but you see what an unhealthful place it is for you. Hereafter be advised by me and stay away."

His only answer was a searching glance, and then he turned and walked swiftly though somewhat unsteadily up the street.

CHAPTER SIX

THE DREAM GIRL

"I have reached these lands but newly
From an ultimate dim Thule."
—Poe

Outside my room sounded a light footstep. The door-knob turned cautiously and slowly; the door opened. I sprang erect with a gasp. Red lips, half parted, dark eyes like limpid seas of wonder, a mass of shimmering hair—framed in my drab doorway stood the girl of my dreams!

She entered, and half turning with a sinuous motion, closed the door. I sprang forward, my hands outstretched, then halted as she put a finger to her lips.

"You must not talk loudly," she almost whispered; "*He* did not say I could not come; yet—"

Her voice was soft and musical, with just a touch of foreign accent which I found delightful. As for the girl herself, every intonation, every movement proclaimed the Orient. She was a fragrant breath from the East. From her night-black hair, piled high above her alabaster forehead, to her little feet, encased in high-heeled pointed slippers, she portrayed the highest ideal of Asiatic loveliness—an effect which was heightened rather than lessened by the English blouse and skirt which she wore.

"You are beautiful!" I said dazedly. "Who are you?"

"I am Zuleika," she answered with a shy smile. "I—I am glad you like me. I am glad you no longer dream hashish dreams."

Strange that so small a thing should set my heart to leaping wildly!

"I owe it all to you, Zuleika," I said huskily. "Had not I dreamed of you every hour since you first lifted me from the gutter, I had lacked the power of even hoping to be freed from my curse."

She blushed prettily and intertwined her white fingers as if in nervousness.

"You leave England tomorrow?" she said suddenly.

"Yes. Hassim has not returned with my ticket—" I hesitated suddenly, remembering the command of silence.

"Yes, I know, I know!" she whispered swiftly, her eyes widening. "And John Gordon has been here! He saw you!"

"Yes!"

She came close to me with a quick lithe movement.

"You are to impersonate some man! Listen, while you are doing this, you must not ever let Gordon see you! He would know you, no matter what your disguise! He is a terrible man!"

"I don't understand," I said, completely bewildered. "How did the Master break me of my hashish craving? Who is this Gordon and why did he come here? Why does the Master go disguised as a leper—and who is he? Above all, why am I to impersonate a man I never saw or heard of?"

"I cannot—I dare not tell you!" she whispered, her face paling. "I—"

Somewhere in the house sounded the faint tones of a Chinese gong. The girl started like a frightened gazelle.

"I must go! *He* summons me!"

She opened the door, darted through, halted a moment to electrify me with her passionate exclamation: "Oh, be careful, be very careful, sahib!" Then she was gone.

CHAPTER SEVEN
THE MAN OF THE SKULL

"What the hammer? what the chain?
In what furnace was thy brain?
What the anvil? what dread grasp
Dare its deadly terrors clasp?"
—Blake

A while after my beautiful and mysterious visitor had left, I sat in meditation. I believed that I had at last stumbled on to an explanation of a part of the enigma, at any rate. This was the conclusion I had reached: Yun Shatu, the opium lord, was simply the agent or servant of some organization or individual whose work was on a far larger scale than merely supplying dope addicts in the Temple of Dreams. This man or these men needed co-workers among all classes of people; in other words, I was being let in with a group of opium smugglers on a gigantic scale. Gordon no doubt had been investigating the case, and his presence alone showed that it was no ordinary one, for I knew that he held a high position with the English government, though just what, I did not know.

Opium or not, I determined to carry out my obligation to the Master. My moral sense had been blunted by the dark ways I had traveled, and the thought of despicable crime did not enter my head. I was indeed hardened.

More, the mere debt of gratitude was now increased a thousandfold, by the thought of the girl.

To the Master I owed it that I was still able to stand up on my feet and look into her clear eyes as a man should. So if he wished my services as a smuggler of dope, he should have them. No doubt I was to impersonate some man so high in governmental esteem that the usual actions of the customs officers would be deemed unnecessary; was I to bring some rare dream-producer into England somehow?

These thoughts were in my mind as I went downstairs, but ever back of them hovered other and more alluring suppositions—what was the reason for the girl, here in this vile dive—a rose in a garbage-heap—and who was she?

As I entered the outer bar, Hassim came in, his brows set in a dark scowl of anger, and, I believed, fear. He carried a newspaper in his hand, folded.

"I told you to wait in opium room," he snarled.

"You were gone so long that I went up to my room. Have you the ticket?"

He merely grunted and pushed on past me into the opium room; and standing at the door I saw him cross the floor and disappear into the rear room. I stood there, my bewilderment increasing. For as Hassim had brushed past me, I had noted an item on the face of the paper, against which his black thumb was tightly pressed as if to mark that special column of news.

And with the unnatural celerity of action and judgment which seemed to be mine those days, I had in that fleeting instant read the following:

AFRICAN SPECIAL COMMISSIONER
FOUND MURDERED!

The body of Major Fairlan Morley was yesterday discovered in a rotting ship's hold at Bordeaux...

No more I saw of the details, but that alone was enough to make me think!

The affair seemed to be taking, on an ugly aspect. Yet—

Another day passed. To my inquiries, Hassim snarled that the plans had been changed and I was not to go to France. Then, late in the evening, he came to bid me once more to the room of mystery.

I stood before the lacquer screen, the yellow smoke acrid in my nostrils, the woven dragons writhing along the tapestries, the palm-trees rearing thick and oppressive.

"A change has come in our plans," said the voice. "You will not sail as was decided before. But I have other work that you may do. Mayhap this will be more to your type of usefulness for I admit you have somewhat disappointed me in regard to subtlety. You interfered the other day in such manner as will no doubt cause me great inconvenience in the future."

I said nothing, but a feeling of resentment began to stir in me.

"Even after the assurance of one of my most trusted servants," the toneless voice continued, with no mark of any emotion save a slightly rising note, "you insisted on releasing my most deadly enemy. Be more circumspect in the future."

"I saved your life!" I said angrily.

"And for that reason alone I overlook your mistake—this time!"

A slow fury suddenly surged up inside of me.

"This time! Make the best of it this time, for I assure you there will be no next time. I owe you a greater debt than I can ever hope to pay, but that does not make me your slave. I have saved your life—the debt is as near paid as a man can pay it. Go your way and I go mine!"

A low, hideous laugh answered me, like a reptilian hiss.

"You fool! You will pay with your whole life's toil! You say you are not my slave? I say you are—just as black Hassim there beside you is my slave—just as the girl Zuleika is my slave, who has bewitched you with her wonderful beauty."

These words sent a wave of hot blood to my brain and I was conscious of a flood of fury which completely engulfed my reason for a second. Just as all my moods and senses seemed sharpened and exaggerated those days, so now this burst of rage transcended every moment of anger I had ever had in my life before.

"Hell's fiends!" I shrieked. "You devil—who are you and what is your hold on me? I'll see you or die!"

Hassim sprang at me, but I hurled him backward and with one stride reached the screen and flung it aside with an incredible effort of strength. Then I shrank back, hands outflung, shrieking. A tall, gaunt figure stood before me, a figure arrayed grotesquely in a silk brocaded gown which fell stiffly to the floor.

From the sleeves of this gown protruded hands which filled me with crawling horror—long, predatory hands, with thin bony fingers and curved talons—withered skin of a parchment brownish-yellow, like the hands of a man long dead.

The hands—but, oh God, the face! A skull to which no vestige of flesh seemed to remain but on which taut brownish-yellow skin grew fast, etching out every detail of that terrible death's-head. The forehead was high and in a way magnificent, but the head was curiously narrow through the temples, and from under penthouse brows great eyes glimmered like pools of yellow fire. The nose was high-bridged and very thin; the mouth was a mere colorless gash between thin, cruel lips. A long, bony neck supported this frightful vision and completed the effect of a reptilian demon from some medieval hell.

I was face to face with the skull-faced man of my dreams!

CHAPTER EIGHT
BLACK WISDOM

The terrible spectacle drove for the instant all thoughts of rebellion from my mind. My very blood froze in my veins and I stood motionless. I heard Hassim laugh grimly behind me. The eyes in the cadaverous face blazed fiendishly at me and I blanched from the concentrated satanic fury I saw in them.

Then the horror laughed sibilantly, wickedly.

"I do you a great honor, Mr. Costigan; among a very few, even of my own servants, you may say that you saw my face and lived. I think you will be more useful to me living than dead."

I was silent, completely unnerved. It was difficult to believe that this man lived, for his appearance certainly belied the thought. He seemed horribly like a mummy. Yet his lips moved when he spoke and his eyes flamed with hideous life.

"You will do as I say," he said abruptly, and his voice, had taken on a note of command. "You doubtless know, or know of, Sir Haldred Frenton?"

"Yes."

Every man of culture in Europe and America was familiar with the travel books of Sir Haldred Frenton, author and soldier of fortune.

"You will go to Sir Haldred's estate tonight—"

"Yes?"

"*And kill him!*"

I staggered, literally. This order was incredible—unspeakable! I had sunk low, low enough to smuggle opium, but to deliberately murder a man I had never seen, a man noted for his kindly deeds!

That was too monstrous, I thought, even to contemplate.

"You do not refuse?"

The tone was as loathing and as mocking as the hiss of a serpent.

"Refuse?" I screamed, finding my voice at last. "Refuse? You incarnate devil! Of course I refuse! You—"

Something in the cold assurance of his manner halted me—froze me into apprehensive silence.

"You fool!" he said calmly. "I broke the hashish chains—do you know how? Four minutes from now you will know and curse the day you were born! Have you not thought it strange, the swiftness of brain, the resilience of body—the brain that should be rusty and slow, the body that should be weak and sluggish from years of abuse? That blow that felled John Gordon—have you not wondered at its might? The ease with which you mastered Major Morley's records—have you not wondered at that? You fool, you are bound to me by chains of steel and blood and fire! I have kept you alive and sane—I alone. Each day the life-saving elixir has been given you in your wine. You could not live and keep your reason without it. And I and only I know its secret!"

He glanced at a queer timepiece which stood on a table at his elbow.

"This time I had Yun Shatu leave the elixir out—I anticipated rebellion. The time is near—ha, it strikes!"

Something else he said, but I did not hear. I did not see, nor did I feel in the human sense of the word. I was writhing at his feet, screaming and gibbering in the flames of such hells as men have never dreamed of.

Aye, I knew now! He had simply given me a dope so much stronger that it drowned the hashish. My unnatural ability was explainable now—I had simply been acting under the stimulus of something which combined all the hells in its make-up, which stimulated, something like heroin, but whose effect was unnoticed by the victim. What it was, I had no idea, nor did I believe anyone knew save that hellish being who stood watching me with grim amusement. But it had held my brain together, instilling into my system a need for it, and now my frightful craving tore my soul asunder.

Never, in my moments of worst shell-shock or my moments of hashish craving, have I ever experienced anything like that, I burned with the heat of a thousand hells and froze with an iciness that was colder than any ice, a hundred times, I swept down to the deepest pits of torture and up to the highest crags of torment—a million yelling devils hemmed me in, shrieking and stabbing. Bone by bone, vein by vein, cell by cell I felt my body disintegrate and fly in bloody atoms all over the universe—and each separate cell was an entire system of quivering, screaming nerves. And they gathered from far voids and reunited with a greater torment.

Through the fiery bloody mists I heard my own voice screaming, a monotonous yammering.

Then, with distended eyes I saw a golden goblet, held by a clawlike hand, swim into view—a goblet filled with a clear amber liquid.

With a bestial screech I seized it with both hands, being dimly aware that the metal stem gave beneath my fingers and brought the brim to my lips. I drank in frenzied haste, the liquid slopping down onto my breast.

CHAPTER NINE
KATHULOS OF EGYPT

"Night shall be thrice night over you.
And Heaven an iron cope."
—Chesterton

The Skull-faced One stood watching me critically as I sat panting on a couch, completely exhausted. He held in his hand the goblet and surveyed the golden stem, which was crushed out of all shape. This my maniac fingers had done in the instant of drinking.

"Superhuman strength, even for a man in your condition," he said with sort of creaky pedantry. "I doubt if even Hassim here could equal it. Are you ready for your instructions now?"

I nodded, wordless. Already the hellish strength of the elixir was flowing through my veins, renewing my burnt-out force. I wondered how long a man could live as I lived being constantly burned out and artificially rebuilt.

"You will be given a disguise and will go alone to the Frenton estate. No one suspects any design against Sir Haldred and your entrance into the estate and the house itself should be a matter of comparative ease. You will not don the disguise—which will be of unique nature—until you are ready to enter the estate. You will then proceed to Sir Haldred's room and kill him, breaking his neck with your bare hands—this is essential—"

The voice droned on, giving its ghastly orders in a frightfully casual and matter-of-fact way. The cold sweat beaded my brow.

"You will then leave the estate, taking care to leave the imprint of your hand somewhere plainly visible, and the automobile, which will be waiting for you at some safe place near by, will bring you back here, you having first removed the disguise. I have, in case of later complications, any amount of men who will swear that you spent the entire night in the Temple of Dreams and never left it. But there must be no detection! Go warily and perform your task surely, for you know the alternative."

I did not return to the opium house but was taken through winding corridors, hung with heavy tapestries, to a small room containing only an Oriental couch. Hassim gave me to understand that I was to remain there until after nightfall and then left me. The door was closed but I made no effort to discover if it was locked. The Skull-faced Master held me with stronger shackles than locks and bolts.

Seated upon the couch in the bizarre setting of a chamber which might have been a room in an Indian zenana, I faced fact squarely and fought out my battle. There was still in me some trace of manhood left—more than the fiend had reckoned, and added to this were black despair and desperation. I chose and determined on my only course.

Suddenly the door opened softly. Some intuition told me whom to expect, nor was I disappointed. Zuleika stood, a glorious vision before me—a vision which mocked me, made blacker my despair and yet thrilled me with wild yearning and reasonless joy.

She bore a tray of food which she set beside me, and then she seated herself on the couch, her large eyes fixed upon my face. A flower in a serpent den she was, and the beauty of her look, took hold of my heart.

"Steephen!" she whispered and I thrilled as she spoke my name for the first time.

Her luminous eyes suddenly shone with tears and she laid her little hand on my arm. I seized it in both my rough hands.

"They have set you a task which you fear and hate!" she faltered.

"Aye!" I almost laughed. "But I'll fool them yet! Zuleika, tell me—what is the meaning of all this?"

She glanced fearfully around her.

"I do not know all." She hesitated. "Your plight is all my fault but I—I hoped—Steephen, I have watched you every time you came to Yun Shatu's for months. You did not see me but I saw you, and I saw in you, not the broken sot your rags proclaimed, but a wounded soul, a soul bruised terribly on the ramparts of life. And from my heart I pitied you. Then when Hassim abused you that day"—again tears started to her eyes—"I could not bear it and I knew how you suffered for want of hashish. So I paid Yun Shatu, and going to the Master I—I—oh, you will hate me for this!" she sobbed.

"No—no—never—"

"I told him that you were a man who might be of use to him and begged him to have Yun Shatu supply you with what you needed. He had already noticed you, for his is the eye of the slaver and all the world is his slave market! So he bade Yun Shatu do as I asked: and now—better if you had remained as you were, my friend."

"No! No!" I exclaimed. "I have known a few days of regeneration, even if it was false! I have stood before you as a man, and that is worth all else!"

And all that I felt for her must have looked forth from my eyes, for she dropped hers and flushed. Ask me not how love comes to a man: but I knew that I loved Zuleika—had loved this mysterious Oriental girl since first I saw her—and somehow I felt that she, in a measure, returned my affection. This realization made blacker and more barren the road I had chosen, yet—for pure love must ever strengthen a man—it nerved me to do what I must do.

"Zuleika," I said, speaking hurriedly, "time flies and there are things I must learn: tell me—who are you and why do you remain in this den of Hades?"

"I am Zuleika—that is all I know. I am Circassian by blood and birth. When I was very little I was captured in a Turkish raid and raised in a Stamboul harem. While I was yet too young to marry, my master gave me as a present to—to *Him.*"

"And who is he—this skull-faced man?"

"He is Kathulos of Egypt—that is all I know. My master."

"An Egyptian? Then what is he doing in London—why all this mystery?"

She intertwined her fingers nervously.

"Steephen, please speak lower; always there is someone listening everywhere. I do not know who the Master is or why he is here or why he does these things; I swear by Allah! If I knew I would tell you. Sometimes distinguished-looking men come here to the room where the Master receives them—not the room where you saw him—and he makes me dance before them and afterward flirt with them a little. And always I must repeat exactly what they say to me. That is what I must always do—in Turkey, in the Barbary States, in Egypt, in France and in England. The Master taught me French and English and educated me in many ways himself. He is the greatest sorcerer in all the world and knows all ancient magic and everything."

"Zuleika," I said, "my race is soon run, but let me get you out of this—come with me and I swear I'll get you away from this fiend!"

She shuddered and hid her face.

"No, no, I cannot!"

"Zuleika," I asked gently, "what hold has he over you, child—dope also?"

"No, no!" she whimpered. "I do not know—I do not know—but I cannot—I never can escape him!"

I sat, baffled for a few moments; then I asked, "Zuleika, where are we right now?"

"This building is a deserted storehouse back of the Temple of Silence."

"I thought so. What is in the chests in the tunnel?"

"I do not know."

Then suddenly she began weeping softly. "You too, a slave, like me—you who are so strong and kind—oh, Steephen, I cannot bear it!"

I smiled. "Lean closer, Zuleika, and I will tell you how I am going to fool this Kathulos."

She glanced apprehensively at the door.

"You must speak low. I will lie in your arms and while you pretend to caress me, whisper your words to me."

She glided into my embrace, and there on the dragon-worked couch in that house of horror I first knew the glory of Zuleika's slender form nestling in my arms—of Zuleika's soft cheek pressing my breast. The fragrance of her was in my nostrils, her hair in my eyes, and my senses reeled. Then with my lips hidden by her silky hair I whispered, swiftly:

"I am going to warn Sir Haldred Frenton—then to find John Gordon and tell him of this den. I will lead the police here and you must watch closely and be ready to hide from *Him*—until we can break through and kill or capture him. Then you will be free."

"But you!" she gasped, paling. "You must have the elixir, and only he—"

"I have a way of outdoing him, child," I answered.

She went pitifully white and her woman's intuition sprang to the right conclusion.

"You are going to kill yourself!"

And much as it hurt me to see her emotion, I yet felt a torturing thrill that she should feel so on my account. Her arms tightened about my neck.

"Don't, Steephen!" she begged. "It is better to live, even—"

"No, not at that price. Better to go out clean while I have the manhood left."

She stared at me wildly for an instant; then, pressing her red lips suddenly to mine, she sprang up and fled from the room. Strange, strange are the ways of love. Two stranded ships on the shores of life, we had drifted inevitably together, and though no word of love had passed between us, we knew each other's heart. Through grime and rags, and through accouterments of the slave, we knew each other's heart and from the first loved as naturally and as purely as it was intended from the beginning of Time.

The beginning of life now and the end for me, for as soon as I had completed my task, ere I felt again the torments of my curse, love and life and beauty and torture should be blotted out together in the stark finality of a pistol ball scattering my rotting brain. Better a clean death than—

The door opened again and Yussef Ali entered.

"The hour arrives for departure," he said briefly. "Rise and follow."

I had no idea, of course, as to the time. No window opened from the room I occupied—I had seen no outer window whatever. The rooms were lighted by tapers in censers swinging from the ceiling. As I rose the slim young Moor slanted a sinister glance in my direction.

"This lies between you and me," he said sibilantly. "Servants of the same Master we—but this concerns ourselves alone. Keep your distance from Zuleika—the Master has promised her to me in the days of the empire."

My eyes narrowed to slits as I looked into the frowning, handsome face of the Oriental, and such hate surged up in me as I have seldom known. My fingers involuntarily opened and closed, and the Moor, marking the action, stepped back, hand in his girdle.

"Not now—there is work for us both—later perhaps"; then in a sudden cold gust of hatred, "Swine! Ape-man! When the Master is finished with you, I shall quench my dagger in your heart!"

I laughed grimly.

"Make it soon, desert-snake, or I'll crush your spine between my hands."

CHAPTER TEN
THE DARK HOUSE

"Against all man-made shackles and
a man-made Hell—
Alone—at last—unaided—I rebel!"
—Mundy

I followed Yussef Ali along the winding hallways, down the steps—Kathulos was not in the idol-room—and along the tunnel. Then through the rooms of the Temple of Dreams and out into the street, where the street lamps gleamed drearily through the fogs and a slight drizzle. Across the street stood an automobile, curtains closely drawn.

"That is yours," said Hassim, who had joined us. "Saunter across natural-like. Don't act suspicious. The place may be watched. The driver knows what to do."

Then he and Yussef Ali drifted back into the bar and I took a single step toward the curb.

"Steephen!"

A voice that made my heart leap spoke my name! A white hand beckoned from the shadows of the doorway. I stepped quickly there.

"Zuleika!"

"Shh!"

She clutched my arm, slipped something into my hand; I made out vaguely a small flask of gold.

"Hide this quick!" came her urgent whisper.

"Don't come back, go away and hide. This is full of elixir—I will try to get you some more before that is all gone. You must find a way of communicating with me."

"Yes, but how did you get this?" I asked amazedly.

"I stole it from the Master! Now please, I must go before he misses me."

And she sprang back into the doorway and vanished. I stood undecided. I was sure that she had risked nothing less than her life in doing this and I was torn by the fear of what Kathulos might do to her, were the theft discovered. But to return to the house of mystery would certainly invite suspicion, and I might carry out my plan and strike back before the Skull-faced One learned of his slave's duplicity.

So I crossed the street to the waiting automobile. The driver was a Negro whom I had never seen before, a lanky man of medium height. I stared hard at him, wondering how much he had seen. He gave no evidence of having seen anything, and I decided that even if he had noticed me step back into the shadows he could not have seen what passed there nor have been able to recognize the girl.

He merely nodded as I climbed in the back seat, and a moment later we were speeding away down the deserted and fog-haunted streets. A bundle beside me I concluded to be the disguise mentioned by the Egyptian.

To recapture the sensations I experienced as I rode through the rainy, misty night would be impossible. I felt as if I were already dead and the bare and dreary streets about me were the roads of death over which my ghost had been doomed to roam forever. A torturing joy was in my heart, and bleak despair—the despair of a doomed man. Not that death itself was so repellent—a dope victim dies too many deaths to shrink from the last—but it was hard to go out just as love had entered my barren life. And I was still young.

A sardonic smile crossed my lips—they were young, too, the men who died beside me in No Man's Land. I drew back my sleeve and clenched my fists, tensing my muscles. There was no surplus weight on my frame, and much of the firm flesh had wasted away, but the cords of the great biceps still stood out like knots of iron, seeming to indicate massive strength. But I knew my might was false, that in reality I was a broken husk of a man, animated by the artificial fire of the elixir, without which a frail girl might topple me over.

The automobile came to a halt among some trees. We were on the outskirts of an exclusive suburb and the hour was past midnight. Through the trees I saw a large house looming darkly against the distant flares of night-time London.

"This is where I wait," said the Negro. "No one can see the automobile from the road or from the house."

Holding a match so its light could not be detected outside the car, I examined the "disguise" and was hard put to restrain an insane laugh. The disguise was the complete hide of a gorilla! Gathering the bundle under my arm I trudged toward the wall which surrounded the Frenton estate. A few steps and the trees where the Negro hid with the car merged into one dark mass. I did not believe he could see me, but for safety's sake, I made, not for the high iron gate at the front but for the wall at the side where there was no gate.

No light showed in the house. Sir Haldred was a bachelor and I was sure that the servants were all in bed long ago. I negotiated the wall with ease and stole across the dark lawn to a side door, still carrying the grisly "disguise" under my arm. The door was locked, as I anticipated, and I did not wish to arouse anyone until I was safely in the house, where the sound of voices would not carry to one who might have followed me. I took hold of the knob with both hands, and exerting slowly the inhuman strength that was mine, began to twist. The shaft turned in my hands and the lock within shattered suddenly, with a noise that was like the crash of a cannon in the stillness. An instant more and I was inside and had closed the door behind me.

I took a single stride in the darkness in the direction I believed the stair to be, then halted as a beam of light flashed into my face. At the side of the beam I caught the glimmer of a pistol muzzle. Beyond, a lean shadowy, face floated.

"Stand where you are and put up your hands!"

I lifted my hands, allowing the bundle to slip to the floor. I had heard that voice only once but I recognized it—knew instantly that the man who held that light was John Gordon.

"How many are with you?"

His voice was sharp, commanding.

"I am alone," I answered. "Take me into a room where a light cannot be seen from the outside and, I'll tell you some things you want to know."

He was silent; then, bidding me take up the bundle I had dropped, he stepped to one side and motioned me to precede him into the next room. There he directed me to a stairway and at the top landing opened a door and switched on lights.

I found myself in a room whose curtains were closely drawn. During this journey Gordon's alertness had not relaxed, and now he stood still covering me with his revolver. Clad in conventional garments, he stood revealed a tall, leanly but powerfully built man, taller than I but not so heavy—with steel-gray eyes and clean-cut features. Something about the man attracted me, even as I noted a bruise on his jawbone where my fist had struck in our last meeting.

"I cannot believe," he said crisply, "that this apparent clumsiness and lack of subtlety is real. Doubtless you have your own reasons for wishing me to be in a secluded room at this time, but Sir Haldred is efficiently protected even now. Stand still."

Muzzle pressed against my chest, he ran his hand over my garments for concealed weapons, seeming slightly surprised when he found none.

"Still," he murmured as if to himself, "a man who can burst an iron lock with his bare hands has scant need of weapons."

"You are wasting valuable time," I said impatiently. "I was sent here tonight to kill Sir Haldred Frenton—"

"By whom?" the question was shot at me.

"By the man who sometimes goes disguised as a leper."

He nodded, a gleam in his scintillant eyes.

"My suspicions were correct, then."

"Doubtless. Listen to me closely—do you desire the death or arrest of that man?"

Gordon laughed grimly.

"To one who wears the mark of the scorpion on his hand, my answer would be superfluous."

"Then follow my directions and your wish shall be granted."

His eyes narrowed suspiciously.

"So that was the meaning of this open entry and non-resistance," he said slowly. "Does the dope which dilates your eyeballs so warp your mind that you think to lead me into ambush?"

I pressed my hands against my temples. Time was racing and every moment was precious—how could I convince this man of my honesty?

"Listen; my name is Stephen Costigan of America. I was a frequenter of Yun Shatu's dive and a hashish addict—as you have guessed, but just now a slave of stronger dope. By virtue of this slavery, the man you know as a false leper, whom Yun Shatu and his friends call 'Master', gained dominance over me and sent me here to murder Sir Haldred—why, God only knows. But I have gained a space of respite by coming into possession of some of this dope which I must have in order to live, and I fear and hate this Master. Listen to me and I swear, by all things holy and unholy, that before the sun rises the false leper shall be in your power!"

I could tell that Gordon was impressed in spite of himself.

"Speak fast!" he rapped.

Still I could sense his disbelief and a wave of futility swept over me.

"If you will not act with me," I said, "let me go and somehow I'll find a way to get to the Master and kill him. My time is short—my hours are numbered and my vengeance is yet to be realized."

"Let me hear your plan, and talk fast," Gordon answered.

"It is simple enough. I will return to the Master's lair and tell him I have accomplished that which he sent me to do. You must follow closely with your men and while I engage the Master in conversation surround the house. Then, at the signal, break in and kill or seize him."

Gordon frowned. "Where is this house?"

"The warehouse back of Yun Shatu's has been converted into a veritable Oriental palace."

"The warehouse!" he exclaimed. "How can that be? I had thought of that first, but I have carefully examined it from without. The widows are closely barred and spiders have built webs across them. The doors are nailed fast on the outside and the seals that mark the warehouse as deserted were never broken."

"They tunneled up from beneath," I answered. "The Temple of Dreams is directly connected with the warehouse. A tunnel connects the building, with one door in the rear room of Yun Shatu's and the other in the idol-room of the warehouse."

"I have been in Yun Shatu's back room and found no such door."

"The table rests upon it. You noted the heavy table in the center of the room? Had you turned it around, the secret door would have opened in the floor. Now this is my plan: I will go in through the Temple of Dreams and meet the Master in the idol-room. You will have men secretly stationed in front of the warehouse and others upon the other street, in front of the Temple of Dreams.

"Yun Shatu's building, as you know, faces the waterfront, while the warehouse, fronting the opposite direction, faces a narrow street running parallel with the river. At the signal let the men in this street break open the front of the warehouse and rush in, while simultaneously those in front of Yun Shatu's make an invasion through the Temple of Dreams. Let these make for the rear room, shooting without mercy any who may seek to deter them, and there open the secret door as I have said.

"There being, to the best of my knowledge, no other exit from the Master's lair, he and his servants will necessarily seek to make their escape through the tunnel. Thus we will have them on both sides."

"This may be a snare," he muttered, "or an attempt to draw me away from Sir Haldred, but—"

I held my breath.

"I am a gambler by nature," he said slowly. "I am going to follow what you Americans call a hunch—but God help you if you are lying to me!"

I sprang erect.

"Thank God! Now aid me with this suit, for I must be wearing it when I return to the automobile waiting for me."

His eyes narrowed as I shook out the horrible masquerade and prepared to don it.

"This shows, as always, the touch of the master hand. You were doubtless instructed to leave marks of your hands, encased in those hideous gauntlets?"

"Yes—though I have no idea why."

"I think I have—the Master is famed for leaving no real clues to mark his crimes—a great ape escaped from a neighboring zoo earlier in the evening and it seems too obvious for mere chance, in the light of this disguise. The ape would have gotten the blame of Sir Haldred's death."

The thing was easily gotten into and the illusion of reality it created was so perfect as to draw a shudder from me as I viewed myself in a mirror.

"It is now two o'clock," said Gordon. "Allowing for the time it will take you to get back to Limehouse and the time it will take me to get my men stationed, I promise you that at half-past four the house will be closely surrounded. Give me a start—wait here until I have left this house, so I will arrive at least as soon as you."

"Good!" I impulsively grasped his hand. "There will doubtless be a girl there who is in no way implicated with the Master's evil doings, but only a victim of circumstances such as I have been. Deal gently with her."

"It shall be done. What signal shall I look for?"

"I have no way of signaling for you and I doubt if any sound in the house could be heard on the street. Let your men make their raid on the stroke of five."

I turned to go.

"A man is waiting for you with a car, I take it? Is he likely to suspect anything?"

"I have a way of finding out, and if he does," I replied grimly, "I will return alone to the Temple of Dreams."

CHAPTER ELEVEN

FOUR THIRTY-FOUR

"Doubting, dreaming dreams no
mortal ever dared to dream before."

The door closed softly behind me, the great dark house looming up more starkly than ever. Stooping, I crossed the wet lawn at a run, a grotesque and unholy figure, I doubt not, since any man had at a glance sworn me to be not a man but a giant ape.

So craftily had the Master devised!

I clambered the wall, dropped to the earth beyond and made my way through the darkness and the drizzle to the group of trees which masked the automobile.

The Negro driver leaned out of the front seat.

I was breathing hard and sought in various ways to simulate the actions of a man who has just murdered in cold blood and fled the scene of his crime.

"You heard nothing, no sound, no scream?" I hissed, gripping his arm.

"No noise except a slight crash when you first went in," he answered. "You did a good job—nobody passing along the road could have suspected anything."

"Have you remained in the car all the time?" I asked. And when he replied that he had, I seized his ankle and ran my hand over the soles of his shoe; it was perfectly dry, as was the cuff of his trouser leg. Satisfied, I climbed into the back seat. Had he taken a step on the earth, shoe and garment would have showed it by the telltale dampness.

I ordered him to refrain from starting the engine until I had removed the apeskin, and then we sped through the night and I fell victim to doubts and uncertainties. Why should Gordon put any trust in the word of a stranger and a former ally of the Master's? Would he not put my tale down as the ravings of a dope-crazed addict, or a lie to ensnare or befool him?

Still, if he had not believed me, why had he let me go?

I could but trust. At any rate, what Gordon did or did not do would scarcely affect my fortunes ultimately, even though Zuleika had furnished me with that which would merely extend the number of my days. My thoughts centered on her, and more than my hope of vengeance on Kathulos was the hope that Gordon might be able to save her from the clutches of the fiend. At any rate, I thought grimly if Gordon failed me, I still had my hands and if I might lay them upon the bony frame of the Skull-faced One—

Abruptly I found myself thinking of Yussef Ali and his strange words, the import of which just occurred to me:

"*The Master, has promised her to me in the days of the empire!*"

The days of the empire—what could that mean?

The automobile at last drew up in front of the building which hid the Temple of Silence—now dark and still. The ride had seemed interminable and as I dismounted I glanced at the timepiece on the dashboard of the car. My heart leaped—it was four thirty-four, and unless my eyes tricked me, I saw a movement in the shadows across the street, out of the flare of the street lamp. At this time of night it could mean only one of two things—some menial of the Master watching for my return or else Gordon had kept his word. The Negro drove away and I opened the door, crossed the deserted bar and entered the opium room. The bunks and the floor were littered with the dreamers, for such places as these knew nothing of day or night as normal people know, but all lay deep in that well-known sottish slumber.

The lamps glimmered through the smoke and a silence hung mistily over all.

CHAPTER TWELVE

THE STROKE OF FIVE

"He saw gigantic tracks of death,
And many a shape of doom."
—Chesterton

Two of the China boys squatted among the smudge fires, staring at me unwinkingly as I threaded my way among the recumbent bodies and made my way to the rear door. For the first time I traversed the corridor alone and found time to wonder again as to the contents of the strange chests which lined the walls.

Four raps on the under side of the floor, and a moment later I stood in the idol-room. I gasped in amazement—the fact that across a table from me sat Kathulos in all his horror was not the cause of my exclamation. Except for the table, the chair on which the Skull-face sat and the altar—now bare of incense—the room was perfectly bare! Drab, unlovely, the unused warehouse met my gaze instead of the costly tapestries I had become accustomed to. The palms, the idol, the lacquered screens—all were gone.

"Ah, Mr. Costigan, you are wondering, no doubt."

The dead voice of the Master broke in on my thoughts. His serpent eyes glittered balefully. The long yellow fingers-twined sinuously upon the table.

"You thought me to be a trusting fool, no doubt!" he rapped suddenly. "Did you think I would not have you followed? You fool, Yussef Ali was at your heels every moment!"

An instant I stood speechless, frozen by the crash of these words against my brain; then as their import sank home, I launched myself forward with a roar. At the same instant, before my clutching fingers could close on the mocking horror on the other side of the table, men rushed from every side. I whirled, and with the clarity of hate, from the swirl of savage faces I singled out Yussef Ali, and crashed my right fist against his temple with every ounce of my strength. Even as he dropped, Hassim struck me to my knees and a Chinaman flung a man-net over my shoulders. I heaved erect, bursting the stout cords as if they were strings, and then a blackjack in the hands of Ganra Singh stretched me stunned and bleeding on the floor.

Lean sinewy hands seized and bound me with cords that cut cruelly into my flesh. Emerging from the mists of semi-unconsciousness, I found myself lying on the altar with the masked Kathulos towering over me like a gaunt ivory tower. About in a semicircle stood Ganra Singh, Yar Khan, Yun Shatu and several others whom I knew as frequenters of the Temple of Dreams. Beyond them—and the sight cut me to the heart—I saw Zuleika crouching in a doorway, her face white and her hands pressed against her cheeks, in an attitude of abject terror.

"I did not fully trust you," said Kathulos sibilantly, "so I sent Yussuf Ali to follow you. He reached the group of trees before you and, following you into the estate, heard your very interesting conversation with John Gordon—for he scaled the house-wall like a cat and clung to the window-ledge! Your driver delayed purposely so as to give Yussuf Ali plenty of time to get back—I have decided to change my abode anyway. My furnishings are already on their way to another house—and as soon as we have disposed of the traitor—you—we shall depart also, leaving a little surprise for your friend Gordon when he arrives at five-thirty."

My heart gave a sudden leap of hope. Yussef Ali had misunderstood, and Kathulos lingered here in false security while the London detective force had already silently surrounded the house. Over my shoulder I saw Zuleika vanish from the door.

I eyed Kathulos, absolutely unaware of what he was saying. It was not long until five—if he dallied longer—then I froze as the Egyptian spoke a word and Li Kung, a gaunt, cadaverous Chinaman, stepped from the silent semicircle and drew from his sleeve a long thin dagger. My eyes sought the time-piece that still rested on the table and my heart sank. It was still ten minutes until five. My death did not matter so much since it simply hastened the inevitable, but in my mind's eye I could see Kathulos and his murderers escaping while the police awaited the stroke of five.

The Skull-face halted in some harangue, and stood in a listening attitude. I believe his uncanny intuition warned him of danger. He spoke a quick staccato command to Li Kung and the Chinaman sprang forward, dagger lifted above my breast.

The air was suddenly supercharged with dynamic tension. The keen dagger-point hovered high above me—loud and clear sounded the skirl of a police whistle and on the heels of the sound there came a terrific crash from the front of the warehouse!

Kathulos leaped into frenzied activity. Hissing orders like a cat spitting, he sprang for the hidden door and the rest followed him. Things happened with the speed of a nightmare. Li Kung had followed the rest, but Kathulos flung a command over his shoulder and the Chinaman turned back and came rushing toward the altar where I lay, dagger high, desperation in his countenance.

A scream broke through the clamor and as I twisted desperately about to avoid the descending dagger, I caught a glimpse of Kathulos dragging Zuleika away. Then with a frenzied wrench I toppled from the altar just as Li Kung's dagger, grazing my breast, sank inches deep into the dark-stained surface and quivered there.

I had fallen on the side next to the wall and what was taking place in the room I could not see, but it seemed as if far away I could hear men screaming faintly and hideously. Then Li Kung wrenched his blade free and sprang, tigerishly, around the end of the altar. Simultaneously a revolver cracked from the doorway—the Chinaman spun clear around, the dagger flying from his hand—he slumped to the floor.

Gordon, came running from the doorway where a few moments earlier Zuleika had stood, his pistol still smoking in his hand. At his heels were three rangy, clean-cut men in plainclothes. He cut my bonds and dragged me upright.

"Quick! Where have they gone?"

The room was empty of life save for myself, Gordon and his men, though two dead men lay on the floor.

I found the secret door and after a few seconds' search located the lever which opened it. Revolvers drawn, the men groped about me and peered nervously into the dark stairway. Not a sound came up from the total darkness.

"This is uncanny!" muttered Gordon. "I suppose the Master and his servants went this way when they left the building—as they are certainly not here now!—and Leary and his men should have stopped them either in the tunnel itself or in the rear room of Yun Shatu's. At any rate, in either event they should have communicated with us by this time."

"Look out, sir!" one of the men exclaimed suddenly, and Gordon, with an ejaculation, struck out with his pistol barrel and crushed the life from a huge snake which had crawled silently up the steps from the blackness beneath.

"Let us see into this matter," said he, straightening.

But before he could step onto the first stair, I halted him; for flesh crawling, I began dimly to understand something of what had happened—I began to understand the silence in the tunnel, the absence of detectives, the screams I had heard some minutes previously while I lay on the altar. Examining the lever which opened the door, I found another smaller lever—I began to believe I knew what those mysterious chests in the tunnel contained.

"Gordon," I said hoarsely, "have you an electric torch?"

One of the men produced a large one.

"Direct the light into the tunnel, but as you value your life, do not put a foot upon the steps."

The beam of light struck through the shadows, lighting the tunnel, etching out boldly a scene that will haunt my brain all the rest of my life. On the floor of the tunnel, between the chests which now gaped open, lay two men who were members of London's finest secret service. Limbs twisted and faces horribly distorted they lay, and above and about them writhed, in long glittering scaly shimmerings, scores of hideous reptiles.

The clock struck five.

CHAPTER THIRTEEN

THE BLIND BEGGAR WHO RODE

"He seemed a beggar such as lags
Looking for crusts and ale."
—Chesterton

The cold gray dawn was stealing over the river as we stood in the deserted bar of the Temple of Dreams. Gordon was questioning the two men who had remained on guard outside the building while their unfortunate companions went in to explore the tunnel.

"As soon as we heard the whistle, sir, Leary and Murken rushed the bar and broke into the opium room, while we waited here at the bar door according to orders. Right away several ragged elopers came tumbling out and we grabbed them. But no one else came out and we heard nothing from Leary and Murken; so we just waited until you came, sir."

"You saw nothing of a giant Negro, or of the Chinaman Yun Shatu?"

"No, sir. After a while the patrolmen arrived and we threw a cordon around the house, but no one was seen."

Gordon shrugged his shoulders; a few cursory questions had satisfied him that the captives were harmless addicts and he had them released.

"You are sure no one else came out?"

"Yes, sir—no, wait a moment. A wretched old blind beggar did come out, all rags and dirt and with a ragged girl leading him. We stopped him but didn't hold him—a wretch like that couldn't be harmful.".

"No?" Gordon jerked out. "Which way did he go?"

"The girl led him down the street to the next block and then an automobile stopped and they got in and drove off, sir."

Gordon glared at him.

"The stupidity of the London detective has rightfully become an international jest," he said acidly. "No doubt it never occurred to you as being strange that a Limehouse beggar should ride about in his own automobile."

Then impatiently waving aside the man, who sought to speak further, he turned to me.

"Mr. Costigan, if you will come to my apartment we may be able to clear up some new things."

CHAPTER FOURTEEN
THE BLACK EMPIRE

"Oh the new spears dipped in life-blood
as the woman shrieked in vain!
Oh the days before the English!
When will those days come again?"
—Mundy

Gordon struck a match and absently allowed it to flicker and go out in his hand. His Turkish cigarette hung unlighted between his fingers.

"This is the most logical conclusion to be reached," he was saying. "The weak link in our chain was lack of men. But curse it, one cannot round up an army at two o'clock in the morning, even with the aid of Scotland Yard. I went on to Limehouse, leaving orders for a number of patrolmen to follow me as quickly as they could be got together, and to throw a cordon about the house.

"They arrived too late to prevent the Master's servants slipping out of the side doors and windows, as they could easily do, with only Finnegan and Hansen on guard at the front of the building. However, they arrived in time to prevent the Master himself from slipping out in that way—no doubt he lingered to effect his disguise and was caught in that manner. He owes his escape to his craft and boldness and to the carelessness of Finnegan and Hansen. The girl who accompanied him—"

"She was Zuleika, I am sure."

I answered listlessly, wondering anew what shackles bound her inexorably to the Egyptian sorcerer.

"You owe your life to her," Gordon rapped out, lighting another match. "We were standing in the shadows in front of the warehouse, waiting for the hour to strike, and of course ignorant as to what was going on in the house, when a girl appeared at one of the barred windows and begged us for God's sake to do something; that a man was being murdered. So we broke in at once. However, she was not to be seen anywhere when we entered."

"She probably returned to the room," I muttered, "and was forced to accompany the Master. God grant he knows nothing of her trickery."

"I do not know," said Gordon, dropping the charred match stem, "whether she guessed at our true identity or whether she just made the appeal in desperation.

"However, the main point is this: evidence points to the fact that, on hearing the whistle, Leary and Murken invaded Yun Shatu's from the front at the same instant my three men and I made our attack on the warehouse front. As it took us some seconds to batter down the door, it is logical to suppose that they found the secret door and entered the tunnel before we effected an entrance into the warehouse.

"The Master, knowing our plans before hand, and being aware that an invasion would be made through the tunnel and having long ago made preparations for such an exigency—"

An involuntary shudder shook me.

"—the Master worked the lever that opened the chests—the screams you heard as you lay upon the altar were the death shrieks of Leary and Murken. Then, leaving the Chinaman behind to finish you, the Master and the rest descended into the tunnel—incredible as it seems—and threading their way unharmed among the serpents, entered Yun Shatu's house and escaped therefrom as I have said."

"That seems impossible. Why should not the snakes turn on them?"

Gordon finally ignited his cigarette and puffed a few seconds before replying.

"The reptiles might still have been giving their full and hideous attention to the dying men, or else—I have on previous occasions been confronted with indisputable proof of the Master's dominance over beasts and reptiles of even the lowest and most dangerous orders. How he and his slaves passed unhurt among those scaly fiends must remain, at present, one of the many unsolved mysteries pertaining to that strange man."

I stirred restlessly in my chair. This brought up a point which I had come to Gordon's neat but bizarre apartments to clear up.

"You have not yet told me," I said abruptly, "who this man is and what is his mission."

"As to who he is, I can only say that he is known as you name him—the Master. I have never seen him unmasked, nor do I know his real name nor his nationality."

"I can enlighten you to an extent there," I broke in. "I have seen him unmasked and have heard the name his slaves call him."

Gordon's eyes blazed and he leaned forward.

"His name," I continued, "is Kathulos and he claims to be an Egyptian."

"Kathulos!" Gordon repeated. "You say he claims to be an Egyptian—have you any reason for doubting his claim to that nationality?"

"He may be of Egypt," I answered slowly, "but he is different, somehow, from any human I ever saw or hope to see. Great age might account for some of his peculiarities, but there are certain lineal differences that my anthropological studies tell me have been present since birth—features which would be abnormal to any other man but which are perfectly normal in Kathulos. That sounds paradoxical, I admit, but to appreciate fully the horrid inhumanness of the man, you would have to see him yourself."

Gordon sat all attention while I swiftly sketched the appearance of the Egyptian as I remembered him—and that appearance was indelibly etched on my brain forever.

As I finished he nodded.

"As I have said, I never saw Kathulos except when disguised as a beggar, a leper or some such thing—when he was fairly swathed in rags. Still, I too have been impressed with a strange *difference* about him—something that is not present at all in other men."

Gordon tapped his knee with his fingers—a habit of his when deeply engrossed by a problem.

"You have asked as to the mission of this man," he began slowly. "I will tell you all I know."

"My position with the British Government is a unique and peculiar one. I hold what might be called a roving commission—an office created solely for the purpose of suiting my special needs. As a secret service official during the first World War, I convinced the powers of a need of such an office and of my ability to fill it.

"Somewhat over seventeen months ago I was sent to South Africa to investigate the unrest which has been growing among the natives of the interior ever since the World War and which has of late assumed alarming proportions. There I first got on the track of this man Kathulos. I found in roundabout ways, that Africa was a seething cauldron of rebellion from Morocco to Cape Town. The old, old vow had been made again—the Negroes and the Mohammedans, banded together, should drive the white men into the sea.

"This pact has been made before but always, hitherto, broken. Now, however, I sensed a giant intellect and a monstrous genius behind the veil, a genius powerful enough to accomplish this union and hold it together. Working entirely on hints and vague whispered clues, I followed the trail up through Central Africa and into Egypt. There, at last, I came upon definite evidence that such a man existed. The whispers hinted of a living dead man—a *skull-faced* man. I learned that this man was the high priest of the mysterious Scorpion society of northern Africa. He was spoken of variously as Skull-face, the Master, and the Scorpion.

"Following a trail of bribed officials and filched state secrets, I at last trailed him to Alexandria, where I had my first sight of him in a dive in the native quarter—disguised as a leper. I heard him distinctly addressed as 'mighty Scorpion' by the natives, but he escaped me.

"All trace vanished then; the trail ran out entirely until rumors of strange happenings in London reached me and I came back to England to investigate an apparent leak in the war office.

"As I thought, the Scorpion had preceded me. This man, whose education and craft transcend anything I ever met with, is simply the leader and instigator of a world-wide movement such as mankind has never seen before. He plots, in a word, the overthrow of the white races!

"His ultimate aim is a black empire, with himself as emperor of the world! And to that end he has banded together in one monstrous conspiracy the black, the brown and the yellow."

"I understand now what Yussef Ali meant when he said 'the days of the empire,'" I muttered.

"Exactly," Gordon rapped with suppressed excitement. "Kathulos' power is unlimited and unguessed. Like an octopus his tentacles stretch to the high places of civilization and to the far corners of the world. And his main weapon is—dope! He has flooded Europe and no doubt America with opium and hashish, and in spite of all effort it has been impossible to discover the break in the barriers through which the hellish stuff is coming. With this he ensnares and enslaves men and women.

"You have told me of the aristocratic men and women you saw coming to Yun Shatu's dive. Without doubt they were dope addicts—for, as I said, the habit lurks in high places—holders of governmental positions, no doubt, coming to trade for the stuff they craved and giving in return state secrets, inside information and promise of protection for the Master's crimes.

"Oh, he does not work haphazardly! Before ever the black flood breaks, he will be prepared; if he has his way, the governments of the white races will be honeycombs of corruption—the strongest men of the white races will be dead. The white men's secrets of war will be his. When it comes, I look for a simultaneous uprising against white supremacy, of all the colored races—races who, in the last war, learned the white men's ways of battle, and who, led by such a man as Kathulos and armed with the white man's finest weapons, will be almost invincible.

"A steady stream of rifles and ammunition has been pouring into East Africa and it was not until I discovered the source that it was stopped. I found that a staid and reliable Scotch firm was smuggling these arms among the natives and I found more: the manager of this firm was an opium slave. That was enough. I saw Kathulos' hand in the matter. The manager was arrested and committed suicide in his cell—that is only one of the many situations with which I am called upon to deal.

"Again the case of Major Fairlan Morley. He, like myself, held a very flexible commission and had been sent to the Transvaal to work upon the same case. He sent to London a number of secret papers for safe-keeping. They arrived some weeks ago and were put in a bank vault. The letter accompanying them gave explicit instructions that they were to be delivered to no one but the major himself, when he called for them in person, or in event of his death, to myself.

"As soon as I learned that he had sailed from Africa I sent trusted men to Bordeaux, where he intended to make his first landing in Europe. They did not succeed in saving the major's life, but they certified his death, for they found his body in a deserted ship whose hulk was stranded on the beach. Efforts were made to keep the affair a secret but somehow it leaked into the papers with the result—"

"I began to understand why I was to impersonate the unfortunate major," I interrupted.

"Exactly. A false beard furnished you, and your black hair dyed blond, you would have presented yourself at the bank, received the papers from the banker, who knew Major Morley just intimately enough to be deceived by your appearance, and the papers would have then fallen into the hands of the Master.

"I can only guess at the contents of those papers, for events have been taking place too swiftly for me to call for and obtain them. But they must deal with subjects closely connected with the activities of Kathulos. How he learned of them and of the provisions of the letter accompanying them, I have no idea, but as I said, London is honeycombed with his spies.

"In my search for clues, I often frequented Limehouse disguised as you first saw me. I went often to the Temple of Dreams and even managed once to enter the back room, for I suspected some sort of rendezvous in the rear of the building. The absence of any exit baffled me and I had no time to search for secret doors before I was ejected by the giant black man Hassim, who had no suspicion of my true identity. I noticed that very often the leper entered or left Yun Shatu's, and finally it was borne on me that this supposed leper was the Scorpion himself.

"That night you discovered me on the couch in the opium room, I had come there with no especial plan in mind. Seeing Kathulos leaving, I determined to rise and follow him, but you spoiled that."

He fingered his chin and laughed grimly.

"I was an amateur boxing champion in Oxford," said he, "but Tom Cribb himself could not have withstood that blow—or have dealt it."

"I regret it as I regret few things."

"No need to apologize. You saved my life immediately afterward—I was stunned, but not too much to know that that brown devil Yussef Ali was burning to cut out my heart."

"How did you come to be at Sir Haldred Frenton's estate? And how is it that you did not raid Yun Shatu's dive?"

"I did not have the place raided because I knew somehow Kathulos would be warned and our efforts would come to naught. I was at Sir Haldred's that night because I have contrived to spend at least part of each night with him since he returned from the Congo. I anticipated an attempt upon his life when I learned from his own lips that he was preparing, from the studies he made on this trip, a treatise on the secret native societies of West Africa. He hinted that the disclosures he intended to make therein might prove sensational, to say the least. Since it is to Kathulos' advantage to destroy such men as might be able to arouse the Western world to its danger, I knew that Sir Haldred was a marked man. Indeed, two distinct attempts were made upon his life on his journey to the coast from the African interior. So I put two trusted men on guard and they are at their post even now.

"Roaming about the darkened house, I heard the noise of your entry, and, warning my men, I strode down to intercept you. At the time of our conversation, Sir Haldred was sitting in his unlighted study, a Scotland Yard man with drawn pistol on each side of him. Their vigilance no doubt accounts for Yussef Ali's failure to attempt what you were sent to do.

"Something in your manner convinced me in spite of yourself," he meditated. "I will admit I had some bad moments of doubt as I waited in the darkness that precedes dawn, outside the warehouse."

Gordon rose suddenly and going to a strong-box which stood in a corner of the room, drew thence a thick envelope.

"Although Kathulos has checkmated me at almost every move," he said, "I have not been entirely idle. Noting the frequenters of Yun Shatu's, I have compiled a partial list of the Egyptian's right-hand men, and their records. What you have told me has enabled me to complete that list. As we know, his henchmen are scattered all over the world, and there are possibly hundreds of them here, in London. However, this is a list of those I believe to be in his closest council, now with him in England. He told you himself that few even of his followers ever saw him unmasked."

We bent together over the list, which contained the following names: "Yun Shatu, Hongkong Chinese, suspected opium smuggler—keeper of Temple of Dreams—resident of Limehouse seven years. Hassim—ex-Senegalese chief—wanted in French Congo for murder. Santiago, Negro—fled from Haiti under suspicion of voodoo worship atrocities. Yar Khan, Afridi, record unknown. Yussef Ali, Moor, slave-dealer in Morocco—suspected of being a German spy in the World War—an instigator of the Fellaheen Rebellion on the upper Nile. Ganra Singh, Lahore, India, Sikh—smuggler of arms into Afghanistan—took an active part in the Lahore and Delhi riots—suspected of murder on two occasions—a dangerous man. Stephen Costigan, American—resident of England since the war—hashish addict—man of remarkable strength. Li Kung, northern China, opium smuggler."

Lines were drawn significantly through three names—mine, Li Kung's and Yussef Ali's. Nothing was written next to mine, but following Li Kung's name was scrawled briefly in Gordon's rambling character: "Shot by John Gordon during the raid on Yun Shatu's." And following the name of Yussef Ali: "Killed by Stephen Costigan during the Yun Shatu raid."

I laughed mirthlessly. Black empire or not, Yussef Ali would never hold Zuleika in his arms, for he had never risen from where I felled him.

"I know not," said Gordon somberly as he folded the list and replaced it in the envelope, "what power Kathulos has that draws together black men and yellow men to serve him—that unites world-old foes. Hindoo, Moslem, and pagan are among his followers. And back in the mists of the East where mysterious and gigantic forces are at work, this uniting is culminating on a monstrous scale."

He glanced at his watch.

"It is nearly ten. Make yourself at home here, Mr. Costigan, while I visit Scotland Yard and see if any clue has been found as to Kathulos' new quarters. I believe that the webs are closing on him, and with your aid I promise you we will have the gang located within a week at most."

CHAPTER FIFTEEN
THE MARK OF THE TULWAR

"The fed world curls by his drowsy mate
In a tight-trod earth; but the lean wolves wait."
—Mundy

I sat alone in John Gordon's apartments and laughed mirthlessly. In spite of the elixir's stimulus, the strain of the previous night, with its loss of sleep and its heartrending action, was telling on me. My mind was a chaotic whirl wherein the faces of Gordon, Kathulos and Zuleika shifted with numbing swiftness. All the mass of information Gordon had given to me seemed jumbled and incoherent.

Through this state of being, one fact stood out boldly, I must find the latest hiding-place of the Egyptian and get Zuleika out of his hands—if indeed she still lived.

A week, Gordon had said—I laughed again—a week and I would be beyond aiding anyone. I had found the proper amount of elixir to use—knew the minimum amount my system required—and knew that I could make the flask last me four days at most. Four days! Four days in which to comb the rat-holes of Limehouse and Chinatown—four days in which to ferret out, somewhere in the mazes of East End, the lair of Kathulos.

I burned with impatience to begin, but nature rebelled, and staggering to a couch, I fell upon it and was asleep instantly.

Then someone was shaking me.

"Wake up, Mr. Costigan!"

I sat up, blinking. Gordon stood over me, his face haggard.

"There's devil's work done, Costigan! The Scorpion has struck again!"

I sprang up, still half asleep and only partly realizing what he was saying. He helped me into my coat, thrust my hat at me, and then his firm grip on my arm was propelling me out of his door and down the stairs. The street lights were blazing; I had slept an incredible time.

"A logical victim!" I was aware that my companion was saying. "He should have notified me the instant of his arrival!"

"I don't understand—" I began dazedly.

We were at the curb now and Gordon hailed a taxi, giving the address of a small and unassuming hotel in a staid and prim section of the city.

"The Baron Rokoff," he rapped as we whirled along at reckless speed, "a Russian free-lance, connected with the war office. He returned from Mongolia yesterday and apparently went into hiding. Undoubtedly he had learned something vital in regard to the slow waking of the East. He had not yet communicated with us, and I had no idea that he was in England until just now."

"And you learned—"

"The baron was found in his room, his dead body mutilated in a frightful manner!"

The respectable and conventional hotel which the doomed baron had chosen for his hiding place was in a state of wild uproar, being suppressed by the police. The management had attempted to keep the matter quiet, but somehow the guests had learned of the atrocity and many were leaving in haste—or preparing to, as the police were planning to hold all for investigation.

The baron's room, which was on the top floor, was in a state to defy description. Not even in the great war have I seen a more complete shambles. Nothing had been touched; all remained just as the chamber-maid had found it a half hour since. Tables and chairs lay shattered on the floor, and the furniture, floor and walls were spattered with blood. The baron, a tall, muscular man in life, lay in the middle of the room, a fearful spectacle. His skull had been cleft to the brows, a deep gash under his left armpit had shorn through his ribs, and his left arm hung by a shred of flesh. The cold bearded face was set in a look of indescribable horror.

"Some heavy, curved weapon must have been used," said Gordon, "something like a saber, wielded with terrific force. See where a chance blow sank inches deep into the window-sill. And again, the thick back of this heavy chair has been split like a shingle. A saber, surely."

"A tulwar," I muttered, somberly. "Do you not recognize the handiwork of the Central Asian butcher? Yar Khan has been here."

"The Afghan! He came across the roofs, of course, and descended to the window-ledge by means of a knotted rope made fast to something on the edge of the roof. About one-thirty the maid, passing through the corridor, heard a terrific commotion in the baron's room—smashing of chairs and a sudden short shriek which died abruptly into a ghastly gurgle and then ceased—to the sound of heavy blows, curiously muffled, such as a sword might make when driven deep into human flesh. Then all noises stopped suddenly.

"She called the manager and they tried the door and, finding it locked, and receiving no answer to their shouts, opened it with the desk key. Only the corpse was there, but the window was open. This is strangely unlike Kathulos' usual procedure. It lacks subtlety. Often his victims appear to have died from natural causes. I scarcely understand."

"I see little difference in the outcome," I answered. "There is nothing that can be done to apprehend the murderer as it is."

"True," Gordon scowled. "We know who did it but there is no proof—not even a fingerprint. Even if we knew where the Afghan is hiding and arrested him, we could prove nothing—there would be a score of men to swear alibis for him. The baron returned only yesterday. Kathulos probably did not know of his arrival until tonight. He knew that, tomorrow, Rokoff would make known his presence to me and impart what he learned in northern Asia. The Egyptian knew he must strike quickly, and lacking time to prepare a safer and more elaborate form of murder, he sent the Afridi with his tulwar. There is nothing we can do, at least not until we discover the Scorpion's hiding-place. What the baron had learned in Mongolia, we shall never know, but that it dealt with the plans and aspirations of Kathulos, we may be sure."

We went down the stairs again and out on the street accompanied by one of the Scotland Yard men, Hansen. Gordon suggested that we walk back to his apartment, and I greeted the opportunity to let the cool night air blow some of the cobwebs out of my mazed brain.

As we walked along the deserted streets, Gordon suddenly cursed savagely.

"This is a veritable labyrinth we are following, leading nowhere! Here, in the very heart of civilization's metropolis, the direct enemy of that civilization commits crimes of the most outrageous nature and goes free! We are children, wandering in the night, struggling with an unseen evil—dealing with an incarnate devil, of whose true identity we know nothing and whose true ambitions we can only guess.

"Never have we managed to arrest one of the Egyptian's direct henchmen, and the few dupes and tools of his we have apprehended have died mysteriously before they could tell us anything. Again I repeat: what strange power has Kathulos that dominates these men of different creeds and races? The men in London with him are, of course, mostly renegades, slaves of dope, but his tentacles stretch all over the East. Some dominance is his: the power that sent the Chinaman, Li Kung, back to kill you, in the face of certain death; that sent Yar Khan and Moslem over the roofs of London to do murder; that holds Zuleika the Circassian in unseen bonds of slavery.

"Of course we know," he continued after a brooding silence, "that the East has secret societies which are behind and above all considerations of creeds. There are cults in Africa and the Orient whose origin dates back to Ophir and the fall of Atlantis. This man must be a power in some or possibly all of these societies. An Egyptian by his own word, he controls the lives and destinies of orthodox Moslems, Hindoos, Shintos and devil-worshippers. It's unnatural.

"Have you ever"—he turned to me abruptly—"heard the ocean mentioned in connection with Kathulos?"

"Never."

"There is a widespread superstition in northern Africa, based on a very ancient legend, that the great leader of the colored races would come out of the sea! And I once heard a Berber speak of the Scorpion as 'The Son of the Ocean'."

"That is a term of respect among that tribe, is it not?"

"Yes; still I wonder sometimes."

CHAPTER SIXTEEN
THE MUMMY WHO LAUGHED

"Laughing as littered skulls that lie
After lost battles turn to the sky
An everlasting laugh."
—Chesterton

"A shop open this late!" Gordon remarked suddenly.

A fog had descended on London and along the quiet street we were traversing the lights glimmered with the peculiar reddish haze characteristic of such atmospheric conditions. Our footfalls echoed drearily. Even in the heart of a great city there are always sections which seem overlooked and forgotten. Such a street was this. Not even a policeman was in sight.

The shop which had attracted Gordon's attention was just in front of us, on the same side of the street. There was no sign over the door, merely some sort of emblem something like a dragon. Light flowed from the open doorway and the small show windows on each side. As it was neither a café nor the entrance to a hotel, we found ourselves idly speculating over its reason for being open. Ordinarily, I suppose neither of us would have given the matter a thought, but our nerves were so keyed up that we found ourselves instinctively suspicious of anything out of the ordinary. Then something occurred which was distinctly out of the ordinary.

A tall, very thin man, considerably stooped, suddenly loomed up out of the fog in front of us, and beyond the shop. I had only a glance of him—an impression of incredible gauntness, of worn, wrinkled garments, a high silk, hat drawn close over the brows, a face hidden by a muffler; then he turned aside and entered the shop. A cold wind whispered down the street, twisting the fog into wispy ghosts, but the coldness that came upon me transcended the wind's.

"Gordon!" I exclaimed in a fierce, low voice. "My senses are no longer reliable or else Kathulos himself has just gone into that house!"

Gordon's eyes blazed. We were now close to the shop, and lengthening his strides into a run, he hurled himself into the door, the detective and I close upon his heels.

A weird assortment of merchandise met our eyes. Antique weapons covered the walls, and the floor was piled high with curious things. Maori idols shouldered Chinese josses, and suits of mediaeval armor bulked darkly against stacks of rare Oriental rugs and Latin-made shawls. The place was an antique shop. Of the figure who had aroused our interest we saw nothing.

An old man clad bizarrely in red fez, brocaded jacket and Turkish slippers came from the back of the shop; he was a Levantine of some sort.

"You wish something, sirs?"

"You keep open rather late," Gordon said abruptly, his eyes traveling swiftly over the shop for some secret hiding-place that might conceal the object of our search.

"Yes, sir. My customers number many eccentric professors and students who keep very irregular hours. Often the night boats unload special pieces for me and very often I have customers later than this. I remain open all night, sir."

"We are merely looking around," Gordon returned, and in an aside to Hansen: "Go to the back and stop anyone who tries to leave that way."

Hansen nodded and strolled casually to the rear of the shop. The back door was clearly visible to our view, through a vista of antique furniture and tarnished hangings strung up for exhibition. We had followed the Scorpion—if he it was—so closely that I did not believe he would have had time to traverse the full length of the shop and make his exit without our having seen him as we came in. For our eyes had been on the rear door ever since we had entered.

Gordon and I browsed around casually among the curios, handling and discussing some of them, but I have no idea as to their nature. The Levantine had seated himself cross-legged on a Moorish mat close to the center of the shop and apparently took only a polite interest in our explorations.

After a time Gordon whispered to me, "There is no advantage in keeping up this pretense. We have looked everywhere the Scorpion might be hiding, in the ordinary manner. I will make known my identity and authority and we will search the entire building openly."

Even as he spoke, a truck drew up outside the door and two burly Negroes entered. The Levantine seemed to have expected them, for he merely waved them toward the back of the shop and they responded with a grunt of understanding.

Gordon and I watched them closely as they made their way to a large mummy-case which stood upright against the wall not far from the back. They lowered this to a level position and then started for the door, carrying it carefully between them.

"Halt!" Gordon stepped forward, raising his hand authoritatively.

"I represent Scotland Yard," he said swiftly, "and have sanction for anything I choose to do. Set that mummy down; nothing leaves this shop until we have thoroughly searched it."

The Negroes obeyed without a word, and my friend turned to the Levantine, who, apparently not perturbed or even interested, sat smoking a Turkish water-pipe.

"Who was that tall man who entered just before we did, and where did he go?"

"No one entered before you, sir. Or, if anyone did, I was at the back of the shop and did not see him. You are certainly at liberty to search my shop, sir."

And search it we did, with the combined craft of a secret service expert and a denizen of the underworld—while Hansen stood stolidly at his post, the two Negroes standing over the carved mummy-case watched us impassively. And the Levantine sat like a sphinx on his mat, puffing a fog of smoke into the air. The whole thing had a distinct effect of unreality.

At last, baffled, we returned to the mummy-case, which was certainly long enough to conceal even a man of Kathulos' height. The thing did not appear to be sealed as is the usual custom, and Gordon opened it without difficulty. A formless shape, swathed in moldering wrappings, met our eyes. Gordon parted some of the wrappings and revealed an inch or so of withered, brownish, leathery arm. He shuddered involuntarily as he touched it, as a man will do at the touch of a reptile or some inhumanly cold thing. Taking a small metal idol from a stand near by, he rapped on the shrunken breast and the arm. Each gave out a solid thumping, like some sort of wood.

Gordon shrugged his shoulders. "Dead for two thousand years, anyway, and I don't suppose I should risk destroying a valuable mummy simply to prove that which we know to be true."

He closed the case again.

"The mummy may have crumbled some, even from this much exposure, but perhaps it did not."

This last was addressed to the Levantine, who replied merely by a courteous gesture of his hand, and the Negroes once more lifted the case and carried it to the truck, where they loaded it on, and a moment later mummy, truck and Negroes had vanished in the fog.

Gordon still nosed about the shop, but I stood stock-still in the center of the floor. To my chaotic and dope-ridden brain I attributed it, but the sensation had been mine, that through the wrappings of the mummy's face, great eyes had burned into mine, eyes like pools of yellow fire, that seared my soul and froze me where I stood. And as the case had been carried through the door, I knew that the lifeless thing in it, dead, God only knows how many centuries, was *laughing*, hideously and silently.

CHAPTER SEVENTEEN
THE DEAD MAN FROM THE SEA

Gordon puffed savagely at his Turkish cigarette, staring abstractedly and unseeingly at Hansen, who was sitting opposite him.

"I suppose we must chalk up another failure against ourselves. That Levantine, Kamonos, is evidently a creature of the Egyptian's, and the walls and floors of his shop are probably honeycombed with secret panels and doors which would baffle a magician."

Hansen made some answer but I said nothing. Since our return to Gordon's apartment, I had been conscious of a feeling of intense languor and sluggishness which not even my condition could account for. I knew that my system was full of the elixir—but my mind seemed strangely slow and hard of comprehension in direct contrast with the average state of my mentality when stimulated by the hellish dope.

This condition was slowly leaving me, like mist floating from the surface of a lake, and I felt as if I were waking gradually from a long and unnaturally sound sleep.

Gordon was saying, "I would give a good deal to know if Kamonos is really one of Kathulos' slaves or if the Scorpion managed to make his escape through some natural exit as we entered."

"Kamonos is his servant, true enough," I found myself saying slowly, as if searching for the proper words. "As we left, I saw his gaze light upon the scorpion which is traced on my hand. His eyes narrowed, and as we were leaving he contrived to brush close against me—and to whisper in a quick low voice: 'Soho, Forty-eight.'"

Gordon came erect like a loosened steel bow.

"Indeed!" he rapped. "Why did you not tell me at the time?"

"I don't know."

My friend eyed me sharply.

"I noticed you seemed like a man intoxicated all the way from the shop," said he. "I attributed it to some aftermath of hashish. But no. Kathulos is undoubtedly a masterful disciple of Mesmer—his power over venomous reptiles shows that, and I am beginning to believe it is the real source of his power over humans.

"Somehow, the Master caught you off your guard in that shop and partly asserted his dominance over your mind. From what hidden nook he sent his thought waves to shatter your brain, I do not know, but Kathulos was somewhere in that shop, I am sure."

"He was. He was in the mummy-case."

"The mummy-case!" Gordon exclaimed rather impatiently. "That is impossible! The mummy quite filled it and not even such a thin being as the Master could have found room there."

I shrugged my shoulders, unable to argue the point but somehow sure of the truth of my statement.

"Kamonos," Gordon continued, "doubtless is not a member of the inner circle and does not know of your change of allegiance. Seeing the mark of the scorpion, he undoubtedly supposed you to be a spy of the Master's. The whole thing may be a plot to ensnare us, but I feel that the man was sincere—Soho, Forty-eight can be nothing less than the Scorpion's new rendezvous."

I, too, felt that Gordon was right, though a suspicion lurked in my mind.

"I secured the papers of Major Morley yesterday," he continued, "and while you slept, I went over them. Mostly they but corroborated what I already knew—touched on the unrest of the natives and repeated the theory that one vast genius was behind all: But there was one matter which interested me greatly and which I think will interest you also."

From his strongbox he took a manuscript written in the close, neat characters of the unfortunate major, and, in a monotonous droning which betrayed little of his intense excitement, he read the following nightmarish narrative:

"This matter I consider worth jotting down—as to whether it has any bearing oh the case at hand, further developments will show: At Alexandria, where I spent some weeks seeking further clues as to the identity of the man known as the Scorpion, I made the acquaintance, through my friend Ahmed Shah, of the noted Egyptologist, Professor Ezra Schuyler of New York. He verified the statement made by various laymen, concerning the legend of the "ocean-man." This myth, handed down from generation to generation, stretches back into the very mists of antiquity and is, briefly, that some day a man shall come up out of the sea and shall lead the people of Egypt to victory over all others.

"This legend has spread over the continent so that now all black races consider that it deals with the coming of a universal emperor. Professor Schuyler gave it as his opinion that the myth was somehow connected with the lost Atlantis, which, he maintains, was located between the African and South American continents and to whose inhabitants the ancestors of the Egyptians were tributary. The reasons for his connection are too lengthy and vague to note here, but following the line of his theory he told me a strange and fantastic tale.

"He said that a close friend of his, Von Lorfmon of Germany, a sort of free-lance scientist, now dead, was sailing off the coast of Senegal some years ago, for the purpose of investigating and classifying the rare specimens of sealife found there. He was using for his purpose a small trading vessel, manned by a crew of Moors, Greeks and Negroes.

"Some days out of sight of land, something floating was sighted, and this object, being grappled and brought aboard, proved to be a *mummy-case of a most curious kind*. Professor Schuyler explained to me the features whereby it differed from the ordinary Egyptian style, but from his rather technical account I merely got the impression that it was a strangely shaped affair carved with characters neither cuneiform nor hieroglyphic. The case was heavily lacquered, being watertight and air-tight, and Von Lorfmon had considerable difficulty in opening it.

"However, he managed to do so without damaging the case, and a most unusual mummy was revealed. Schuyler said that he never saw either the mummy or the case, but that from descriptions given him by the Greek skipper who was present at the opening of the case, the mummy differed as much from the ordinary man as the case differed from the conventional type.

"Examination proved that the subject had not undergone the usual procedure of mummification. All parts were intact just as in life, but the whole form was shrunk and hardened to a wood-like consistency. Cloth wrappings swathed the thing and they crumbled to dust and vanished the instant air was let in upon them.

"Von Lorfmon was impressed by the effect upon the crew. The Greeks showed no interest beyond that which would ordinarily be shown by any man, but the Moors, and even more the Negroes, seemed to be rendered temporarily insane! As the case was hoisted on board, they all fell prostrate on the deck and raised a sort of worshipful chant, and it was necessary to use force in order to exclude them from the cabin wherein the mummy was exposed.

"A number of fights broke out between them and the Greek element of the crew, and the skipper and Von Lorfmon thought best to put back to the nearest port in all haste. The skipper attributed it to the natural aversion of seamen toward having a corpse on board, but Von Lorfmon seemed to sense a deeper meaning."

"They made port in Lagos, and that very night Von Lorfmon was murdered in his stateroom and the mummy and its case vanished. All the Moor and Negro sailors deserted ship the same night. Schuyler said—and here the matter took on a most sinister and mysterious aspect—that immediately afterward this widespread unrest among the natives began to smolder and take tangible form; he connected it in some manner with the old legend.

"An aura of mystery, also, hung over Von Lorfmon's death. He had taken the mummy into his stateroom, and anticipating an attack from the fanatical crew, had carefully barred and bolted door and portholes. The skipper, a reliable man, swore that it was virtually impossible to effect an entrance from without. And what signs were presented pointed to the fact that the locks had been worked from *within*. The scientist was killed by a dagger which formed part of his collection and which was left in his breast.

"As I have said, immediately afterward the African cauldron began to seethe. Schuyler said that in his opinion the natives considered the ancient prophecy fulfilled. The mummy was *the man from the sea*.

"Schuyler gave as his opinion that the thing was the work of Atlanteans and that the man in the mummy-case was a native of lost Atlantis.

"How the case came to float up through the fathoms of water which cover the forgotten land, he does not venture to offer a theory. He is sure that somewhere in the ghost-ridden mazes of the African jungles the mummy has been enthroned as a god, and, inspired by the dead thing, the black warriors are gathering for a wholesale massacre. He believes, also, that some crafty Moslem is the direct moving power of the threatened rebellion."

Gordon ceased speaking and looked up at me.

"Mummies seem to weave a weird dance through the warp of the tale," he said. "The German scientist took several pictures of the mummy with his camera, and it was after seeing these—which strangely enough were not stolen along with the thing—that Major Morley began to think himself on the brink of some monstrous discovery. His diary reflects his state of mind and becomes incoherent—his condition seems to have bordered on insanity. What did he learn to unbalance him so? Do you suppose that the mesmeric spells of Kathulos were used in some way against him?"

"These pictures—" I began.

"They fell into Schuyler's hands and he gave one to Morley. I found it among the manuscripts."

He handed the thing to me, watching me narrowly.

I stared, then rose unsteadily and poured myself a tumbler of wine.

"Not a dead idol in a voodoo hut," I said shakily, "but a monster animated by fearsome life, roaming the world for victims. Morley had seen the Master—that is why his brain crumbled. Gordon, as I hope to live again, that face is the face of Kathulos!"

Gordon stared wordlessly at me.

"The Master hand, Gordon!" I laughed. A certain grim enjoyment penetrated the mists of my horror, at the sight of the steel-nerved Englishman struck speechless, doubtless for the first time in his life.

He moistened his lips and said in a scarcely recognizable voice, "Then, in God's name, Costigan, nothing is stable or certain, and mankind hovers at the brink of untold abysses of nameless horror. If that dead monster found by Von Lorfmon is in truth the Scorpion, brought to life in some hideous fashion, what can mortal effort accomplish against him?"

"The mummy at Kamonos'—" I began, but he interrupted.

"Aye, the man whose flesh, hardened by a thousand years of nonexistence—that must have been Kathulos himself! He would have just had time to strip, wrap himself in the linens and step into the case before we entered. You remember that the case, leaning upright against the wall, stood partly concealed by a large Burmese idol, which obstructed our view and doubtless gave him time to accomplish his purpose. My God, Costigan, with what horror of the prehistoric world are we dealing?"

"I have heard of Hindoo fakirs who could induce a condition closely resembling death," I began. "Is it not possible that Kathulos, a shrewd and crafty Oriental, could have placed himself in this state and his followers have placed the case in the ocean where it was sure to be found? And might not he have been in this shape tonight at Kamonos'?"

Gordon shook his head.

"No. I have seen these fakirs. None of them ever feigned death to the extent of becoming shriveled and hard—in a word, dried up. Morley, narrating in another place the description of the mummy-case as jotted down by Von Lorfmon and passed on to Schuyler, mentions the fact that large portions of seaweed adhered to it—seaweed of a kind found only at great depths, on the bottom of the ocean. The wood, too, was of a kind which Von Lorfmon failed to recognize or classify, in spite of the fact that he was one of the greatest living authorities on flora. And his notes again and again emphasize the enormous *age* of the thing. He admitted that there was no way of telling how old the mummy was, but his hints intimate that he believed it to be not thousands of years old, but millions of years!

"No. We must face the facts. Since you are positive that the picture of the mummy is the picture of Kathulos—and there is little room for fraud—one of two things is practically certain. The Scorpion was never dead but ages ago was placed in that mummy-case and his life preserved in some manner, or else—he was dead and has been brought to life! Either of these theories, viewed in the cold light of reason, is absolutely untenable. Are we all insane?"

"Had you ever walked the road to hashish land," I said somberly, "you could believe anything to be true. Had you ever gazed into the terrible reptilian eyes of Kathulos the sorcerer, you would not doubt that he was both dead and alive."

Gordon gazed out the window, his fine face haggard in the gray light.

"At any rate," said he, "there are two places which I intend exploring thoroughly before the sun rises again—Kamonos' antique shop and Soho, Forty-eight."

CHAPTER EIGHTEEN
THE GRIP OF THE SCORPION

"While from a proud tower in the town
Death looks gigantically down."
—Poe

Hansen snored on the bed as I paced the room. Another day had passed over London and again the street lamps glimmered through the fog. Their lights affected me strangely. They seemed to beat, solid waves of energy, against my brain. They twisted the fog into strange sinister shapes. Footlights of the stage that is the streets of London, how many grisly scenes had they lighted?

Gordon I had not seen since dawn. Following the clue of "Soho 48" he had gone forth to arrange a raid upon the place and he thought it best that I should remain under cover. He anticipated an attempt upon my life, and again he feared that if I went searching among the dives I formerly frequented it would arouse suspicion.

Hansen snored on. I seated myself and began to study the Turkish shoes which clothed my feet. Zuleika had worn Turkish slippers—how she floated through my waking dreams, gilding prosaic things with her witchery! Her face smiled at me from the fog; her phantom footfalls re-echoed through the misty chambers of my skull.

They beat an endless tattoo, luring and haunting till it seemed that these echoes found echoes, soft and stealthy, in the hallway outside the room where I stood. A sudden rap at the door, and I started.

Hansen slept on as I crossed the room and flung the door swiftly open. A swirling wisp of fog had invaded the corridor, and through it, like a silver veil, I saw her—Zuleika stood before me with her shimmering hair and her red lips parted and her great dark eyes.

Like a speechless fool I stood and she glanced quickly down the hallway and then stepped inside and closed the door.

"Gordon!" she whispered in a thrilling undertone. "Your friend! The Scorpion has him!"

Hansen had awakened and now sat gaping stupidly at the strange scene which met his eyes.

Zuleika did not heed him.

"And, oh, Steephen!" she cried, and tears shone in her eyes, "I have tried so hard to secure some more elixir, but I could not."

"Never mind that." I finally found my speech. "Tell me about Gordon."

"He went back to Kamonos' alone, and Hassim and Ganra Singh took him captive and brought him to the Master's house. Tonight assemble a great host of the people of the Scorpion for the sacrifice."

"Sacrifice!" A grisly thrill of horror coursed down my spine. Was there no limit to the ghastliness of this business?

"Quick, Zuleika, where is this house of the Master's?"

"Soho, Forty-eight. You must summon the police and send many men to surrounded it, but you must not go yourself—"

Hansen sprang up, quivering for action, but I turned to him. My brain was clear now, or seemed to be, and racing unnaturally.

"Wait!" I turned back to Zuleika. "When is this sacrifice to take place?"

"At the rising of the moon."

"That is only a few hours before dawn. Time to save him, but if we raid the house they'll kill him before we can reach them. And God only knows how many diabolical things guard all approaches."

"I do not know," Zuleika whimpered. "I must go now, or the Master will kill me."

Something gave way in my brain at that; something like a flood of wild and terrible exultation swept over me.

"The Master will kill no one!" I shouted, flinging my arms on high. "Before ever the east turns red for dawn, the Master dies! By all things holy and unholy I swear it!"

Hansen stared wildly at me, and Zuleika shrank back as I turned on her. To my dope-inspired brain had come a sudden burst of light, true and unerring.

I knew Kathulos was a mesmerist—that he understood fully the secret of dominating another's mind and soul. And I knew that at last I had hit upon the reason of his power over the girl. Mesmerism! As a snake fascinates and draws to him a bird, so the Master held Zuleika to him with unseen shackles. So absolute was his rule over her that it held even when she was out of his sight, working over great distances.

There was but one thing which would break that hold: the magnetic power of some other person whose control was stronger with her than Kathulos'. I laid my hands on her slim little shoulders and made her face me.

"Zuleika," I said commandingly, "here you are safe; you shall not return to Kathulos. There is no need of it. Now you are free."

But I knew I had failed before I ever started. Her eyes held a look of amazed, unreasoning fear and she twisted timidly in my grasp.

"Steephen, please let me go!" she begged. "I must—I must!"

I drew her over to the bed and asked Hansen for his handcuffs. He handed them to me wonderingly, and I fastened one cuff to the bedpost and the other to her slim wrist. The girl whimpered but made no resistance, her limpid eyes seeking mine in mute appeal.

It cut me to the quick to enforce my will upon her in this apparently brutal manner, but I steeled myself.

"Zuleika," I said tenderly, "you are now my prisoner. The Scorpion cannot blame you for not returning to him when you are unable to do so—and before dawn you shall be free of his rule entirely."

I turned to Hansen and spoke in a tone which admitted of no argument.

"Remain here, just without the door, until I return. On no account allow any strangers to enter—that is, anyone whom you do not personally know. And I charge you, on your honor as a man, do not release this girl, no matter what she may say. If neither I nor Gordon have returned by ten o'clock tomorrow, take her to this address—that family once were friends of mine and will take care of a homeless girl. I am going to Scotland Yard."

"Steephen," Zuleika wailed, "you are going to the Master's lair? You will be killed. Send the police, do not go!"

I bent, drew her into my arms, felt her lips against mine, then tore myself away.

The fog plucked at me with ghostly fingers, cold as the hands of dead men, as I raced down the street, I had no plan, but one was forming in my mind, beginning to seethe in the stimulated cauldron that was my brain. I halted at the sight of a policeman pacing his beat, and beckoning him to me, scribbled a terse note on a piece of paper torn from a notebook, and handed it to him.

"Get this to Scotland Yard; it's a matter of life and death and it has to do with the business of John Gordon."

At that name, a gloved hand came up in swill assent, but his assurance of haste died out behind me as I renewed my flight. The note stated briefly that Gordon was a prisoner at Soho Forty-eight and advised an immediate raid in force—advised, nay, in Gordon's name, commanded it.

My reason for my actions was simple; I knew that the first noise of the raid sealed John Gordon's doom. Somehow I first must reach him and protect or free him before the police arrived.

The time seemed endless, but at last the grim gaunt outlines of the house that was Soho Forty-eight rose up before me, a giant ghost in the fog. The hour grew late; few people dared the mists and the dampness as I came to a halt in the street before this forbidding building. No lights showed from the windows, either upstairs or down. It seemed deserted. But the lair of the scorpion often seems deserted until the silent death strikes suddenly.

Here I halted and a wild thought struck me. One way or another, the drama would be over by dawn. Tonight was the climax of my career, the ultimate top of life. Tonight I was the strongest link in the strange chain of events. Tomorrow it would not matter whether I lived or died. I drew the flask of elixir from my pocket and gazed at it. Enough for two more days if properly eked out. Two more days of life! Or—I needed stimulation as I never needed it before; the task in front of me was one no mere human could hope to accomplish.

If I drank the entire remainder of the elixir, I had no idea as to the duration of its effect, but it would last the night through. And my legs were shaky; my mind had curious periods of utter vacuity; weakness of brain and body assailed me. I raised the flask and with one draft drained it.

For an instant I thought it was death. Never had I taken such an amount.

Sky and world reeled, and I felt as if I would fly into a million vibrating fragments, like the bursting of a globe of brittle steel. Like fire, like hell-fire, the elixir raced along my veins and I was a giant! Monster! A superman!

Turning, I strode to the menacing, shadowy doorway. I had no plan; I felt the need of none. As a drunken man walks blithely into danger, I strode to the lair of the Scorpion, magnificently aware of my superiority, imperially confident of my stimulation and sure as the unchanging stars that the way would open before me.

Oh, there never was a superman like that who knocked commandingly on the door of Soho Forty-eight that night in the rain and the fog!

I knocked four times, the old signal that we slaves had used to be admitted into the idol room at Yun Shatu's. An aperture opened in the center of the door, and slanted eyes looked warily out. They slightly widened as the owner recognized me, then narrowed wickedly.

"You fool!" I said angrily. "Don't you see the mark?"

I held my hand to the aperture.

"Don't you recognize me? Let me in, curse you!"

I think the very boldness of the trick made for its success. Surely by now all the Scorpion's slaves knew of Stephen Costigan's rebellion, knew that he was marked for death. And the very fact that I came there, inviting doom, confused the doorman.

The door opened, and I entered. The man who had admitted me was a tall, lank Chinaman I had known as a servant at Kathulos'. He closed the door behind me, and I saw we stood in a sort of vestibule, lighted by a dim lamp whose glow could not be seen from the street for the reason that the windows were heavily curtained. The Chinaman glowered at me, undecided. I looked at him, tensed. Then suspicion flared in his eyes and his hand flew, to his sleeve. But at the instant I was on him and his lean neck broke like a rotten bough between my hands.

I eased his corpse to the thickly carpeted floor, and listened. No sound broke the silence. Stepping as stealthily as a wolf, fingers spread like talons, I stole into the next room. This was furnished in Oriental style, with couches and rugs and gold-worked drapery, but was empty of human life. I crossed it and went into the next one. Light flowed softly from the censers which were swung from the ceiling, and the Eastern rugs deadened the sound of my footfalls; I seemed to be moving through a castle of enchantment.

Every moment I expected a rush of silent assassins from the doorways or from behind the curtains or screen with their writhing dragons. Utter silence reigned. Room after room I explored, and at last halted at the foot of the stairs. The inevitable censer shed an uncertain light, but most of the stairs were veiled in shadows. What horrors awaited me above?

But fear and the elixir are strangers and I mounted that stair of lurking terror as boldly as I had entered that house of terror. The upper rooms I found to be much like those below, and with them they had this fact in common: they were empty of human life. I sought an attic but there seemed no door letting into one. Returning to the first floor, I made a search for an entrance into the basement, but again my efforts were fruitless. The amazing truth was borne in upon me: except for myself and that dead man who lay sprawled so grotesquely in the outer vestibule, there were no men in that house, dead or living.

I could not understand it. Had the house been bare of furniture I should have reached the natural conclusion that Kathulos had fled—but no signs of flight met my eye. This was unnatural, uncanny. I stood in the great shadowy library and pondered. No. I had made no mistake in the house.

Even if the broken corpse in the vestibule were not there to furnish mute testimony, everything in the room pointed toward the presence of the Master. There were the artificial palms, the lacquered screen, the tapestries, even the idol, though now no incense smoke rose before it. About the walls were ranged long shelves of books, bound in strange and costly fashion—books in every language in the world, I found from a swift examination, and on every subject—outré and bizarre, most of them.

Remembering the secret passage in the Temple of Dreams, I investigated the heavy mahogany table which stood in the center of the room. But nothing resulted. A sudden blaze of fury surged up in me, primitive and unreasoning. I snatched a statuette from the table and dashed it against the shelf-covered wall. The noise of its breaking would surely bring the gang from their hiding-place. But the result was much more startling than that!

The statuette struck the edge of a shelf and instantly the whole section of shelves with their load of books swung silently outward, revealing a narrow doorway! As in the other secret door, a row of steps led downward. At another time I would have shuddered at the thought of descending, with the horrors of the other tunnel fresh in my mind, but inflamed as I was by the elixir, I strode forward without an instant's hesitancy.

Since there was no one in the house, they must be somewhere in the tunnel or in whatever lair to which the tunnel led. I stepped through the doorway, leaving the door open. The police might find it that way and follow me, though somehow I felt as if mine would be a lone hand from the start to grim finish.

I went down a considerable distance and then the stair debouched into a level corridor some twenty feet wide—a remarkable thing. In spite of the width, the ceiling was rather low and from it hung small, curiously shaped, lamps which flung a dim light. I stalked hurriedly along the corridor like old Death seeking victims, and as I went I noted the work of the thing. The floor was of great broad flags and the walls seemed to be of huge blocks of evenly set stone. This passage was clearly no work of modern days; the slaves of Kathulos never tunneled there. Some secret way of mediaeval times, I thought—and after all, who knows what catacombs lie below London, whose secrets are greater and darker than those of Babylon and Rome?

On and on I went, and now I knew that I must be far below the earth. The air was dank and heavy, and cold moisture dripped from the stones of walls and ceiling. From time to time I saw smaller passages leading away in the darkness, but I determined to keep to the larger main one.

A ferocious impatience gripped me. I seemed to have been walking for hours, and still only dank damp walls and bare flags and guttering lamps met my eyes. I kept a close watch for sinister-appearing chests or the like—saw no such things.

Then as I was about to burst into savage curses, another stair loomed up in the shadows in front of me.

CHAPTER NINETEEN
DARK FURY

"The ringed wolf glared the circle round
Through baleful, blue-lit eye,
Not unforgetful of his debt.
Quoth he, 'I'll do some damage yet
Or ere my turn to die.'"
—Mundy

Like a lean wolf, I glided up the stairs. Some twenty feet up there was a sort of landing from which other corridors diverged, much like the lower one by which I had come. The thought came to me that the earth below London must be honeycombed with such secret passages, one above the other. Some feet above this landing the steps halted at a door, and here I hesitated, uncertain as to whether I should chance knocking or not. Even as I meditated, the door began to open. I shrank back against the wall, flattening myself out as much as possible. The door swung wide and a Moor came through. Only a glimpse I had of the room beyond, out of the corner of my eye, but my unnaturally alert senses registered the fact that the room was empty.

And on the instant, before he could turn, I smote the Moor a single deathly blow behind the angle of the jawbone, and he toppled headlong down the stairs, to lie in a crumpled heap on the landing, his limbs tossed grotesquely about.

My left hand caught the door as it started to slam shut, and in an instant I was through and standing in the room beyond. As I had thought, there was no occupant of this room. I crossed it swiftly and entered the next. These rooms were furnished in a manner before which the furnishings of the Soho house paled into insignificance.

Barbaric, terrible, unholy—these words alone convey some slight idea of the ghastly sights which met my eyes. Skulls, bones and complete skeletons formed much of the decorations, if such they were. Mummies leered from their cases and mounted reptiles ranged the walls. Between these sinister relics hung African shields of hide and bamboo, crossed with assagais and war daggers. Here and there reared obscene idols, black and horrible.

And in between and scattered about among these evidences of savagery and barbarism were vases, screens, rugs and hangings of the highest Oriental workmanship; a strange and incongruous effect.

I had passed through two of these rooms without seeing a human being, when I came to stairs leading upward. Up these I went, several flights, until I came to a door in a ceiling. I wondered if I were still under the earth. Surely the first stairs had led into a house of some sort. I raised the door cautiously. Starlight met my eyes, and I drew myself warily up and out. There I halted. A broad flat roof stretched away on all sides, and beyond its rim on all sides glimmered the lights of London. Just what building I was on, I had no idea, but that it was a tall one, I could tell, for I seemed to be above most of the lights I saw. Then I saw that I was not alone.

Over against the shadows of the ledge that, ran around the roof's edge, a great menacing form bulked in starlight. A pair of eyes glinted at me with a light not wholly sane; the starlight glanced silver from a curving length of steel. Yar Khan, the Afghan killer, fronted me in the silent shadows.

A fierce wild exultation surged over me. Now I could begin to pay the debt I owed Kathulos and all his hellish band! The dope fired my veins and sent waves of inhuman power and dark fury through me. A spring, and I was on my feet in a silent, deathly rush.

Yar Khan was a giant, taller and bulkier than I. He held a tulwar, and from the instant I saw him, I knew that he was full of the dope to the use of which he was addicted—heroin.

As I came in, he swung his heavy weapon high in air, but before he could strike I seized his sword wrist in an iron grip, and with my free hand drove smashing blows into his midriff.

Of that hideous battle, fought in silence above the sleeping city with only the stars to see, I remember little. I remember tumbling back and forth, locked in a death embrace. I remember the stiff beard rasping my flesh as his dope-fired eyes gazed wildly into mine. I remember the taste of hot blood in my mouth, the tang of fearful exultation in my soul, the onrushing and upsurging of inhuman strength and fury.

God, what a sight for a human eye, had anyone looked upon that grim roof where two human leopards, dope maniacs, tore each other to pieces!

I remember his arm breaking like rotten wood in my grip, and the tulwar falling from his useless hand. Handicapped as he was by a broken arm, the end was inevitable, and with one wild uproaring flood of might, I rushed him to the edge of the roof and bent him backward far out over the ledge. An instant, we struggled there; then I tore loose his hold and hurled him over, and one single shriek came up as he hurtled into the darkness below.

I stood upright, arms hurled up toward the stars, a terrible statue of primordial triumph. And down my breast trickled streams of blood from the long wounds left by the Afghan's frantic nails, on neck and face.

Then I turned with the craft of the maniac. Had no one heard the sound of that battle? My eyes were on the door through which I had come, but a noise made me turn; and for the first time I noticed a small affair like a tower jutting up from the roof. There was no window there, but there was a door, and even as I looked that door opened and a huge black form framed itself in the light that streamed from within. Hassim!

He stepped out on the roof and closed the door, his shoulders hunched and neck outthrust as he glanced this way and that. I struck him senseless to the roof with one hate-driven smash. I crouched over him, waiting some sign of returning consciousness. Then, away in the sky, close to the horizon, I saw a faint red tint. The rising of the moon!

Where in God's name was Gordon? Even as I stood undecided, a strange noise reached me. It was curiously like the droning of many bees.

Striding in the direction from which it seemed to come, I crossed the roof and leaned over the ledge. A sight nightmarish and incredible met my eyes.

Some twenty feet below the level of the roof on which I stood, there was another roof, of the same size and clearly a part of the same building. On one side it was bounded by the wall; on the other three sides a parapet several feet high took the place of a ledge.

A great throng of people stood, sat and squatted, close-packed on the roof—and without exception they were *Negroes*! There were hundreds of them, and it was their low-voiced conversation which I had heard. But what held my gaze was that upon which their eyes were fixed.

About the center of the roof rose a sort of teocalli some ten feet high, almost exactly like those found in Mexico and on which the priests of the Aztecs sacrificed human victims. This, allowing for its infinitely smaller scale, was an exact type of those sacrificial pyramids. On the flat top of it was a curiously carved altar, and beside it stood a lank, dusky form whom even the ghastly mask he wore could not disguise to my gaze—Santiago, the Haiti voodoo fetish man. On the altar lay John Gordon, stripped to the waist and bound hand and foot, but conscious.

I reeled back from the roof edge, rent in twain by indecision. Even the stimulus of the elixir was not equal to this. Then a sound brought me about to see Hassim struggling dizzily to his knees. I reached him with two long strides, and ruthlessly smashed him down again. Then I noticed a queer sort of contrivance dangling from his girdle. I bent and examined it. It was a mask similar to that worn by Santiago. Then my mind leaped, swift and sudden, to a wild desperate plan, which to my dope-ridden brain seemed not at all wild or desperate.

I stepped softly to the tower and, opening the door, peered inward. I saw no one who might need to be silenced, but I saw a long silken robe hanging upon a peg in the wall. The luck of the dope fiend! I snatched it and closed the door again. Hassim showed no signs of consciousness, but I gave him another smash on the chin to make sure and, seizing his mask, hurried to the ledge.

A low guttural chant floated up to me, jangling, barbaric, with an undertone of maniacal blood-lust. The Negroes, men and women, were swaying back and forth to the wild rhythm of their death chant. On the teocalli, Santiago stood like a statue of black basalt, facing the east, dagger held high—a wild and terrible sight, naked as he was save for a wide silken girdle and that inhuman mask on his face. The moon thrust a red rim above the eastern horizon and a faint breeze stirred the great black plumes which nodded above the voodoo man's mask. The chant of the worshippers dropped to a low, sinister whisper.

I hurriedly slipped on the death mask, gathered the robe close about me and prepared for the descent. I was prepared to drop the full distance, being sure in the superb confidence of my insanity that I would land unhurt, but as I climbed over the ledge I found a steel ladder leading down. Evidently Hassim, one of the voodoo priests, intended descending this way. So down I went, and in haste, for I knew that the instant the moon's lower rim cleared the city's skyline, that motionless dagger would descend into Gordon's breast.

Gathering the robe close about me so as to conceal my white skin, I stepped down upon the roof, and strode forward through rows of black worshippers who shrank aside to let me through. To the foot of the teocalli I stalked and up the stairs that ran about it, until I stood beside the death altar and marked the dark red stains upon it. Gordon lay on his back, his eyes open, his face drawn and haggard, but his gaze dauntless and unflinching.

Santiago's eyes blazed at me through the slits of his mask, but I read no suspicion in his gaze until I reached forward and took the dagger from his hand. He was too much astonished to resist, and the black throng fell suddenly silent. That he saw my hand was not that of a Negro it is certain, but he was simply struck speechless with astonishment. Moving swiftly I cut Gordon's bonds and hauled him erect. Then Santiago, with a shriek, leaped upon me—shrieked again and, arms flung high, pitched headlong from the teocalli, with his own dagger burred to the hilt in his breast.

Then the black worshippers were on us with a screech and a roar—leaping on the steps of the teocalli like black leopards in the moonlight, knives flashing, eyes gleaming whitely.

I tore mask and robe from me and answered Gordon's exclamation with a wild laugh. I had hoped that by virtue of my disguise I might get us both safely away, but now I was content to die there at his side.

He tore a great metal ornament from the altar, and as the attackers came he wielded this. A moment, we held them at bay, and then they flowed over us like a black wave. This to me was Valhalla! Knives stung me, and blackjacks smashed against me, but I laughed and drove my iron fists in straight, steam-hammer smashes that shattered flesh and bone. I saw Gordon's crude weapon rise and fall, and each time a man went down. Skulls shattered and blood splashed and the dark fury swept over me. Nightmare faces swirled about me, and I was on my knees; up again, and the faces crumpled before my blows. Through far mists, I seemed to hear a hideous familiar voice raised in imperious command. Gordon was swept away from me, but from the sounds I knew that the work of death still went on. The stars reeled through fogs of blood, but hell's exaltation was on me, and I reveled in the dark tides of fury, until a darker deeper tide swept over me and I knew no more.

CHAPTER TWENTY
ANCIENT HORROR

"Here now in his triumph where all things falter
Stretched out on the spoils that his own hand spread,
As a God self-slain on his own strange altar,
Death lies dead."
—Swinburne

Slowly, I drifted back into life—slowly, slowly. A mist held me, and in the mist I saw a Skull—

I lay in a steel cage like a captive wolf, and the bars were too strong, I saw, even for my strength. The cage seemed to be set in a sort of niche in the wall, and I was looking into a large room. This room was under the earth; for the floor was of stone flags and the walls and ceiling were composed of gigantic blocks of the same material. Shelves ranged the walls, covered with weird appliances, apparently of a scientific nature, and more were on the great table that stood in the center of the room. Beside this sat Kathulos.

The Sorcerer was clad in a snaky yellow robe, and those hideous hands and that terrible head were more pronouncedly reptilian than ever. He turned his great yellow eyes toward me, like pools of livid fire, and his parchment-thin lips moved in what probably, passed for a smile.

I staggered erect and gripped the bars, cursing.

"Gordon, curse you, where is Gordon?"

Kathulos took a test-tube from the table, eyed it closely and emptied it into another.

"Ah, my friend awakes," he murmured in his voice—the voice of a living dead man.

He thrust his hands into his long sleeves and turned fully to me.

"I think in you," he said distinctly, "I have created a Frankenstein monster. I made of you a superhuman creature to serve my wishes and you broke from me. You are the bane of my might, worse than Gordon, even. You have killed valuable servants and interfered with my plans. However, your evil comes to an end tonight. Your friend Gordon broke away but he is being hunted through the tunnels and cannot escape.

"You," he continued with the sincere interest of the scientist, "are a most interesting subject. Your brain must be formed differently from any other man that ever lived. I will make a close study of it and add it to my laboratory. How a man with apparent need of the elixir in his system, has managed to go on for two days still stimulated by the last draft, is more than I can understand."

My heart leaped. With all his wisdom, little Zuleika had tricked him, and he evidently did not know that she had filched a flask of the life-giving stuff from him.

"The last draft you had from me," he went on, "was sufficient only for some eight hours. I repeat, it has me puzzled. Can you offer any suggestion?"

I snarled wordlessly. He sighed.

"As always the barbarian. Truly the proverb speaks: 'Jest with the wounded tiger and warm the adder in your bosom before you seek to lift the savage from his savagery!'"

He meditated awhile in silence. I watched him uneasily. There was about him a vague and curious indifference—his long fingers emerging from the sleeves drummed on the chair arms, and some hidden exultation strummed at the back of his voice, lending it unaccustomed vibrancy.

"And you might have been king of the new regime," he said suddenly. "Aye, the new—new and inhumanly old!"

He bent his head as if listening. From far off seemed to come a hum of guttural voices. His lips writhed in a smile.

"My black children," he murmured. "They tear my enemy Gordon to pieces in the tunnels. They, Mr. Costigan, are my real henchmen, and it was for their edification tonight that I laid John Gordon on the sacrificial stone. I would have preferred to have made some experiments with him, based on certain scientific theories, but my children must be humored. Later, under my tutelage, they will outgrow their childish superstitions and throw aside their foolish customs, but now they must be led gently by the hand.

"How do you like these under-the-earth corridors, Mr. Costigan?" he switched suddenly. "You thought of them—what? No doubt that the white savages of your Middle Ages built them? Faugh? These tunnels are older than your world! They were brought into being by mighty kings, too many eons ago for your mind to grasp, when an imperial city towered where now this crude village of London stands. All trace of that metropolis has crumbled to dust and vanished but these corridors were built by more than human skill—ha! ha! Of all the teeming thousands who move daily above them, none knows of their existence save my servants—and not all of them. Zuleika, for instance, does not know of them, for of late I have begun to doubt her loyalty and shall doubtless soon make of her an example."

At that I hurled myself blindly against the side of the cage, a red wave of hate and fury tossing me in its grip. I seized the bars and strained until the veins stood out on my forehead and the muscles bulged and crackled in my arms and shoulders. And the bars bent before my onslaught—a little but no more, and finally the power flowed from my limbs and I sank down trembling and weakened.

"The bars hold," he announced with something almost like relief in his tone. "Frankly, I prefer to be on the opposite side of them. You are a human ape if there was ever one."

He laughed suddenly and wildly.

"But why do you seek to oppose me?" he shrieked unexpectedly. "Why defy me, who am Kathulos, the Sorcerer, great even in the days of the old empire? Today, invincible! A magician, a scientist, among ignorant savages! Ha, ha!"

I shuddered, and sudden blinding light broke in on me. Kathulos himself was an addict, and was fired by the stuff of his choice! What hellish concoction was strong enough, terrible enough to thrill the Master and inflame him, I do not know, nor do I wish to know. Of all the uncanny knowledge that was his, I, knowing the man as I did, count this the most weird and grisly.

"You, you paltry fool!" he was ranting, his face lit supernaturally. "Know you who I am? Kathulos of Egypt! Bah! They knew me in the old days! I reigned in the dim misty sea lands ages and ages before the sea rose and engulfed the land. I died, not as men die; the magic draft of life everlasting was ours! I drank deep and slept. Long I slept in my lacquered case! My flesh withered and grew hard: my blood dried in my veins. I became as one dead. But still within me burned the spirit of life, sleeping but anticipating the awakening. The great cities crumbled to dust. The sea drank the land. The tall shrines and the lofty spires sank beneath the green waves. All this I knew as I slept, as a man knows in dreams. Kathulos of Egypt? Faugh!*Kathulos of Atlantis*!"

I uttered a sudden involuntary cry. This was too grisly for sanity.

"Aye, the magician, the Sorcerer.

"And down the long years of savagery, through which the barbaric races struggled to rise without their masters, the legend came of the day of empire, when one of the Old Race would rise up from the sea. Aye, and lead to victory the black people who are our slaves in the old days.

"These brown and yellow people, what care I for them? The blacks were the slaves of my race, and I am their god today. They will obey me. The yellow and the brown people are fools—I make them my tools and the day will come when my black warriors will turn on them and slay at my word. And you, you white barbarians, whose ape-ancestors forever defied my race and me, your doom is at hand! And when I mount my universal throne, the only whites shall be white slaves!

"The day came as prophesied, when my case, breaking free from the halls where it lay—where it had lain when Atlantis was still sovran of the world—where since her empery it had sunk into the green fathoms—when my case, I say, was smitten by the deep sea tides and moved and stirred, and thrust aside the clinging seaweed that masks temples and minarets, and came floating up past the lofty sapphire and golden spires, up through the green waters, to float upon the lazy waves of the sea.

"Then came a white fool carrying out the destiny of which he was not aware. The men on his ship, true believers, knew that the time had come. And I—the air entered my nostrils and I awoke from the long, long sleep.

"I stirred and I moved and lived. And rising in the night, I slew the fool that had lifted me from the ocean, and my servants made obeisance to me and took me into Africa, where I abode awhile and learned new languages and new ways of a new world, and became strong.

"The wisdom of your dreary world—ha ha! I who delved deeper in the mysteries of the old than any man dared go! All that men know today, I know, and the knowledge beside that which I have brought down the centuries is as a grain of sand beside a mountain! You should know something of that knowledge! By it I lifted you from one hell to plunge you into a greater! You fool, here at my hand is that which would lift you from this! Aye, would strike from you the chains whereby I have bound you!"

He snatched up a golden vial and shook it before my gaze. I eyed it as men dying in the desert must eye the distant mirages. Kathulos fingered it meditatively. His unnatural excitement seemed to have passed suddenly, and when he spoke again it was in the passionless, measured tones of the scientist.

"That would indeed be an experiment worth while—to free you of the elixir habit and see if your dope-riddled body would sustain life. Nine times out of ten the victim, with the need and stimulus removed, would die—but you are such a giant of a brute—"

He sighed and set the vial down.

"The dreamer opposes the man of destiny. My time is not my own or I should choose to spend my life in my laboratories, carrying out my experiments. But now, as in the days of the old empire when kings sought my counsel, I must work and labor for the good of the race at large. Aye, I must toil and sow the seed of glory against the full coming of the imperial days when the seas give up all their living dead."

I shuddered. Kathulos laughed wildly again. His fingers began to drum his chair arms and his face gleamed with the unnatural light once more. The red visions had begun to seethe in his skull again.

"Under the green seas they lie, the ancient masters, in their lacquered cases, dead as men reckon death, but only sleeping. Sleeping through the long ages as hours, awaiting the day of awakening! The old masters, the wise men, who foresaw the day when the sea would gulp the land, and who made ready. Made ready that they might rise again in the barbaric days to come. As did I. Sleeping they lie, ancient kings and grim wizards, who died as men die, before Atlantis sank. Who, sleeping, sank with her but who shall rise again!

"Mine the glory! I rose first. And I sought out the site of old cities, on shores that did not sink. Vanished, long vanished. The barbarian tide swept over them thousands of years ago as the green waters swept over their elder sister of the deeps. On some, the deserts stretch bare. Over some, as here, young barbarian cities rise."

He halted suddenly. His eyes sought one of the dark openings that marked a corridor. I think his strange intuition warned him of some impending danger but I do not believe that he had any inkling of how dramatically our scene would be interrupted.

As he looked, swift footsteps sounded and a man appeared suddenly in the doorway—a man disheveled, tattered and bloody. *John Gordon*! Kathulos sprang erect with a cry, and Gordon, gasping as from superhuman exertion, brought down the revolver he held in his hand and fired point-blank. Kathulos staggered, clapping his hand to his breast, and then, groping wildly, reeled to the wall and fell against it. A doorway opened and he reeled through, but as Gordon leaped fiercely across the chamber, a blank stone surface met his gaze, which yielded not to his savage hammerings.

He whirled and ran drunkenly to the table where lay a bunch of keys the Master had dropped there.

"The vial!" I shrieked. "Take the vial!" And he thrust it into his pocket.

Back along the corridor through which he had come sounded a faint clamor, growing swiftly like a wolf-pack in full cry. A few precious seconds spent with fumbling for the right key, then the cage door swung open and I sprang out. A sight for the gods we were, the two of us! Slashed, bruised and cut, our garments hanging in tatters—my wounds had ceased to bleed, but now as I moved they began again, and from the stiffness of my hands I knew that my knuckles were shattered. As for Gordon, he was fairly drenched in blood from crown to foot.

We made off down a passage in the opposite direction from the menacing noise, which

I knew to be the black servants of the Master in full pursuit of us. Neither of us was in good shape for running, but we did our best. Where we were going I had no idea. My superhuman strength had deserted me, and I was going on will power alone. We switched off into another corridor, and we had not gone twenty steps when, looking back, I saw the first of the black devils rounding the corner.

A desperate effort increased our lead a trifle, but they had seen us, were in full view now, and a yell of fury broke from them, to be succeeded by a more sinister silence as they bent all efforts to overhauling us.

There, a short distance in front of us, we saw a stair loom suddenly in the gloom. If we might reach that—but we saw something else.

Against the ceiling, between us and the stairs, hung a huge thing like an iron grill, with great spikes along the bottom—a portcullis.

And even as we looked, without halting in our panting strides, it began to move.

"They're lowering the portcullis!" Gordon croaked, his blood-streaked face a mask of exhaustion and will.

Now the blacks were only ten feet behind us—now the huge grate, gaining momentum, with a creak of rusty, unused mechanism, rushed downward. A final spurt, a gasping straining nightmare of pure nerve-strength, hurled us under and through, and the grate crashed behind us!

A moment we lay gasping, not heeding the frenzied horde who raved and screamed on the other side of the grate. So close had that final leap been, that the great spikes in their descent had torn shreds from our clothing.

The blacks were thrusting at us with daggers through the bars, but we were out of reach and it seemed to me that I was content to lie there and die of exhaustion. But Gordon weaved unsteadily erect and hauled me with him.

"Got to get out," he croaked; "got to warn—Scotland Yard—honeycombs in heart of London—high explosives—arms—ammunition."

We blundered up the steps, and in front of us I seemed to hear a sound of metal grating against metal. The stairs ended abruptly, on a landing that terminated in a blank wall. Gordon hammered against this and the inevitable secret doorway opened. Light streamed in, through the bars of a sort of grille. Men in the uniform of London police were sawing at these with hacksaws, and even as they greeted us, an opening was made through which we crawled.

"You're hurt, sir!" One of the men took Gordon's arm.

My companion shook him off.

"There's no time to lose! Out of here, as quick as we can go!"

I saw that we were in a basement of some sort. We hastened up the steps and out into the early dawn which was turning the east scarlet. Over the tops of smaller houses I saw in the distance a great gaunt building on the roof of which, I felt instinctively, that wild drama had been enacted the night before.

"That building was leased some months ago by a mysterious Chinaman," said Gordon, following my gaze. "Office building originally—the neighborhood deteriorated and the building stood vacant for some time. The new tenant added several stories to it but left it apparently empty. Had my eye on it for some time."

This was told in Gordon's jerky swift manner as we started hurriedly along the sidewalk. I listened mechanically, like a man in a trance. My vitality was ebbing fast, and I knew that I was going to crumple at any moment.

"The people living in the vicinity had been reporting strange sights and noises. The man who owned the basement we just left heard queer sounds emanating from the wall of the basement, and called the police. About that time I was racing back and forth among those cursed corridors like a hunted rat, and I heard the police banging on the wall.

"I found the secret door and opened it, but found it barred by a grating. It was while I was telling the astounded policemen to procure a hacksaw that the pursuing Negroes, whom I had eluded for the moment, came in sight, and I was forced to shut the door and run for it again. By pure luck I found you and by pure luck managed to find the way back to the door.

"Now we must get to Scotland Yard. If we strike swiftly, we may capture the entire band of devils. Whether I killed Kathulos or not I do not know, or if he can be killed by mortal weapons. But to the best of my knowledge all of them are now in those subterranean corridors and—"

At that moment the world shook! A brain-shattering roar seemed to break the sky with its incredible detonation; houses tottered and crashed to ruins; a mighty pillar of smoke and flame burst from the earth, and on its wings great masses of débris soared skyward. A black fog of smoke and dust and falling timbers enveloped the world, a prolonged thunder seemed to rumble up from the center of the earth as of walls and ceilings falling, and amid the uproar and the screaming I sank down and knew no more.

CHAPTER TWENTY-ONE
THE BREAKING OF THE CHAIN

"And like a soul belated,
In heaven and hell unmated,
By cloud and mist abated,
Comes out of darkness morn."
—Swinburne

There is little need to linger on the scenes of horror of that terrible London morning. The world is familiar with and knows most of the details attendant to the great explosion which wiped out a tenth of that great city with a resultant loss of lives and property. For such a happening some reason must needs be given; the tale of the deserted building got out, and many wild stories were circulated.

Finally, to still the rumors, the report was unofficially given out that this building had been the rendezvous and secret stronghold of a gang of international anarchists, who had stored its basement full of high explosives and who had supposedly ignited these accidentally. In a way there was a good deal to this tale, as you know, but the threat that had lurked there far transcended that one.

All this was told to me, for when I sank unconscious, Gordon, attributing my condition to exhaustion and a need of the hashish to the use of which he thought I was addicted, lifted me, and with the aid of the stunned policeman, got me to his rooms before returning to the scene of the explosion. At his rooms he found Hansen, and Zuleika handcuffed to the bed as I had left her. He released her and left her to tend to me, for all London was in a terrible turmoil, and he was needed elsewhere.

When I came to myself at last, I looked up into her starry eyes and lay quiet, smiling up at her. She sank down upon my bosom, nestling my head in her arms and covering my face with her kisses.

"Steephen!" she sobbed over and over, as her tears splashed hot on my face.

I was scarcely strong enough to put my arms about her, but I managed it. And we lay there for a space, in silence except for the girl's hard, racking sobs.

"Zuleika, I love you," I murmured.

"And I love you, Steephen," she sobbed. "Oh, it is so hard to part now—but I'm going with you, Steephen; I can't live without you!"

"My dear child," said John Gordon, entering the room suddenly, "Costigan's not going to die. We will let him have enough hashish to tide him along, and when he is stronger we will take him off the habit slowly."

"You don't understand, sahib; it is not hashish Steephen must have. It is something which only the Master knew, and now that he is dead or is fled, Steephen cannot get it and must die."

Gordon shot a quick, uncertain glance at me. His fine face was drawn and haggard, his clothes sooty and torn from his work among the débris of the explosion.

"She's right, Gordon," I said languidly. "I'm dying. Kathulos killed the hashish-craving with a concoction he called the elixir. I've been keeping myself alive on some of the stuff that Zuleika stole from him and gave me, but I drank it all last night."

I was aware of no craving of any kind, no physical or mental discomfort, even. All my mechanism was slowing down fast; I had passed the stage where the need of the elixir would tear and rend me. I felt only a great lassitude and a desire to sleep. And I knew that the moment I closed my eyes, I would die.

"A strange dope, that elixir," I said with growing languor. "It burns and freezes, and then at last the craving kills easily and without torment."

"Costigan, curse it," said Gordon desperately, "you can't go like this! That vial I took from the Egyptian's table—what is in it?"

"The Master swore it would free me of my curse and probably kill me also," I muttered. "I'd forgotten about it. Let me have it; it can no more than kill me, and I'm dying now."

"Yes, quick, let me have it!" exclaimed Zuleika fiercely, springing to Gordon's side, her hands passionately, outstretched. She returned with the vial which he had taken from his pocket, and knelt beside me, holding it to my lips, while she murmured to me gently and soothingly in her own language.

I drank, draining the vial, but feeling little interest in the whole matter. My outlook was purely impersonal, at such a low ebb was my life, and I cannot even remember how the stuff tasted. I only remember feeling a curious sluggish fire burn faintly along my veins, and the last thing I saw was Zuleika crouching over me, her great eyes fixed with a burning intensity on me. Her tense little hand rested inside her blouse, and remembering her vow to take her own life if I died, I tried to lift a hand and disarm her, tried to tell Gordon to take away the dagger she had hidden in her garments. But speech and action failed me and I drifted away into a curious sea of unconsciousness.

Of that period I remember nothing. No sensation fired my sleeping brain to such an extent as to bridge the gulf over which I drifted. They say I lay like a dead man for hours, scarcely breathing, while Zuleika hovered over me, never leaving my side an instant, and fighting like a tigress when anyone tried to coax her away to rest. Her chain was broken.

As I had carried the vision of her into that dim land of nothingness, so her dear eyes were the first thing which greeted my returning consciousness. I was aware of a greater weakness than I thought possible for a man to feel, as if I had been an invalid for months, but the life in me, faint though it was, was sound and normal, caused by no artificial stimulation. I smiled up at my girl, and murmured weakly:

"Throw away your dagger, little Zuleika: I'm going to live."

She screamed and fell on her knees beside me, weeping and laughing at the same time. Women are strange beings, of mixed and powerful emotions, truly.

Gordon entered and grasped the hand which I could not lift from the bed.

"You're a case for an ordinary human physician now, Costigan," he said. "Even a layman like myself can tell that. For the first time, since I've known you, the look in your eyes is entirely sane. You look like a man who has had a complete nervous breakdown, and needs about a year of rest and quiet. Great heavens, man, you've been through enough, outside your dope experience, to last you a lifetime."

"Tell me first," said I, "was Kathulos killed in the explosion?"

"I don't know," answered Gordon somberly. "Apparently the entire system of subterranean passages was destroyed. I know my last bullet—the last bullet that was in the revolver which I wrested from one of my attackers—found its mark in the Master's body, but whether he died from the wound, or whether a bullet can hurt him, I do not know. And whether in his death agonies he ignited the tons and tons of high explosives which were stored in the corridors, or whether the Negroes did it unintentionally, we shall never know.

"My God, Costigan, did you ever see such a honeycomb? And we know not how many miles in either direction the passages reached. Even now Scotland Yard men are combing the subways and basements of the town for secret openings. All known openings, such as the one through which we came and the one in Soho, Forty-eight, were blocked by falling walls. The office building was simply blown to atoms."

"What about the men who raided Soho, Forty-eight?"

"The door in the library wall had been closed. They found the Chinaman you killed, but searched the house without avail. Lucky for them, too, else they had doubtless been in the tunnels when the explosion came, and perished with the hundreds of Negroes who must have died there."

"Every Negro in London must have been there."

"I daresay. Most of them are voodoo worshippers at heart, and the power the Master wielded was incredible."

My tale draws to a close. The months that followed passed uneventfully, except for the growing happiness which to me was paradise, but which would bore you were I to relate it. But one day Gordon and I again discussed the mysterious happenings that had had their being under the grim hand of the Master.

"Since that day," said Gordon, "the world has been quiet. Africa has subsided and the East seems to have returned to her ancient sleep. There can be but one answer—living or dead, Kathulos was destroyed that morning when his world crashed all about him."

"Gordon," said I, "what is the answer to that greatest of all mysteries?"

My friend shrugged his shoulders.

"I have come to believe that mankind eternally hovers on the brinks of secret oceans of which it knows nothing. Races have lived and vanished before our race rose out of the slime of the primitive, and it is likely still others will live upon the earth after ours has vanished. Scientists have long upheld the theory that the Atlanteans possessed a higher civilization than our own and on very different lines. Certainly Kathulos himself was proof that our boasted culture and knowledge were nothing beside that of whatever fearful civilization produced him."

"I have him to thank for two things," I said slowly: "the regaining of my lost manhood—and Zuleika. Kathulos, then, is dead, as far as any mortal thing can die. But what of those others—those 'ancient masters' who still sleep in the sea?"

Gordon shuddered.

"As I said, perhaps mankind loiters on the brink of unthinkable chasms of horror. But a fleet of gunboats is even now patrolling the oceans unobtrusively, with orders to destroy instantly any strange case that may be found."

"At night I dream of them, sometimes," I muttered, "sleeping in their lacquered cases, which drip with strange seaweed, far down among the green surges—where unholy spires and strange towers rise in the dark ocean."

"We have been face to face with an ancient horror," said Gordon somberly, "with a fear too dark and mysterious for the human brain to cope with. Fortune has been with us; she may not again favor the sons of men. It is best that we be ever on our guard. The universe was not made for humanity alone; life takes strange phases and it is the first instinct of nature for the different species to destroy each other. No doubt we seemed as horrible to the Master as he did to us. We have scarcely tapped the chest of secrets which nature has stored, and I shudder to think of what that chest may hold for the human race."

"That's true," said I, inwardly rejoicing at the vigor which was beginning to course through my wasted veins, "but men will meet obstacles as they come, as men have always risen to meet them. Now, I am beginning to know the full worth of life and love, and not all the devils from all the abysses can hold me."

Gordon smiled.

"You have it coming to you, old comrade. The best thing is to forget all about that dark interlude, for in that course lies light and happiness."

THE WHISPERER IN DARKNESS

BY

H. P. LOVECRAFT

I

Bear in mind closely that I did not see any actual visual horror at the end. To say that a mental shock was the cause of what I inferred—that last straw which sent me racing out of the lonely Akeley farmhouse and through the wild domed hills of Vermont in a commandeered motor at night—is to ignore the plainest facts of my final experience. Notwithstanding the deep extent to which I shared the information and speculations of Henry Akeley, the things I saw and heard, and the admitted vividness of the impression produced on me by these things, I cannot prove even now whether I was right or wrong in my hideous inference. For after all, Akeley's disappearance establishes nothing. People found nothing amiss in his house despite the bullet-marks on the outside and inside. It was just as though he had walked out casually for a ramble in the hills and failed to return. There was not even a sign that a guest had been there, or that those horrible cylinders and machines had been stored in the study. That he had mortally feared the crowded green hills and endless trickle of brooks among which he had been born and reared, means nothing at all, either; for thousands are subject to just such morbid fears. Eccentricity, moreover, could easily account for his strange acts and apprehensions toward the last.

The whole matter began, so far as I am concerned, with the historic and unprecedented Vermont floods of November 3rd, 1927. I was then, as now, an instructor of literature at Miskatonic University in Arkham, Massachusetts, and an enthusiastic amateur student of New England folklore. Shortly after the flood, amidst the varied reports of hardship, suffering, and organized relief which filled the press, there appeared certain odd stories of things found floating in some of the swollen rivers; so that many of my friends embarked on curious discussions and appealed to me to shed what light I could on the subject. I felt flattered at having my folklore study taken so seriously, and did what I could to belittle the wild, vague tales which seemed so clearly an outgrowth of old rustic superstitions. It amused me to find several persons of education who insisted that some stratum of obscure, distorted fact might underlie the rumors.

The tales thus brought to my notice came mostly through newspaper cuttings; though one yarn had an oral source and was repeated to a friend of mine in a letter from his mother in Hardwick, Vermont. The type of thing described was essentially the same in all cases, though there seemed to be three separate instances involved—one connected with the

Winooski River near Montpelier, another attached to the West River in Windham County beyond Newfane, and a third centering in the Passumpsic in Caledonia County above Lyndonville. Of course many of the stray items mentioned other instances, but on analysis they all seemed to boil down to these three. In each case country folk reported seeing one or more very bizarre and disturbing objects in the surging waters that poured down from the unfrequented hills, and there was a widespread tendency to connect these sights with a primitive, half-forgotten cycle of whispered legend which old people resurrected for the occasion.

What people thought they saw were organic shapes not quite like any they had ever seen before. Naturally, there were many human bodies washed along by the streams in that tragic period; but those who described these strange shapes felt quite sure that they were not human, despite some superficial resemblances in size and general outline. Nor, said the witnesses, could they have been any kind of animal known to Vermont. They were pinkish things about five feet long; with crustaceous bodies bearing vast pairs of dorsal fins or membranous wings and several sets of articulated limbs, and with a sort of convoluted ellipsoid, covered with multitudes of very short antennae, where a head would ordinarily be. It was really remarkable how closely the reports from different sources tended to coincide; though the wonder was lessened by the fact that the old legends, shared at one time throughout the hill country, furnished a morbidly vivid picture which might well have colored the imaginations of all the witnesses concerned. It was my conclusion that such witnesses—in every case naive and simple backwoods folk—had glimpsed the battered and bloated bodies of human beings or farm animals in the whirling currents; and had allowed the half-remembered folklore to invest these pitiful objects with fantastic attributes.

The ancient folklore, while cloudy, evasive, and largely forgotten by the present generation, was of a highly singular character, and obviously reflected the influence of still earlier Indian tales. I knew it well, though I had never been in Vermont, through the exceedingly rare monograph of Eli Davenport, which embraces material orally obtained prior to 1839 among the oldest people of the state. This material, moreover, closely coincided with tales which I had personally heard from elderly rustics in the mountains of New Hampshire. Briefly summarized, it hinted at a hidden race of monstrous beings which lurked somewhere among the remoter hills—in the deep woods of the highest peaks, and the dark valleys where streams trickle from unknown sources. These beings were seldom glimpsed, but evidences of their presence were reported by those who had ventured farther than usual up the slopes of certain mountains or into certain deep, steep-sided gorges that even the wolves shunned.

There were queer footprints or claw-prints in the mud of brook-margins and barren patches, and curious circles of stones, with the grass around them worn away, which did not seem to have been placed or entirely shaped by Nature. There were, too, certain caves of problematical depth in the sides of the hills; with mouths closed by boulders in a manner scarcely accidental, and with more than an average quota of the queer prints leading both toward and away from them—if indeed the direction of these prints could be justly estimated. And worst of all, there were the things which adventurous people had seen very rarely in the twilight of the remotest valleys and the dense perpendicular woods above the limits of normal hill-climbing.

It would have been less uncomfortable if the stray accounts of these things had not agreed so well. As it was, nearly all the rumors had several points in common; averring that the creatures were a sort of huge, light-red crab with many pairs of legs and with two great bat-like wings in the middle of the back. They sometimes walked on all their legs, and sometimes on the hindmost pair only, using the others to convey large objects of indeterminate nature. On one occasion they were spied in considerable numbers, a detachment of them wading along a shallow woodland watercourse three abreast in evidently disciplined formation. Once a specimen was seen flying—launching itself from the top of a bald, lonely hill at night and vanishing in the sky after its great flapping wings had been silhouetted an instant against the full moon.

These things seemed content, on the whole, to let mankind alone; though they were at times held responsible for the disappearance of venturesome individuals—especially persons who built houses too close to certain valleys or too high up on certain mountains. Many localities came to be known as inadvisable to settle in, the feeling persisting long after the cause was forgotten. People would look up at some of the neighboring mountain-precipices with a shudder, even when not recalling how many settlers had been lost, and how many farmhouses burned to ashes, on the lower slopes of those grim, green sentinels.

But while according to the earliest legends the creatures would appear to have harmed only those trespassing on their privacy; there were later accounts of their curiosity respecting men, and of their attempts to establish secret outposts in the human world. There were tales of the queer claw-prints seen around farmhouse windows in the morning, and of occasional disappearances in regions outside the obviously haunted areas. Tales, besides, of buzzing voices in imitation of human speech which made surprising offers to lone travelers on roads and cart-paths in the deep woods, and of children frightened out of their wits by things seen or heard where the primal forest pressed close upon their dooryards. In the final layer of legends—the layer just preceding the decline of superstition and the abandonment of close contact with the dreaded places—there are shocked references to hermits and remote farmers who at some period of life appeared to have undergone a repellent mental change, and who were shunned and whispered about as mortals who had sold themselves to the strange beings. In one of the northeastern counties it seemed to be a fashion about 1800 to accuse eccentric and unpopular recluses of being allies or representatives of the abhorred things.

As to what the things were—explanations naturally varied. The common name applied to them was "those ones," or "the old ones," though other terms had a local and transient use. Perhaps the bulk of the Puritan settlers set them down bluntly as familiars of the devil, and made them a basis of awed theological speculation. Those with Celtic legendry in their heritage—mainly the Scotch-Irish element of New Hampshire, and their kindred who had settled in Vermont on Governor Wentworth's colonial grants—linked them vaguely with the malign fairies and "little people" of the bogs and raths, and protected themselves with scraps of incantation handed down through many generations. But the Indians had the most fantastic theories of all. While different tribal legends differed, there was a marked consensus of belief in certain vital particulars; it being unanimously agreed that the creatures were not native to this earth.

The Pennacook myths, which were the most consistent and picturesque, taught that the Winged Ones came from the Great Bear in the sky, and had mines in our earthly hills whence they took a kind of stone they could not get on any other world. They did not live here, said the myths, but merely maintained outposts and flew back with vast cargos of stone to their own stars in the north. They harmed only those earth-people who got too near them or spied upon them. Animals shunned them through instinctive hatred, not because of being hunted. They could not eat the things and animals of earth, but brought their own food from the stars. It was bad to get near them, and sometimes young hunters who went into their hills never came back. It was not good, either, to listen to what they whispered at night in the forest with voices like a bee's that tried to be like the voices of men. They knew the speech of all kinds of men—Pennacooks, Hurons, men of the Five Nations—but did not seem to have or need any speech of their own. They talked with their heads, which changed color in different ways to mean different things.

All the legendry, of course, white and Indian alike, died down during the nineteenth century, except for occasional atavistical flare-ups. The ways of the Vermonters became settled; and once their habitual paths and dwellings were established according to a certain fixed plan, they remembered less and less what fears and avoidances had determined that plan, and even that there had been any fears or avoidances. Most people simply knew that certain hilly regions were considered as highly unhealthy, unprofitable, and generally unlucky to live in, and that the farther one kept from them the better off one usually was. In time the ruts of custom and economic interest became so deeply cut in approved places that there was no longer any reason for going outside them, and the haunted hills were left deserted by accident rather than by design. Save during infrequent local scares, only wonder-loving grandmothers and retrospective nonagenarians ever whispered of beings dwelling in those hills; and even such whisperers admitted that there was not much to fear from those things now that they were used to the presence of houses and settlements, and now that human beings let their chosen territory severely alone.

All this I had known from my reading, and from certain folk tales picked up in New Hampshire; hence when the flood-time rumors began to appear, I could easily guess what imaginative background had evolved them. I took great pains to explain this to my friends, and was correspondingly amused when several contentious souls continued to insist on a possible element of truth in the reports. Such persons tried to point out that the early legends had a significant persistence and uniformity, and that the virtually unexplored nature of the Vermont hills made it unwise to be dogmatic about what might or might not dwell among them; nor could they be silenced by my assurance that all the myths were of a well-known pattern common to most of mankind and determined by early phases of imaginative experience which always produced the same type of delusion.

It was of no use to demonstrate to such opponents that the Vermont myths differed but little in essence from those universal legends of natural personification which filled the ancient world with fauns and dryads and satyrs, suggested the *kallikantzaroi* of modern Greece, and gave to wild Wales and Ireland their dark hints of strange, small, and terrible hidden races of troglodytes and burrowers. No use, either, to point out the even more startlingly similar belief of the Nepalese hill tribes in the dreaded *Mi-Go* or "Abominable Snow-Men" who lurk hideously amidst the ice and rock pinnacles of the Himalayan summits. When I brought up this evidence, my opponents turned it against me by claiming that it must imply some actual historicity for the ancient tales; that it must argue the real existence of some queer elder earth-race, driven to hiding after the advent and dominance of mankind, which might very conceivably have survived in reduced numbers to relatively recent times—or even to the present.

The more I laughed at such theories, the more these stubborn friends asseverated them; adding that even without the heritage of legend the recent reports were too clear, consistent, detailed, and sanely prosaic in manner of telling, to be completely ignored. Two or three fanatical extremists went so far as to hint at possible meanings in the ancient Indian tales which gave the hidden beings a non-terrestrial origin; citing the extravagant books of

Charles Fort with their claims that voyagers from other worlds and outer space have often visited earth. Most of my foes, however, were merely romanticists who insisted on trying to transfer to real life the fantastic lore of lurking "little people" made popular by the magnificent horror-fiction of Arthur Machen.

II

As was only natural under the circumstances, this piquant debating finally got into print in the form of letters to the *Arkham Advertiser*; some of which were copied in the press of those Vermont regions whence the flood-stories came. The *Rutland Herald* gave half a page of extracts from the letters on both sides, while the *Brattleboro Reformer* reprinted one of my long historical and mythological summaries in full, with some accompanying comments in "The Pendrifter's" thoughtful column which supported and applauded my skeptical conclusions. By the spring of 1928 I was almost a well-known figure in Vermont, notwithstanding the fact that I had never set foot in the state. Then came the challenging letters from Henry Akeley which impressed me so profoundly, and which took me for the first and last time to that fascinating realm of crowded green precipices and muttering forest streams.

Most of what I now know of Henry Wentworth Akeley was gathered by correspondence with his neighbors, and with his only son in California, after my experience in his lonely farmhouse. He was, I discovered, the last representative on his home soil of a long, locally distinguished line of jurists, administrators, and gentlemen-agriculturists. In him, however, the family mentally had veered away from practical affairs to pure scholarship; so that he had been a notable student of mathematics, astronomy, biology, anthropology, and folklore at the University of Vermont. I had never previously heard of him, and he did not give many autobiographical details in his communications; but from the first I saw he was a man of character, education, and intelligence, albeit a recluse with very little worldly sophistication.

Despite the incredible nature of what he claimed, I could not help at once taking Akeley more seriously than I had taken any of the other challengers of my views. For one thing, he was really close to the actual phenomena—visible and tangible—that he speculated so grotesquely about; and for another thing, he was amazingly willing to leave his conclusions in a tentative state like a true man of science. He had no personal preferences to advance, and was always guided by what he took to be solid evidence. Of course I began by considering him mistaken, but gave him credit for being intelligently mistaken; and at no time did I emulate some of his friends in attributing his ideas, and his fear of the lonely green hills, to insanity. I could see that there was a great deal to the man, and knew that what he reported must surely come from strange circumstances deserving investigation, however little it might have to do with the fantastic causes he assigned. Later on I received from him certain material proofs which placed the matter on a somewhat different and bewilderingly bizarre basis.

I cannot do better than transcribe in full, so far as is possible, the long letter in which Akeley introduced himself, and which formed such an important landmark in my own intellectual history. It is no longer in my possession, but my memory holds almost every word of its portentous message; and again I affirm my confidence in the sanity of the man who wrote it. Here is the text—a text which reached me in the cramped, archaic-looking scrawl of one who had obviously not mingled much with the world during his sedate, scholarly life.

R.F.D. #2, Townshend, Windham Co., Vermont
May 5th, 1928

Albert N. Wilmarth, Esq.,
118 Saltonstall St,
Arkham, Mass,

My dear Sir:—
I have read with great interest the *Brattleboro Reformer's* reprint (Apr. 23, '28) of your letter on the recent stories of strange bodies seen floating in our flooded streams last fall, and on the curious folklore they so well agree with. It is easy to see why an outlander would take the position you take, and even why "Pendrifter" agrees with you. That is the attitude generally taken by educated persons both in and out of Vermont, and was my own attitude as a young man (I am now 57) before my studies, both general and in Davenport's book, led me to do some exploring in parts of the hills hereabouts not usually visited.

I was directed toward such studies by the queer old tales I used to hear from elderly farmers of the more ignorant sort, but now I wish I had let the whole matter alone. I might say, with all proper modesty, that the subject of anthropology and folklore is by no means strange to me. I took a good deal of it at college, and am familiar with most of the standard authorities such as Tylor, Lubbock, Frazer, Quatrefages, Murray, Osborn, Keith, Boule, G. Elliot

Smith, and so on. It is no news to me that tales of hidden races are as old as all mankind. I have seen the reprints of letters from you, and those arguing with you, in the *Rutland Herald*, and guess I know about where your controversy stands at the present time.

What I desire to say now is, that I am afraid your adversaries are nearer right than yourself, even though all reason seems to be on your side. They are nearer right than they realize themselves—for of course they go only by theory, and cannot know what I know. If I knew as little of the matter as they, I would not feel justified in believing as they do. I would be wholly on your side.

You can see that I am having a hard time getting to the point, probably because I really dread getting to the point; but the upshot of the matter is that *I have certain evidence that monstrous things do indeed live in the woods on the high hills which nobody visits. I* have not seen any of the things floating in the rivers, as reported, *but I have seen things like them* under circumstances I dread to repeat. I have seen footprints, and of late have seen them nearer my own home (I live in the old Akeley place south of Townshend Village, on the side of Dark Mountain) than I dare tell you now. And I have overheard voices in the woods at certain points that I will not even begin to describe on paper.

At one place I heard them so much that I took a phonograph there—with a dictaphone attachment and wax blank—and I shall try to arrange to have you hear the record I got. I have run it on the machine for some of the old people up here, and one of the voices had nearly scared them paralyzed by reason of its likeness to a certain voice (that buzzing voice in the woods which Davenport mentions) that their grandmothers have told about and mimicked for them. I know what most people think of a man who tells about "hearing voices"—but before you draw conclusions just listen to this record and ask some of the older backwoods people what they think of it. If you can account for it normally, very well; but there must be something behind it. *Ex nihilo nihil fit*, you know.

Now my object in writing you is not to start an argument, but to give you information which I think a man of your tastes will find deeply interesting. *This is private. Publicly I am on your side*, for certain things shew me that it does not do for people to know too much about these matters. My own studies are now wholly private, and I would not think of saying anything to attract people's attention and cause them to visit the places I have explored. It is true—terribly true—that there are non-human creatures watching us all the time; with spies among us gathering information. It is from a wretched man who, if he was sane (as I think he was), was one of those spies, that I got a large part of my clues to the matter. He later killed himself, but I have reason to think there are others now.

The things come from another planet, being able to live in interstellar space and fly through it on clumsy, powerful wings which have a way of resisting the aether but which are too poor at steering to be of much use in helping them about on earth. I will tell you about this later if you do not dismiss me at once as a madman. They come here to get metals from mines that go deep under the hills, *and I think I know where they come from.* They will not hurt us if we let them alone, but no one can say what will happen if we get too curious about them. Of course a good army of men could wipe out their mining colony. That is what they are afraid of. But if that happened, more would come from *outside*—any number of them. They could easily conquer the earth, but have not tried so far because they have not needed to. They would rather leave things as they are to save bother.

I think they mean to get rid of me because of what I have discovered. There is a great black stone with unknown hieroglyphics half worn away which I found in the woods on Round Hill, east of here; and after I took it home everything became different. If they think I suspect too much they will either kill me *or take me off the earth to where they come from.* They like to take away men of learning once in a while, to keep informed on the state of things in the human world.

This leads me to my secondary purpose in addressing you—namely, to urge you to hush up the present debate rather than give it more publicity. *People must be kept away from these hills*, and in order to effect this, their curiosity ought not to be aroused any further. Heaven knows there is peril enough anyway, with promoters and real estate men flooding Vermont with herds of summer people to overrun the wild places and cover the hills with cheap bungalows.

I shall welcome further communication with you, and shall try to send you that phonograph record and black stone (which is so worn that photographs don't show much) by express if you are willing. I say "try" because I think those creatures have a way of tampering with things around here. There is a sullen, furtive fellow named Brown, on a farm near the village, who I think is their spy. Little by little they are trying to cut me off from our world because I know too much about their world.

They have the most amazing way of finding out what I do. You may not even get this letter. I think I shall have to leave this part of the country and go to live with my son in San Diego, Cal., if things get any worse, but it is not easy to give up the place you were born in, and where your family has lived for six generations. Also, I would hardly dare sell this house to anybody now that the *creatures* have taken notice of it. They seem to be trying to get the black stone back and destroy the phonograph record, but I shall not let them if I can help it. My great police dogs always hold them back, for there are very few here as yet, and they are clumsy in getting about. As I have said, their wings are not much use for short flights on earth. I am on the very brink of deciphering that stone—in a very terrible way—and with your knowledge of folklore you may be able to supply missing links enough to help me. I suppose you know all about the fearful myths antedating the coming of man to the earth—the Yog-Sothoth and Cthulhu cycles—which are hinted at in the *Necronomicon*. I had access to a copy of that once, and hear that you have one in your college library under lock and key.

To conclude, Mr. Wilmarth, I think that with our respective studies we can be very useful to each other. I don't wish to put you in any peril, and suppose I ought to warn you that possession of the stone and the record won't be very safe; but I think you will find any risks worth running for the sake of knowledge. I will drive down to Newfane or Brattleboro to send whatever you authorize me to send, for the express offices there are more to be trusted. I might say that I live quite alone now, since I can't keep hired help any more. They won't stay because of the things that try to get near the house at night, and that keep the dogs barking continually. I am glad I didn't get as deep as this into the business while my wife was alive, for it would have driven her mad.

Hoping that I am not bothering you unduly, and that you will decide to get in touch with me rather than throw this letter into the waste basket as a madman's raving, I am

Yrs. very truly,
HENRY W. AKELEY

P.S. I am making some extra prints of certain photographs taken by me, which I think will help to prove a number of the points I have touched on. The old people think they are monstrously true. I shall send you these very soon if you are interested. H.W.A.

It would be difficult to describe my sentiments upon reading this strange document for the first time. By all ordinary rules, I ought to have laughed more loudly at these extravagances than at the far milder theories which had previously moved me to mirth; yet something in the tone of the letter made me take it with paradoxical seriousness. Not that I believed for a moment in the hidden race from the stars which my correspondent spoke of; but that, after some grave preliminary doubts, I grew to feel oddly sure of his sanity and sincerity, and of his confrontation by some genuine though singular and abnormal phenomenon which he could not explain except in this imaginative way. It could not be as he thought it, I reflected, yet on the other hand it could not be otherwise than worthy of investigation. The man seemed unduly excited and alarmed about something, but it was hard to think that all cause was lacking. He was so specific and logical in certain ways—and after all, his yarn did fit in so perplexingly well with some of the old myths—even the wildest Indian legends.

That he had really overheard disturbing voices in the hills, and had really found the black stone he spoke about, was wholly possible despite the crazy inferences he had made—inferences probably suggested by the man who had claimed to be a spy of the outer beings and had later killed himself. It was easy to deduce that this man must have been wholly insane, but that he probably had a streak of perverse outward logic which made the naive Akeley—already prepared for such things by his folklore studies—believe his tale. As for the latest developments—it appeared from his inability to keep hired help that Akeley's humbler rustic neighbors were as convinced as he that his house was besieged by uncanny things at night. The dogs really barked, too.

And then the matter of that phonograph record, which I could not but believe he had obtained in the way he said. It must mean something; whether animal noises deceptively like human speech, or the speech of some hidden, night-haunting human being decayed to a state not much above that of lower animals. From this my thoughts went back to the black hieroglyphed stone, and to speculations upon what it might mean. Then, too, what of the photographs which Akeley said he was about to send, and which the old people had found so convincingly terrible?

As I re-read the cramped handwriting I felt as never before that my credulous opponents might have more on their side than I had conceded. After all, there might be some queer and perhaps hereditarily misshapen outcasts in those shunned hills, even though no such race of star-born monsters as folklore claimed. And if there were, then the presence of strange bodies in the flooded streams would not be wholly beyond belief. Was it too presumptuous to suppose that both the old legends and the recent reports had this much of reality behind them? But even as I harbored these doubts I felt ashamed that so fantastic a piece of bizarrerie as Henry Akeley's wild letter had brought them up.

In the end I answered Akeley's letter, adopting a tone of friendly interest and soliciting further particulars. His reply came almost by return mail; and contained, true to promise, a number of Kodak views of scenes and objects illustrating what he had to tell. Glancing at these pictures as I took them from the envelope, I felt a curious sense of fright and nearness to forbidden things; for in spite of the vagueness of most of them, they had a damnably suggestive power which was intensified by the fact of their being genuine photographs—actual optical links with what they portrayed, and the product of an impersonal transmitting process without prejudice, fallibility, or mendacity.

The more I looked at them, the more I saw that my serious estimate of Akeley and his story had not been unjustified. Certainly, these pictures carried conclusive evidence of something in the Vermont hills which was at least vastly outside the radius of our common knowledge and belief. The worst thing of all was the footprint—a view taken where the sun shone on a mud patch somewhere in a deserted upland. This was no cheaply counterfeited thing, I could see at a glance; for the sharply defined pebbles and grass-blades in the field of vision gave a clear index of scale and left no possibility of a tricky double exposure. I have called the thing a "footprint," but "claw-print" would be a better term. Even now I can scarcely describe it save to say that it was hideously crab-like, and that there seemed to be some ambiguity about its direction. It was not a very deep or fresh print, but seemed to be about the size of an average man's foot. From a central pad, pairs of saw-toothed nippers projected in opposite directions—quite baffling as to function, if indeed the whole object were exclusively an organ of locomotion.

Another photograph—evidently a time-exposure taken in deep shadow—was of the mouth of a woodland cave, with a boulder of rounded regularity choking the aperture. On the bare ground in front of it one could just discern a dense network of curious tracks, and when I studied the picture with a magnifier I felt uneasily sure that the tracks were like the one in the other view. A third picture showed a druid-like circle of standing stones on the summit of a wild hill. Around the cryptic circle the grass was very much beaten down and worn away, though I could not detect any footprints even with the glass. The extreme remoteness of the place was apparent from the veritable sea of tenantless mountains which formed the background and stretched away toward a misty horizon.

But if the most disturbing of all the views was that of the footprint, the most curiously suggestive was that of the great black stone found in the Round Hill woods. Akeley had photographed it on what was evidently his study table, for I could see rows of books and a bust of Milton in the background. The thing, as nearly as one might guess, had faced the camera vertically with a somewhat irregularly curved surface of one by two feet; but to say anything definite about that surface, or about the general shape of the whole mass, almost defies the power of language. What outlandish geometrical principles had guided its cutting—for artificially cut it surely was—I could not even begin to guess; and never before had I seen anything which struck me as so strangely and unmistakably alien to this world. Of the hieroglyphics on the surface I could discern very few, but one or two that I did see gave me rather a shock. Of course they might be fraudulent, for others besides myself had read the monstrous and abhorred *Necronomicon* of the mad Arab Abdul Alhazred; but it nevertheless made me shiver to recognize certain ideographs which study had taught me to link with the most blood-curdling and blasphemous whispers of things that had had a kind of mad half-existence before the earth and the other inner worlds of the solar system were made.

Of the five remaining pictures, three were of swamp and hill scenes which seemed to bear traces of hidden and unwholesome tenancy. Another was of a queer mark in the ground very near Akeley's house, which he said he had photographed the morning after a night on which the dogs had barked more violently than usual. It was very blurred, and one could really draw no certain conclusions from it; but it did seem fiendishly like that other mark or claw-print photographed on the deserted upland. The final picture was of the Akeley place itself; a trim white house of two stories and attic, about a century and a quarter old, and with a well-kept lawn and stone-bordered path leading up to a tastefully carved Georgian doorway. There were several huge police dogs on the lawn, squatting near a pleasant-faced man with a close-cropped gray beard whom I took to be Akeley himself—his own photographer, one might infer from the tube-connected bulb in his right hand.

From the pictures I turned to the bulky, closely written letter itself; and for the next three hours was immersed in a gulf of unutterable horror. Where Akeley had given only outlines before, he now entered into minute details; presenting long transcripts of words overheard in the woods at night, long accounts of monstrous pinkish forms spied in thickets at twilight on the hills, and a terrible cosmic narrative derived from the application of profound and varied scholarship to the endless bygone discourses of the mad self-styled spy who had killed himself. I found myself faced by names and terms that I had heard elsewhere in the most hideous of connections—Yuggoth, Great Cthulhu, Tsathoggua, Yog-Sothoth, R'lyeh, Nyarlathotep, Azathoth, Hastur, Yian, Leng, the Lake of Hali, Bethmoora, the Yellow Sign, L'mur-Kathulos, Bran, and the Magnum Innominandum—and was drawn back through nameless eons and inconceivable dimensions to worlds of elder, outer entity at which the crazed author of the *Necronomicon* had only guessed in the vaguest way. I was told of the pits of primal life, and of the streams that had trickled down therefrom; and finally, of the tiny rivulet from one of those streams which had become entangled with the destinies of our own earth.

My brain whirled; and where before I had attempted to explain things away, I now began to believe in the most abnormal and incredible wonders. The array of vital evidence was damnably vast and overwhelming; and the cool, scientific attitude of Akeley—an attitude removed as far as imaginable from the demented, the fanatical, the hysterical, or even the extravagantly speculative—had a tremendous effect on my thought and judgment. By the time I laid the frightful letter aside I could understand the fears he had come to entertain, and was ready to do anything in my power to keep people away from those wild, haunted hills. Even now, when time has dulled the impression and made me half question my own experience and horrible doubts, there are things in that letter of Akeley's which I would not quote, or even form into words on paper. I am almost glad that the letter and record and photographs are gone now—and I wish, for reasons I shall soon make clear, that the new planet beyond Neptune had not been discovered.

With the reading of that letter my public debating about the Vermont horror permanently ended. Arguments from opponents remained unanswered or put off with promises, and eventually the controversy petered out into oblivion. During late May and June I was in constant correspondence with Akeley; though once in a while a letter would be lost, so that we would have to retrace our ground and perform considerable laborious copying. What we were trying to do, as a whole, was to compare notes in matters of obscure mythological scholarship and arrive at a clearer correlation of the Vermont horrors with the general body of primitive world legend.

For one thing, we virtually decided that these morbidities and the hellish Himalayan *Mi-Go* were one and the same order of incarnated nightmare. There were also absorbing zoological conjectures, which I would have referred to Professor Dexter in my own college but for Akeley's imperative command to tell no one of the matter before us. If I seem to disobey that command now, it is only because I think that at this stage a warning about those farther Vermont hills—and about those Himalayan peaks which bold explorers are more and more determined to ascend—is more conducive to public safety than silence would be. One specific thing we were leading up to was a deciphering of the hieroglyphics on that infamous black stone—a deciphering which might well place us in possession of secrets deeper and more dizzying than any formerly known to man.

III

Toward the end of June the phonograph record came—shipped from Brattleboro, since Akeley was unwilling to trust conditions on the branch line north of there. He had begun to feel an increased sense of espionage, aggravated by the loss of some of our letters; and said much about the insidious deeds of certain men whom he considered tools and agents of the hidden beings. Most of all he suspected the surly farmer Walter Brown, who lived alone on a run-down hillside place near the deep woods, and who was often seen loafing around corners in Brattleboro, Bellows Falls, Newfane, and South Londonderry in the most inexplicable and seemingly unmotivated way. Brown's voice, he felt convinced, was one of those he had overheard on a certain occasion in a very terrible conversation; and he had once found a footprint or claw-print near Brown's house which might possess the most ominous significance. It had been curiously near some of Brown's own footprints—footprints that faced toward it.

So the record was shipped from Brattleboro, whither Akeley drove in his Ford car along the lonely Vermont back roads. He confessed in an accompanying note that he was beginning to be afraid of those roads, and that he would not even go into Townshend for supplies now except in broad daylight. It did not pay, he repeated again and again, to know too much unless one were very remote from those silent and problematical hills. He would be going to California pretty soon to live with his son, though it was hard to leave a place where all one's memories and ancestral feelings centered.

Before trying the record on the commercial machine which I borrowed from the college administration building I carefully went over all the explanatory matter in Akeley's various letters. This record, he had said, was obtained about 1 a.m. on May 1st, 1915, near the closed mouth of a cave where the wooded west slope of Dark Mountain rises out of Lee's Swamp. The place had always been unusually plagued with strange voices, this being the reason he had brought the phonograph, dictaphone, and blank in expectation of results. Former experience had told him that May Eve—the hideous Sabbat-night of underground European legend—would probably be more fruitful than any other date, and he was not disappointed. It was noteworthy, though, that he never again heard voices at that particular spot.

Unlike most of the overheard forest voices, the substance of the record was quasi-ritualistic, and included one palpably human voice which Akeley had never been able to place. It was not Brown's, but seemed to be that of a man of greater cultivation. The second voice, however, was the real crux of the thing—for this was the accursed *buzzing* which had no likeness to humanity despite the human words which it uttered in good English grammar and a scholarly accent.

The recording phonograph and dictaphone had not worked uniformly well, and had of course been at a great disadvantage because of the remote and muffled nature of the overheard ritual; so that the actual speech secured was very fragmentary. Akeley had given me a transcript of what he believed the spoken words to be, and I glanced through this again as I prepared the machine for action. The text was darkly mysterious rather than openly horrible, though a knowledge of its origin and manner of gathering gave it all the associative horror which any words could well possess. I will present it here in full as I remember it—and I am fairly confident that I know it correctly by heart, not only from reading the transcript, but from playing the record itself over and over again. It is not a thing which one might readily forget!

(INDISTINGUISHABLE SOUNDS)

(A CULTIVATED MALE HUMAN VOICE)

... is the Lord of the Woods, even to... and the gifts of the men of Leng... so from the wells of night to the gulfs of space, and from the gulfs of space to the wells of night, ever the praises of Great Cthulhu, of Tsathoggua, and of Him Who is not to be Named. Ever Their praises, and abundance to the Black Goat of the Woods. Iä! Shub-Niggurath! The Goat with a Thousand Young!

(A BUZZING IMITATION OF HUMAN SPEECH)

Iä! Shub-Niggurath! The Black Goat of the Woods with a Thousand Young!

(HUMAN VOICE)

And it has come to pass that the Lord of the Woods, being... seven and nine, down the onyx steps... (tri)butes to Him in the Gulf, Azathoth, He of Whom Thou hast taught us marv(els)... on the wings of night out beyond space, out beyond th... to That whereof Yuggoth is the youngest child, rolling alone in black aether at the rim...

(BUZZING VOICE)

... go out among men and find the ways thereof, that He in the Gulf may know. To Nyarlathotep, Mighty Messenger, must all things be told. And He shall put on the semblance of men, the waxen mask and the robe that hides, and come down from the world of Seven Suns to mock...

(HUMAN VOICE)

... (Nyarl)athotep, Great Messenger, bringer of strange joy to Yuggoth through the void, Father of the Million Favored Ones, Stalker among...

(SPEECH CUT OFF BY END OF RECORD)

Such were the words for which I was to listen when I started the phonograph. It was with a trace of genuine dread and reluctance that I pressed the lever and heard the preliminary scratching of the sapphire point, and I was glad that the first faint, fragmentary words were in a human voice—a mellow, educated voice which seemed vaguely Bostonian in accent, and which was certainly not that of any native of the Vermont hills. As I listened to the tantalizingly feeble rendering, I seemed to find the speech identical with Akeley's carefully prepared transcript. On it chanted, in that mellow Bostonian voice, "... Iä! Shub-Niggurath! The Goat with a Thousand Young!..."

And then I heard *the other voice*. To this hour I shudder retrospectively when I think of how it struck me, prepared though I was by Akeley's accounts. Those to whom I have since described the record profess to find nothing but cheap imposture or madness in it; but *could they have heard the accursed thing itself*, or read the bulk of Akeley's correspondence (especially that terrible and encyclopedic second letter), I know they would think differently. It is, after all, a tremendous pity that I did not disobey Akeley and play the record for others—a tremendous pity, too, that all of his letters were lost. To me, with my first-hand impression of the actual sounds, and with my knowledge of the background and surrounding circumstances, the voice was a monstrous thing. It swiftly followed the human voice in ritualistic response, but in my imagination it was a morbid echo winging its way across unimagin-able abysses from unimaginable outer hells. It is more than two years now since I last ran off that blasphemous waxen cylinder; but at this moment, and at all other moments, I can still hear that feeble, fiendish buzzing as it reached me for the first time.

Iä! Shub-Niggurath! The Black Goat of the Woods with a Thousand Young!

But though that voice is always in my ears, I have not even yet been able to analyze it well enough for a graphic description. It was like the drone of some loathsome, gigantic insect ponderously shaped into the articulate speech of an alien species, and I am perfectly certain that the organs producing it can have no resemblance to the vocal organs of man, or indeed to those of any of the mammalia. There were singularities in timbre, range, and overtones which placed this phenomenon wholly outside the sphere of humanity and earth-life. Its sudden advent that first time almost stunned me, and I heard the rest of the record through in a sort of abstracted daze. When the longer passage of buzzing came, there was a sharp intensification of that feeling of blasphemous infinity which had struck me during the shorter and earlier passage. At last the record ended abruptly, during an unusually clear speech of the human and Bostonian voice; but I sat stupidly staring long after the machine had automatically stopped.

I hardly need say that I gave that shocking record many another playing, and that I made exhaustive attempts at analysis and comment in comparing notes with Akeley. It would be both useless and disturbing to repeat here all that we concluded; but I may hint that we agreed in believing we had secured a clue to the source of some of the most repulsive primordial customs in the cryptic elder religions of mankind. It seemed plain to us, also, that there were ancient and elaborate alliances between the hidden outer creatures and certain members of the human race. How extensive these alliances were, and how their state today might compare with their state in earlier ages, we had no means of guessing; yet at best there was room for a limitless amount of horrified speculation. There seemed to be an awful, immemorial linkage in several definite stages betwixt man and nameless infinity. The blasphemies which appeared on earth, it was hinted, came from the dark planet Yuggoth, at the rim of the solar system; but this was itself merely the populous outpost of a frightful interstellar race whose ultimate source must lie far outside even the Einsteinian space-time continuum or greatest known cosmos.

Meanwhile we continued to discuss the black stone and the best way of getting it to Arkham—Akeley deeming it inadvisable to have me visit him at the scene of his nightmare studies. For some reason or other, Akeley was afraid to trust the thing to any ordinary or expected transportation route. His final idea was to take it across county to Bellows Falls and ship it on the Boston and Maine system through Keene and Winchendon and Fitchburg, even though this would necessitate his driving along somewhat lonelier and more forest-traversing hill roads than the main highway to Brattleboro. He said he had noticed a man around the express office at Brattleboro when he had sent the phonograph record, whose actions and expression had been far from reassuring. This man had seemed too anxious to talk with the clerks, and had taken the train on which the record was shipped. Akeley confessed that he had not felt strictly at ease about that record until he heard from me of its safe receipt.

About this time—the second week in July—another letter of mine went astray, as I learned through an anxious communication from Akeley. After that he told me to address him no more at Townshend, but to send all mail in care of the General Delivery at Brattleboro; whither he would make frequent trips either in his car or on the motor-coach line which had lately replaced passenger service on the lagging branch railway. I could see that he was getting more and more anxious, for he went into much detail about the increased barking of the dogs on moonless nights, and about the fresh claw-prints he sometimes found in the road and in the mud at the back of his farmyard when morning came. Once he told about a veritable army of prints drawn up in a line facing an equally thick and resolute line of dog-tracks, and sent a loathsomely disturbing Kodak picture to prove it. That was after a night on which the dogs had outdone themselves in barking and howling.

On the morning of Wednesday, July 18th, I received a telegram from Bellows Falls, in which Akeley said he was expressing the black stone over the B. & M. on Train No. 5508, leaving Bellows Falls at 12:15 p.m., standard time, and due at the North Station in Boston at 4:12 p.m. It ought, I calculated, to get up to Arkham at least by the next noon; and accordingly I stayed in all Thursday morning to receive it. But noon came and went without its advent, and when I telephoned down to the express office I was informed that no shipment for me had arrived. My next act, performed amidst a growing alarm, was to give a long-distance call to the express agent at the Boston North Station; and I was scarcely surprised to learn that my consignment had not appeared. Train No. 5508 had pulled in only 35 minutes late on the day before, but had contained no box addressed to me. The agent promised, however, to institute a searching inquiry; and I ended the day by sending Akeley a night-letter outlining the situation.

With commendable promptness a report came from the Boston office on the following afternoon, the agent telephoning as soon as he learned the facts. It seemed that the railway express clerk on No. 5508 had been able to recall an incident which might have much bearing on my loss—an argument with a very curious-voiced man, lean, sandy, and rustic-looking, when the train was waiting at Keene, NH, shortly after one o'clock standard time.

The man, he said, was greatly excited about a heavy box which he claimed to expect, but which was neither on the train nor entered on the company's books. He had given the name of Stanley Adams, and had had such a queerly thick droning voice, that it made the clerk abnormally dizzy and sleepy to listen to him. The clerk could not remember quite how the conversation had ended, but recalled starting into a fuller awakeness when the train began to move. The Boston agent added that this clerk was a young man of wholly unquestioned veracity and reliability, of known antecedents and long with the company.

That evening I went to Boston to interview the clerk in person, having obtained his name and address from the office. He was a frank, prepossessing fellow, but I saw that he could add nothing to his original account. Oddly, he was scarcely sure that he could even recognize the strange inquirer again. Realizing that he had no more to tell, I returned to Arkham and sat up till morning writing letters to Akeley, to the express company, and to the police department and station agent in Keene. I felt that the strange-voiced man who had so queerly affected the clerk must have a pivotal place in the ominous business, and hoped that Keene station employees and telegraph-office records might tell something about him and about how he happened to make his inquiry when and where he did.

I must admit, however, that all my investigations came to nothing. The queer-voiced man had indeed been noticed around the Keene station in the early afternoon of July 18th, and one lounger seemed to couple him vaguely with a heavy box; but he was altogether unknown, and had not been seen before or since. He had not visited the telegraph office or received any message so far as could be learned, nor had any message which might justly be considered a notice of the black stone's presence on No. 5508 come through the office for anyone. Naturally Akeley joined with me in conducting these inquiries, and even made a personal trip to Keene to question the people around the station; but his attitude toward the matter was more fatalistic than mine. He seemed to find the loss of the box a portentous and menacing fulfillment of inevitable tendencies, and had no real hope at all of its recovery. He spoke of the undoubted telepathic and hypnotic powers of the hill creatures and their agents, and in one letter hinted that he did not believe the stone was on this earth any longer. For my part, I was duly enraged, for I had felt there was at least a chance of learning profound and astonishing things from the old, blurred hieroglyphs. The matter would have rankled bitterly in my mind had not Akeley's immediate subsequent letters brought up a new phase of the whole horrible hill problem which at once seized all my attention.

IV

The unknown things, Akeley wrote in a script grown pitifully tremulous, had begun to close in on him with a wholly new degree of determination. The nocturnal barking of the dogs whenever the moon was dim or absent was hideous now, and there had been attempts to molest him on the lonely roads he had to traverse by day. On the second of August, while bound for the village in his car, he had found a tree-trunk laid in his path at a point where the highway ran through a deep patch of woods; while the savage barking of the two great dogs he had with him told all too well of the things which must have been lurking near. What would have happened had the dogs not been there, he did not dare guess—but he never went out now without at least two of his faithful and powerful pack. Other road experiences had occurred on August 5th and 6th; a shot grazing his car on one occasion, and the barking of the dogs telling of unholy woodland presences on the other.

On August 15th I received a frantic letter which disturbed me greatly, and which made me wish Akeley could put aside his lonely reticence and call in the aid of the law. There had been frightful happenings on the night of the 12th–13th, bullets flying outside the farmhouse, and three of the twelve great dogs being found shot dead in the morning. There were myriads of claw-prints in the road, with the human prints of Walter Brown among them. Akeley had started to telephone to Brattleboro for more dogs, but the wire had gone dead before he had a chance to say much. Later he went to Brattleboro in his car, and learned there that linemen had found the main telephone cable neatly cut at a point where it ran through the deserted hills north of Newfane. But he was about to start home with four fine new dogs, and several cases of ammunition for his big-game repeating rifle. The letter was written at the post office in Brattleboro, and came through to me without delay.

My attitude toward the matter was by this time quickly slipping from a scientific to an alarmedly personal one. I was afraid for Akeley in his remote, lonely farmhouse, and half afraid for myself because of my now definite connection with the strange hill problem. The thing was *reaching out* so. Would it suck me in and engulf me? In replying to his letter I urged him to seek help, and hinted that I might take action myself if he did not. I spoke of visiting Vermont in person in spite of his wishes, and of helping him explain the situation to the proper authorities. In return, however, I received only a telegram from Bellows Falls which read thus:

> APPRECIATE YOUR POSITION BUT CAN DO NOTHING. TAKE NO ACTION YOURSELF FOR IT COULD ONLY HARM BOTH. WAIT FOR EXPLANATION.
>
> HENRY AKELY

But the affair was steadily deepening. Upon my replying to the telegram I received a shaky note from Akeley with the astonishing news that he had not only never sent the wire, but had not received the letter from me to which it was an obvious reply. Hasty inquiries by him at Bellows Falls had brought out that the message was deposited by a strange sandy-haired man with a curiously thick, droning voice, though more than this he could not learn. The clerk showed him the original text as scrawled in pencil by the sender, but the handwriting was wholly unfamiliar. It was noticeable that the signature was misspelled—A-K-E-L-Y, without the second "E." Certain conjectures were inevitable, but amidst the obvious crisis he did not stop to elaborate upon them.

He spoke of the death of more dogs and the purchase of still others, and of the exchange of gunfire which had become a settled feature each moonless night. Brown's prints, and the prints of at least one or two more shod human figures, were now found regularly among the claw-prints in the road, and at the back of the farmyard. It was, Akeley admitted, a pretty bad business; and before long he would probably have to go to live with his California son whether or not he could sell the old place. But it was not easy to leave the only spot one could really think of as home. He must try to hang on a little longer; perhaps he could scare off the intruders—especially if he openly gave up all further attempts to penetrate their secrets.

Writing Akeley at once, I renewed my offers of aid, and spoke again of visiting him and helping him convince the authorities of his dire peril. In his reply he seemed less set against that plan than his past attitude would have led one to predict, but said he would like to hold off a little while longer—long enough to get his things in order and reconcile himself to the idea of leaving an almost morbidly cherished birthplace. People looked askance at his studies and speculations, and it would be better to get quietly off without setting the countryside in a turmoil and creating widespread doubts of his own sanity. He had had enough, he admitted, but he wanted to make a dignified exit if he could.

This letter reached me on the 28th of August, and I prepared and mailed as encouraging a reply as I could. Apparently the encouragement had effect, for Akeley had fewer terrors to report when he acknowledged my note. He was not very optimistic, though, and expressed the belief that it was only the full moon season which was holding the creatures off. He hoped there would not be many densely cloudy nights, and talked vaguely of boarding in Brattleboro when the moon waned. Again I wrote him encouragingly, but on September 5th there came a fresh communication which had obviously crossed my letter in the mails; and to this I could not give any such hopeful response. In view of its importance I believe I had better give it in full—as best I can do from memory of the shaky script. It ran substantially as follows:

Monday

Dear Wilmarth—

A rather discouraging P.S. to my last. Last night was thickly cloudy—though no rain—and not a bit of moonlight got through. Things were pretty bad, and I think the end is getting near, in spite of all we have hoped. After midnight something landed on the roof of the house, and the dogs all rushed up to see what it was. I could hear them snapping and tearing around, and then one managed to get on the roof by jumping from the low ell. There was a terrible fight up there, and I heard a frightful *buzzing* which I'll never forget. And then there was a shocking smell. About the same time bullets came through the window and nearly grazed me. I think the main line of the hill creatures had got close to the house when the dogs divided because of the roof business. What was up there I don't know yet, but I'm afraid the creatures are learning to steer better with their space wings. I put out the light and used the windows for loopholes, and raked all around the house with rifle fire aimed just high enough not to hit the dogs. That seemed to end the business, but in the morning I found great pools of blood in the yard, beside pools of a green sticky stuff that had the worst odor I have ever smelled. I climbed up on the roof and found more of the sticky stuff there. Five of the dogs were killed—I'm afraid I hit one by aiming too low, for he was shot in the back. Now I am setting the panes the shots broke, and am going to Brattleboro for more dogs. I guess the men at the kennels think I am crazy. Will drop another note later. Suppose I'll be ready for moving in a week or two, though it nearly kills me to think of it.

Hastily—
AKELEY

But this was not the only letter from Akeley to cross mine. On the next morning—September 6th—still another came; this time a frantic scrawl which utterly unnerved me and put me at a loss what to say or do next. Again I cannot do better than quote the text as faithfully as memory will let me.

Tuesday

Clouds didn't break, so no moon again—and going into the wane anyhow. I'd have the house wired for electricity and put in a searchlight if I didn't know they'd cut the cables as fast as they could be mended.

I think I am going crazy. It may be that all I have ever written you is a dream or madness. It was bad enough before, but this time it is too much. *They talked to me last night*—talked in that cursed buzzing voice and told me things that I dare not repeat to you. I heard them plainly over the barking of the dogs, and once when they were drowned out *a human voice helped them*. Keep out of this, Wilmarth—it is worse than either you or I ever suspected. *They don't mean to let me get to California now—they want to take me off alive, or what theoretically and mentally amounts to alive*—not only to Yuggoth, but beyond that—away outside the galaxy *and possibly beyond the last curved rim of space*. I told them I wouldn't go where they wish, *or in the terrible way they propose to take me*, but I'm afraid it will be no use. My place is so far out that they may come by day as well as by night before long. Six more dogs killed, and I felt presences all along the wooded parts of the road when I drove to Brattleboro today.

It was a mistake for me to try to send you that phonograph record and black stone. Better smash the record before it's too late. Will drop you another line tomorrow if I'm still here. Wish I could arrange to get my books and things to Brattleboro and board there. I would run off without anything if I could, but something inside my mind holds me back. I can slip out to Brattleboro, where I ought to be safe, but I feel just as much a prisoner there as at the house. And I seem to know that I couldn't get much farther even if I dropped everything and tried. It is horrible—don't get mixed up in this.

Yrs—AKELEY

I did not sleep at all the night after receiving this terrible thing, and was utterly baffled as to Akeley's remaining degree of sanity. The substance of the note was wholly insane, yet the manner of expression—in view of all that had gone before—had a grimly potent quality of convincingness. I made no attempt to answer it, thinking it better to wait until Akeley might have time to reply to my latest communication. Such a reply indeed came on the following day, though the fresh material in it quite overshadowed any of the points brought up by the letter it nominally answered. Here is what I recall of the text, scrawled and blotted as it was in the course of a plainly frantic and hurried composition.

Wednesday

W—

Yr letter came, but it's no use to discuss anything any more. I am fully resigned. Wonder that I have even enough will power left to fight them off. Can't escape even if I were willing to give up everything and run. They'll get me.

Had a letter from them yesterday—R.F.D. man brought it while I was at Brattleboro. Typed and postmarked Bellows Falls. Tells what they want to do with me—I can't repeat it. Look out for yourself, too! Smash that record. Cloudy nights keep up, and moon waning all the time. Wish I dared to get help—it might brace up my will power—but everyone who would dare to come at all would call me crazy unless there happened to be some proof. Couldn't ask people to come for no reason at all—am all out of touch with everybody and have been for years.

But I haven't told you the worst, Wilmarth. Brace up to read this, for it will give you a shock. I am telling the truth, though. It is this—*I have seen and touched one of the things, or part of one of the things*. God, man, but it's awful! It was dead, of course. One of the dogs had it, and I found it near the kennel this morning. I tried to save it in the woodshed to convince people of the whole thing, but it all evaporated in a few hours. Nothing left. You know, all those things in the rivers were seen only on the first morning after the flood. And here's the worst. I tried to photograph it for you, but when I developed the film *there wasn't anything visible except the woodshed*. What can the thing have been made of? I saw it and felt it, and they all leave footprints. It was surely made of matter—but what kind of matter? The shape can't be described. It was a great crab with a lot of pyramided fleshy rings or knots of thick, ropy stuff covered with feelers where a man's head would be. That green sticky stuff is its blood or juice. And there are more of them due on earth any minute.

Walter Brown is missing—hasn't been seen loafing around any of his usual corners in the villages here-abouts. I must have got him with one of my shots, though the creatures always seem to try to take their dead and wounded away.

Got into town this afternoon without any trouble, but am afraid they're beginning to hold off because they're sure of me. Am writing this in Brattleboro P.O. This may be goodbye—if it is, write my son George Goodenough Akeley, 176 Pleasant St, San Diego, Cal., *but don't come up here*. Write the boy if you don't hear from me in a week, and watch the papers for news.

I'm going to play my last two cards now—if I have the will power left. First to try poison gas on the things (I've got the right chemicals and have fixed up masks for myself and the dogs) and then if that doesn't work, tell the sheriff. They can lock me in a madhouse if they want to—it'll be better than what the *other creatures* would do. Perhaps I can get them to pay attention to the prints around the house—they are faint, but I can find them every morning. Suppose, though, police would say I faked them somehow; for they all think I'm a queer character.

Must try to have a state policeman spend a night here and see for himself—though it would be just like the creatures to learn about it and hold off that night. They cut my wires whenever I try to telephone in the night—the linemen think it is very queer, and may testify for me if they don't go and imagine I cut them myself. I haven't tried to keep them repaired for over a week now.

I could get some of the ignorant people to testify for me about the reality of the horrors, but everybody laughs at what they say, and anyway, they have shunned my place for so long that they don't know any of the new events. You couldn't get one of those run-down farmers to come within a mile of my house for love or money. The mail-carrier hears what they say and jokes me about it—God! If I only dared tell him how real it is! I think I'll try to get him to notice the prints, but he comes in the afternoon and they're usually about gone by that time. If I kept one by setting a box or pan over it, he'd think surely it was a fake or joke.

Wish I hadn't gotten to be such a hermit, so folks don't drop around as they used to. I've never dared show the black stone or the Kodak pictures, or play that record, to anybody but the ignorant people. The others would say I faked the whole business and do nothing but laugh. But I may yet try showing the pictures. They give those claw-prints clearly, even if the things that made them can't be photographed. What a shame nobody else saw that *thing* this morning before it went to nothing!

But I don't know as I care. After what I've been through, a madhouse is as good a place as any. The doctors can help me make up my mind to get away from this house, and that is all that will save me.

Write my son George if you don't hear soon. Goodbye, smash that record, and don't mix up in this.

Yrs—AKELEY

The letter frankly plunged me into the blackest of terror. I did not know what to say in answer, but scratched off some incoherent words of advice and encouragement and sent them by registered mail. I recall urging Akeley to move to Brattleboro at once, and place himself under the protection of the authorities; adding that I would come to that town with the phonograph record and help convince the courts of his sanity. It was time, too, I think I wrote, to alarm the people generally against this thing in their midst. It will be observed that at this moment of stress my own belief in all Akeley had told and claimed was virtually complete, though I did think his failure to get a picture of the dead monster was due not to any freak of Nature but to some excited slip of his own.

V

Then, apparently crossing my incoherent note and reaching me Saturday afternoon, September 8th, came that curiously different and calming letter neatly typed on a new machine; that strange letter of reassurance and invitation which must have marked so prodigious a transition in the whole nightmare drama of the lonely hills. Again I will quote from memory—seeking for special reasons to preserve as much of the flavor of the style as I can. It was postmarked Bellows Falls, and the signature as well as the body of the letter was typed—as is frequent with beginners in typing. The text, though, was marvelously accurate for a tyro's work; and I concluded that Akeley must have used a machine at some previous period—perhaps in college. To say that the letter relieved me would be only fair, yet beneath my relief lay a substratum of uneasiness. If Akeley had been sane in his terror, was he now sane in his deliverance? And the sort of "improved rapport" mentioned... what was it? The entire thing implied such a diametrical reversal of Akeley's previous attitude! But here is the substance of the text, carefully transcribed from a memory in which I take some pride.

Townshend, Vermont,
Thursday, Sept. 6th, 1928.

My dear Wilmarth:—

It gives me great pleasure to be able to set you at rest regarding all the silly things I've been writing you. I say "silly," although by that I mean my frightened attitude rather than my descriptions of certain phenomena. Those phenomena are real and important enough; my mistake had been in establishing an anomalous attitude toward them.

I think I mentioned that my strange visitors were beginning to communicate with me, and to attempt such communication. Last night this exchange of speech became actual. In response to certain signals I admitted to the house a messenger from those outside—a fellow-human, let me hasten to say. He told me much that neither you nor I had even begun to guess, and showed clearly how totally we had misjudged and misinterpreted the purpose of the Outer Ones in maintaining their secret colony on this planet.

It seems that the evil legends about what they have offered to men, and what they wish in connection with the earth, are wholly the result of an ignorant misconception of allegorical speech—speech, of course, molded by cultural backgrounds and thought-habits vastly different from anything we dream of. My own conjectures, I freely own, shot as widely past the mark as any of the guesses of illiterate farmers and savage Indians. What I had thought morbid and shameful and ignominious is in reality awesome and mind-expanding and even *glorious*—my previous estimate being merely a phase of man's eternal tendency to hate and fear and shrink from the *utterly different*.

Now I regret the harm I have inflicted upon these alien and incredible beings in the course of our nightly skirmishes. If only I had consented to talk peacefully and reasonably with them in the first place! But they bear me no grudge, their emotions being organized very differently from ours. It is their misfortune to have had as their human agents in Vermont some very inferior specimens—the late Walter Brown, for example. He prejudiced me vastly against them. Actually, they have never knowingly harmed men, but have often been cruelly wronged and spied upon by our species. There is a whole secret cult of evil men (a man of your mystical erudition will understand me when I link them with Hastur and the Yellow Sign) devoted to the purpose of tracking them down and injuring them on behalf of monstrous powers from other dimensions. It is against these aggressors—not against normal humanity—that the drastic precautions of the Outer Ones are directed. Incidentally, I learned that many of our lost letters were stolen not by the Outer Ones but by the emissaries of this malign cult.

All that the Outer Ones wish of man is peace and non-molestation and an increasing intellectual rapport. This latter is absolutely necessary now that our inventions and devices are expanding our knowledge and motions, and making it more and more impossible for the Outer Ones' necessary outposts to exist secretly on this planet. The alien beings desire to know mankind more fully, and to have a few of mankind's philosophic and scientific leaders know more about them. With such an exchange of knowledge all perils will pass, and a satisfactory modus vivendi be established. The very idea of any attempt to *enslave* or *degrade* mankind is ridiculous.

As a beginning of this improved rapport, the Outer Ones have naturally chosen me—whose knowledge of them is already so considerable—as their primary interpreter on earth. Much was told me last night—facts of the most stupendous and vista-opening nature—and more will be subsequently communicated to me both orally and in writing. I shall not be called upon to make any trip *outside* just yet, though I shall probably wish to do so later on—employing special means and transcending everything which we have hitherto been accustomed to regard as human experience. My house will be besieged no longer. Everything has reverted to normal, and the dogs will have no further occupation. In place of terror I have been given a rich boon of knowledge and intellectual adventure which few other mortals have ever shared.

The Outer Beings are perhaps the most marvelous organic things in or beyond all space and time—members of a cosmos-wide race of which all other life-forms are merely degenerate variants. They are more vegetable than animal, if these terms can be applied to the sort of matter composing them, and have a somewhat fungoid structure; though the presence of a chlorophyll-like substance and a very singular nutritive system differentiate them altogether from true cormophytic fungi. Indeed, the type is composed of a form of matter totally alien to our part of space—with electrons having a wholly different vibration—rate. That is why the beings cannot be photographed on the *ordinary* camera films and plates of our known universe, even though our eyes can see them. With proper knowledge, however, any good chemist could make a photographic emulsion which would record their images.

The genus is unique in its ability to traverse the heatless and airless interstellar void in full corporeal form, and some of its variants cannot do this without mechanical aid or curious surgical transpositions. Only a few species have the aether-resisting wings characteristic of the Vermont variety. Those inhabiting certain remote peaks in the Old World were brought in other ways. Their external resemblance to animal life, and to the sort of structure we understand as material, is a matter of parallel evolution rather than of close kinship. Their brain-capacity exceeds that of any other surviving life-form, although the winged types of our hill country are by no means the most highly developed. Telepathy is their usual means of discourse, though they have rudimentary vocal organs which, after a slight operation (for surgery is an incredibly expert and everyday thing among them), can roughly duplicate the speech of such types of organism as still use speech.

Their main *immediate* abode is a still undiscovered and almost lightless planet at the very edge of our solar system—beyond Neptune, and the ninth in distance from the sun. It is, as we have inferred, the object mystically hinted at as "Yuggoth" in certain ancient and forbidden writings; and it will soon be the scene of a strange focusing of thought upon our world in an effort to facilitate mental rapport. I would not be surprised if astronomers became sufficiently sensitive to these thought-currents to discover Yuggoth when the Outer Ones wish them to do so. But Yuggoth, of course, is only the stepping-stone. The main body of the beings inhabits strangely organized abysses wholly beyond the utmost reach of any human imagination. The space-time globule which we recognize as the totality of all cosmic entity is only an atom in the genuine infinity which is theirs. *And as much of this infinity as any human brain can hold is eventually to be opened up to me, as it has been to not more than fifty other men since the human race has existed.*

You will probably call this raving at first, Wilmarth, but in time you will appreciate the titanic opportunity I have stumbled upon. I want you to share as much of it as is possible, and to that end must tell you thousands of things that won't go on paper. In the past I have warned you not to come to see me. Now that all is safe, I take pleasure in rescinding that warning and inviting you.

Can't you make a trip up here before your college term opens? It would be marvelously delightful if you could. Bring along the phonograph record and all my letters to you as consultative data—we shall need them in piecing together the whole tremendous story. You might bring the Kodak prints, too, since I seem to have mislaid the negatives and my own prints in all this recent excitement. But what a wealth of facts I have to add to all this groping and tentative material—*and what a stupendous device I have to supplement my additions*!

Don't hesitate—I am free from espionage now, and you will not meet anything unnatural or disturbing. Just come along and let my car meet you at the Brattleboro station—prepare to stay as long as you can, and expect many an evening of discussion of things beyond all human conjecture. Don't tell anyone about it, of course—for this matter must not get to the promiscuous public.

The train service to Brattleboro is not bad—you can get a timetable in Boston. Take the B. & M. to Greenfield, and then change for the brief remainder of the way. I suggest your taking the convenient 4:10 p.m.—standard—from Boston. This gets into Greenfield at 7:35, and at 9:19 a train leaves there which reaches Brattleboro at 10:01. That is weekdays. Let me know the date and I'll have my car on hand at the station.

Pardon this typed letter, but my handwriting has grown shaky of late, as you know, and I don't feel equal to long stretches of script. I got this new Corona in Brattleboro yesterday—it seems to work very well.

Awaiting word, and hoping to see you shortly with the phonograph record and all my letters—and the Kodak prints.

I am
Yours in anticipation,
HENRY W. AKELEY

To Albert N. Wilmarth, Esq.,
Miskatonic University, Arkham, Mass

The complexity of my emotions upon reading, re-reading, and pondering over this strange and unlooked-for letter is past adequate description. I have said that I was at once relieved and made uneasy, but this expresses only crudely the overtones of diverse and largely subconscious feelings which comprised both the relief and the uneasiness. To begin with, the thing was so antipodally at variance with the whole chain of horrors preceding it—the change of mood from stark terror to cool complacency and even exultation was so unheralded, lightning-like, and complete! I could scarcely believe that a single day could so alter the psychological perspective of one who had written that final frenzied bulletin of Wednesday, no matter what relieving disclosures that day might have brought. At certain moments a sense of conflicting unrealities made me wonder whether this whole distantly reported drama of fantastic forces were not a kind of half-illusory dream created largely within my own mind. Then I thought of the phonograph record and gave way to still greater bewilderment.

The letter seemed so unlike anything which could have been expected! As I analyzed my impression, I saw that it consisted of two distinct phases. First, granting that Akeley had been sane before and was still sane, the indicated change in the situation itself was so swift and unthinkable. And secondly, the change in Akeley's own manner, attitude, and language was so vastly beyond the normal or the predictable. The man's whole personality seemed to have undergone an insidious mutation—a mutation so deep that one could scarcely reconcile his two aspects with the supposition that both represented equal sanity. Word-choice, spelling—all were subtly different. And with my academic sensitiveness to prose style, I could trace profound divergences in his commonest reactions and rhythm-responses. Certainly, the emotional cataclysm or revelation which could produce so radical an overturn must be an extreme one indeed! Yet in another way the letter seemed quite characteristic of Akeley. The same old passion for infinity—the same old scholarly inquisitiveness. I could not a moment—or more than a moment—credit the idea of spuriousness or malign substitution. Did not the invitation—the willingness to have me test the truth of the letter in person—prove its genuineness?

I did not retire Saturday night, but sat up thinking of the shadows and marvels behind the letter I had received. My mind, aching from the quick succession of monstrous conceptions it had been forced to confront during the last four months, worked upon this startling new material in a cycle of doubt and acceptance which repeated most of the steps experienced in facing the earlier wonders; till long before dawn a burning interest and curiosity had begun to replace the original storm of perplexity and uneasiness. Mad or sane, metamorphosed or merely relieved, the chances were that Akeley had actually encountered some stupendous change of perspective in his hazardous research; some change at once diminishing his danger—real or fancied—and opening dizzy new vistas of cosmic and superhuman knowledge. My own zeal for the unknown flared up to meet his, and I felt myself touched by the contagion of the morbid barrier-breaking. To shake off the maddening and wearying limitations of time and space and natural law—to be linked with the vast *outside*—to come close to the nighted and abysmal secrets of the infinite and the ultimate—surely such a thing was worth the risk of one's life, soul, and sanity! And Akeley had said there was no longer any peril—he had invited me to visit him instead of warning me away as before. I tingled at the thought of what he might now have to tell me—there was an almost paralyzing fascination in the thought of sitting in that lonely and lately beleaguered farmhouse with a man who had talked with actual emissaries from outer space; sitting there with the terrible record and the pile of letters in which Akeley had summarized his earlier conclusions.

So late Sunday morning I telegraphed Akeley that I would meet him in Brattleboro on the following Wednesday—September 12th—if that date were convenient for him. In only one respect did I depart from his suggestions, and that concerned the choice of a train. Frankly, I did not feel like arriving in that haunted Vermont region late at night; so instead of accepting the train he chose I telephoned the station and devised another arrangement. By rising early and taking the 8:07 a.m. (standard) into Boston, I could catch the 9:25 for Greenfield; arriving there at 12:22 noon. This connected exactly with a train reaching Brattleboro at 1:08 p.m.—a much more comfortable hour than 10:01 for meeting Akeley and riding with him into the close-packed, secret-guarding hills.

I mentioned this choice in my telegram, and was glad to learn in the reply which came toward evening that it had met with my prospective host's endorsement. His wire ran thus:

> ARRANGEMENT SATISFACTORY. WILL MEET 1:08 TRAIN
> WEDNESDAY. DON'T FORGET RECORD AND LETTERS AND PRINTS.
> KEEP DESTINATION QUIET. EXPECT GREAT REVELATIONS.
>
> AKELEY

Receipt of this message in direct response to one sent to Akeley—and necessarily delivered to his house from the Townshend station either by official messenger or by a restored telephone service—removed any lingering sub-conscious doubts I may have had about the authorship of the perplexing letter. My relief was marked—indeed, it was greater than I could account for at that time; since all such doubts had been rather deeply buried. But I slept soundly and long that night, and was eagerly busy with preparations during the ensuing two days.

VI

On Wednesday I started as agreed, taking with me a valise full of simple necessities and scientific data, including the hideous phonograph record, the Kodak prints, and the entire file of Akeley's correspondence. As requested, I had told no one where I was going; for I could see that the matter demanded utmost privacy, even allowing for its most favorable turns. The thought of actual mental contact with alien, outside entities was stupefying enough to my trained and somewhat prepared mind; and this being so, what might one think of its effect on the vast masses of uninformed laymen? I do not know whether dread or adventurous expectancy was uppermost in me as I changed trains in Boston and began the long westward run out of familiar regions into those I knew less thoroughly. Waltham—Concord—Ayer—Fitchburg—Gardner—Athol—

My train reached Greenfield seven minutes late, but the northbound connecting express had been held. Transferring in haste, I felt a curious breathlessness as the cars rumbled on through the early afternoon sunlight into territories I had always read of but had never before visited. I knew I was entering an altogether older-fashioned and more primitive New England than the mechanized, urbanized coastal and southern areas where all my life had been spent; an unspoiled, ancestral New England without the foreigners and factory-smoke, billboards and concrete roads, of the sections which modernity has touched. There would be odd survivals of that continuous native life whose deep roots make it the one authentic outgrowth of the landscape—the continuous native life which keeps alive strange ancient memories, and fertilizes the soil for shadowy, marvelous, and seldom-mentioned beliefs.

Now and then I saw the blue Connecticut River gleaming in the sun, and after leaving Northfield we crossed it. Ahead loomed green and cryptical hills, and when the conductor came around I learned that I was at last in Vermont. He told me to set my watch back an hour, since the northern hill country will have no dealings with new-fangled daylight time schemes. As I did so it seemed to me that I was likewise turning the calendar back a century.

The train kept close to the river, and across in New Hampshire I could see the approaching slope of steep Wantastiquet, about which singular old legends cluster. Then streets appeared on my left, and a green island showed in the stream on my right. People rose and filed to the door, and I followed them. The car stopped, and I alighted beneath the long train-shed of the Brattleboro station.

Looking over the line of waiting motors I hesitated a moment to see which one might turn out to be the Akeley Ford, but my identity was divined before I could take the initiative. And yet it was clearly not Akeley himself who advanced to meet me with an outstretched hand and a mellowly phrased query as to whether I was indeed Mr. Albert N. Wilmarth of Arkham. This man bore no resemblance to the bearded, grizzled Akeley of the snapshot; but was a younger and more urban person, fashionably dressed, and wearing only a small, dark mustache. His cultivated voice held an odd and almost disturbing hint of vague familiarity, though I could not definitely place it in my memory.

As I surveyed him I heard him explaining that he was a friend of my prospective host's who had come down from Townshend in his stead. Akeley, he declared, had suffered a sudden attack of some asthmatic trouble, and did not feel equal to making a trip in the outdoor air. It was not serious, however, and there was to be no change in plans regarding my visit. I could not make out just how much this Mr. Noyes—as he announced himself—knew of Akeley's researches and discoveries, though it seemed to me that his casual manner stamped him as a comparative outsider. Remembering what a hermit Akeley had been, I was a trifle surprised at the ready availability of such a friend; but did not let my puzzlement deter me from entering the motor to which he gestured me. It was not the small ancient car I had expected from Akeley's descriptions, but a large and immaculate specimen of recent pattern—apparently Noyes's own, and bearing Massachusetts license plates with the amusing "sacred codfish" device of that year. My guide, I concluded, must be a summer transient in the Townshend region.

Noyes climbed into the car beside me and started it at once. I was glad that he did not overflow with conversation, for some peculiar atmospheric tensity made me feel disinclined to talk. The town seemed very attractive in the afternoon sunlight as we swept up an incline and turned to the right into the main street. It drowsed like the older New England cities which one remembers from boyhood, and something in the collocation of roofs and steeples and chimneys and brick walls formed contours touching deep viol-strings of ancestral emotion. I could tell that I was at the gateway of a region half-bewitched through the piling-up of unbroken time-accumulations; a region where old, strange things have had a chance to grow and linger because they have never been stirred up.

As we passed out of Brattleboro my sense of constraint and foreboding increased, for a vague quality in the hill-crowded countryside with its towering, threatening, close-pressing green and granite slopes hinted at obscure secrets and immemorial survivals which might or might not be hostile to mankind. For a time our course followed a broad, shallow river which flowed down from unknown hills in the north, and I shivered when my companion told me it was the West River. It was in this stream, I recalled from newspaper items, that one of the morbid crab-like beings had been seen floating after the floods.

Gradually the country around us grew wilder and more deserted. Archaic covered bridges lingered fearsomely out of the past in pockets of the hills, and the half-abandoned railway track paralleling the river seemed to exhale a nebulously visible air of desolation. There were awesome sweeps of vivid valley where great cliffs rose, New England's virgin granite showing gray and austere through the verdure that scaled the crests. There were gorges where untamed streams leaped, bearing down toward the river the unimagined secrets of a thousand pathless peaks. Branching away now and then were narrow, half-concealed roads that bored their way through solid, luxuriant masses of forest among whose primal trees whole armies of elemental spirits might well lurk. As I saw these I thought of how Akeley had been molested by unseen agencies on his drives along this very route, and did not wonder that such things could be.

The quaint, sightly village of Newfane, reached in less than an hour, was our last link with that world which man can definitely call his own by virtue of conquest and complete occupancy. After that we cast off all allegiance to immediate, tangible, and time-touched things, and entered a fantastic world of hushed unreality in which the narrow, ribbon-like road rose and fell and curved with an almost sentient and purposeful caprice amidst the tenantless green peaks and half-deserted valleys. Except for the sound of the motor, and the faint stir of the few lonely farms we passed at infrequent intervals, the only thing that reached my ears was the gurgling, insidious trickle of strange waters from numberless hidden fountains in the shadowy woods.

The nearness and intimacy of the dwarfed, domed hills now became veritably breath-taking. Their steepness and abruptness were even greater than I had imagined from hearsay, and suggested nothing in common with the prosaic objective world we know. The dense, unvisited woods on those inaccessible slopes seemed to harbor alien and incredible things, and I felt that the very outline of the hills themselves held some strange and eon-forgotten meaning, as if they were vast hieroglyphs left by a rumored titan race whose glories live only in rare, deep dreams. All the legends of the past, and all the stupefying imputations of Henry Akeley's letters and exhibits, welled up in my memory to heighten the atmosphere of tension and growing menace. The purpose of my visit, and the frightful abnormalities it postulated, struck me all at once with a chill sensation that nearly overbalanced my ardor for strange delvings.

My guide must have noticed my disturbed attitude; for as the road grew wilder and more irregular, and our motion slower and more jolting, his occasional pleasant comments expanded into a steadier flow of discourse. He spoke of the beauty and weirdness of the country, and revealed some acquaintance with the folklore studies of my prospective host. From his polite questions it was obvious that he knew I had come for a scientific purpose, and that I was bringing data of some importance; but he gave no sign of appreciating the depth and awfulness of the knowledge which Akeley had finally reached.

His manner was so cheerful, normal, and urbane that his remarks ought to have calmed and reassured me; but oddly enough, I felt only the more disturbed as we bumped and veered onward into the unknown wilderness of hills and woods. At times it seemed as if he were pumping me to see what I knew of the monstrous secrets of the place, and with every fresh utterance that vague, teasing, baffling *familiarity* in his voice increased. It was not an ordinary or healthy familiarity despite the thoroughly wholesome and cultivated nature of the voice. I somehow linked it with forgotten nightmares, and felt that I might go mad if I recognized it. If any good excuse had existed, I think I would have turned back from my visit. As it was, I could not well do so—and it occurred to me that a cool, scientific conversation with Akeley himself after my arrival would help greatly to pull me together.

Besides, there was a strangely calming element of cosmic beauty in the hypnotic landscape through which we climbed and plunged fantastically. Time had lost itself in the labyrinths behind, and around us stretched only the flowering waves of faery and the recaptured loveliness of vanished centuries—the hoary groves, the untainted pastures edged with gay autumnal blossoms, and at vast intervals the small brown farmsteads nestling amidst huge trees beneath vertical precipices of fragrant brier and meadow-grass. Even the sunlight assumed a supernal glamor, as if some special atmosphere or exhalation mantled the whole region. I had seen nothing like it before save in the magic vistas that sometimes form the backgrounds of Italian primitives. Sodoma and Leonardo conceived such expanses, but only in the distance, and through the vaultings of Renaissance arcades. We were now burrowing bodily through the midst of the picture, and I seemed to find in its necromancy a thing I had innately known or inherited, and for which I had always been vainly searching.

Suddenly, after rounding an obtuse angle at the top of a sharp ascent, the car came to a standstill. On my left, across a well-kept lawn which stretched to the road and flaunted a border of whitewashed stones, rose a white, two-and-a-half-story house of unusual size and elegance for the region, with a congeries of contiguous or arcade-linked barns, sheds, and windmill behind and to the right. I recognized it at once from the snapshot I had received, and was not surprised to see the name of Henry Akeley on the galvanized-iron mailbox near the road. For some distance back of the house a level stretch of marshy and sparsely wooded land extended, beyond which soared a steep, thickly forested hillside ending in a jagged leafy crest. This latter, I knew, was the summit of Dark Mountain, half way up which we must have climbed already.

Alighting from the car and taking my valise, Noyes asked me to wait while he went in and notified Akeley of my advent. He himself, he added, had important business elsewhere, and could not stop for more than a moment. As he briskly walked up the path to the house I climbed out of the car myself, wishing to stretch my legs a little before settling down to a sedentary conversation. My feeling of nervousness and tension had risen to a maximum again now that I was on the actual scene of the morbid beleaguering described so hauntingly in Akeley's letters, and I honestly dreaded the coming discussions which were to link me with such alien and forbidden worlds.

Close contact with the utterly bizarre is often more terrifying than inspiring, and it did not cheer me to think that this very bit of dusty road was the place where those monstrous tracks and that fetid green ichor had been found after moonless nights of fear and death. Idly I noticed that none of Akeley's dogs seemed to be about. Had he sold them all as soon as the Outer Ones made peace with him? Try as I might, I could not have the same confidence in the depth and sincerity of that peace which appeared in Akeley's final and queerly different letter. After all, he was a man of much simplicity and with little worldly experience. Was there not, perhaps, some deep and sinister undercurrent beneath the surface of the new alliance?

Led by my thoughts, my eyes turned downward to the powdery road surface which had held such hideous testimonies. The last few days had been dry, and tracks of all sorts cluttered the rutted, irregular highway despite the unfrequented nature of the district. With a vague curiosity I began to trace the outline of some of the heterogeneous impressions, trying meanwhile to curb the flights of macabre fancy which the place and its memories suggested. There was something menacing and uncomfortable in the funereal stillness, in the muffled, subtle trickle of distant brooks, and in the crowding green peaks and black-wooded precipices that choked the narrow horizon.

And then an image shot into my consciousness which made those vague menaces and flights of fancy seem mild and insignificant indeed. I have said that I was scanning the miscellaneous prints in the road with a kind of idle curiosity—but all at once that curiosity was shockingly snuffed out by a sudden and paralyzing gust of active terror. For though the dust tracks were in general confused and overlapping, and unlikely to arrest any casual gaze, my restless vision had caught certain details near the spot where the path to the house joined the highway; and had recognized beyond doubt or hope the frightful significance of those details. It was not for nothing, alas, that I had pored for hours over the Kodak views of the Outer Ones' claw-prints which Akeley had sent. Too well did I know the marks of those loathsome nippers, and that hint of ambiguous direction which stamped the horrors as no creatures of this planet. No chance had been left me for merciful mistake. Here, indeed, in objective form before my own eyes, and surely made not many hours ago, were at least three marks which stood out blasphemously among the surprising plethora of blurred footprints leading to and from the Akeley farmhouse. *They were the hellish tracks of the living fungi from Yuggoth.*

I pulled myself together in time to stifle a scream. After all, what more was there than I might have expected, assuming that I had really believed Akeley's letters? He had spoken of making peace with the things. Why, then, was it strange that some of them had visited his house? But the terror was stronger than the reassurance. Could any man be expected to look unmoved for the first time upon the claw-marks of animate beings from outer depths of space? Just then I saw Noyes emerge from the door and approach with a brisk step. I must, I reflected, keep command of myself, for the chances were this genial friend knew nothing of Akeley's profoundest and most stupendous probings into the forbidden.

Akeley, Noyes hastened to inform me, was glad and ready to see me; although his sudden attack of asthma would prevent him from being a very competent host for a day or two. These spells hit him hard when they came, and were always accompanied by a debilitating fever and general weakness. He never was good for much while they lasted—had to talk in a whisper, and was very clumsy and feeble in getting about. His feet and ankles swelled, too, so that he had to bandage them like a gouty old beef-eater. Today he was in rather bad shape, so that I would have to attend very largely to my own needs; but he was none the less eager for conversation. I would find him in the study at the left of the front hall—the room where the blinds were shut. He had to keep the sunlight out when he was ill, for his eyes were very sensitive.

As Noyes bade me adieu and rode off northward in his car I began to walk slowly toward the house. The door had been left ajar for me; but before approaching and entering I cast a searching glance around the whole place, trying to decide what had struck me as so intangibly queer about it. The barns and sheds looked trimly prosaic enough, and I noticed Akeley's battered Ford in its capacious, unguarded shelter. Then the secret of the queerness reached me. It was the total silence. Ordinarily a farm is at least moderately murmurous from its various kinds of livestock, but here all signs of life were missing. What of the hens and the hogs? The cows, of which Akeley had said he possessed several, might conceivably be out to pasture, and the dogs might possibly have been sold; but the absence of any trace of cackling or grunting was truly singular.

I did not pause long on the path, but resolutely entered the open house door and closed it behind me. It had cost me a distinct psychological effort to do so, and now that I was shut inside I had a momentary longing for precipitate retreat. Not that the place was in the least sinister in visual suggestion; on the contrary, I thought the graceful late-colonial hallway very tasteful and wholesome, and admired the evident breeding of the man who had furnished it. What made me wish to flee was something very attenuated and indefinable. Perhaps it was a certain odd odor which I thought I noticed—though I well knew how common musty odors are in even the best of ancient farmhouses.

VII

Refusing to let these cloudy qualms overmaster me, I recalled Noyes's instructions and pushed open the six-paneled, brass-latched white door on my left. The room beyond was darkened, as I had known before; and as I entered it I noticed that the queer odor was stronger there. There likewise appeared to be some faint, half-imaginary rhythm or vibration in the air. For a moment the closed blinds allowed me to see very little, but then a kind of apologetic hacking or whispering sound drew my attention to a great easy-chair in the farther, darker corner of the room. Within its shadowy depths I saw the white blur of a man's face and hands; and in a moment I had crossed to greet the figure who had tried to speak. Dim though the light was, I perceived that this was indeed my host. I had studied the Kodak picture repeatedly, and there could be no mistake about this firm, weather-beaten face with the cropped, grizzled beard.

But as I looked again my recognition was mixed with sadness and anxiety; for certainly, this face was that of a very sick man. I felt that there must be something more than asthma behind that strained, rigid, immobile expression and unwinking glassy stare; and realized how terribly the strain of his frightful experiences must have told on him. Was it not enough to break any human being—even a younger man than this intrepid delver into the forbidden? The strange and sudden relief, I feared, had come too late to save him from something like a general breakdown. There was a touch of the pitiful in the limp, lifeless way his lean hands rested in his lap. He had on a loose dressing-gown, and was swathed around the head and high around the neck with a vivid yellow scarf or hood.

And then I saw that he was trying to talk in the same hacking whisper with which he had greeted me. It was a hard whisper to catch at first, since the gray mustache concealed all movements of the lips, and something in its timbre disturbed me greatly; but by concentrating my attention I could soon make out its purport surprisingly well. The accent was by no means a rustic one, and the language was even more polished than correspondence had led me to expect.

"Mr. Wilmarth, I presume? You must pardon my not rising. I am quite ill, as Mr. Noyes must have told you; but I could not resist having you come just the same. You know what I wrote in my last letter—there is so much to tell you tomorrow when I shall feel better. I can't say how glad I am to see you in person after all our many letters. You have the file with you, of course? And the Kodak prints and record? Noyes put your valise in the hall—I suppose you saw it. For tonight I fear you'll have to wait on yourself to a great extent. Your room is upstairs—the one over this—and you'll see the bathroom door open at the head of the staircase. There's a meal spread for you in the dining-room—right through this door at your right—which you can take whenever you feel like it. I'll be a better host tomorrow—but just now weakness leaves me helpless.

"Make yourself at home—you might take out the letters and pictures and record and put them on the table here before you go upstairs with your bag. It is here that we shall discuss them—you can see my phonograph on that corner stand.

"No, thanks—there's nothing you can do for me. I know these spells of old. Just come back for a little quiet visiting before night, and then go to bed when you please. I'll rest right here—perhaps sleep here all night as I often do. In the morning I'll be far better able to go into the things we must go into. You realize, of course, the utterly stupendous nature of the matter before us. To us, as to only a few men on this earth, there will be opened up gulfs of time and space and knowledge beyond anything within the conception of human science and philosophy.

"Do you know that Einstein is wrong, and that certain objects and forces *can* move with a velocity greater than that of light? With proper aid I expect to go backward and forward in time, and actually *see* and *feel* the earth of remote past and future epochs. You can't imagine the degree to which those beings have carried science. There is nothing they can't do with the mind and body of living organisms. I expect to visit other planets, and even other stars and galaxies. The first trip will be to Yuggoth, the nearest world fully peopled by the beings. It is a strange dark orb at the very rim of our solar system—unknown to earthly astronomers as yet. But I must have written you about this. At the proper time, you know, the beings there will direct thought-currents toward us and cause it to be discovered—or perhaps let one of their human allies give the scientists a hint.

"There are mighty cities on Yuggoth—great tiers of terraced towers built of black stone like the specimen I tried to send you. That came from Yuggoth. The sun shines there no brighter than a star, but the beings need no light. They have other, subtler senses, and put no windows in their great houses and temples. Light even hurts and hampers and confuses them, for it does not exist at all in the black cosmos outside time and space where they came from originally. To visit Yuggoth would drive any weak man mad—yet I am going there. The black rivers of pitch that flow under those mysterious Cyclopean bridges—things built by some elder race extinct and forgotten before the things came to Yuggoth from the ultimate voids—ought to be enough to make any man a Dante or Poe if he can keep sane long enough to tell what he has seen.

"But remember—that dark world of fungoid gardens and windowless cities isn't really terrible. It is only to us that it would seem so. Probably this world seemed just as terrible to the beings when they first explored it in the primal age. You know they were here long before the fabulous epoch of Cthulhu was over, and remember all about sunken R'lyeh when it was above the waters. They've been inside the earth, too—there are openings which human beings know nothing of—some of them in these very Vermont hills—and great worlds of unknown life down there; blue-litten K'n-yan, red-litten Yoth, and black, lightless N'kai. It's from N'kai that frightful Tsathoggua came—you know, the amorphous, toad-like god-creature mentioned in the Pnakotic Manuscripts and the *Necronomicon* and the Commoriom myth-cycle preserved by the Atlantean high-priest Klarkash-Ton.

"But we will talk of all this later on. It must be four or five o'clock by this time. Better bring the stuff from your bag, take a bite, and then come back for a comfortable chat."

Very slowly I turned and began to obey my host; fetching my valise, extracting and depositing the desired articles, and finally ascending to the room designated as mine. With the memory of that roadside claw-print fresh in my mind, Akeley's whispered paragraphs had affected me queerly; and the hints of familiarity with this unknown world of fungous life—forbidden Yuggoth—made my flesh creep more than I cared to own. I was tremendously sorry about Akeley's illness, but had to confess that his hoarse whisper had a hateful as well as pitiful quality. If only he wouldn't gloat so about Yuggoth and its black secrets!

My room proved a very pleasant and well-furnished one, devoid alike of the musty odor and disturbing sense of vibration; and after leaving my valise there I descended again to greet Akeley and take the lunch he had set out for me. The dining-room was just beyond the study, and I saw that a kitchen ell extended still farther in the same direction. On the dining-table an ample array of sandwiches, cake, and cheese awaited me, and a Thermos-bottle beside a cup and saucer testified that hot coffee had not been forgotten. After a well-relished meal I poured myself a liberal cup of coffee, but found that the culinary standard had suffered a lapse in this one detail. My first spoonful revealed a faintly unpleasant acrid taste, so that I did not take more. Throughout the lunch I thought of Akeley sitting silently in the great chair in the darkened next room.

Once I went in to beg him to share the repast, but he whispered that he could eat nothing as yet. Later on, just before he slept, he would take some malted milk—all he ought to have that day.

After lunch I insisted on clearing the dishes away and washing them in the kitchen sink—incidentally emptying the coffee which I had not been able to appreciate. Then returning to the darkened study I drew up a chair near my host's corner and prepared for such conversation as he might feel inclined to conduct. The letters, pictures, and record were still on the large center-table, but for the nonce we did not have to draw upon them. Before long I forgot even the bizarre odor and curious suggestions of vibration.

I have said that there were things in some of Akeley's letters—especially the second and most voluminous one—which I would not dare to quote or even form into words on paper. This hesitancy applies with still greater force to the things I heard whispered that evening in the darkened room among the lonely haunted hills. Of the extent of the cosmic horrors unfolded by that raucous voice I cannot even hint. He had known hideous things before, but what he had learned since making his pact with the Outside Things was almost too much for sanity to bear. Even now I absolutely refuse to believe what he implied about the constitution of ultimate infinity, the juxtaposition of dimensions, and the frightful position of our known cosmos of space and time in the unending chain of linked cosmos-atoms which makes up the immediate super-cosmos of curves, angles, and material and semi-material electronic organization.

Never was a sane man more dangerously close to the arcana of basic entity—never was an organic brain nearer to utter annihilation in the chaos that transcends form and force and symmetry. I learned whence Cthulhu *first* came, and why half the great temporary stars of history had flared forth. I guessed—from hints which made even my informant pause timidly—the secret behind the Magellanic Clouds and globular nebulae, and the black truth veiled by the immemorial allegory of Tao. The nature of the Doels was plainly revealed, and I was told the essence (though not the source) of the Hounds of Tindalos. The legend of Yig, Father of Serpents, remained figurative no longer, and I started with loathing when told of the monstrous nuclear chaos beyond angled space which the *Necronomicon* had mercifully cloaked under the name of Azathoth. It was shocking to have the foulest nightmares of secret myth cleared up in concrete terms whose stark, morbid hatefulness exceeded the boldest hints of ancient and medieval mystics. Ineluctably I was led to believe that the first whisperers of these accursed tales must have had discourse with Akeley's Outer Ones, and perhaps have visited outer cosmic realms as Akeley now proposed visiting them.

I was told of the Black Stone and what it implied, and was glad that it had not reached me. My guesses about those hieroglyphics had been all too correct! And yet Akeley now seemed reconciled to the whole fiendish system he had stumbled upon; reconciled and eager to probe farther into the monstrous abyss. I wondered what beings he had talked with since his last letter to me, and whether many of them had been as human as that first emissary he had mentioned. The tension in my head grew insufferable, and I built up all sorts of wild theories about the queer, persistent odor and those insidious hints of vibration in the darkened room.

Night was falling now, and as I recalled what Akeley had written me about those earlier nights I shuddered to think there would be no moon. Nor did I like the way the farmhouse nestled in the lee of that colossal forested slope leading up to Dark Mountain's unvisited crest. With Akeley's permission I lighted a small oil lamp, turned it low, and set it on a distant bookcase beside the ghostly bust of Milton; but afterward I was sorry I had done so, for it made my host's strained, immobile face and listless hands look damnably abnormal and corpse-like. He seemed half-incapable of motion, though I saw him nod stiffly once in a while.

After what he had told, I could scarcely imagine what profounder secrets he was saving for the morrow; but at last it developed that his trip to Yuggoth and beyond—*and my own possible participation in it*—was to be the next day's topic. He must have been amused by the start of horror I gave at hearing a cosmic voyage on my part proposed, for his head wobbled violently when I showed my fear. Subsequently he spoke very gently of how human beings might accomplish—and several times had accomplished—the seemingly impossible flight across the interstellar void. It seemed that *complete human bodies did not indeed make the trip,* but that the prodigious surgical, biological, chemical, and mechanical skill of the Outer Ones had found a way to convey human brains without their concomitant physical structure.

There was a harmless way to extract a brain, and a way to keep the organic residue alive during its absence. The bare, compact cerebral matter was then immersed in an occasionally replenished fluid within an ether-tight cylinder of a metal mined in Yuggoth, certain electrodes reaching through and connecting at will with elaborate instruments capable of duplicating the three vital faculties of sight, hearing, and speech. For the winged fungus-beings to carry the brain-cylinders intact through space was an easy matter. Then, on every planet covered by their civilization, they would find plenty of adjustable faculty-instruments capable of being connected with the encased brains; so that after a little fitting these traveling intelligences could be given a full sensory and articulate life—albeit a bodiless and mechanical one—at each stage of their journeying through and beyond the space-time continuum. It was as simple as carrying a phonograph record about and playing it wherever a phonograph of the corresponding make exists. Of its success there could be no question. Akeley was not afraid. Had it not been brilliantly accomplished again and again?

For the first time one of the inert, wasted hands raised itself and pointed to a high shelf on the farther side of the room. There, in a neat row, stood more than a dozen cylinders of a metal I had never seen before—cylinders about a foot high and somewhat less in diameter, with three curious sockets set in an isosceles triangle over the front convex surface of each. One of them was linked at two of the sockets to a pair of singular-looking machines that stood in the background. Of their purport I did not need to be told, and I shivered as with ague. Then I saw the hand point to a much nearer corner where some intricate instruments with attached cords and plugs, several of them much like the two devices on the shelf behind the cylinders, were huddled together.

"There are four kinds of instruments here, Wilmarth," whispered the voice. "Four kinds—three faculties each—makes twelve pieces in all. You see there are four different sorts of beings presented in those cylinders up there. Three humans, six fungoid beings who can't navigate space corporeally, two beings from Neptune (God! if you could see the body this type has on its own planet!), and the rest entities from the central caverns of an especially interesting dark star beyond the galaxy. In the principal outpost inside Round Hill you'll now and then find more cylinders and machines—cylinders of extra-cosmic brains with different senses from any we know—allies and explorers from the uttermost Outside—and special machines for giving them impressions and expression in the several ways suited at once to them and to the comprehensions of different types of listeners. Round Hill, like most of the beings' main outposts all through the various universes, is a very cosmopolitan place! Of course, only the more common types have been lent to me for experiment.

"Here—take the three machines I point to and set them on the table. That tall one with the two glass lenses in front—then the box with the vacuum tubes and sounding-board—and now the one with the metal disc on top. Now for the cylinder with the label 'B-67' pasted on it. Just stand in that Windsor chair to reach the shelf. Heavy? Never mind! Be sure of the number—B-67. Don't bother that fresh, shiny cylinder joined to the two testing instruments—the one with my name on it. Set B-67 on the table near where you've put the machines—and see that the dial switch on all three machines is jammed over to the extreme left.

"Now connect the cord of the lens machine with the upper socket on the cylinder—there! Join the tube machine to the lower left-hand socket, and the disc apparatus to the outer socket. Now move all the dial switches on the machines over to the extreme right—first the lens one, then the disc one, and then the tube one. That's right. I might as well tell you that this is a human being—just like any of us. I'll give you a taste of some of the others tomorrow."

To this day I do not know why I obeyed those whispers so slavishly, or whether I thought Akeley was mad or sane. After what had gone before, I ought to have been prepared for anything; but this mechanical mummery seemed so like the typical vagaries of crazed inventors and scientists that it struck a chord of doubt which even the preceding discourse had not excited. What the whisperer implied was beyond all human belief—yet were not the other things still farther beyond, and less preposterous only because of their remoteness from tangible concrete proof?

As my mind reeled amidst this chaos, I became conscious of a mixed grating and whirring from all three machines lately linked to the cylinder—a grating and whirring which soon subsided into a virtual noiselessness. What was about to happen? Was I to hear a voice? And if so, what proof would I have that it was not some cleverly concocted radio device talked into by a concealed but closely watching speaker? Even now I am unwilling to swear just what I heard, or just what phenomenon really took place before me. But something certainly seemed to take place.

To be brief and plain, the machine with the tubes and sound-box began to speak, and with a point and intelligence which left no doubt that the speaker was actually present and observing us. The voice was loud, metallic, lifeless, and plainly mechanical in every detail of its production. It was incapable of inflection or expressiveness, but scraped and rattled on with a deadly precision and deliberation.

"Mr. Wilmarth," it said, "I hope I do not startle you. I am a human being like yourself, though my body is now resting safely under proper vitalizing treatment inside Round Hill, about a mile and a half east of here. I myself am here with you—my brain is in that cylinder and I see, hear, and speak through these electronic vibrators. In a week I am going across the void as I have been many times before, and I expect to have the pleasure of Mr. Akeley's company. I wish I might have yours as well; for I know you by sight and reputation, and have kept close track of your correspondence with our friend. I am, of course, one of the men who have become allied with the outside beings visiting our planet. I met them first in the Himalayas, and have helped them in various ways. In return they have given me experiences such as few men have ever had.

"Do you realize what it means when I say I have been on thirty-seven different celestial bodies—planets, dark stars, and less definable objects—including eight outside our galaxy and two outside the curved cosmos of space and time? All this has not harmed me in the least. My brain has been removed from my body by fissions so adroit that it would be crude to call the operation surgery. The visiting beings have methods which make these extractions easy and almost normal—and one's body never ages when the brain is out of it. The brain, I may add, is virtually immortal with its mechanical faculties and a limited nourishment supplied by occasional changes of the preserving fluid.

"Altogether, I hope most heartily that you will decide to come with Mr. Akeley and me. The visitors are eager to know men of knowledge like yourself, and to show them the great abysses that most of us have had to dream about in fanciful ignorance. It may seem strange at first to meet them, but I know you will be above minding that. I think Mr. Noyes will go along, too—the man who doubtless brought you up here in his car. He has been one of us for years—I suppose you recognized his voice as one of those on the record Mr. Akeley sent you."

At my violent start the speaker paused a moment before concluding. "So, Mr. Wilmarth, I will leave the matter to you; merely adding that a man with your love of strangeness and folklore ought never to miss such a chance as this. There is nothing to fear. All transitions are painless, and there is much to enjoy in a wholly mechanized state of sensation. When the electrodes are disconnected, one merely drops off into a sleep of especially vivid and fantastic dreams.

"And now, if you don't mind, we might adjourn our session till tomorrow. Good night—just turn all the switches back to the left; never mind the exact order, though you might let the lens machine be last. Good night, Mr. Akeley—treat our guest well! Ready now with those switches?"

That was all. I obeyed mechanically and shut off all three switches, though dazed with doubt of everything that had occurred. My head was still reeling as I heard Akeley's whispering voice telling me that I might leave all the apparatus on the table just as it was. He did not essay any comment on what had happened, and indeed no comment could have conveyed much to my burdened faculties. I heard him telling me I could take the lamp to use in my room, and deduced that he wished to rest alone in the dark. It was surely time he rested, for his discourse of the afternoon and evening had been such as to exhaust even a vigorous man. Still dazed, I bade my host good night and went upstairs with the lamp, although I had an excellent pocket flashlight with me.

I was glad to be out of that downstairs study with the queer odor and vague suggestions of vibration, yet could not of course escape a hideous sense of dread and peril and cosmic abnormality as I thought of the place I was in and the forces I was meeting. The wild, lonely region, the black, mysteriously forested slope towering so close behind the house, the footprints in the road, the sick, motionless whisperer in the dark, the hellish cylinders and machines, and above all the invitations to strange surgery and stranger voyagings—these things, all so new and in such sudden succession, rushed in on me with a cumulative force which sapped my will and almost undermined my physical strength.

To discover that my guide Noyes was the human celebrant in that monstrous bygone Sabbat-ritual on the phonograph record was a particular shock, though I had previously sensed a dim, repellent familiarity in his voice. Another special shock came from my own attitude toward my host whenever I paused to analyze it; for much as I had instinctively liked Akeley as revealed in his correspondence, I now found that he filled me with a distinct repulsion. His illness ought to have excited my pity; but instead, it gave me a kind of shudder. He was so rigid and inert and corpse-like—and that incessant whispering was so hateful and unhuman!

It occurred to me that this whispering was different from anything else of the kind I had ever heard; that, despite the curious motionlessness of the speaker's mustache-screened lips, it had a latent strength and carrying-power remarkable for the wheezings of an asthmatic. I had been able to understand the speaker when wholly across the room, and once or twice it had seemed to me that the faint but penetrant sounds represented not so much weakness as deliberate repression—for what reason I could not guess. From the first I had felt a disturbing quality in their timbre. Now, when I tried to weigh the matter, I thought I could trace this impression to a kind of subconscious familiarity like that which had made Noyes's voice so hazily ominous. But when or where I had encountered the thing it hinted at, was more than I could tell.

One thing was certain—I would not spend another night here. My scientific zeal had vanished amidst fear and loathing, and I felt nothing now but a wish to escape from this net of morbidity and unnatural revelation. I knew enough now. It must indeed be true that cosmic linkages do exist—but such things are surely not meant for normal human beings to meddle with.

Blasphemous influences seemed to surround me and press chokingly upon my senses. Sleep, I decided, would be out of the question; so I merely extinguished the lamp and threw myself on the bed fully dressed. No doubt it was absurd, but I kept ready for some unknown emergency; gripping in my right hand the revolver I had brought along, and holding the pocket flashlight in my left. Not a sound came from below, and I could imagine how my host was sitting there with cadaverous stiffness in the dark.

Somewhere I heard a clock ticking, and was vaguely grateful for the normality of the sound. It reminded me, though, of another thing about the region which disturbed me—the total absence of animal life. There were certainly no farm beasts about, and now I realized that even the accustomed night-noises of wild living things were absent. Except for the sinister trickle of distant unseen waters, that stillness was anomalous—interplanetary—and I wondered what star-spawned, intangible blight could be hanging over the region. I recalled from old legends that dogs and other beasts had always hated the Outer Ones, and thought of what those tracks in the road might mean.

VIII

Do not ask me how long my unexpected lapse into slumber lasted, or how much of what ensued was sheer dream. If I tell you that I awaked at a certain time, and heard and saw certain things, you will merely answer that I did not wake then; and that everything was a dream until the moment when I rushed out of the house, stumbled to the shed where I had seen the old Ford, and seized that ancient vehicle for a mad, aimless race over the haunted hills which at last landed me—after hours of jolting and winding through forest-threatened labyrinths—in a village which turned out to be Townshend.

You will also, of course, discount everything else in my report; and declare that all the pictures, record-sounds, cylinder-and-machine sounds, and kindred evidences were bits of pure deception practiced on me by the missing Henry Akeley. You will even hint that he conspired with other eccentrics to carry out a silly and elaborate hoax—that he had the express shipment removed at Keene, and that he had Noyes make that terrifying wax record. It is odd, though, that Noyes has not even yet been identified; that he was unknown at any of the villages near Akeley's place, though he must have been frequently in the region. I wish I had stopped to memorize the license-number of his car—or perhaps it is better after all that I did not. For I, despite all you can say, and despite all I sometimes try to say to myself, know that loathsome outside influences must be lurking there in the half-unknown hills—and that those influences have spies and emissaries in the world of men. To keep as far as possible from such influences and such emissaries is all that I ask of life in future.

When my frantic story sent a sheriff's posse out to the farmhouse, Akeley was gone without leaving a trace. His loose dressing-gown, yellow scarf, and foot-bandages lay on the study floor near his corner easy-chair, and it could not be decided whether any of his other apparel had vanished with him. The dogs and livestock were indeed missing, and there were some curious bullet-holes both on the house's exterior and on some of the walls within; but beyond this nothing unusual could be detected. No cylinders or machines, none of the evidences I had brought in my valise, no queer odor or vibration-sense, no footprints in the road, and none of the problematical things I glimpsed at the very last.

I stayed a week in Brattleboro after my escape, making inquiries among people of every kind who had known Akeley; and the results convince me that the matter is no figment of dream or delusion. Akeley's queer purchases of dogs and ammunition and chemicals, and the cutting of his telephone wires, are matters of record; while all who knew him—including his son in California—concede that his occasional remarks on strange studies had a certain consistency. Solid citizens believe he was mad, and unhesitatingly pronounce all reported evidences mere hoaxes devised with insane cunning and perhaps abetted by eccentric associates; but the lowlier country folk sustain his statements in every detail. He had showed some of these rustics his photographs and black stone, and had played the hideous record for them; and they all said the footprints and buzzing voice were like those described in ancestral legends.

They said, too, that suspicious sights and sounds had been noticed increasingly around Akeley's house after he found the black stone, and that the place was now avoided by everybody except the mail man and other casual, tough-minded people. Dark Mountain and Round Hill were both notoriously haunted spots, and I could find no one who had ever closely explored either. Occasional disappearances of natives throughout the district's history were well attested, and these now included the semi-vagabond Walter Brown, whom Akeley's letters had mentioned. I even came upon one farmer who thought he had personally glimpsed one of the queer bodies at flood-time in the swollen West River, but his tale was too confused to be really valuable.

When I left Brattleboro I resolved never to go back to Vermont, and I feel quite certain I shall keep my resolution. Those wild hills are surely the outpost of a frightful cosmic race—as I doubt all the less since reading that a new ninth planet has been glimpsed beyond Neptune, just as those influences had said it would be glimpsed. Astronomers, with a hideous appropriateness they little suspect, have named this thing "Pluto." I feel, beyond question, that it is nothing less than nighted Yuggoth—and I shiver when I try to figure out the real reason why its monstrous denizens wish it to be known in this way at this especial time. I vainly try to assure myself that these daemoniac creatures are not gradually leading up to some new policy hurtful to the earth and its normal inhabitants.

But I have still to tell of the ending of that terrible night in the farmhouse. As I have said, I did finally drop into a troubled doze; a doze filled with bits of dream which involved monstrous landscape-glimpses. Just what awaked me I cannot yet say, but that I did indeed awake at this given point I feel very certain. My first confused impression was of stealthily creaking floor-boards in the hall outside my door, and of a clumsy, muffled fumbling at the latch. This, however, ceased almost at once; so that my really clear impressions began with the voices heard from the study below. There seemed to be several speakers, and I judged that they were controversially engaged.

By the time I had listened a few seconds I was broad awake, for the nature of the voices was such as to make all thought of sleep ridiculous. The tones were curiously varied, and no one who had listened to that accursed phonograph record could harbor any doubts about the nature of at least two of them. Hideous though the idea was, I knew that I was under the same roof with nameless things from abysmal space; for those two voices were unmistakably the blasphemous buzzings which the Outside Beings used in their communication with men. The two were individually different—different in pitch, accent, and tempo—but they were both of the same damnable general kind.

A third voice was indubitably that of a mechanical utterance-machine connected with one of the detached brains in the cylinders. There was as little doubt about that as about the buzzings; for the loud, metallic, lifeless voice of the previous evening, with its inflectionless, expressionless scraping and rattling, and its impersonal precision and deliberation, had been utterly unforgettable. For a time I did not pause to question whether the intelligence behind the scraping was the identical one which had formerly talked to me; but shortly afterward I reflected that any brain would emit vocal sounds of the same quality if linked to the same mechanical speech-producer; the only possible differences being in language, rhythm, speed, and pronunciation. To complete the eldritch colloquy there were two actually human voices—one the crude speech of an unknown and evidently rustic man, and the other the suave Bostonian tones of my erstwhile guide Noyes.

As I tried to catch the words which the stoutly fashioned floor so bafflingly intercepted, I was also conscious of a great deal of stirring and scratching and shuffling in the room below; so that I could not escape the impression that it was full of living beings—many more than the few whose speech I could single out. The exact nature of this stirring is extremely hard to describe, for very few good bases of comparison exist. Objects seemed now and then to move across the room like conscious entities; the sound of their footfalls having something about it like a loose, hard-surfaced clattering—as of the contact of ill-coordinated surfaces of horn or hard rubber. It was, to use a more concrete but less accurate comparison, as if people with loose, splintery wooden shoes were shambling and rattling about on the polished board floor. On the nature and appearance of those responsible for the sounds, I did not care to speculate.

Before long I saw that it would be impossible to distinguish any connected discourse. Isolated words—including the names of Akeley and myself—now and then floated up, especially when uttered by the mechanical speech-producer; but their true significance was lost for want of continuous context. Today I refuse to form any definite deductions from them, and even their frightful effect on me was one of *suggestion* rather than of *revelation.* A terrible and abnormal conclave, I felt certain, was assembled below me; but for what shocking deliberations I could not tell. It was curious how this unquestioned sense of the malign and the blasphemous pervaded me despite Akeley's assurances of the Outsiders' friendliness.

With patient listening I began to distinguish clearly between voices, even though I could not grasp much of what any of the voices said. I seemed to catch certain typical emotions behind some of the speakers. One of the buzzing voices, for example, held an unmistakable note of authority; whilst the mechanical voice, notwithstanding its artificial loudness and regularity, seemed to be in a position of subordination and pleading. Noyes's tones exuded a kind of conciliatory atmosphere. The others I could make no attempt to interpret. I did not hear the familiar whisper of Akeley, but well knew that such a sound could never penetrate the solid flooring of my room.

I will try to set down some of the few disjointed words and other sounds I caught, labeling the speakers of the words as best I know how. It was from the speech-machine that I first picked up a few recognizable phrases.

(THE SPEECH-MACHINE)

"... brought it on myself... sent back the letters and the record... end on it... taken in... seeing and hearing... damn you... impersonal force, after all... fresh, shiny cylinder... great God..."

(FIRST BUZZING VOICE)

"... time we stopped... small and human... Akeley... brain... saying..."

(SECOND BUZZING VOICE)

"... Nyarlathotep... Wilmarth... records and letters... cheap imposture..."

(NOYES)

"... (an unpronounceable word or name, possibly N'gah-Kthun)... harmless... peace... couple of weeks... theatrical... told you that before..."

(FIRST BUZZING VOICE)

"... no reason... original plan... effects... Noyes can watch... Round Hill... fresh cylinder... Noyes's car..."

(NOYES)

"... well... all yours... down here... rest... place..."

(SEVERAL VOICES AT ONCE IN INDISTINGUISHABLE SPEECH)

(MANY FOOTSTEPS, INCLUDING THE PECULIAR LOOSE STIRRING OR CLATTERING)

(A CURIOUS SORT OF FLAPPING SOUND)

(THE SOUND OF AN AUTOMOBILE STARTING AND RECEDING)

(SILENCE)

That is the substance of what my ears brought me as I lay rigid upon that strange upstairs bed in the haunted farmhouse among the daemoniac hills—lay there fully dressed, with a revolver clenched in my right hand and a pocket flashlight gripped in my left. I became, as I have said, broad awake; but a kind of obscure paralysis nevertheless kept me inert till long after the last echoes of the sounds had died away. I heard the wooden, deliberate ticking of the ancient Connecticut clock somewhere far below, and at last made out the irregular snoring of a sleeper. Akeley must have dozed off after the strange session, and I could well believe that he needed to do so.

Just what to think or what to do was more than I could decide. After all, what *had* I heard beyond things which previous information might have led me to expect? Had I not known that the nameless Outsiders were now freely admitted to the farmhouse? No doubt Akeley had been surprised by an unexpected visit from them. Yet something in that fragmentary discourse had chilled me immeasurably, raised the most grotesque and horrible doubts, and made me wish fervently that I might wake up and prove everything a dream. I think my subconscious mind must have caught something which my consciousness has not yet recognized. But what of Akeley? Was he not my friend, and would he not have protested if any harm were meant me? The peaceful snoring below seemed to cast ridicule on all my suddenly intensified fears.

Was it possible that Akeley had been imposed upon and used as a lure to draw me into the hills with the letters and pictures and phonograph record? Did those beings mean to engulf us both in a common destruction because we had come to know too much? Again I thought of the abruptness and unnaturalness of that change in the situation which must have occurred between Akeley's penultimate and final letters. Something, my instinct told me, was terribly wrong. All was not as it seemed. That acrid coffee which I refused—had there not been an attempt by some hidden, unknown entity to drug it? I must talk to Akeley at once, and restore his sense of proportion. They had hypnotized him with their promises of cosmic revelations, but now he must listen to reason. We must get out of this before it would be too late. If he lacked the will power to make the break for liberty, I would supply it. Or if I could not persuade him to go, I could at least go myself. Surely he would let me take his Ford and leave it in a garage at Brattleboro. I had noticed it in the shed—the door being left unlocked and open now that peril was deemed past—and I believed there was a good chance of its being ready for instant use. That momentary dislike of Akeley which I had felt during and after the evening's conversation was all gone now. He was in a position much like my own, and we must stick together. Knowing his indisposed condition, I hated to wake him at this juncture, but I knew that I must. I could not stay in this place till morning as matters stood.

At last I felt able to act, and stretched myself vigorously to regain command of my muscles. Arising with a caution more impulsive than deliberate, I found and donned my hat, took my valise, and started downstairs with the flashlight's aid. In my nervousness I kept the revolver clutched in my right hand, being able to take care of both valise and flashlight with my left. Why I exerted these precautions I do not really know, since I was even then on my way to awaken the only other occupant of the house.

As I half tiptoed down the creaking stairs to the lower hall I could hear the sleeper more plainly, and noticed that he must be in the room on my left—the living-room I had not entered. On my right was the gaping blackness of the study in which I had heard the voices. Pushing open the unlatched door of the living-room I traced a path with the flashlight toward the source of the snoring, and finally turned the beams on the sleeper's face. But in the next second I hastily turned them away and commenced a cat-like retreat to the hall, my caution this time springing from reason as well as from instinct. For the sleeper on the couch was not Akeley at all, but my quondam guide Noyes.

Just what the real situation was, I could not guess; but common sense told me that the safest thing was to find out as much as possible before arousing anybody. Regaining the hall, I silently closed and latched the living-room door after me; thereby lessening the chances of awaking Noyes. I now cautiously entered the dark study, where I expected to find Akeley, whether asleep or awake, in the great corner chair which was evidently his favorite resting-place. As I advanced, the beams of my flashlight caught the great center-table, revealing one of the hellish cylinders with sight and hearing machines attached, and with a speech-machine standing close by, ready to be connected at any moment. This, I reflected, must be the encased brain I had heard talking during the frightful conference; and for a second I had a perverse impulse to attach the speech-machine and see what it would say.

It must, I thought, be conscious of my presence even now; since the sight and hearing attachments could not fail to disclose the rays of my flashlight and the faint creaking of the floor beneath my feet. But in the end I did not dare meddle with the thing. I idly saw that it was the fresh, shiny cylinder with Akeley's name on it, which I had noticed on the shelf earlier in the evening and which my host had told me not to bother. Looking back at that moment, I can only regret my timidity and wish that I had boldly caused the apparatus to speak. God knows what mysteries and horrible doubts and questions of identity it might have cleared up! But then, it may be merciful that I let it alone.

From the table I turned my flashlight to the corner where I thought Akeley was, but found to my perplexity that the great easy-chair was empty of any human occupant asleep or awake. From the seat to the floor there trailed voluminously the familiar old dressing-gown, and near it on the floor lay the yellow scarf and the huge foot-bandages I had thought so odd. As I hesitated, striving to conjecture where Akeley might be, and why he had so suddenly discarded his necessary sick-room garments, I observed that the queer odor and sense of vibration were no longer in the room. What had been their cause? Curiously it occurred to me that I had noticed them only in Akeley's vicinity. They had been strongest where he sat, and wholly absent except in the room with him or just outside the doors of that room. I paused, letting the flashlight wander about the dark study and racking my brain for explanations of the turn affairs had taken.

Would to heaven I had quietly left the place before allowing that light to rest again on the vacant chair. As it turned out, I did not leave quietly; but with a muffled shriek which must have disturbed, though it did not quite awake, the sleeping sentinel across the hall. That shriek, and Noyes's still-unbroken snore, are the last sounds I ever heard in that morbidity-choked farmhouse beneath the black-wooded crest of a haunted mountain—that focus of trans-cosmic horror amidst the lonely green hills and curse-muttering brooks of a spectral rustic land.

It is a wonder that I did not drop flashlight, valise, and revolver in my wild scramble, but somehow I failed to lose any of these. I actually managed to get out of that room and that house without making any further noise, to drag myself and my belongings safely into the old Ford in the shed, and to set that archaic vehicle in motion toward some unknown point of safety in the black, moonless night. The ride that followed was a piece of delirium out of Poe or Rimbaud or the drawings of Doré, but finally I reached Townshend. That is all. If my sanity is still unshaken, I am lucky. Sometimes I fear what the years will bring, especially since that new planet Pluto has been so curiously discovered.

As I have implied, I let my flashlight return to the vacant easy-chair after its circuit of the room; then noticing for the first time the presence of certain objects in the seat, made inconspicuous by the adjacent loose folds of the empty dressing-gown. These are the objects, three in number, which the investigators did not find when they came later on. As I said at the outset, there was nothing of actual visual horror about them. The trouble was in what they led one to infer. Even now I have my moments of half-doubt—moments in which I half-accept the skepticism of those who attribute my whole experience to dream and nerves and delusion.

The three things were damnably clever constructions of their kind, and were furnished with ingenious metallic clamps to attach them to organic developments of which I dare not form any conjecture. I hope—devoutly hope—that they were the waxen products of a master artist, despite what my inmost fears tell me. Great God! That whisperer in darkness with its morbid odor and vibrations! Sorcerer, emissary, changeling, outsider... that hideous repressed buzzing... and all the time in that fresh, shiny cylinder on the shelf... poor devil... "prodigious surgical, biological, chemical, and mechanical skill..."

For the things in the chair, perfect to the last, subtle detail of microscopic resemblance—or identity—were the face and hands of Henry Wentworth Akeley.

NIGHTMARE-TOUCH

BY

LAFCADIO HEARN

I

What *is* the fear of ghosts among those who believe in ghosts?

All fear is the result of experience—experience of the individual or of the race—experience either of the present life or of lives forgotten. Even the fear of the unknown can have no other origin. And the fear of ghosts must be a product of past pain.

Probably the fear of ghosts, as well as the belief in them, had its beginning in dreams. It is a peculiar fear. No other fear is so intense; yet none is so vague. Feelings thus voluminous and dim are super-individual mostly—feelings inherited—feelings made within us by the experience of the dead.

What experience?

Nowhere do I remember reading a plain statement of the reason why ghosts are feared. Ask any ten intelligent persons of your acquaintance, who remember having once been afraid of ghosts, to tell you exactly why they were afraid—to define the fancy behind the fear;—and I doubt whether even one will be able to answer the question. The literature of folk-lore—oral and written—throws no clear light upon the subject. We find, indeed, various legends of men torn asunder by phantoms; but such gross imaginings could not explain the peculiar quality of ghostly fear. It is not a fear of bodily violence. It is not even a reasoning fear—not a fear that can readily explain itself—which would not be the case if it were founded upon definite ideas of physical danger. Furthermore, although primitive ghosts may have been imagined as capable of tearing and devouring, the common idea of a ghost is certainly that of a being intangible and imponderable.[1]

Now I venture to state boldly that the common fear of ghosts is *the fear of being touched by ghosts*—or, in other words, that the imagined Supernatural is dreaded mainly because of its imagined power to touch. Only to *touch*, remember!—not to wound or to kill.

But this dread of the touch would itself be the result of experience—chiefly, I think, of prenatal experience stored up in the individual by inheritance, like the child's fear

1 I may remark here that in many old Japanese legends and ballads, ghosts are represented as having power to *pull off* people's heads. But so far as the origin of the fear of ghosts is concerned, such stories explain nothing—since the experiences that evolved the fear must have been real, not imaginary, experiences.

of darkness. And who can ever have had the sensation of being touched by ghosts? The answer is simple:—*Everybody who has been seized by phantoms in a dream.*

Elements of primeval fears—fears older than humanity—doubtless enter into the child-terror of darkness. But the more definite fear of ghosts may very possibly be composed with inherited results of dream-pain—ancestral experience of nightmare. And the intuitive terror of supernatural touch can thus be evolutionally explained.

Let me now try to illustrate my theory by relating some typical experiences.

II

When about five years old I was condemned to sleep by myself in a certain isolated room, thereafter always called the Child's Room. (At that time I was scarcely ever mentioned by name, but only referred to as "the Child.") The room was narrow, but very high, and, in spite of one tall window, very gloomy. It contained a fire-place wherein no fire was ever kindled; and the Child suspected that the chimney was haunted.

A law was made that no light should be left in the Child's Room at night—simply because the Child was afraid of the dark. His fear of the dark was judged to be a mental disorder requiring severe treatment. But the treatment aggravated the disorder. Previously I had been accustomed to sleep in a well-lighted room, with a nurse to take care of me. I thought that I should die of fright when sentenced to lie alone in the dark, and—what seemed to me then abominably cruel—actually *locked* into my room, the most dismal room of the house. Night after night when I had been warmly tucked into bed, the lamp was removed; the key clicked in the lock; the protecting light and the footsteps of my guardian receded together. Then an agony of fear would come upon me. Something in the black air would seem to gather and grow—(I thought that I could even *hear* it grow)—till I had to scream. Screaming regularly brought punishment; but it also brought back the light, which more than consoled for the punishment. This fact being at last found out, orders were given to pay no further heed to the screams of the Child.

Why was I thus insanely afraid? Partly because the dark had always been peopled for me with shapes of terror. So far back as memory extended, I had suffered from ugly dreams; and when aroused from them I could always *see* the forms dreamed of, lurking in the shadows of the room. They would soon fade out; but for several moments they would appear like tangible realities. And they were always the same figures.... Sometimes, without any preface of dreams, I used to see them at twilight-time—following me about from room to room, or reaching long dim hands after me, from story to story, up through the interspaces of the deep stairways.

I had complained of these haunters only to be told that I must never speak of them, and that they did not exist. I had complained to everybody in the house; and everybody in the house had told me the very same thing. But there was the evidence of my eyes! The denial of that evidence I could explain only in two ways:—Either the shapes were afraid of big people, and showed themselves to me alone, because I was little and weak; or else the entire household had agreed, for some ghastly reason, to say what was not true. This latter theory seemed to me the more probable one, because I had several times perceived the shapes when I was not unattended;—and the consequent appearance of secrecy frightened me scarcely less than the visions did. Why was I forbidden to talk about what I saw, and even heard—on creaking stairways—behind wavering curtains?

"Nothing will hurt you,"—this was the merciless answer to all my pleadings not to be left alone at night. But the haunters *did* hurt me. Only—they would wait until after I had fallen asleep, and so into their power—for they possessed occult means of preventing me from rising or moving or crying out.

Needless to comment upon the policy of locking me up alone with these fears in a black room. Unutterably was I tormented in that room—for years! Therefore I felt relatively happy when sent away at last to a children's boarding-school, where the haunters very seldom ventured to show themselves.

They were not like any people that I had ever known. They were shadowy dark-robed figures, capable of atrocious self-distortion—capable, for instance, of growing up to the ceiling, and then across it, and then lengthening themselves, head-downwards, along the opposite wall. Only their faces were distinct; and I tried not to look at their faces. I tried also in my dreams—or thought that I tried—to awaken myself from the sight of them by pulling at my eyelids with my fingers; but the eyelids would remain closed, as if sealed.... Many years afterwards, the frightful plates in Orfila's *Traité des Exhumés*, beheld for the first time, recalled to me with a sickening start the dream-terrors of childhood. But to understand the Child's experience, you must imagine Orfila's drawings intensely alive, and continually elongating or distorting, as in some monstrous anamorphosis.

Nevertheless the mere sight of those nightmare-faces was not the worst of the experiences in the Child's Room. The dreams always began with a suspicion, or sensation of something heavy in the air—slowly quenching will—slowly numbing my power to move. At such times I usually found myself alone in a large unlighted apartment; and, almost simultaneously with the first sensation of fear, the atmosphere of the room would become suffused, half-way to the ceiling, with a sombre-yellowish glow, making objects dimly visible—though the ceiling itself remained pitch-black. This was not a true appearance of light: rather it seemed as if the black air were changing color from beneath.... Certain terrible aspects of sunset, on the eve of storm, offer like effects of sinister color.... Forthwith I would try to escape—(feeling at every step a sensation *as of wading*)—and would sometimes succeed in struggling half-way across the room;—but there I would always find myself brought to a standstill—paralyzed by some innominable opposition. Happy voices I could hear in the next room;—I could see light through the transom over the door that I had vainly endeavored to reach;—I knew that one loud cry would save me. But not even by the most frantic effort could I raise my voice above a whisper.... And all this signified only that the Nameless was coming—was nearing—was mounting the stairs. I could hear the step—booming like the sound of a muffled drum—and I wondered why nobody else heard it. A long, long time the haunter would take to come—malevolently pausing after each ghastly footfall. Then, without a creak, the bolted door would open—slowly, slowly—and the thing would enter, gibbering soundlessly—and put out hands—and clutch me—and toss me to the black ceiling—and catch me descending to toss me up again, and again, and again.... In those moments the feeling was not fear: fear itself had been torpified by the first seizure. It was a sensation that has no name in the language of the living. For every touch brought a shock of something infinitely worse than pain—something that thrilled into the innermost secret being of me—a sort of abominable electricity, discovering unimagined capacities of suffering in totally unfamiliar regions of sentiency.... This was commonly the work of a single tormentor; but I can also remember having been caught by a group, and tossed from one to another—seemingly for a time of many minutes.

IIII

Whence the fancy of those shapes? I do not know. Possibly from some impression of fear in earliest infancy; possibly from some experience of fear in other lives than mine. That mystery is forever insoluble. But the mystery of the shock of the touch admits of a definite hypothesis.

First, allow me to observe that the experience of the sensation itself cannot be dismissed as "mere imagination." Imagination means cerebral activity: its pains and its pleasures are alike inseparable from nervous operation, and their physical importance is sufficiently proved by their physiological effects. Dream-fear may kill as well as other fear; and no emotion thus powerful can be reasonably deemed undeserving of study.

One remarkable fact in the problem to be considered is that the sensation of seizure in dreams differs totally from all sensations familiar to ordinary waking life. Why this differentiation? How interpret the extraordinary massiveness and depth of the thrill?

I have already suggested that the dreamer's fear is most probably not a reflection of relative experience, but represents the incalculable total of ancestral experience of dream-fear. If the sum of the experience of active life be transmitted by inheritance, so must likewise be transmitted the summed experience of the life of sleep. And in normal heredity either class of transmissions would probably remain distinct.

Now, granting this hypothesis, the sensation of dream-seizure would have had its beginnings in the earliest phases of dream-consciousness—long prior to the apparition of man. The first creatures capable of thought and fear must often have dreamed of being caught by their natural enemies. There could not have been much imagining of pain in these primal dreams. But higher nervous development in later forms of being would have been accompanied with larger susceptibility to dream-pain. Still later, with the growth of reasoning-power, ideas of the supernatural would have changed and intensified the character of dream-fear. Furthermore, through all the course of evolution, heredity would have been accumulating the experience of such feeling. Under those forms of imaginative pain evolved through reaction of religious beliefs, there would persist some dim survival of savage primitive fears, and again, under this, a dimmer but incomparably deeper substratum of ancient animal-terrors. In the dreams of the modern child all these latencies might quicken—one below another—unfathomably—with the coming and the growing of nightmare.

It may be doubted whether the phantasms of any particular nightmare have a history older than the brain in which they move. But the shock of the touch would seem to indicate *some point of dream-contact with the total race-experience of shadowy seizure.* It may be that profundities of Self—abysses never reached by any ray from the life of sun—are strangely stirred in slumber, and that out of their blackness immediately responds a shuddering of memory, measureless even by millions of years.

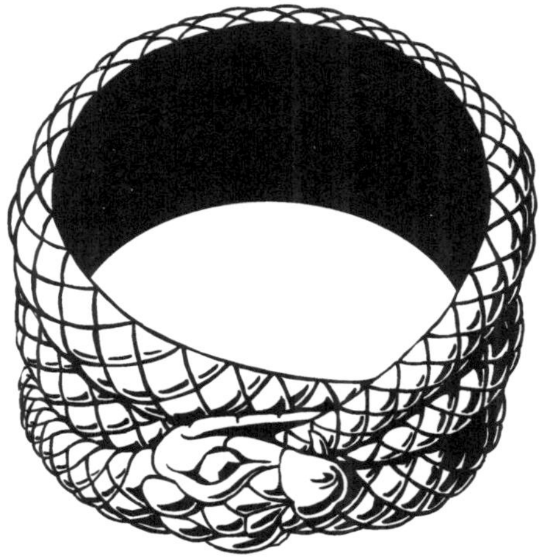

THE HAUNTER OF THE RING

BY

ROBERT E. HOWARD

As I entered John Kirowan's study I was too much engrossed in my own thoughts to notice, at first, the haggard appearance of his visitor, a big, handsome young fellow well known to me.

"Hello, Kirowan," I greeted. "Hello, Gordon. Haven't seen you for quite a while. How's Evelyn?" And before he could answer, still on the crest of the enthusiasm which had brought me there, I exclaimed: "Look here, you fellows, I've got something that will make you stare! I got it from that robber Ahmed Mektub, and I paid high for it, but it's worth it. Look!" From under my coat I drew the jewel-hilted Afghan dagger which had fascinated me as a collector of rare weapons.

Kirowan, familiar with my passion, showed only polite interest, but the effect on Gordon was shocking.

With a strangled cry he sprang up and backward, knocking the chair clattering to the floor. Fists clenched and countenance livid he faced me, crying: "Keep back! Get away from me, or—"

I was frozen in my tracks.

"What in the—" I began bewilderedly, when Gordon, with another amazing change of attitude, dropped into a chair and sank his head in his hands. I saw his heavy shoulders quiver. I stared helplessly from him to Kirowan, who seemed equally dumbfounded.

"Is he drunk?" I asked.

Kirowan shook his head, and filling a brandy glass, offered it to the man. Gordon looked up with haggard eyes, seized the drink and gulped it down like a man half famished. Then he straightened up and looked at us shamefacedly.

"I'm sorry I went off my handle, O'Donnel" he said. "It was the unexpected shock of you drawing that knife."

"Well," I retorted, with some disgust, "I suppose you thought I was going to stab you with it!"

"Yes, I did!" Then, at the utterly blank expression on my face, he added: "Oh, I didn't actually *think* that; at least, I didn't reach that conclusion by any process of reasoning. It was just the blind primitive instinct of a hunted man, against whom anyone's hand may be turned."

His strange words and the despairing way he said them sent a queer shiver of nameless apprehension down my spine.

"What are you talking about?" I demanded uneasily. "Hunted? For what? You never committed a crime in your life."

"Not in this life, perhaps," he muttered.

"What do you mean?"

"What if retribution for a black crime committed in a previous life were hounding me?" he muttered.

"That's nonsense," I snorted.

"Oh, is it?" he exclaimed, stung. "Did you ever hear of my great-grandfather, Sir Richard Gordon of Argyle?"

"Sure; but what's that got to do with—"

"You've seen his portrait: doesn't it resemble me?"

"Well, yes," I admitted, "except that your expression is frank and wholesome whereas his is crafty and cruel."

"He murdered his wife," answered Gordon. "Suppose the theory of reincarnation were true? Why shouldn't a man suffer in one life for a crime committed in another?"

"You mean you think you are the reincarnation of your great-grandfather? Of all the fantastic—well, since he killed his wife, I suppose you'll be expecting Evelyn to murder you!" This last was delivered in searing sarcasm, as I thought of the sweet, gentle girl Gordon had married. His answer stunned me.

"My wife," he said slowly, "has tried to kill me three times in the past week."

There was no reply to that. I glanced helplessly at John Kirowan. He sat in his customary position, chin resting on his strong, slim hands; his white face was immobile, but his dark eyes gleamed with interest. In the silence I heard a clock ticking like a death-watch.

"Tell us the full story, Gordon," suggested Kirowan, and his calm, even voice was like a knife that cut a strangling, relieving the unreal tension.

"You know we've been married less than a year," Gordon began, plunging into the tale as though he were bursting for utterance; his words stumbled and tripped over one another. "All couples have spats, of course, but we've never had any real quarrels. Evelyn is the best-natured girl in the world.

"The first thing out of the ordinary occurred about a week ago. We had driven up in the mountains, left the car, and were wandering around picking wild flowers. At last we came to a steep slope, some thirty feet in height, and Evelyn called my attention to the flowers which grew thickly at the foot. I was looking over the edge and wondering if I could climb down without tearing my clothes to ribbons, when I felt a violent shove from behind that toppled me over.

"If it had been a sheer cliff, I'd have broken my neck. As it was, I went tumbling down, rolling and sliding, and brought up at the bottom scratched and bruised, with my garments in rags. I looked up and saw Evelyn staring down, apparently frightened half out of her wits.

"'Oh Jim!' she cried. 'Are you hurt? How came you to fall?'

"It was on the tip of my tongue to tell her that there was such a thing as carrying a joke too far, but these words checked me. I decided that she must have stumbled against me unintentionally, and actually didn't know it was she who precipitated me down the slope.

"So I laughed it off, and went home. She made a great fuss over me, insisted on swabbing my scratches with iodine, and lectured me for my carelessness! I hadn't the heart to tell her it was her fault.

"But four days later, the next thing happened. I was walking along our driveway, when I saw her coming up it in the automobile. I stepped out on the grass to let her by, as there isn't any curb along the driveway. She was smiling as she approached me, and slowed down the car, as if to speak to me. Then, just before she reached me, a most horrible change came over her expression. Without warning the car leaped at me like a living thing as she drove her foot down on the accelerator. Only a frantic leap backward saved me from being ground under the wheels. The car shot across the lawn and crashed into a tree. I ran to it and found Evelyn dazed and hysterical, but unhurt. She babbled of losing control of the machine.

"I carried her into the house and sent for Doctor Donnelly. He found nothing seriously wrong with her, and attributed her dazed condition to fright and shock. Within half an hour she regained her normal senses, but she's refused to touch the wheel since. Strange to say, she seemed less frightened on her own account than on mine. She seemed vaguely to know that she'd nearly run me down, and grew hysterical again when she spoke of it. Yet she seemed to take it for granted that I knew the machine had got out of her control. But I distinctly saw her wrench the wheel around, and I know she deliberately tried to hit me—why, God alone knows."

"Still I refused to let my mind follow the channel it was getting into. Evelyn had never given any evidence of any psychological weakness or 'nerves'; she's always been a level-headed girl, wholesome and natural. But I began to think she was subject to crazy impulses. Most of us have felt the impulse to leap from tall buildings. And sometimes a person feels a blind, childish and utterly reasonless urge to harm someone. We pick up a pistol, and the thought suddenly enters our mind how easy it would be to send our friend, who sits smiling and unaware, into eternity with a touch of the trigger. Of course we don't do it, but the impulse is there. So I thought perhaps some lack of mental discipline made Evelyn susceptible to these unguided impulses, and unable to control them."

"Nonsense," I broke in. "I've known her since she was a baby. If she has any such trait, she's developed it since she married you."

It was an unfortunate remark. Gordon caught it up with a despairing gleam in his eyes. "That's just it—since she married me! It's a curse—a black, ghastly curse, crawling like a serpent out of the past! I tell you, I was Richard Gordon and she—she was Lady Elizabeth, his murdered wife!" His voice sank to a blood-freezing whisper.

I shuddered; it is an awful thing to look upon the ruin of a keen clean brain, and such I was certain that I surveyed in James Gordon. Why or how, or by what grisly chance it had come about I could not say, but I was certain the man was mad.

"You spoke of three attempts." It was John Kirowan's voice again, calm and stable amid the gathering webs of horror and unreality.

"Look here!" Gordon lifted, his arm, drew back the sleeve and displayed a bandage, the cryptic significance of which was intolerable.

"I came into the bathroom this morning looking for my razor," he said. "I found Evelyn just on the point of using my best shaving implement for some feminine purpose—to cut out a pattern, or something. Like many women she can't seem to realize the difference between a razor and a butcher-knife or a pair of shears.

"I was a bit irritated, and I said: 'Evelyn, how many times have I told you not to use my razors for such things? Bring it here; I'll give you my pocket-knife.'

"'I'm sorry, Jim,' she said. 'I didn't know it would hurt the razor. Here it is.'

"She was advancing, holding the open razor toward me. I reached for it—then something warned me. It was the same look in her eyes, just as I had seen it the day she nearly ran over me. That was all that saved my life, for I instinctively threw up my hand just as she slashed at my throat with all her power. The blade gashed my arm as you see, before I caught her wrist. For an instant she fought me like a wild thing; her slender body was taut as steel beneath my hands. Then she went limp and the look in her eyes was replaced by a strange dazed expression. The razor slipped out of her fingers.

"I let go of her and she stood swaying as if about to faint. I went to the lavatory—my wound was bleeding in a beastly fashion—and the next thing I heard her cry out, and she was hovering over me.

"'Jim!' she cried. 'How did you cut yourself so terribly?'"

Gordon shook his head and sighed heavily. "I guess I was a bit out of my head. My self-control snapped.

"'Don't keep up this pretense, Evelyn,' I said. 'God knows what's got into you, but you know as well as I that you've tried to kill me three times in the past week.'

"She recoiled as if I'd struck her, catching at her breast and staring at me as if at a ghost. She didn't say a word—and just what I said I don't remember. But when I finished I left her standing there white and still as a marble statue. I got my arm bandaged at a drug store, and then came over here, not knowing what else to do.

"Kirowan—O'Donnel—it's damnable! Either my wife is subject to fits of insanity—" He choked on the word. "No, I can't believe it. Ordinarily her eyes are too clear and level—too utterly sane. But every time she has an opportunity to harm me, she seems to become a temporary maniac."

He beat his fists together in his impotence and agony.

"But it isn't insanity! I used to work in a psychopathic ward, and I've seen every form of mental unbalance. My wife is *not* insane!"

"Then what—" I began, but he turned haggard eyes on me.

"Only one alternative remains," he answered. "It is the old curse—from the days when I walked the earth with a heart as black as hell's darkest pits, and did evil in the sight of man and of God. *She* knows, in fleeting snatches of memory. People have *seen* before—have glimpsed forbidden things in momentary liftings of the veil, which bars life from life. She was Elizabeth Douglas, the ill-fated bride of Richard Gordon, whom he murdered in jealous frenzy, and the vengeance is hers. I shall die by her hands, as it was meant to be. And she—" he bowed his head in his hands.

"Just a moment." It was Kirowan again. "You have mentioned a strange look in your wife's eyes. What sort of a look? Was it of maniacal frenzy?"

Gordon shook his head. "It was an utter blankness. All the life and intelligence simply vanished, leaving her eyes dark wells of emptiness."

Kirowan nodded, and asked a seemingly irrelevant question. "Have you any enemies?"

"Not that I know of."

"You forget Joseph Roelocke," I said. "I can't imagine that elegant sophisticate going to the trouble of doing you actual harm, but I have an idea that if he could discomfort you without any physical effort on his part, he'd do it with a right good will."

Kirowan turned on me an eye that had suddenly become piercing.

"And who is this Joseph Roelocke?"

"A young exquisite who came into Evelyn's life and nearly rushed her off her feet for a while. But in the end she came back to her first love—Gordon here. Roelocke took it pretty hard. For all his suaveness there's a streak of violence and passion in the man that might have cropped out but for his infernal indolence and blasé indifference."

"Oh, there's nothing to be said against Roelocke," interrupted Gordon impatiently. "He must know that Evelyn never really loved him. He merely fascinated her temporarily with his romantic Latin air."

"Not exactly Latin, Jim," I protested. "Roelocke does look foreign, but it isn't Latin. It's almost Oriental."

"Well, what has Roelocke to do with this matter?" Gordon snarled with the irascibility of frayed nerves. "He's been as friendly as a man could be since Evelyn and I were married. In fact, only a week ago he sent her a ring which he said was a peace-offering and a belated wedding gift; said that after all, her jilting him was a greater misfortune for her than it was for him—the conceited jackass!"

"A ring?" Kirowan had suddenly come to life; it was as if something hard and steely had been sounded in him. "What sort of a ring?"

"Oh, a fantastic thing—copper, made like a scaly snake coiled three times, with its tail in its mouth and yellow jewels for eyes. I gather he picked it up somewhere in Hungary."

"He has traveled a great deal in Hungary?"

Gordon looked surprized at this questioning but answered: "Why, apparently the man's traveled everywhere. I put him down as the pampered son of a millionaire. He never did any work, so far as I know."

"He's a great student," I put in. "I've been up to his apartment several times, and I never saw such a collection of books—"

Gordon leaped to his feet with an oath, "Are we all crazy?" he cried. "I came up here hoping to get some help—and you fellows fall to talking of Joseph Roelocke. I'll go to Doctor Donnelly—"

"Wait!" Kirowan stretched out a detaining hand. "If you don't mind, we'll go over to your house. I'd like to talk to your wife."

Gordon dumbly acquiesced. Harried and haunted by grisly forebodings, he knew not which way to turn, and welcomed anything that promised aid.

We drove over in his car, and scarcely a word was spoken on the way. Gordon was sunk in moody ruminations, and Kirowan had withdrawn himself into some strange aloof domain of thought beyond my ken. He sat like a statue, his dark vital eyes staring into space, not blankly, but as one who looks with understanding into some far realm.

Though I counted the man as my best friend, I knew but little of his past. He had come into my life as abruptly and unannounced as Joseph Roelocke had come into the life of Evelyn Ash. I had met him at the Wanderer's Club, which is composed of the drift of the world, travelers, eccentrics, and all manner of men whose paths lie outside the beaten tracks of life. I had been attracted to him, and intrigued by his strange powers and deep knowledge. I vaguely knew that he was the black sheep younger son of a titled Irish family, and that he had walked many strange ways. Gordon's mention of Hungary struck a chord in my memory; one phase of his life Kirowan had once let drop fragmentarily. I only knew that he had once suffered a bitter grief and a savage wrong, and that it had been in Hungary. But the nature of the episode I did not know.

At Gordon's house Evelyn met us calmly, showing inner agitation only by the over-restraint of her manner. I saw the beseeching look she stole at her husband. She was a slender, soft-spoken girl, whose dark eyes were always vibrant and alight with emotion. That child try to murder her adored husband? The idea was monstrous. Again I was convinced that James Gordon himself was deranged.

Following Kirowan's lead, we made a pretense of small talk, as if we had casually dropped in, but I felt that Evelyn was not deceived. Our conversation rang false and hollow, and presently Kirowan said: "Mrs. Gordon, that is a remarkable ring you are wearing. Do you mind if I look at it?"

"I'll have to give you my hand," she laughed. "I've been trying to get it off today, and it won't come off."

She held out her slim white hand for Kirowan's inspection, and his face was immobile as he looked at the metal snake that coiled about her slim finger. He did not touch it. I myself was aware of an unaccountable repulsion. There was something almost obscene about that dull copperish reptile wound about the girl's white finger.

"It's evil-looking, isn't it?" She involuntarily shivered. "At first I liked it, but now I can hardly bear to look at it. If I can get it off I intend to return it to Joseph—Mr. Roelocke."

Kirowan was about to make some reply, when the doorbell rang. Gordon jumped as if shot, and Evelyn rose quickly.

"I'll answer it, Jim—I know who it is."

She returned an instant later with two more mutual friends, those inseparable cronies, Doctor Donnelly, whose burly body, jovial manner and booming voice were combined with as keen a brain as any in the profession, and Bill Bain, elderly, lean, wiry, acidly witty. Both were old friends of the Ash family. Doctor Donnelly had ushered Evelyn into the world, and Bain was always Uncle Bill to her.

"Howdy, Jim! Howdy, Mr. Kirowan!" roared Donnelly. "Hey, O'Donnel, have you got any firearms with you? Last time your nearly blew my head off showing me an old flintlock pistol that wasn't supposed to be loaded!"

"Doctor Donnelly!"

We all turned. Evelyn was standing beside a wide table, holding it as if for support. Her face was white. Our badinage ceased instantly. A sudden tension was in the air.

"Doctor Donnelly," she repeated, holding her voice steady by an effort, "I sent for you and Uncle Bill—for the same reason for which I know Jim has brought Mr. Kirowan and Michael. There is a matter Jim and I can no longer deal with alone. There is something between us—something black and ghastly and terrible."

"What are you talking about, girl?" All the levity was gone from Donnelly's great voice.

"My husband—" She choked, then went blindly on: "My husband has accused me of trying to murder him."

The silence that fell was broken by Bain's sudden and energetic rise. His eyes blazed and his fists quivered.

"You young pup!" he shouted at Gordon. "I'll knock the living daylights—"

"Sit down, Bill!" Donnelly's huge hand crushed his smaller companion back into his chair. "No use goin' off half cocked. Go ahead, honey."

"We need help. We can not carry this thing alone." A shadow crossed her comely face. "This morning Jim's arm was badly cut. He said I did it. I don't know. I was handing him the razor. Then I must have fainted. At least, everything faded away. When I came to myself he was washing his arm in the lavatory—and—and he accused me of trying to kill him."

"Why, the young fool!" barked the belligerent Bain. "Hasn't he sense enough to know that if you did cut him, it was an accident?"

"Shut up, won't you?" snorted Donnelly. "Honey, did you say you fainted? That isn't like you."

"I've been having fainting spells," she answered. "The first time was when we were in the mountains and Jim fell down a cliff. We were standing on the edge—then everything went black, and when my sight cleared, he was rolling down the slope." She shuddered at the recollection.

"Then when I lost control of the car and it crashed into the tree. You remember—Jim called you over."

Doctor Donnelly nodded his head ponderously.

"I don't remember you ever having fainting spells before."

"But Jim says I pushed him over the cliff!" she cried hysterically. "He says I tried to run him down in the car! He says I purposely slashed him with the razor!"

Doctor Donnelly turned perplexedly, toward the wretched Gordon.

"How about it, son?"

"God help me," Gordon burst out in agony; "it's true!"

"Why, you lying hound!" It was Bain who gave tongue, leaping again to his feet. "If you want a divorce, why don't you get it in a decent way, instead of resorting to these despicable tactics—"

"Damn you!" roared Gordon, lunging up, and losing control of himself completely. "If you say that I'll tear your jugular out!"

Evelyn screamed; Donnelly grabbed Bain ponderously and banged him back into his chair with no overly gentle touch, and Kirowan laid a hand lightly on Gordon's shoulder. The man seemed to crumple into himself. He sank back into his chair and held out his hands gropingly toward his wife.

"Evelyn," he said, his voice thick with laboring emotion, "you know I love you. I feel like a dog. But God help me, it's true. If we go on this way, I'll be a dead man, and you—"

"Don't say it!" she screamed. "I know you wouldn't lie to me, Jim. If you say I tried to kill you, I know I did. But I swear, Jim, I didn't do it consciously. Oh, I must be going mad! That's why my dreams have been so wild and terrifying lately—"

"Of what have you dreamed, Mrs. Gordon?" asked Kirowan gently.

She pressed her hands to her temples and stared dully at him, as if only half comprehending.

"A black thing," she muttered. "A horrible faceless black thing that mows and mumbles and paws over me with apish hands. I dream of it every night. And in the daytime I try to kill the only man I ever loved. I'm going mad! Maybe I'm already crazy and don't know it."

"Calm yourself, honey." To Doctor Donnelly, with all his science, it was only another case of feminine hysteria. His matter-of-fact voice seemed to soothe her, and she sighed and drew a weary hand through her damp locks.

"We'll talk this all over, and everything's goin' to be okay," he said, drawing a thick cigar from his vest pocket. "Gimme a match, honey."

She began mechanically to feel about the table, and just as mechanically Gordon said: "There are matches in the drawer, Evelyn."

She opened the drawer and began groping in it, when suddenly, as if struck by recollection and intuition, Gordon sprang up, white-faced, and shouted: "No, no! Don't open that drawer-don't—"

Even as he voiced that urgent cry, she stiffened, as if at the feel of something in the drawer. Her change of expression held us all frozen, even Kirowan. The vital intelligence vanished from her eyes like a blown-out flame, and into them came the look Gordon had described as blank. The term was descriptive. Her beautiful eyes were dark wells of emptiness, as if the soul had been withdrawn from behind them.

Her hand came out of the drawer holding a pistol, and she fired point-blank. Gordon reeled with a groan and went down, blood starting from his head. For a flashing instant she looked down stupidly at the smoking gun in her hand, like one suddenly waking from a nightmare. Then her wild scream of agony smote our ears.

"Oh God, I've killed him! Jim! *Jim!* "

She reached him before any of us, throwing herself on her knees and cradling his bloody head in her arms, while she sobbed in an unbearable passion of horror and anguish. The emptiness was gone from her eyes; they were alive and dilated with grief and terror.

I was making toward my prostrate friend with Donnelly and Bain, but Kirowan caught my arm. His face was no longer immobile; his eyes glittered with a controlled savagery.

"Leave him to them!" he snarled. "We are hunters, not healers! Lead me to the house of Joseph Roelocke!"

I did not question him. We drove there in Gordon's car.

I had the wheel, and something about the grim face of my companion caused me to hurl the machine recklessly through the traffic. I had the sensation of being part of a tragic drama which was hurtling with headlong speed toward a terrible climax.

I wrenched the car to a grinding halt at the curb before the building where Roelocke lived in a bizarre apartment high above the city. The very elevator that shot us skyward seemed imbued with something of Kirowan's driving urge for haste. I pointed out Roelocke's door, and he cast it open without knocking and shouldered his way in. I was close at his heels.

Roelocke, in a dressing-gown of Chinese silk worked with dragons, was lounging on a divan, puffing quickly at a cigarette. He sat up, overturning a wine-glass which stood with a half-filled bottle at his elbow.

Before Kirowan could speak, I burst out with our news. "James Gordon has been shot!"

He sprang to his feet. "Shot? When? When did she kill him?"

"*She?*" I glared in bewilderment. "How did you know—"

With a steely hand Kirowan thrust me aside, and as the men faced each other, I saw recognition flare up in Roelocke's face. They made a strong contrast: Kirowan, tall, pale with some white-hot passion; Roelocke, slim, darkly handsome, with the saracenic arch of his slim brows above his black eyes. I realized that whatever else occurred, it lay between those two men. They were not strangers; I could sense like a tangible thing the hate that lay between them.

"John Kirowan!" softly whispered Roelocke.

"You remember me, Yosef Vrolok!" Only an iron control kept Kirowan's voice steady. The other merely stared at him without speaking.

"Years ago," said Kirowan more deliberately, "when we delved in the dark mysteries together in Budapest, I saw whither you were drifting. I drew back; I would not descend to the foul depths of forbidden occultism and diabolism to which you sank. And because I would not, you despised me, and you robbed me of the only woman I ever loved; you turned her against me by means of your vile arts, and then you degraded and debauched her, sank her into your own foul slime. I had killed you with my hands then, Yosef Vrolok—vampire by nature as well as by name that you are—but your arts protected you from physical vengeance. But you have trapped yourself at last!"

Kirowan's voice rose in fierce exultation. All his cultured restraint had been swept away from him, leaving a primitive, elemental man, raging and gloating over a hated foe.

"You sought the destruction of James Gordon and his wife, because she unwittingly escaped your snare; you—"

Roelocke shrugged his shoulders and laughed. "You are mad. I have not seen the Gordons for weeks. Why blame me for their family troubles?"

Kirowan snarled. "Liar as always. What did you say just now when O'Donnel told you Gordon had been shot? 'When did *she* kill him?' You were expecting to hear that the girl had killed her husband. Your psychic powers had told you that a climax was close at hand. You were nervously awaiting news of the success of your devilish scheme.

"But I did not need a slip of your tongue to recognize your handiwork. I knew as soon as I saw the ring on Evelyn Gordon's finger; the ring she could not remove; the ancient and accursed ring of Thoth-amon, handed down by foul cults of sorcerers since the days of forgotten Stygia, I knew that ring was yours, and I knew by what ghastly rites you came to possess it. And I knew its power. Once she put it on her finger, in her innocence and ignorance, she was in your power. By your black magic you summoned the black elemental spirit, *the haunter of the ring*, out of the gulfs of Night and the ages. Here in your accursed chamber you performed unspeakable rituals to drive Evelyn Gordon's soul from her body, and to cause that body to be possessed by that godless sprite from *outside* the human universe.

"She was too clean and wholesome, her love for her husband too strong, for the fiend to gain complete and permanent possession of her body; only for brief instants could it drive her own spirit into the void and animate her form. But that was enough for your purpose. But you have brought ruin upon yourself by your vengeance!"

Kirowan's voice rose to a feline screech.

"What was the price demanded by the fiend you drew from the Pits? Ha, you blench! Yosef Vrolok is not the only man to have learned forbidden secrets! After I left Hungary, a broken man, I took up again the study of the black arts, to trap you, you cringing serpent! I explored the ruins of Zimbabwe, the lost mountains of inner Mongolia, and the forgotten jungle islands of the southern seas. I learned what sickened my soul so that I forswore occultism for ever—but I learned of the black spirit that deals death by the hand of a beloved one, and is controlled by a master of magic.

"But, Yosef Vrolok, you are not an adept! You have not the power to control the fiend you have invoked. And you have sold your soul!"

The Hungarian tore at his collar as if it were a strangling noose. His face had changed, as if a mask had dropped away; he looked much older.

"You lie!" he panted. "I did not promise him my soul—"

"I do not lie!" Kirowan's shriek was shocking in its wild exultation. "I know the price a man must pay for calling forth the nameless shape that roams the gulfs of Darkness. Look! There in the corner behind you! A nameless, sightless thing is laughing—is mocking you! It has fulfilled its bargain, and it has come for you, Yosef Vrolok!"

"No! No!" shrieked Vrolok, tearing his limp collar away from his sweating throat. His composure had crumpled, and his demoralization was sickening to see. "I tell you it was not *my* soul—I promised it a soul, but not *my* soul—he must take the soul of the girl, or of James Gordon."

"Fool!" roared Kirowan. "Do you think *he* could take the souls of innocence? That he would not know they were beyond his reach? The girl and the youth he could kill; their souls were not his to take or yours to give. But *your* black soul is not beyond his reach, and he will have his wage. Look! He is materializing behind you! He is growing out of thin air!"

Was it the hypnosis inspired by Kirowan's burning words that caused me to shudder and grow cold, to feel an icy chill that was not of earth pervade the room? Was it a trick of light and shadow that seemed to produce the effect of a black anthropomorphic shadow on the wall behind the Hungarian? *No*, by heaven! It grew, it swelled-Vrolok had not turned. He stared at Kirowan with eyes starting from his head, hair standing stiffly on his scalp, sweat dripping from his livid face.

Kirowan's cry started shudders down my spine.

"Look behind you, fool! *I see him!* He has come! He is here! His grisly mouth gapes in awful laughter! His mis-shapen paws reach for you!"

And then at last Vrolok wheeled, with an awful shriek, throwing his arms above his head in a gesture of wild despair. And for one brain-shattering instant he was *blotted out* by a great black shadow—Kirowan grasped my arm and we fled from that accursed chamber, blind with horror.

The same paper which bore a brief item telling of James Gordon having suffered a slight scalp-wound by the accidental discharge of a pistol in his home, headlined the sudden death of Joseph Roelocke, wealthy and eccentric clubman, in his sumptuous apartments—apparently from heart-failure.

I read it at breakfast, while I drank cup after cup of black coffee, from a hand that was not too steady, even after the lapse of a night. Across the table from me Kirowan likewise seemed to lack appetite. He brooded, as if he roamed again through bygone years.

"Gordon's fantastic theory of reincarnation was wild enough," I said at last. "But the actual facts were still more incredible. Tell me, Kirowan, was that last scene the result of hypnosis? Was it the power of your words that made me seem to see a black horror grow out of the air and rip Yosef Vrolok's soul from his living body?"

He shook his head. "No human hypnotism would strike that black-hearted devil dead on the floor. No; there are beings outside the ken of common humanity, foul shapes of transcosmic evil. Such a one it was with which Vrolok dealt."

"But how could it claim his soul?" I persisted. "If indeed such an awful bargain had been struck, it had not fulfilled its part, for James Gordon was not dead, but merely knocked senseless."

"Vrolok did not know it," answered Kirowan. "He thought that Gordon was dead, and I convinced him that he himself had been trapped, and was doomed. In his demoralization he fell easy prey to the thing he called forth. *It*, of course, was always watching for a moment of weakness on his part. The powers of Darkness never deal fairly with human beings; he who traffics with them is always cheated in the end."

"It's a mad nightmare," I muttered. "But it seems to me, then, that you as much as anything else brought about Vrolok's death."

"It is gratifying to think so," Kirowan answered. "Evelyn Gordon is safe now; and it is a small repayment for what he did to another girl, years ago, and in a far country."